# Praise for Jennifer St. Giles's
## *Midnight Secrets*

"Jennifer St. Giles creates multi-faceted characters that throb with strong emotions... It is a fantastic love story that brings a dreary, dark era to a close at Killdaren Castle and sets things right for a happy-ever-after."

~ *The Long and the Short of It*

# Look for these titles by
## *Jennifer St. Giles*

*Now Available:*

*Killdaren Series*
Midnight Secrets
Darkest Dreams

# Midnight Secrets

*Jennifer St. Giles*

SAMHAIN
PUBLISHING

Samhain Publishing, Ltd.
11821 Mason Montgomery Road, 4B
Cincinnati, OH 45249
www.samhainpublishing.com

Midnight Secrets
Copyright © 2012 by Jennifer St. Giles
Print ISBN: 978-1-60928-439-8
Digital ISBN: 978-1-60928-375-9

Editing by Tera Kleinfelter
Cover by Kanaxa

*This book has been previously published.*

First Samhain Publishing, Ltd. electronic publication: April 2011
First Samhain Publishing, Ltd. print publication: March 2012

# Dedication

To all those who fill my heart, thank you for your love, encouragement and understanding. Because of you I can dream, believe, create, love and hopefully inspire.

"Hope is the thing with feathers
That perches in the soul,
And sings the tune without the words,
And never stops at all..."
~Emily Dickinson

"Behold, I show you a mystery;
We shall not all sleep, but we shall all be changed,
In a moment, in the twinkling of an eye..."
I Corinthians 15:51-52

# Chapter One

*May 1879*
*Oxford, England*

"*I left our shells on the rocks! I'll be right back.*"

"*Cassie! No! They're too far out. The waves are coming in too fast.*"

"*And you worry too much. I'll hurry.*" Turning, I dashed into the cool sea, laughing at the salty spray splashing my face and bonnet. Within a few steps I knew Mary was right. The sea swirled deeper and more wildly than earlier, but confidence spurred me on. I hurried to the rocks and snatched up our precious pheasant shells moments before a wave swelled over their resting place. Triumphant, I held up my hand. Mary and I had spent the entire morning searching for two shells that exactly matched. We were twins in spirit, though only cousins by blood, and since our faces were dissimilar, our shells had to be alike.

My smile died to a gasp of surprise to see Mary stumbling toward me through the water, horror on her face. She pointed at something behind me. I spun around, grasping for balance as the sea sucked the sand out from under my feet. A burgeoning wave nearly twice my height rushed toward us. I screamed, running for Mary, but the rushing tide caught my flannel gown, billowing it like a sail in a stiff wind, pulling me out to sea. I fought, crying in frustration as I saw Mary floundering too.

"*Go back,*" I yelled at her.

"*No! Not without you! We're twins. Everything together, remember?*"

*The sea roared and crashed around me. I had only moments before I would be swept under by its churning power.*

*"Cassie! Cassie! Oh Cassie!" Mary cried as if grieving deeply for me.*

*I reached for her. Just as our fingers touched, the wall of water slammed into her, and she hung, suspended in the wave for a moment as her beautiful, golden hair floated like a halo about her head before she disappeared into darkness.*

"Mary! Mary! Mary!"

Waking with my own cries echoing in the stillness of the dawn, I shivered with dread. The few dreams I'd had in my life had not been of fanciful fairytales or princes and castles. They'd been omens of trouble or death. Always. My hands trembled as I clasped them together, praying for Mary and myself, because no matter how hard I tried to erase this abnormal darkness from my life, it continued to haunt me.

This time, my dream confused me, though. Much of it had been an accurate memory of the moment Mary's life and my life had irrevocably changed when we were ten. And this dream had been unlike my other dreams, where I'd follow my nanny or my grandparents through a long tunnel, calling to them continuously as they disappeared into darkness. Soon after those dreams, usually the next day, news would come that they had died.

Pale gray light filtered through my lace curtains, casting a fractured pattern of shadows over the Asian carpet and the watered silk of my walls. I rose and opened a window, drawing in deep breaths of air, hoping the morning songs of the birds and the scent of spring blossoms would chase away the darkness. They didn't. Very little of the sun's warmth seeped though the dawn and the cold inside me grew, tightening a band of worry around my heart.

Going to my vanity, I picked up the pheasant shell from amongst my treasured combs and perfumes. I ran my fingertip over the rippled surface and the carved M in it, remembering. That day, Mary had come after me in the sea. There had been a huge wave, and Mary had nearly drowned trying to save me, just as I had dreamed. But we'd both lived through the experience. So why had I dreamed differently now?

Had I, for the first time in my life, had a normal dream? Or was the dream a reflection of what had happened in Mary's life and in mine since that day? Mary never went into the sea again, yet she frequently painted its glory and fury, unable to look away from it for long, as if held fascinated by the power that had almost killed her. Her obsession with capturing the sea on canvas and her need to help those who couldn't help themselves had drawn her far from her family. Last year she'd accepted a post in Cornwall to teach a blind child at an isolated estate by the sea.

For me, the changes in my life had been subtler, but just as deep. I still ventured into the sea, to my ankles at the most, though. And I still gathered shells, but only from the sand, far beyond the grasp of the sea. In short, I firmly adhered to all things safe, practical and proper, exactly as a lady should.

Sliding the shell into my pocket, I dressed, taking care to erase any worry from my expression. *Never let your dreams be known, Cassie,* my mother had said to me all of my life. Just as she told Andromeda to never reveal her ability to read another person's thoughts with only a touch of her hand. There were people who wouldn't understand my sister and me, and I didn't question my mother's advice, for I'd seen the harshness with which the world treated those who were different. Only our family knew of my dreams and Andromeda's gift and we rarely, if ever, spoke of them.

Upon leaving my room, I ordered a telegram sent immediately to my Aunt Lavinia in Brighton, inquiring if she'd heard from Mary recently then went in search of my sisters. There was nothing more I could do about my dream.

I found Andromeda and Gemini in the breakfast room, discussing the plans for the day.

"Cassie! You must talk some sense into Andrie. I need you both to attend the Eversmores' tea with me this afternoon and she won't come!"

9

Andromeda knitted her brow. "I don't see why I should have to spend a boring afternoon pretending that I'm the least bit interested in gossip or fashion. I'm expecting father's next shipment of artifacts to arrive any day now, and I want to be here when it comes."

Father often said God had blessed him with all the gold a man could want in three golden-haired daughters, but he still chased after the promise of riches rather than being a staid professor. A treasure hunter at heart, he satisfied his urgings under the guise of archeology, and my mother followed happily in his wake. Currently, they sought a gold temple Alexander the Great had built to procure Apollo's favor.

"You should have mentioned this earlier, Gemmi. I can't go either. I have fifty posts to read and answer today. 'Cassiopeia's Corner' doesn't write itself."

*And news of Mary to wait for,* I thought then shook off a chill and forced a smile. To my surprise Gemini burst into tears and buried her face in her hands. Andromeda looked at me and shrugged.

Being the practical, sane voice in the midst of the Andrews family chaos was a lonely post and mine to bear. My parents traveled to numerous exotic ports on a budget, sending artifacts for Andromeda to study, and Gemini flitted to what limited social opportunities our position as daughters of a professor at Oxford afforded us. Between the responsibility and drama in caring for my sisters, I spent my time writing a proper etiquette column for *The Exemplary Ladies Journal*, an endeavor which added to the family's meager coffers, rather than drain them.

"Gemmi, whatever is the matter?" I slid my arm around her shoulders and handed her a napkin.

She grabbed the cloth and dabbed at her eyes. "Now that I'm old enough to attend parties, neither of you go anymore. I'm sure we'd receive more invitations, perhaps even to a ball or house party, if you and Andrie would bother to attend anything. And today, well I just need your help!"

"Heavens, Gemmi. You know you can always count on our help." But I feared she was setting herself up for heartbreak. No matter how much proper polish I applied to our family with my column, it would never cover our lack of bloodlines or bohemian-like lifestyle. "What do you need for Andrie and me to do? And why must we attend the tea to do it?"

"I need you to keep Lucinda Swaith away from Lord Percy so that I might have a few moments of his attention without her running up and batting her lashes at him. She's been doing it constantly since he returned from London. I truly think he's interested in me, but Lucinda keeps intruding."

"Two weeks constant? It's a wonder her eyelids haven't fallen off." Andromeda batted her eyes causing Gemini to giggle through her tears. "If you want my opinion, Gemmi, if Lord Percy's attentions are so easily swayed, then you are better off without them."

Gemini wailed again at that remark. Heavens. Andromeda and I had never been this distraught over a man's affections on any level. But then, we were different than others, different than Gemini, and maybe she needed our support in this matter even more than she needed Lord Percy's attentions.

"I don't think Gemmi wants to hear that right now." I bit my lip in consternation because that is exactly what I would have advised in "Cassiopeia's Corner". Apparently, advice didn't help a smidge with feelings. "One hour. Andrie and I will come and keep Lucinda occupied. Then you'll be on your own."

"Cassie!" Andromeda cried, almost close to tears herself now. "I just know the artifacts will arrive! And I won't be here!"

"They've lain in the dirt for centuries. An hour or two longer in a crate isn't going to harm them."

Andromeda gasped as if I had blasphemed, and Gemini giggled, her storm of tears already over.

The day was not off to a promising start, and the Eversmores' tea was everything Andromeda had predicted, an endless showcase for gossip and fashion, upon both of which Lucinda appeared to be an expert.

At least it was turning out to be a success for Gemini. Lord Percy had spent the better part of the past hour at her side.

Later, I would have to inform Gemini that Lucinda constantly batted her eyes at anyone with whom she spoke. And I could readily see how distracting conversation with her would be for anyone. I couldn't keep my eyes off her face, not because of its pleasantness, but because I kept looking, waiting for her *not* to blink. It was dizzying.

Finally, I turned my thoughts back to my dream and Mary, distracting myself enough from the blinking to be able to glance about the room only to see Andromeda rushing toward me, clearly distressed.

*She must have news of Mary,* I thought. Our housekeeper would have forwarded any messages to us here.

Andromeda grabbed my hand before I could clear my mind of my worry that death had claimed someone I loved and my sister gasped as if I'd struck her when she read my mind. She released my hand and turned as white as the lace on her blue damask dress. "You had a dream," she whispered.

"Yes." I sighed and looked at Lucinda. "Excuse us." I motioned for Andromeda to follow me to the corner where we wouldn't be overheard.

"Mother and Father?" Andromeda asked, her hands already shaking.

"No. I dreamed of Mary." I set my hand on hers and she didn't pull away. "But this dream was different than the others, so I'm not sure what it means."

She exhaled and gave my fingers a reassuring squeeze. "Perhaps it's just like when you dreamed of me. Remember? The only thing that happened was I became ill with a lung ailment."

Remember? I would never forget the terror I'd felt, nor the look in my mother's eyes when I told her I'd dreamed of Andromeda dying. It was the first time in my life my mother had stepped away from me rather than comfort me. "Let's hope. What were you coming to tell me? It looked important."

Anger stiffened her face. "It is important. We need to get Gemmi away from Lord Percy and never let her near him again. His intentions are not honorable."

"What makes you say that? Did you...did you touch his

hand and read his mind?" To Andromeda, her gift was a terrible curse to bear. The stronger a person's emotions, the easier and clearer she could read their thoughts. As a child, she had readily interacted with others, but once we grew older, she shied away from being with people at all.

"No. Thank heavens. If I had been close to Lord Percy when I learned this, I most likely would have hit him. I overheard Lord Chauncey tell some other dandy that Lord Percy had to marry an heiress or face ruin from his gambling debts."

"But Gemmi is no heiress."

"Lord Percy has learned of Father's expedition. And since Gemmi's so pretty, he's staying close enough to sweep her off her feet should Father find gold. He's also seeing an heiress in London, too."

"Well, it is a good thing we came to the tea after all. Honestly, I was already questioning Lord Percy's attention to Gemmi. I mean, I know she is very pretty, but with no dowry and only academic titles in our lineage...Dear me, we must break this to her gently, Andrie." Unfortunately, as I glanced at Gemini across the room and saw her eyes alight with adoration for Lord Percy, I didn't think there would be any easy way to tell her.

We returned home to find several crates filling the drawing room. I settled on the sofa with my correspondence for "Cassiopeia's Corner" and let Andromeda and Gemini unpack the artifacts. Our house would never be the model of sophisticated style I'd seen in the Eversmores' gilded and white décor with everything properly perfect and in its place. We had too many stuffed animals and partial skeletons in the corners of our rooms. Not to mention a shrunken head or two displayed with the china. Anyone coming to our home surely left questioning our sanity. It occurred to me that one way to solve Gemini's problem with Lord Percy was to invite him to tea and serve the shrunken heads on a platter with the scones. But then my sterling reputation for being perfectly proper would go up in flames, and that was something I wasn't willing to risk.

Gemini pulled a broken vase from the crate and looked at me, her eyes shining with hope. "Father is going to find gold this time and our dearest wishes will come true. We'll all have the biggest, most beautiful weddings ever."

Andromeda met my gaze over the top of Gemini's head. How much of Gemini's heart was set on Lord Percy? And had Gemini herself given Lord Percy his fortune-hunting ideas?

"Gemmi, in thirty years of excavations, Father hasn't found more than what you have in your hand, so don't hold your breath or count on some grand dream."

"Do you always have to be so practical, Cassie?"

"Yes."

She pouted. "Well, you're wrong. Things are about to be hugely different for us. I know it." She set the vase on the floor, and I frowned at her, finding her choice of words disturbing. What was Gemini not saying?

"Don't put that treasure there!" Andromeda picked up the broken vase as if it were a crown jewel. She moved to the next room, setting it on the dining room table. Gemini and I both rolled our eyes at that because we knew what was next.

Andromeda would cover every flat surface in the house as she extensively studied and catalogued each item before sending them on to the archeological department at the University. We'd be lucky to find a place to eat even in the tiny breakfast nook for months to come now.

To be fair, if the treasures had come from the Celts, then I'd be the one sighing with pleasure over broken pottery. The legends and heroes of that time in history had burrowed in my heart ever since hearing stories of dragons and fairies and merrows and selkies on my grandfather's lap. His deep voice and soothing Irish lilt had made the stories magical for me, all of which was completely impractical to be thinking about now. I had work to do. I forced the memories to the back of my mind as I always did and I focused on the task at hand, despite my sisters' chatter.

I knew the answers to the questions in the letters before me by heart.

*"A decorous and practical lady never acts in haste or takes any action which might impugn her reputation. She must always keep in mind her deportment and her attention to proper etiquette and dress."*

*"A decorous and practical lady would never, on any occasion, be alone with a gentleman."*

*"In the matter of love at first sight, a decorous and practical lady judiciously bides her time for at least a year before acknowledging her affection. This allows the gentleman in question ample time to prove himself worthy and shows him she has the patience and discretion needed to make a proper wife."*

"Cassie! Oh, Cassie!" Looking up at my sisters' horrified cries I saw a telegram in Andromeda's hands. I was so focused I must have missed the knock at the door. Standing, I clasped the pheasant shell in my pocket tightly, making my palm sting. I knew what had happened. I didn't know how, or when, but I knew what. Joining my sisters, I read the telegram, my hands shaking.

*Dear Ones,*

*Mary has supposedly drowned, her body swept out to sea. I am at Seafarer's Inn, Dartmoor's End, waiting for the sea to return her to me.*

*Sorrowfully,*

*Aunt Lavinia*

My body went numb and my heart hurt with every beat. I'd known from the moment I'd awakened that Mary was lost and I hated the part of me that dreamed of death always too late for me to change anything. They were the most painful moments of my life.

"How could she?" I blinked back my tears and startled everyone when I threw the letter down. I paced across the room, anger and doubt staving off my grief. "How could she possibly have drowned? She hasn't gone into the sea in years."

"She knew something bad would happen in the sea and now it has," Gemini cried, tears streaming down her cheeks.

All I could see in my mind was Mary running into the water to save me. "I'm going. I don't know what I can do about this, but I'm going to Cornwall. I have to know why she went into the sea."

"I'm going with you. Aunt Lavinia needs us." Andromeda folded her arms and furrowed her brow.

"Me too," Gemini added. They both glared at me ready for battle, for it would be no small expense.

"We will all go." My agreement shocked them. Usually my sisters and I argued for hours when it came to making practical decisions and carting everyone to the wilds of Cornwall was utterly impractical.

They didn't give me a second to change my mind. They immediately packed and we left for the Cornish coast within hours. I sent a note to our parents informing them Mary had drowned and we were going to be with Aunt Lavinia at Dartmoor's End. Then I spent the entire journey focused on one question. How had Mary drowned?


*Dartmoor's End, England*

"Miss Andrews, I don't mean to be rude, but you have said all of this before." Constable Poole slashed his dark brows at me from where he sat behind his desk. I didn't have to see beneath his bushy mustache to know he frowned; indignant irritation had his back ramrod straight. He hadn't bothered to stand when I entered his office for the third time today, but then, I hadn't bothered to wait for his assistant to escort me in this time either.

"You may be hearing me, Constable, but you aren't understanding me at all." I paced toward him. "Mary was deathly afraid of the sea. She did not go swimming and drown."

He stood, this time trying to quell my persistence with a disdainful stare. "Until I have specific evidence to prove otherwise, my conclusion of this matter remains as cited in my report."

"What about her employer, Sean Killdaren? I've heard

alarming stories about him and his brother, the Viscount of Blackmoor."

Sean Killdaren had also snubbed Aunt Lavinia's every attempt to speak with him, thus raising serious questions in my mind.

The constable flicked his hand as if I were a fly in his face. "Rumors only."

"I'd hardly call one of them being suspect in the death of Lady Helen Kennedy a rumor," I persisted. "What do you know of the case? Were you constable at the time?"

"Yes, an assistant. And there is nothing about the case that needs to concern you."

"You don't think it odd that while working for the Killdarens my cousin has suddenly disappeared?"

"Lady Helen died eight years ago. She did not die easy. I hardly see a connection with your cousin's drowning."

I threw my hands up. "You don't know that she *did* drown! There is no body. And how can you expect to find a connection between Mary and Lady Helen if you aren't investigating the matter?"

We glared at each other. After a week of hard travel and several days of searching, I knew little more about Mary's death than I had upon receiving the telegram. Mary had supposedly drowned while swimming alone.

"Constable, you aren't giving the facts of this case serious consideration. Apart from Mary's fear of the sea, why would a woman go swimming alone in the chilly May water? Why has her body never washed ashore?"

"Since you're asking me to spell it out for you, Miss Andrews, she may have deliberately drowned herself. And not all things the sea claims find their way to the shore. I can tell you this, though. After this long in the water, you don't want her body to return to you. Now, I have a number of things left to do today. So unless you have evidence implicating someone in your cousin's death, I suggest you refrain from wasting my time or spreading any more rumors. The Earl of Dartraven doesn't take kindly to anyone who besmirches the reputations of his sons."

Dizzied by anger, I grasped the edge of his desk. "So, their wealth rules the law here?"

His dark eyes glittered. "Woman, you try my patience. Shall I have you escorted out?"

"Unnecessary, sir. You'll have your evidence." I marched from his office, my heart and cheeks burning with ire. I didn't know the least thing about investigating a crime, but I was certain something terrible had happened to Mary—and I refused to return to the inn where Andromeda and Gemini comforted Aunt Lavinia until I had more than Constable Poole's obstinacy to report.

For the past six years as a journalist, I'd made it my business to read a great many newspapers, some concerning crime. With those in mind, I went directly to the mercantile store and perused the available publications. *The Police Chronicles* caught my gaze first. Glancing through the front page article, I found a detailed account of the investigation into the murder of a prominent business man in London. That should help me to investigate Mary's death.

Noticing the clerk eye me with suspicion, I picked up *The Crime Gazette* and *The London Report* as well and made my way to the counter.

"Ya asked about that teacher a day or two ago, didn't ya?" The clerk surprised me, for I'd given up on finding out about Mary from the villagers. I'd asked a number of people who only said that Mary had rarely visited the town.

My pulse raced with hoped. "Yes. Did you learn more about her disappearance?"

Her gaze darted between me and the newspapers I clutched, then her eyes grew wider than a king's gold piece. "Yar one of those fancy newspaper reporters, aren't ya. Had a few of them around years ago when Lady Helen was murdered. They were men, though." She spoke as if being a woman wasn't proper then she lowered her voice. "It's the maze, I tell ya. My bet is that teacher went in there and never was seen again and the Killdaren doesn't want folks to know."

"The Killdaren?" I wondered what sort of man could evoke such awe—or was it fear?

"Mister Sean Killdaren. He's the second son of the Earl of Dartraven by only a blink of an eye. Ye'll know why folks call him *the* Killdaren rather than mister iffen you ever catch a glimpse of him."

"Did someone see Mary go into the maze?"

Shrugging hard enough to bounce her sausage ringlets, she leaned on the counter. "Well, not first hand that I've heard, mind ya. But that would be a place anyone could disappear from. Iffen the sea had taken her seems like she'd have washed ashore like most things."

The shop bell clanged and two women dressed in simple worn muslins entered. "Wouldn't you say so, Berta?" The clerk addressed one of the women.

"What's that, Camile?"

"That teacher they say drowned up at the castle. I betcha she wandered into the maze, I do."

"Don't know if it were the maze or the sea, and I don't care to know." She nodded to the other woman who'd entered with her. "Betsy, here, says that ol' hag housekeeper who's always running off the help is now trying to hire a downstairs maid. Imagine that. As if anyone would want to work for her. I'd have to be starvin' to take on that job. All that work and nothin' for it. Yer practically invisible when it comes to gettin' anythin' extra by working downstairs, too. No cast off gowns or tips from gentry with that thankless job. Why it's worse than a scullery maid, I tell ya."

"Wouldn't get no tips, no how. No one dares to visit the Killdarens. Now the Wellworths are where ya need to be getting a position. My cousin said he made handfuls of shillings a day during the last hunting party, he did." The other woman continued on with more about the hunting party, but I wasn't listening. One word had stuck in my mind and an entire plan revolved itself around it.

*Maid.*

# Chapter Two

My heart raced as if I were off to commit a crime. The path leading from the village cut along the edge of the wild sand dunes where dark shadows from the maritime forest lurked and shifted with the inland breeze. A chill stole through the warmth of the late afternoon sun, promising there would be a cold bite to the coming night. I pulled the edges of a worn cloak closer to my breasts. Minutes after leaving the mercantile store, I'd bought it and a ragged potato sack from an elderly woman selling herbs at the end of the street. After mussing my neat chignon, I now looked like a woman desperately needing work.

The walk between Dartmoor's End and Killdaren's castle took longer than I thought it would and only added to my frustrations. The area was so isolated that my skin crawled.

How could Constable Poole ever believe a woman would go swimming alone on this empty stretch of sand and sea? But he didn't believe that, did he? He believed Mary had taken her own life.

She would never have done that. I knew it as surely as I knew myself. So why had Mary's shoes and basket been found on this stretch of beach? What had happened?

The castle loomed ahead as I crested the rise of a dune. Even with the sun shining upon it, the stone walls were dark and begged me to ask what sinister secrets lay hidden in the shadows.

Like some mythological creature the Killdaren's home was half manor-like and half castle-like in appearance. From the moment I'd arrived in Dartmoor's End days ago and had seen the castle from afar, it had captivated me, as did the stories about the castle's rarely seen owner, Sean Killdaren and his brother, Alexander, the Viscount of Blackmoor—a man who resided farther down the coast in Dragon's Cove.

The brothers had nearly killed each other the same night Lady Helen Kennedy had been murdered and they hadn't spoken to each other since. There had also been mutterings about a Dragon's Curse plaguing the family, but none of the villagers wanted to say what that meant.

The Killdarens' wealth and position had kept the twin sons of the family from a hangman's noose once. As I made my way down the hill, following the craggy path to their land, I wondered if one of them had murdered again.

Once I reached the estate, an understanding of the vastness of the Killdarens' fortune dawned. I passed an elaborate, two-story stable, large enough to be a manor house itself. Then I skirted the edge of the a massive formal garden, where dozens of statues and a riot of color from blooming phlox, pansies, rhododendron and gladiolas did little to ease my spirit. The sun glistening off the marble and showering the flowers reminded me of Mary. She loved flowers and sunlight. I could almost picture her in the gardens, her cheeks flushed with pleasure and her arms laden with blooms.

Cresting a knoll, I took in the full scope of the estate and saw that the darkness behind the gardens wasn't the maritime forest, but a large, elaborate maze that eventually lost itself into a thick expanse of trees. I stopped and stared at the high hedges of the maze, seeing just how obscuring the looming green labyrinth was and I shivered. In just a few steps, a woman *could* disappear.

I moved on and saw an odd building jutting from the castle's main structure. Three-storied and glass-domed, it cast a shadow over half of the garden, marring its beauty. No light, no matter how bright, could alter the building's frightening façade. Dark gray stone walls were topped with sinister gargoyles and black curtains covered the encircling windows, shrouding it like a tomb.

A face flashed in the nearest window then was gone, but the sensation that someone continued to secretly watch me lingered. I hurried to the servants' door and quickly rapped the knocker before I could change my mind. The people inside these walls were the last to see Mary alive, and I had to learn what they knew, even if I had to use deceit to do so.

The Killdarens' affluence put them not only above the law, but also socially beyond any persons of my acquaintance. Why, even calling the intricately carved brass and mahogany door a servants' entrance seemed ludicrous, for its grandness could grace the front of any opulent residence I'd ever entered.

The door opened with a yawning creak.

I don't know exactly what I expected, but it wasn't a jaunty smile and a twinkling gaze.

"And I thought me bonnie lived over the sea." The look in the man's eyes practically undressed me on the spot.

I stepped back, barely remembering to curb my admonishing response to such an improper and personal greeting. "Beg your pardon, sir, but I'm Cassie Andrews. I hear you are in need of a maid."

He stared at me for a long moment before he called to someone inside. "Ma, you've a visitor."

"Stuart Frye! Did you take any scones?" The sharp voice cut abrasively through the air.

"She's all bark and no bite," the man whispered, then winked as he bit into a scone. A smile tugged at the corners of my mouth. Dressed in a worn cotton shirt and pants the color of old leather, he had a rugged appeal that went well with his familiar manner.

The woman's voice from inside grew louder. "What did you say? No boy of mine had better be talking behind my back or he'll end up in more trouble than he can handle."

"Promise to be nice to the pretty maid and I'll behave. She looks like a dose of pure sunshine dropped on our doorstep."

Heat flagged my cheeks. How could he flirt so outlandishly with his mother right behind him?

Mrs. Frye appeared in the doorway, brandishing a formidable scowl and a wooden spoon. Her stone gray hair was twisted into a hard knot at the top of her head and pulled so tightly back from her face that I felt the pain of it in a glance. She wore a black uniform relieved only by the plain lines of a white apron and her pale face—a face which might have been pretty but for her icy sternness. She smacked her son on the shoulder with the spoon. "You keep those roving eyes to yourself."

"Bake me scones and I'll be nice." He laughed and held up an entire handful of goodies as he brushed a kiss to the prickly woman's cheek before strolling down the steps.

"Those scones are for Miss Prudence's tea!"

"You tell her I stole them. Maybe that will get her to step a dainty foot outside, and bring Rebecca with her. It isn't right to keep a child all locked up."

Goodness! I jerked my gaze between the two of them, recognizing the name of the blind child Mary had come to teach.

"Don't go exaggerating circumstances. Rebecca's delicate and needs special care."

"Not any more than Jamie, and look how well he turned out."

I saw a crack in Mrs. Frye's harsh armor. Her features softened, and for a brief moment she appeared almost motherly. "Whatever else you've done, you did right by your brother. Now stop wasting time." She shot her gaze to me. "Well, missy, are you here for work?"

I nodded.

Narrowing her eyes, she leaned in close to my face. "You aren't from around here, and you don't look like a scullery maid. What trouble are you in?"

"No trouble, ma'am." I crossed my fingers, hoping God would forgive me for lying. "My father's ill and we've little money left. He lost his post as a vicar. I need work."

"Humph. I don't know if you'll do or not. I won't be putting up with no airs and no consorting. You must live here so you can be watched, and you're forbidden from any wild celebrations with the villagers. Sneak out at night and you'll be searching for a new post by morning."

"Yes, ma'am. Please, ma'am. I need the work."

"Be here at dawn tomorrow with your things." She scowled and then slammed the door in my face. I stood on the step, blinking, wondering if I'd imagined the whole incident. Darkening shadows and a brisker wind soon convinced me I hadn't. Upon leaving the castle grounds, I practically ran to Seafarer's Inn, somewhat stunned but elated as well. I couldn't believe I'd secured the post.

Unfortunately, when I told my family, they couldn't believe it either and went immediately into hysterics that seemed to have no end.

Andromeda pressed her palm to my forehead. "My word, Cassie, has your grief driven you insane?"

"This is a disaster! A parlor maid? The scandal! I can't believe you've done this." Aunt Lavinia wailed as if the world had come to an end.

I drew a deep breath. "If everyone would calm down and think about this for a moment, all of you would realize this is the perfect answer. I'll be able to speak with people who worked with Mary."

"Don't they hang spies when they catch them?" Gemini sounded entirely too curious about the matter.

"The gallows!" Aunt Lavinia fell back upon the sofa, looking as if she would faint as she held up her hand. "No. It'll be worse than that. They'll brand you a fallen woman and cut off your hair. You'll never be able to marry."

Though I knew it to be utter nonsense, the image of me shorn and hanging from one of Killdaren's Castle's high stone turrets flitted across my mind. "Hush this insanity. Working as a maid is no less honorable than working as a governess. And should they discover I am searching for the truth about Mary, the worse that can happen is I'll be dismissed. And what's more, I've no desire to marry anyway. I want a career as a journalist." I didn't even know that myself until the words burst from me.

I had long resigned myself to spinsterhood, for surely no man could love a woman who dreamed of people's deaths. But I hadn't a set course for my future either, I hadn't imagined doing anything other than what I had done every day for years. Now I realized I wanted to accomplish more than what my etiquette column offered.

"Not marry!" Aunt Lavinia gasped as if that was the most shocking thing she'd heard yet.

"You already are a journalist," Andromeda said.

"Writing 'Cassiopeia's Corner' hardly qualifies as being a journalist. A real journalist is one that discovers stories and writes about them."

Andromeda grabbed my hand. "I didn't know you were unhappy."

I swallowed the sudden lump in my throat. "I'm not. And this isn't about me. It is about Mary. Somewhere behind the stone walls is the answer to what happened to her, and I won't rest until I find it."

"What if something bad did happen to Mary? Wouldn't you be in danger?" Andromeda turned my way, her heart in her eyes. She'd said the first sane words since the discussion began.

"I'll have Father's pistol. I'll be careful. Besides, all I am going to do is to scrub a few floors and ask a few questions. How hard or dangerous can that be?"

I slipped silently from the Seafarer's Inn a little before dawn, tiptoeing out with a few of my belongings stuffed into the potato sack along with the pistol, something I prayed I wouldn't need but was prepared to use. I didn't wake my aunt and sisters. Another tearful barrage would do little to help either of us, so I left a note instead, telling them I would contact them as soon as possible. Despite my family's misgivings, I did not think this to be a rash or deadly move, for unlike Mary, I entered Killdaren's Castle armed and aware there might be danger lurking in its shadows.

As I made my way in the dawn's glowing light, a strange

anticipation for discovering what lay beyond the castle's stone walls fluttered inside me and filled me with guilt. How could I find excitement in investigating my cousin's death? It was not a very flattering observation and made me want to ignore the practical and starkly honest conscience I'd always heeded.

Thankfully, I soon crested the sand dunes separating the seaside inn from the view of the castle and paused to breathe deeply of the salty air. The sun rose like a fiery god from the wavy, blue horizon. Tangy sea breezes tugged at my knotted chignon and whipped at the skirts of the homespun wool dress I had purchased from one of the inn's maids last night. The early morning mists and the sound of the sea wrapped around me, tightening the sorrow squeezing my heart. I reached into my pocket and rubbed the pheasant shell, wondering if Mary had had her matching shell with her when she disappeared. I knew she'd brought it to Cornwall from a letter she'd written earlier this year.

"Mary, are you out there?" I whispered softly.

Arcing overhead, a gull cried a sharp, plaintive note as if answering me before diving to the right and drawing my gaze toward my destination. This morning, the pinkish-gold hues of dawn painted the gray stone walls and cast an eerie beauty over the castle's forbidding façade, almost making me doubt I had seen a face in the window yesterday afternoon. Almost, but not quite. Nothing could brighten the darkness of the maze or the looming presence of the stone gargoyles. I kept my gaze focused on the back door, determined to ignore the urge to run knotting my stomach.

Before I could knock, the door flung open. Mrs. Frye stood there with her hands planted on her hips. "You're late!"

I glanced at the rising sun. "I apologize, ma'am."

"Well, what are you waiting for? You've chores that need doing. Impoverished vicar's daughter or not, you'll get no special treatment here. Your only time off will be half-days Sunday, so you can rightly serve the Lord's commands. Otherwise, there'll be no lazing about."

Apparently dawn meant before the light of day and not

minutes after.

"Yes, ma'am." I followed her stiff-backed march into the castle, where the size of the rooms and the height of the ceilings completely swallowed me. An arched doorway joined two kitchens that stretched like a sea of order and cleanliness. Not a speck marred the shine of the wood floor, not a spoon, dish, or knife lay out of place and the copper pots gleamed like mirrors.

Mrs. Frye didn't pause, but moved faster. "The cook, Mrs. Murphy, will be returning from the market soon. Once you and Bridget finish the dining room, you can both assist with the cooking."

"Yes, ma'am." I drew a deep breath and drank in my fill of the hominess. Beneath the smell of fresh scones filling a silver platter on the counter, the welcoming scents of lemon, beeswax and dried spices lingered in the air.

"Besides your assigned duties, you'll do as the upstairs maids and Nurse Tolley ask. They mainly take care of Miss Prudence and her daughter, Rebecca." She took the staircase from the kitchens. "You're to use the servants' stairs at all times. The only time you are anywhere in the house other than in the kitchens and your room is if you're cleaning. Do you understand?"

"Yes, ma'am." We rounded landing after landing until we reached the top floor. The Killdarens were Irish and I kept looking for some bit of Celtic antiquity to show. Though immaculately clean and made of rich, dark wood, the walls of the servants' stairwell were completely bare, and no sounds beyond the brush of our skirts and our muffled steps could be heard. The household seemed unnaturally quiet, almost eerily so. It was like tiptoeing through a graveyard.

"You'll share a room with Bridget, the other downstairs maid. Breakfast for the servants is thirty minutes before sun up. You missed it this morning, so there'll be no meal until later. I'll give you five minutes to settle your things and then I expect you downstairs."

"I'll hurry, ma'am."

"See that you do." She turned to face me and her apparently perpetual scowl deepened. She didn't like what she saw. "You'll need to cover that yellow hair with a mob cap in order to be decent."

I slid my fingers over my chignon, wondering what about my hair was indecent.

"I have fresh uniform dresses in the storage closet, though nothing as small as you. After the chores are done this evening, we'll find two that you can take in. I expect you to be wearing one first thing in the morning. Above all other rules, there are two you must adhere implicitly to. You're to make no noise, and once in your room at night, you're to stay there until morning. I'll not have any roaming about. The Killdaren sleeps during the daytime and is busy during the night. No one is to disturb him, ever. Do you understand?"

"Yes, ma'am." I nearly bit my tongue to keep from asking why. What manner of man slept when all others were awake?

Mrs. Frye left after giving an additional warning not to waste another moment. I hurriedly unpacked my sack, taking time to hide the pistol and my crime publications under the thin, lumpy mattress. The room contained no frills, but was amply furnished with two small cot-like beds, a desk and chair, a washstand and mirror, and a small wardrobe. It reminded me of Mrs. Frye—serviceable, impeccably clean and no character beyond what was necessary to be functional.

Keeping the housekeeper's warning in mind, I hurried downstairs, saving any further reflections for later. Even though I had taken less time than allotted, Mrs. Frye still frowned when I appeared, then led me impatiently to the dining room. Once we exited the kitchens and entered the great room and the entry hall of the castle, I was thrust back in time by the Killdarens' history and wealth swelling around me.

Ornately papered and carved paneled walls climbed twenty feet to patterned and scrolled ceilings where elaborate chandeliers hung. The marbled floor of traditional black and white squares was bordered with intricate designs along its edges. Oil paintings and tapestries lined the walls, depicting scenes of life from ages past. Statues and vases and delicate artifacts filled every spare space. I was so overwhelmed, so fascinated, that I had to focus my gaze on Mrs. Frye's unrelenting back or risk being lured to linger, a gaffe that would have had me dismissed, I'm sure.

She passed through a set of paneled doors and I followed then abruptly halted in the doorway.

Great heavens. This was the dining room? A banquet hall fit for a king was a more apt description. The long mahogany table, topped with silver candelabras, cut down the center of the room. It was surrounded by padded chairs covered in burgundy damask with chair backs crested by a pair of carved dragons, giving the room an almost medieval flare. As richly appointed as the great hall and entryway, with dark green silk and wood paneling on the walls and a black marble mantel, it had to be the most elegant room I had ever seen.

"Bridget?" Mrs. Frye called out.

"'ere, Mrs. Frye." The muffled reply was followed a moment later by a pretty, young woman with wisps of fiery red hair escaping her mob cap. She peeped over the table, her blue eyes as bright as stars. "I'm 'alf-way finished with the chairs."

"I've brought help, so I expect you to be done in half the time. This is Cassie. You are to teach her the proper way to clean the downstairs. She'll be sharing your room as well. Now, no more dawdling, understood?"

"Yes, ma'am." I moved toward Bridget as Mrs. Frye exited the room.

"Lord must've 'eard me prayers!" Bridget smile and stuffed a lemon-scented rag into my hand.

"Thank you." I stared at the huge table and the numerous chairs.

"Don't ya worry none, Cassie. This isn't as 'ard as it looks. The two of us will 'ave thin's done quick." Her manner was as warm as her hair was red.

Climbing under the table with her, I began polishing. After my fifth chair, I sat back and drew a breath and patted the perspiration on my brow with the sleeve of my dress. My arms ached and the unfamiliar feel of the rough wool dress irritated my skin. It amazed me that Bridget had already done twenty-five of the chairs before I had arrived. When I glanced up, I saw she, too, had stopped work to study me.

"I was just wondering who had fifty people to dinner at once."

She laughed. "Ach, no one eats in 'ere at all, leastways not while I've been 'ere and my sister Flora before me as well. That'd be at least five years. Yet we polish and scrub every week as if the Queen herself were coming." She leaned closer to me, her brow furrowing. "Ya aren't from around 'ere, are ya, miss?"

I cleared my throat, for I had forgotten to speak as a maid would. "No. I'm from further North. Hard times have me working."

"No shame in that, at all. Hard times 'ave us all working. My sister Flora's goin' to change that for us McGowans one day real soon. But for now we best get busy. Mrs. Frye doesn't put up with much chatter. She'll most likely be back in an hour and 'ave our necks if we aren't done with the table and workin' on the silver by then."

We set to work, finished polishing the table, and had just started on the silver when Mrs. Frye appeared. She grunted at our progress and pointed out a spot that needed more polishing, then left.

"So, why does the family never use the dining room?"

Bridget's eyes grew huge. "Ya mean ya don't know?"

"Is there something I should know?"

"They're cursed, the Dragon's Curse, ya know. Cursed since their birth to murder each other. Most folks are too afraid to even socialize with 'em. A right shame if you ask me, too. Men as handsome as the Killdaren and the viscount shouldn't be cursed."

"Handsome are they?" Who had cursed them and why?

"Like princes." She looked cautiously about. "Come with me quick, and I'll let ya peek at the Killdaren's picture. It's all I 'ave ever seen of him."

Her words shocked me. "How many years have you worked

here?"

"Three." Rising quietly, she motioned me to follow her. As I did, my thoughts raced. Mary had only been here a year. Had she even met her employer? In coming here I had assumed Sean Killdaren had known Mary. What if he hadn't ever met her? Exiting the double doors, Bridget tiptoed silently across the intimidating center hall into another room. "We'll not be cleaning in 'ere till tomorrow, but I didn't want ya to 'ave to wait that long to see 'im. The picture's on the far wall. I'll watch for Mrs. Frye while ya go take a peek. Make it quick."

Feeling like a thief, I slipped inside and would have been carried away by the multitude of books filling the massive shelves if I had not seen the painting first. The impact of the image literally stole my breath, and I stepped back from the life-sized portrait hanging above the mantel of a massive stone hearth.

His green eyes, so vibrantly realistic, stared directly at me from beneath dark brows over a chiseled nose and roughly hewn jaw. He wore a black suit, white ruffled shirt, and had a black cape flung over one shoulder. In one black-gloved hand he held a silver walking stick with what I thought was a fanged snake on its tip. But as I moved closer, I saw it was a dragon that curled up the cane. A force greater than my own will held me captive before him. Had he needed the night to hide his sins?

It was the first portrait I'd seen done of someone in the moonlight. Dark shadows surrounded him on all sides. He held his free hand fisted at his side, expressing anger or...pain? A haunting moon and an eerie black sky sharpened the edge of darkness to his character. Even so, the sensual charisma emanating from him would have brought a vibrant warmth to his picture had it not been for the cynical, almost cold smile barely curving his full lips.

"He canna go out into the daylight, they say. It's whispered that he is a vampire."

# Chapter Three

I nearly jumped from my skin. I hadn't heard Bridget leave her post guarding the door to join me in the room before Sean Killdaren's portrait.

"Surely not." I choked out the words, my throat too constricted to add a scoffing laugh to the nonsense. For even I, the voice of reason among my wildly imaginative family, could readily believe Bridget's gossip, provided the man was anything like his portrait. Thankfully, that was something I doubted. The artist had to have embellished the facts. There was no way this was a realistic depiction of the man.

"Whot if it were true?" Bridget asked softly, gazing at the picture so raptly that a fissure of doubt snaked inside of me. "Whot if 'e was a vampire? Would ya let him claim ya? Would ya live forever in the dark o 'the night to be with him?"

A full minute passed before I could assert myself. I shook my head. "No. No man could be that magnetic. No man could have such a mesmerizing appeal as to lure a woman to live forever in darkness. Why do they say he can't go into the daylight?"

"It kills him, is whot I've 'eard. Daylight kills vampires, right?"

"I suppose. Does that have anything to do with the curse?"

Behind us the door opened and we whirled around.

"Blimey, we're caught," Bridget whispered.

Instead of Mrs. Frye's dour countenance and the doom that would have surely followed, two richly dressed gentlemen entered the room. One man looked somewhat like the portrait of Sean Killdaren except less dynamic, with graying temples and bleary blue eyes. The other man, completely gray-haired, sported a fashionable mustache and monocle, and carried a silver walking stick. Both wore top hats, morning coats, and pale trousers. "It's the Earl of Dartraven, the Killdaren's father and his cohort," Bridget said under her breath.

"My Lord, Sir Warwick." Bridget immediately fell into a curtsy.

Keeping silent, I lowered my gaze and curtsied as well.

"Up with you, child. Flora is it?" asked the Earl of Dartraven.

"Dartraven, your memory so lacks these days, it's a wonder you can still distinguish a horse from an ass. Flora of the golden locks left our service, if you recall. This is Bridget, and a new maid if I'm not mistaken. Am I right?"

"Beg your pardon, my name is Cassie, my lord, Sir Warwick." I mimicked Bridget's tone and kept my gaze downcast.

"Well, maids, have Mrs. Frye serve tea." The earl waved his hand, dismissing us as he turned to his friend. "Remembering tedious details is exactly why I tolerate your odious presence, Warwick. And I can tell an ass from a horse easily. I've not a horse in my son's library at the moment, but there is an ass."

Warwick laughed. "The only reason you keep me around is to alleviate your own boredom."

Bridget and I hurried from the library back to the dining room. "Ya get to scrubbin' and I'll find Mrs. Frye. Blimey, but I 'ope she don't learn we were shirking our chores."

"Do they live here?" I whispered. Mrs. Frye hadn't mentioned them earlier.

"Only the earl, part of the year 'til winter. Then 'e goes to 'is estate near 'ampton Court. Sir Warwick lives nearby."

"I'd have thought the coast warmer than the country during the winter."

"Not 'ere, I tell ya. There's no cold like that of the sea and castle."

"You said the Killdarens were cursed. Who cursed them and why?"

"Don't know." Bridget lowered her voice to a whisper. "I 'ear it's always been that way. One of 'em is doomed to die."

I shivered, thinking about Mary lost in the cold sea, her body drifting in the waves. Bridget left and I set to work on the silver. Soon my mind drifted to Sean Killdaren's portrait, his green eyes, the chiseled perfection of his face, and the irresistible magnetism that still had me in its grasp.

How had Bridget worked here for three years and had yet to see him? I closed my eyes and brought more details of his image to mind, the cold curve of his mouth and the clench of his black gloved fist. Perhaps it was a good thing she hadn't.

Bridget returned and we finished the work in the dining room then made our way to the kitchens. That's when the real work began. The kitchen that I had imagined as being warm and cozy became hot and grueling when burning ovens and hard work were involved. We were there hours before we finished.

"It's scandalous of 'er, I say," Bridget muttered with the first hint of discontent I had heard. We were on our way back to our room after hours of scrubbing, polishing, then cooking. "She 'ired us as 'ousemaids, and after our 'ard chores, she puts us to work as scullery maids. She's punishing me for my sister's desertion, I tell ya."

"How so?" I rolled my shoulders, protesting the heavy wool upon my skin and the ache in my arms. I wanted a hot bath.

"Flora started as a scullery maid, and within two years she became Mrs. Murphy's best 'elper, practically running the kitchens for 'er. Everyone thought Flora would take Mrs. Murphy's place when Mrs. Murphy grew too old. But Flora surprised us all, she did. Went after a better life. With 'er 'aving a voice like an angel, though, we should 'ave expected it."

We'd come upstairs to ready ourselves for dinner and had to be back in the kitchens for the evening meal shortly. Bridget flopped back on her bed, and I moved to the window, opening it for a breath of fresh air. "You mentioned your sister earlier. I'm sorry, but I can't remember where you said she went."

"I don't rightly know yet. But I tell ya, anywhere Mrs. Frye ain't has to be a better place."

"She is rather stiff minded." From our room, I had a view of the stables, the gardens, part of the round, gargoyle-guarded room and the maze, which still appeared dark and unnavigable even from this height. I couldn't see the sea, but I could smell its tangy salt in the air and hear the whip of the waves lashing the shore. Dusk blanketed the sky, leaving only a sliver of a red sun on the horizon. Even as I watched, the deep shadows of the night crept closer to the castle's stone walls...and to me.

For the first time in my life I would spend the night away from my family and anything familiar. Apprehension tightened a knot inside me.

"Not the 'alf of it," Bridget said in response. "She 'as plenty of money in the 'ousehold budget to 'ire another scullery maid, too. She's just a wantin' to see me struggle. I've thought about quitin' and takin' me brother and mother to join Flora."

Turning from the window, I focused my attention on Bridget. "Didn't you just say you don't know where she is?"

Bridget sat up, a frown creasing her freckled forehead. "I don't, but I suspect she'll write to me from London shortly. She'll send a letter to the church. Her man promised to write for 'er. She's goin' to be a famous singer, she is. He's promised her a part in a play, earning twice a week's salary in a day."

"Then she went to London with someone from here? What is his name?" Moving over to the washstand, I poured a dab of water into the basin and wet my silk handkerchief, washing my face. After twelve hours of scrubbing the castle and working in the steamy kitchens, dirt and grime increased the discomfort of my wool dress. I was desperate for a bath.

"Don't know his surname and I ain't too sure 'e's from 'ere. She kept it secret, so I'm thinkin' 'e was a bit above us, iffen ya know what I mean. Gentry most likely." Her voice lowered. "Or clergy. She called 'im Jack. In two weeks' time she fell in love and up and moved. He's the best thing that has ever 'appened to 'er, as sad and upset as she was."

Bridget's story bothered me. "Why was she sad? When did she leave for London?"

"I'm only supposing it's London. It could 'ave been Paris. Imagine that." She beamed at the idea, her blue eyes sparkling. "It's been about two weeks, now. Miss Mary drowning 'ad us all upset. That was a sad day, I tell ya. The eve of May Day it was and Flora took the death especially 'ard. Mary was teachin' Flora to speak and sing proper, she was."

My pulse pounded in my ears and I had to force myself to breathe and act no more than mildly curious. "A woman drowned? What happened?"

"Odd thing that was. Mary and the poor wee one—ya don't know about Rebecca yet. She's blind. We all think she's the Killdaren's child since Miss Prudence and Rebecca live 'ere. Not that Miss Prudence 'as never said who Rebecca's father is, mind ya, but that's another story. As I said, Miss Mary and the wee one went on a picnic. 'ours later, the wee one comes back drenched in seawater and covered with sand, crying for her Mary. Stuart found the picnic blanket and Mary's boots and basket up o'er the dunes, nigh coming close to being pulled out to sea themselves. Mary was a one always teachin' and the wee one can be wild. I'm thinkin' Mary drowned either teachin' the wee one to swim, or savin' the wee one from drownin'. Won't never know for sure, though. The wee one goes mad every time she 'ears Mary's name, screams for days and won't talk."

My head spun. I covered my face with my silk handkerchief, quietly dabbing at the tears welling in my eyes and pressing my fingers against them to stem more tears from falling. Was it all as simple as that? Had Mary drowned saving the child? I didn't believe for a minute that Mary had been teaching the child to swim, but I could readily believe she would have gone into the ocean to save a child, just as she had for me.

"Ya all right, Cassie? We need to 'urry or we'll miss the dinner we worked so 'ard to make." Bridget touched my shoulder and I nearly jumped from my skin again.

"Yes." I swallowed the lump of emotion lodged in my throat and snatched the cloth from my face. Exhaustion suddenly weighed upon me. I ached from my fingers to my toes and all I wanted was a bath and to crawl into bed and cry. Having finally heard a plausible reason why Mary would have gone into the sea, my heart wanted to grieve. Instead, I had to keep up pretenses, eat, talk and act as if everything was fine. Before going down, I slipped the pheasant shell into my pocket from where I had placed it under my pillow.

At the huge oak table by the hearth in the second kitchen, I met some of the household servants, and thankfully, learned that Mrs. Frye and the upper servants, except for Mr. and Mrs. Murphy, always dined first. Already too many names and faces blurred before me, though there were surprisingly few servants considering the vastness of the castle and its grounds; but as Bridget explained, with no visitors an army of servants wasn't needed.

I had my back to the warm fire and ate what I knew should be a delicious venison stew, but I couldn't taste a thing. My heart was caught up with visions of Mary being swept out to sea and I had to force myself to focus on the people around me. Even though I may have already found an answer to what happened to her, I still needed to be sure.

Mrs. Murphy had a jovial plumpness that directly opposed Mrs. Frye's prickly, bony nature, and Mr. Murphy, an even plumper and jollier version of his wife, held the position of head butler. He seemed utterly out of character to what I imagined a proper butler for such a rich manor would be. In addition to Stuart, Mrs. Frye had another son named Jamie, who dwarfed everyone in the room. He had yet to say a word, but kept staring at me, making me uncomfortable.

Stuart hadn't helped either. He began the evening winking at me and flirting almost as outrageously as he had at the back door yesterday, but the longer his brother kept staring at me, Stuart's expression turned troubled and he stopped flirting. The odd situation had me fiddling with my hair and brushing my cheeks with the back of my hand, wondering if something about my appearance was amiss.

It wasn't just my imagination, either. Bridget sent funny looks toward Jamie and Stuart which neither of them noticed. Finally, I pulled my mob cap lower and tried to ignore them.

Two other housemaids, sisters named Janet and Adele Oaks, were the only other women present. Dark haired, with a smidgen of gray at their temples, they desperately needed to wear fichus, for their bosoms nearly spilled from their dresses every time they leaned forward to flirt outrageously with Stuart Frye, Will and Simon, men who worked the stables and grounds.

Besides Jamie staring at me and the eye-opening familiarity between the sexes, the lively banter during dinner was like a family meal in the Andrews home and made me long for my sisters.

"I'll tell ya, we've got nothin' out of them fancy laws and stuff. It's a cryin' shame when a pint o' ale will buy ya a life of 'ell. Tom Dickens found a shilling in his ale, and when he fished it out, they carried him to the ship," Will said.

"They took the McGary brothers with the same trick," Stuart said.

"What are they talking about?" I whispered to Bridget.

"Press-gangs," she said. "Men are up and disappearing from the docks and being forced to serve the Queen's navy by trickery. Officers plop a king's shillin' in a tankard and when the surprised fool who's a drinkin' takes it out, they chain 'em to a ship. The officials are claimin' it's all legal 'cause the man had the money in his hand, right? It's the kiss o' death from the sea, iffen ya ask me, toilin' day 'n and day out, battling storms and pirates. Some even say a winsome woman or two 'ave disappeared that way."

"To serve on a ship?"

"Ack no! They force the women to give favors to the men, iffen ya know what I mean. The women lure the men from the safety of the pub, and when they're naked and distracted the women cosh 'em and have 'em carted to the ship."

My stomach roiled. I knew the world to be cruel, but such vileness shocked me. Thoughts of my own aches and discomfort lost importance. Glancing about the table, I shuddered, wondering if Mary could be at some pub forced to lure men and give favors just to stay alive. "I thought press-gangs had been outlawed."

"That's what Will was sayin'. Fancy laws don't buy us folk anythin' but more misery. Instead of just stealin' 'em off the streets, they now trick 'em with their ale. It's a maggot filled barrel of rot that a man can't 'ave a pint without worryin' about his life."

I studied the men and women at the table, wondering about their lives and the perils they faced with no real hope of legal recourse. Their conversation drifted to horse racing and the weather, and my shock dulled beneath the exhaustion weighing down my every muscle. My eyes drooped and my own discomforts soon clamored as loudly as before. I ached. Grime covered me from head to toe, and I still had hours of sewing to do in order to have my uniform ready for the next day.

The meal was nearly over, and I thought to escape unnoticed back to my room when Jamie Frye slammed his fist on the table, making everyone jump in surprise as dishes and mugs rattled.

"How...can...ye all do it?" He spoke very slowly as if each word were a mountain to be scaled before being spoken. "Ye...act as if...she never was!" He pointed a finger directly at me and said, "She...could...die tonight...disappear from her bed, and ye wouldn't care."

Shocked at his violence, I leaned back from the table, fighting the urge to flee as fast as my heart raced.

Everyone sat stunned and disturbingly silent.

"It's all right, Jamie." Stuart Frye finally rose and walked very slowly to his brother, as if Jamie were a wild predator. "We all miss Mary. Her death was an accident that saddens us all."

"No...no...no! It wasn't," Jamie shouted, standing up so fast and so forcefully that he toppled the bench over backward, sending everyone on it to the floor before he thundered out the door. Vibrations from the heavy wood slamming shut, shivered down my spine.

My shock must have been evident, because a second later Stuart Frye stood at my side, his hand on my shoulder. "I'm sorry, Miss Cassie. I shouldn't have made my brother come tonight. It's your hair that upset him, I'm afraid."

"My hair?" I asked, so stunned that I didn't even pull away from the familiarity of his touch.

"It's golden, not unlike Mary's was." He frowned and leaned closer, as if studying my features.

"A common color, I would think," I replied, gathering my wits. Jamie's denial that Mary's death was an accident continued to ring in my ears just as loudly as the immensity of his size and strength shouted at me to be very wary.

"Saint's in 'eaven. I 'aven't seen Jamie this upset since ya came back with Mary's basket and boots the day she died," Bridget said to Stuart.

"I need to go find Jamie. You'll be all right, miss?"

Bridget brushed Stuart's hand from my shoulder, surprising me. I'd forgotten it was there. "Of course, she will, Stuart Frye. And ye need't be taking advantage of 'er innocence, either. As if Mary wasn't enough for ya."

I thought it Divine Providence that I had my bottom planted firmly on a bench, or I might have fainted. Mary and Stuart Frye?

Stuart glared at Bridget for a long, uncomfortable moment. "I wouldn't be spreading rumors about the dead if I were you." He spoke softly, but the anger behind his words rang as loudly as his brother's outburst.

Bridget snubbed her shoulder his way as she turned protectively to me and Stuart Frye left. "Janet and Adele will clean the kitchens for us tonight since ya 'ave a good bit of sewing to do. Come along, and I'll 'elp. Before midnight we'll 'ave your uniform ready for the morn."

"Thank you." I forced a smile, no easy task considering the turmoil of questions roiling inside of me.

It was exactly midnight when we finished sewing my uniform and I could thankfully slip off the rough wool dress I'd worn all day. The first thing I did was to try and rid myself of the feel of grime. Bridget shook her head amusedly at my bathing attempt with the water basin and my handkerchief, then rolled her eyes when I explained I'd not be able to sleep unless refreshed.

She had no such qualms. Having already had her spring bath, she'd wait for summer. After washing her hands and face, she crawled into bed wearing her chemise and went promptly to sleep. I gingerly soothed areas of tenderness on my skin and hands with rose and milk cream. The scent evoked so many memories of home that tears stung my eyes when I slid on my soft cotton nightdress. I crawled onto the lumpy cot, exhausted beyond the point of even yearning for anything but sleep. But my mind wouldn't let me rest. It raced through the events of the day, ending with Jamie Frye's outburst. *She could die tonight, disappear from her bed and ye wouldn't care.*

For some reason, I couldn't accept the explanation that Mary drowned saving Rebecca. Not yet. Not that Mary wouldn't have done such a thing, but because the cloud of tension surrounding me told me something else. Someone was hiding something about Mary's death. Rising, I stuffed my father's pistol beneath my pillow and read several articles from a crime publication by the light of a candle. Then on the margin of the paper, I wrote Sean Killdaren's name down and after a moment added the names of all the men at the castle as well as my impressions of them. I had to make a suspect list and gathering my thoughts on paper would help.

Now that I'd made investigative progress, I thought I'd be able to sleep. But as soon as I shut my eyes, I popped them wide open.

What had happened to Mary's personal belongings? Her sketchbook, her paintings of the sea, her diary and her pheasant shell? I had to ask Aunt Lavinia as soon as I could.

Once more, I tried to settle beneath the covers, but couldn't relax on the lumpy bed. I strained to hear every sound, wary of what might happen if I fell asleep. The castle creaked and groaned, the sea crashed against the shore, and Bridget snored, a sound so unladylike that I cringed even as I found comfort in it. If she could sleep so soundly, then my fears of the night had to be childish, right?

I must have fallen asleep because when I first heard a low, moaning cry, I thought Mary was calling to me in a dream as she had before. The sound grew insistently louder until I realized I wasn't dreaming and the screeching was coming from outside.

Rushing to the window, I saw the glass roof of the gargoyle-guarded building glow like an eerie sun. That's were the sound was coming from. As I stared with my heart pounding, the noise suddenly died.

What had it been? Had it been a woman crying for help? Then the light from the building flickered wildly, as if a huge moth had been pinned over a flame and someone stood watching it flutter in helpless torment.

Had I truly heard moaning screams? I went to Bridget and shook her awake. She blinked at me, clearly confused. "Whot? Who are ya?"

"It's Cassie. Come look, there is something strange outside." I pulled her to the window.

She stood quiet for a moment, blinked several times, then looked at me. "Whot?"

"Don't you see the light from the gargoyle building? I heard a terrible moaning, as if, well, as if it might have been a woman in pain or crying for help."

"Ack, t'was nuthing but the wind. She can make ya think someone's dying, and there's no light now. Must 'ave been the Killdaren. 'e's a strange one, up all night, sleeps all day. Makes ya wonder what 'e does when everyone's a sleeping. Times like this make ya think that 'im being a vampire is more than just a rumor." Bridget crawled back into her bed, settling into her covers like a babe into the arms of a mother. "Best get to sleep and not speak of 'im. Morning'll be 'ere before ya know it."

I peered outside again. The round room sat darkly shrouded again. No screeching rent the night. Only the rhythm of the waves' ebb and flow disturbed the quiet now. The urge to sneak downstairs and to learn exactly what was in the round chamber grabbed at me so strongly I had to clench my fists to be practical and prudent and stay put. I didn't know enough about the castle to search through it alone, and I couldn't ask Bridget, for if we were caught, she could lose her post and her livelihood.

"You're right." I nearly choked on the words as I crawled beneath my thin blanket and huddled there, my body aching. I tried to find some measure of reassurance, but the metal of the pistol beneath my pillow left me cold. I kept hearing Mary call to me and my mind dwelled on the Killdaren. What had he been doing tonight?

As much as I wanted to know, I also faced the fact that I wouldn't be leaving my bed. And in all honesty, prudence and practicality had very little to do with that decision. I was too frightened to venture out. Surely all of my practical inclinations in my life didn't stem from fear?

# Chapter Four

"Cassie, time's a wasting. You'll miss the morning meal iffen ya don't 'urry along."

It seemed as if I'd just shut my eyes when Bridget shook me. For a moment, I didn't know where I was, then everything flooded back to me and I groaned as I moved.

"We've less than five minutes. I've been trying to wake ya, I 'ave, but ya've been sleeping like the dead 'cept for your snorin'."

My aches lost importance; I sat straight up, shocked. "Snores? Did you say I snore?"

Bridget pulled her mob cap on then frowned at me as if I'd lost my mind. "Ya don't 'ave to sound so flabbergasted."

"I'm not." Appalled more aptly described my feelings. "I just never associated myself with the habit."

"Ya 'ave such a funny notion about ya self. What with all the bathin' and a no snorin'. I woke thinkin' I'd wandered into a rose garden during the night, the way ye've dolled yourself up to smell good. Best git movin'. Mrs. Frye don't tolerate tardiness none."

Scooting from the bed, I barely had time to slip the pistol under the bedding and to stuff my hair sufficiently beneath my mob cap before Bridget declared it was time to go.

Both Jamie and Stuart were absent from the breakfast table, and Mrs. Frye seemed sterner than she had before. She delegated the day's tasks in clipped commands accompanied by dire threats of unemployment and reduced wages if her wishes weren't carried out immediately.

"Bet she got an earful of last night's going on," Bridget whispered.

"You mean Jamie's outburst?"

"Rightly so. I fear she's goin' ta blame ya for it, too. Today's goin' to be 'ard, but ya do right and she'll settle 'er ire down soon."

"Bridget!" Mrs. Frye snapped. "You're talking when I'm talking. There'll be no meal tonight for you. I expect your utmost respect and for you to have better manners than this."

"Yes, ma'am," Bridget said.

"B—" I opened my mouth to protest, planning to inform Mrs. Frye that as I was new and Bridget was only explaining my job, but Bridget pinched my arm so hard that my voice escaped in a gasp.

Mrs. Frye glared at me. "You are already causing trouble here. Today you will polish the dining room again by yourself so you will remember exactly how it's done. When you are done with that task then you can help Bridget in the library. I want every book on every shelf dusted."

"Yes, ma'am." Bridget grabbed my arm and pulled me from the kitchen. I had to swallow the words of protest stuck in my throat.

Bridget marched angrily and I followed, realizing that she headed for a closet filled with cleaning supplies. Once there, she shoved rags and a huge tin of polish into my hands.

"I don't believe her," I whispered. "Why—"

"'er!" Bridget hissed. "It's you that I'm not believin'. I've me sickly mama and a little brother to feed, and until I 'ear from Flora, me post 'ere is all that's savin' us from the poor 'ouse. That place is a death sentence for sure, ya 'ear. Don't be takin' on airs that'll cost me."

"But—"

"Just go. If she catches us gabbing, it'll only make thin's worse, I tell ya."

My heart wincing, I went directly to the dining room and

redid everything Bridget and I had done the day before, from polishing the wood to the silver. As I worked, it occurred to me that in my six years of answering questions on women's problems in "Cassiopeia's Corner", I had a very limited view of the world to be giving out advice like I did.

Midday I finished with the dining room and joined Bridget in the library. In just two days of scrubbing, several blisters spotted my now reddened hands. And the aches and pains in my arms had spread all the way to my shoulders and down my back. All I could think about all morning was a hot bath. That is until the moment I walked into the library where Bridget dusted. Thoughts of a bath flew as Sean Killdaren's presence took over. Even though it was just a canvas and paint likeness in the room with me, I couldn't ignore him. The aura of the portrait was almost magical in its ability to capture my attention. Again, I stood before him and just stared at him. I studied the cleft in his chin, the determined angle of his nose, and the glint in his green eyes—eyes that matched the vibrant emerald eyes of the carved dragon on his cane.

He appeared tall in the picture, with an imposing breadth to his shoulders that made me want to step back to make room for him to pass, as if he were an otherworldly prince capable of deciding more than just my earthly future, but the fate of my soul as well.

Impractical nonsense. Utterly ridiculous, I admonished myself. Since I never had the luxury of fanciful dreams, my mind was determined play them out during the day with this man. Otherworldly prince, indeed! I shook my head and set to work. Pulling a book off the shelf, I began dusting and then froze as I read its title. *Powerful Vampires and Their Lovers.*

"Good Lord!" I dropped the book.

Bridget came running over. "Whot is it?"

I pointed at the book, speechless.

She picked it up, dusted it off, and held it out to me, puzzled. "Somethin' wrong with it?"

"Didn't you read the title? *Powerful Vampires and Their Lovers.* Who'd have such a book?"

Bridget reverently ran her finger over the gold embossing. "Blimey, that whot it says?"

I pulled my gaze from the book and my mind back from its wild path. I shouldn't jump to conclusions about the book's content or those who owned it. Why, if someone poured over my books and chose to pull Mary Shelley's *Frankenstein* down, they could suppose any number of horrible things about me. Then the significance of what Bridget said slowly dawned on me.

I gently placed my hand over hers. "You can't read."

She pulled away and slipped the book back onto the shelf. "Never 'ad the time for nonsense such as that, I tell ya. Too much to be done. What would I do with readin'?"

"I'll teach you to read. Pick any book, and I'll teach you to read it, Bridget."

She glanced cautiously at the door then at me. She looked as if she'd been handed her heart's desire, but didn't dare take it because it would disappear if she did.

"Please," I urged. "You've helped me so much already. Please let me do this for you."

"Well..." She glanced at the books as if they were forbidden candy. "Whot titles are 'ere?" She waved to the shelf that held the vampire book.

I pointed to each book, finding all of them intriguing and disturbing. *Powerful Vampires and Their Lovers. The Trail of Blood: Vampires and their Victims. Haunts and Hunts Worthy of a Vampire. Mastery of Druid Magic. The Sacred and Profane Rites and Rituals of the Druids and Their Children. The Druid's Thirst for Humans.*

Reaching, she chose the first book. "*Powerful Vampires and Their Lovers.*" Her eyes danced with a saucy gleam. "Every Sunday I 'ear the Good Book read, but I don't think there's a soul around who'd tell me about vampires and such." She looked at Sean Killdaren's portrait. "I'm thinkin' there's a thing or two I want to know about things I shouldn't."

I followed Bridget's gaze and encountered Sean Killdaren's green eyes and his imposing, black-draped figure. "I know exactly what you mean, Bridget. Tonight we'll read about vampires." I set the book aside until we finished cleaning then hid it in the ample folds of my dress when we went back to our room.

My hopes for more revelations about Mary or to conduct any investigations met a frustrating end my second day in the castle. Mrs. Frye kept Bridget and me so busy we didn't even get a moment's respite, and I couldn't explore. We worked until the evening meal, then Bridget retired to our room and I went to dinner. If not for my plan to steal food for Bridget, I would have gone with her to our room. Jamie did not appear, but Stuart did. He ate quickly and left without saying a word.

I myself could barely swallow the food on my plate. I kept thinking of Bridget alone in our room doing without her meal because of me, and that burned inside. I'd never given much thought to the demands my family made of the handful of servants in our home, or of the power to help or harm that I held as an employer. But in my short time at the castle, I'd quickly learned about the power the upper servants had over the lower servants and the harshness of the servants' world.

I managed to snitch three pieces of cheese and some bread, wrap them in a clean silk handkerchief, and tuck them into my pocket for Bridget. I think Mrs. Murphy caught me, but averted her gaze and went on speaking to Janet and Adele Oaks, asking them if they'd take the clean-up after the meal until the blisters on my hands healed. It surprised me that she noticed my blisters and that the Oak sisters agreed. I knew they had to be exhausted too, and shouldn't have to bear the burden of my work as well. I thanked them and Mrs. Murphy, feeling tears sting my eyes at their kindness. They had so little and worked so hard, yet gave so freely to help another. I couldn't recall many of the ladies in Oxford's social strata who would be that kind under these conditions.

Everyone in some manner or another seemed to be silently protesting Mrs. Frye's judgment against Bridget, but nobody voiced their opposition, and I didn't either, I realized with surprise. My desire to stay employed in the Killdarens' castle outweighed any principle of right I'd be willing to stand upon. At least when it came to the matter of punishing Bridget by taking away a meal. Something more severe I was sure I would have stood up for what was right no matter what.

I'd learned something, though. Had someone written to "Cassiopeia's Corner" about this very situation, I would have advised her to stand on principle. Yet, now that I was in the situation, I had chosen differently. The more I lived of life away from the isolated world of my home and family, the more difficult the answers to even the simplest questions became.

Bridget nearly cried when I handed her the bread and cheese. I wanted to hug her, yet I didn't, sensing she would reject any overtures of comfort on my part. She ate quickly and then we settled on her cot, huddling by the light of a small candle to read the vampire book. We went through the alphabet and the sounds each letter made, many of which Bridget already knew, then we read only five sentences of the vampire book before her eyes drooped and she fell asleep.

I couldn't blame her. The day had been exhausting and the vampire book had offered very little excitement, just a description of an old stone church and a lonely woman entering it to pray. I'd expected that a book about powerful vampires and their lovers would have started out differently and I set it aside disappointed. After tucking Bridget beneath her blanket, I spent the next hour bathing, with only the basin of cold water available to ease my skin irritations and curtail the growing sense of dirt clinging to my body. I desperately longed for a tub of hot water, so I could sink into its comforting heat and feel the soothing bath salts cleanse my skin free of dirt, perspiration, and cleaners. I even went though the difficult task of washing my hair in the basin, using up every ounce of water from the ewer.

When I finished and had smoothed rose and milk cream over my chafed skin and reddened hands, wincing at my blisters, I slipped on an old cotton dress I'd brought with me and put my father's pistol into the pocket. If Mrs. Frye continued to keep me and Bridget working so hard during the day, I would have to accustom myself to investigating at night.

Stuffing my hair into my mob cap for appearances, I quietly tiptoed downstairs as the massive mahogany clock in the center hall chimed the quarter hour. Bits of silver moonlight shone through the portal-like windows, lighting the servants' stairs in gray shadows. The kitchen that bustled with frenzied warmth from dawn to dusk seemed like a dark, shadowed sea after midnight, a place where dragons might lurk, waiting for a tasty meal.

Butterflies flurried in my stomach, as if trying to warn me to go no further, and I almost turned back, but then shook my head and determinedly snatched my imagination back from the folly of its wandering. I could only blame my grandfather's stories for my fanciful thoughts.

Turning down an unlit corridor off the center hall, I nearly jumped when booming male voices reached me in the dark. I ventured closer down the carpeted corridor, wondering if Sean Killdaren was in the room just ahead. My pulse leaped at the thought of seeing him. Flickering light spilled from the room, accompanied by the snap and crackle of a fire in the hearth. After a moment, I realized it was Sir Warwick and the earl, and they were well in their cups, which would explain why I hadn't recognized their voices from earlier. I backed into the shadowed doorway of a room across the way to listen.

"The bloody idiots are determined not to wed. Made a pact to have no heirs so the bloody curse will die with them," the earl said.

Sir Warwick laughed. "It's ironic. Your by-blows will likely leave you a dozen brats and your heirs none."

"There is nothing amusing to the situation. Alexander is as determined as Sean. Were that chit Helen alive today, I'd murder her myself for ruining my sons' lives."

"Why don't you outsmart them and arrange marriages for them both?

"I may have to if I expect to see an heir before I die, though my sons would more likely murder me than wed if I did betroth them. Unfortunately, few fathers will let their chits marry men suspected of murder, at least none with worthy enough dowries."

"I've heard the Bow Street Runners have solved impossible cases. Hire a man to clear the boys' reputation."

"I would if I was sure neither of my sons had killed the chit, but I'm not. The evidence was entirely too damning. I'll—"

A leather gloved hand clamped over my mouth and nose from behind. An arm wrapped around my stomach and arms, trapping me, and jerking me back against the hard body of a large man. I couldn't breathe, I couldn't scream, I couldn't reach my pistol. I could barely move. Terror flamed in my breasts and fired through my veins. The man pulled me deeper into the darkened room, shutting the door. Dear Lord. Is this how Mary disappeared?

Wrenching violently, I tried to free myself, but the man clamped me tighter to him, crushing me with his strength. I pressed my head back, fighting to ease the pressure on my face enough to breathe. In my panic I remembered the size of Jamie Frye, his anger, the veiled threat that if I were to die none would care. Then the hand covering my mouth and nose loosened enough for me to suck in blessed air. I smelled leather, mint and something frighteningly unknown, but compelling enough that I drew another needed breath.

"The scent of roses," a deep, cultured voice with a hint of an Irish burr whispered close to my ear, and I knew it wasn't Jamie. "The feel of a woman." As he spoke, his arm about my stomach slid higher, pressing beneath my bosom, almost caressing the undersides of my breasts a moment. I rammed my spine back, lifting myself to my tiptoes, trying to keep from knowing the warmth of his muscled arm so intimately against me. This brought his mouth and the heat of his breath closer to my ear.

"The actions of a thief." His tone was soft, menacing. My heart thundered harder, more painfully. "Will you come to such an ill fate, lass? 'Like a rose, she has lived as long as roses live...the space of one morning'? Or will it be even less for you?"

Any affinity I had for Malherbe's poetry met a quick death

at that moment. I shook my head, trying to speak, but only managed a muffled squeal.

"Let's see what you've stolen, my rose."

I didn't understand what he meant to do until he moved his gloved hand from beneath my breasts, sliding downward, pressing firmly along the contours of my body all the way down to my hips, then brushing over my intimate flesh as he slid from one dress pocket to the other, and finding my father's pistol. His body jerked with surprise and he drew a sharp breath.

"Run or scream and I will kill you instantly." He pulled the pistol from my pocket. His voice chilled and became deadly. I'd never heard true menace before now.

"Are you an assassin?" He released me, shoving the muzzle of the pistol into my back, urging me deeper into the room.

My legs shook, and my vision blurred. "Assassin? Good God! Please. I don't know what you're talking about. I haven't stolen anything either. The pistol is mine. To keep me safe."

I heard him light a lamp, filling the dark-paneled room with a muted glow. I barely saw the billiard table before me and the numerous game tables beyond that. I was too aware of the man behind me with my pistol to my back.

"Take off your cap," he ordered.

Squeezing my eyes shut, I pulled off my cap, feeling almost as if I was removing my clothes before him. I hadn't taken the time to pin my hair and it spilled down my back.

"Turn around, slowly."

I did as he asked. Opening my eyes to fearful slits, I kept my gaze on the pistol and his large, black-gloved hand. At that moment I wanted to know if and when he would pull the trigger more than who he was or what he looked like. He'd barely eased my pistol back enough to allow me room to turn. As soon as I did, he pressed the muzzle deeper into my breast, directly over my pounding heart.

When he didn't shoot, when he didn't say anything at all, I finally lifted my gaze and met his deadly green stare. Sean Killdaren was everything his portrait promised and more.

"Who are you?"

Swallowing a lump of pure fear, I found my voice. "Cassie Andrews. I'm...the new housemaid."

"I don't know how well you can see, but I assure you, I am not that stupid. You're no more a housemaid than I am a street urchin. The truth."

"'Tis the truth. I am Cassie Andrews, and I...I needed work. Hard times...my father lost his post." I held up my blistered hands.

"Where are you from?"

"Oxford." I cringed, realizing I should have lied.

"You're educated. You can't convince me that between this hell and Oxford there wasn't a single teaching post."

"I left home...there was a...scandal. I had to," I said, desperate. Inferring that I was a fallen woman seemed the only plausible excuse for why an educated woman would seek employment as a housemaid so far from home. I took heart in that every word I'd said was essentially the truth. I considered Mary's death a hidden scandal.

Bolstering myself with that, I met the fire of his gaze as he studied me. Dressed completely in black right down to the cape he wore, he was as dark as his midnight painting had portrayed him and just as dynamic. The cleft of his shadowed chin, the fullness of his mouth, the height and breadth of him in person loomed larger than life, even more so than the painting. Only the fire in his dragon green eyes gleamed brighter than his picture, and I noted a sharper, more sinister edge to him, as if he could very well be a vamp—

I mentally shook the ridiculous thought away.

"Why the pistol?"

I swallowed and shut my eyes. "Protection. The scandal." Heat flooded my face.

"Look at me, lass." He pressed his gloved fingers to my chin.

I met his gaze with trepidation. How could I so unashamedly lead another person to such untruths?

His thumb caressed my cheek and a different sensation besides that of fear, coiled inside of me. The unknown emotion gripped me just as strongly as my terror had, but left me wanting to know what his ungloved touch would feel like against my cheek.

Whatever he looked for, he must have found it in my gaze, for he lifted the pistol from my breast and stepped slightly back, releasing my chin. "You'll not need a weapon in my home, so I will keep it safe for you for now. Before you go, I want to know why you were eavesdropping on my father and Sir Warwick."

"I...got lost. I wanted a book to read."

"And you thought making use of the library a servant's right?"

I shook my head no and lowered my gaze, feeling the sting in his question, but then couldn't stay silent. "Don't you think servants thirst to know things?"

"Perhaps," he said oddly. "The library is down the opposite corridor from here."

I nodded, starting to back away from him.

"I'll escort you."

"That's not necessary."

"You know the way?" He lifted a brow, clearly questioning the validity of everything I'd just said. His gaze bore down on me, and I backed away faster even though he didn't move.

"No. I just...don't think I'll be able to read after...this. I'd like to retire now."

A ghost of a smile seemed to curve his lips, but it came and left so quickly that I thought I imagined it. I kept backing up until I felt the door behind me and found the doorknob. Opening it, I winced at the pain from my blisters. Just before I escaped, he spoke so softly I almost didn't hear him. "Perhaps you'll meet me there some night."

I immediately dismissed the words. Never would I do such an outrageous thing as meet a man alone at night. I moved so quickly with my blood roaring in my ears and my thoughts running so wildly that I didn't see anything of what I passed on my return to my room. Once there, I pressed the door firmly closed and tried to draw an easy breath, but I couldn't. I was too vulnerable. My body burned and shivered in places too intimate to acknowledge.

Bridget slept, softly snoring, completely oblivious to my tumultuous state. I wanted to shake her awake so I wouldn't be alone with *him*, the feel of him, the exotic scent of him, the presence of him that seem to cling to every corner of my mind and body as if a magic spell had been cast over my person. But I was too ashamed to have anyone know, too shocked to speak about the surging, unknown feeling that had coiled inside of me the moment my terror had fled.

Moonlight spilled through the open window, allowing me enough light to see, and I grabbed a spindly chair from a corner, propping it beneath the doorknob. The precaution made me feel only marginally better. For in truth, I had little fear he had followed me. And the vulnerability preying on me had little to do with what might happen and everything to do with what had happened.

I'd dismally failed in my first investigative venture. The man had stolen my father's pistol! He'd touched me, almost intimately, had held me at gunpoint no less, and I was too enamored by the man to even think about Mary and what may have happened to her.

Stripping off my dress in a disgusted huff, I slipped beneath the worn blanket of my cot and willed myself to forget everything and go to sleep, yet couldn't. *He* wouldn't leave me alone. He preyed upon my every thought, and the feel of his gloved touch irritatingly lingered upon my skin as much as the chafing wool.

Eventually, I resorted to whispering nursery rhymes and counting sheep. My mind and body would have none of it, and kept clamoring that I dwell on Sean.

Sean? Not Sean Killdaren or Mister Killdaren, or even The Killdaren, but Sean? Good heavens. Had I lost my mind? I was now even thinking of the man more intimately than propriety would allow. Yet his name and his lilting Irish brogue had delved deep inside me, all the way to the hidden places where I kept my grandfather's stories of fairies and magic.

Desperate, I lit a candle and dug out the vampire book I'd borrowed from the library. Surely a story would wipe the man from my mind.

*The woman entered the dark stone church, fearful of what she would find, but too alone in life to miss speaking to the man again. Earlier, when she'd been at the altar praying for the love she'd never known, he'd arrived. He'd knelt at the altar and prayed aloud, almost jovially, asking for the blessed blood of the Lamb. His comfortable manner with God had brought her prayers to a halt. She'd studied him, noting his dress, all somber black, with an edging of white at his collar.*

*"Is there something that I can pray for you?" he'd asked, startling her.*

*She'd shaken her head. After a long moment her curiosity grew too great to ignore. "You are a minister?"*

*His warm smile broadened, making her examine the dark of his eyes more closely. "In a way. I live here; just beyond those doors there's a stairwell." He'd nodded toward carved wood panels behind her that she'd never noticed before. After he'd spoken with her for some time, he'd stood, citing an important meeting. Then just before leaving, he'd invited her to come back tonight to pray again.*

*And she had.*

*The church was empty when she arrived, but the carved wood doors stood open, inviting yet darkly forbidding. She called out several times, only to hear the echo of her own voice. Peering beyond the doors, she found a stone stairwell, lit by sconces. She hesitated a few moments, watching the candle flames dance upon the walls. Then, taking one last look over her shoulder, she descended the steps, coming unexpectedly to a richly appointed circular room. Ensconced in the center of the chamber upon a raised dais lay a lonely crypt shaped like a man. It reminded her of him in some way, and she wondered if perhaps she'd in some way seen his ghost.*

*Rather than being frightened, she was compelled, drawn by*

*the loneliness in him that matched hers. Tentatively, she approached, reaching out to touch the unfamiliar words and geometric shapes engraved on the crypt. When she did, the stone beneath her fingers began to warm. Surprised, she pressed her palm to the stone, feeling heat throb in rhythm to the beat of her heart. Drawn, unable to do aught but follow the force urging her to explore, she splayed both of her hands against the stone. Vibrations started to shake the crypt, and in an explosion of light, the lid popped open. The man she met earlier, still richly dressed, in black, rose up.*

*"You came." He took hold of her arms, his demeanor much darker than before. She screamed, frightened by the dangerous gleam in his eyes. He pulled her to him, toward the red velvet bed in which he lay. He smiled, showing sharp fangs. "Fear not. Your pleasure will be great. As will mine." His lips sought the throbbing pulse at her throat and she moaned.*

I snapped the book closed, startled by the rekindling of the heat Sean, uh The Killdaren, had seeded within me.

My word, what was happening to me? I stuffed the book into the farthest corner of the room from me and buried it beneath the potato sack that I'd packed my belongings in. Then I firmly blew out the candle and determinedly directed my mind to think only of Mary. The reason I'd come here. My thoughts still drifted toward *him* again, but this time, I focused on what his father, the Earl of Dartraven had said. *I'd hire a runner if I was sure neither of my sons had killed the chit, but I'm not.*

Having now met *him*, I knew without a doubt he could have, and would have killed me, had I given him cause.

# Chapter Five

"Blimey. What did ya think was biting ya last night?" Bridget's red hair, lifted by the sea breeze, fluttered about her mob cap and face. Freckles dotted her nose and her blue eyes sparkled, giving her a striking, almost earthy, beauty. The sea, sun and warm wind bathed the morning in a comforting light, making the sand dunes glisten and the maritime forest lushly green.

"A spider," I muttered, my cheeks flaming. I'd die before telling the truth. The vampire had been dressed in black with fiery green eyes. For the first time in my life, I'd actually had a real dream. Not a dream about someone's death or of trouble as always before, but a real, normal dream. I didn't doubt that it was a dream, because no sense of impending doom had accompanied it. No deep dread filled my heart. And though the vampire had an uncanny resemblance to Sean, I somehow didn't fear for Sean's life. At no point in my dream did he disappear into darkness or die. In fact, I feared more for myself than for him. I'd been naked and he'd been touching me, and the thoughts wouldn't go away no matter how much I willed them to do so.

And maybe deep inside myself I didn't want them to. The man had given me something I'd never had before—a pleasurable dream. Somehow insisting that I continue to think of him as The Killdaren or anything other than Sean was too hypocritical for even my proper driven soul, so I allowed myself the fantasy. But it would be in my mind only, no one would ever know.

The man had captured me in a web of awareness I couldn't escape. I shivered every time I shut my eyes and relived my first sight of him, his touch, the lilt of his voice, and the lure of his scent. He was in my mind and in my thoughts. A man so dangerous that he seemed capable of anything, so why did I have this desire to think of him so intimately? Why was I so curious about him? Why did I want to see him again?

It was Sunday, my first half day off. Five days since I'd met him. Five days since I had unsuccessfully committed myself to forgetting him, at least in terms of my physical reaction to him.

My investigation had progressed very little, but I hadn't ventured from my room to explore again. The things I'd learned about Mary since the night of Jamie's outburst had been subtle remembrances of my cousin that I'd overheard in conversations between the servants. Mary had touched each of them in a special way. Just as she'd been teaching Bridget's sister, Flora, to sing, she done a number of kind things for the others, too.

I had yet to meet the child Mary had come to Killdaren's Castle to teach, and I thought this extremely odd. I'd lived a week in a house, albeit a massive home, but I'd heard nothing from a child. No laughter, no playing, no shouting, nothing. I'd asked Bridget about Rebecca as much as I dared, commenting on how quiet she was, and Bridget would only reply that the child wasn't well. The answer left me wondering what "not well" meant.

My first perceptions of those at Killdaren's Castle hadn't changed, only deepened over the past days. But more importantly, after a week of bathing from a basin, I was desperate for a bath—and even more desperate for any sense of my life before coming to this place. I missed my sisters terribly.

"Now that's a thing to 'ave nightmares o'er, I tell ya."

Glancing up, I saw Bridget nod toward the Killdaren's maze, her expression more fearful than ever. "Have. Remember to try and not drop your h's. Now what do you mean about the maze?"

"Not h...ere," she whispered, pronouncing the h as she glanced about.

I looked and found nothing amiss, yet her furtive response dimmed the brightness of the day and had me checking over my shoulder more than once.

She didn't speak until we were out of sight of the castle, on the lonely path to the village edging the forest. "Makes me shiver just to look at the maze. Ya can't see where yer goin' when yer in it. Ya can't see who's behind ya. Not a good feelin' at all, and whot's worse—" Bridget's voice dropped low as she leaned my way, her eyes big blue saucers, "—it's whispered that *she* died in there, ya know, but no one speaks of it."

I stumbled though the path lay smooth. Bridget caught my elbow, bringing us to a halt. My tongue stuck to the roof of my mouth, slurring my words. "M-m-mary? I thought you said she drowned?"

"Ack. I forgot. Ya wouldn't know about Lady Helen, now would ya. It h-happened a ways back. Wouldn't know much myself except Flora's best friend worked for the Kennedys. Sad thing it were. Her father up and killed himself after it h-happened, too. Their house has lain silent ever since. They say it's 'aunted. The father left a note saying he was going to h-heaven to hear his angel sing. Even the Queen requested Lady Helen to sing for her on occasion. 'er beauty was ten times that of Helen o' Troy. Had to have been, to have every eligible man for miles after h-her hand. And all of them jealous of the other, especially the Killdaren brothers. Golden hair and cornflower eyes, she h-had." Bridget blinked at me several times, her brow creasing to a frown. "Like you, miss, ya might say. And I kept all of my h's, I did."

"You did well." But my thoughts weren't on Bridget's progress, they were on what she'd just said. Golden hair and cornflower eyes. Like you, miss. *And like Mary,* I thought. Mary's hair had been golden. *Except her eyes had been different.* Mary's had been brown, but mine were blue.

I glanced about. Everything appeared normal; still I became uneasy. Finding a commonality between a woman who'd been murdered and my cousin, who I suspected had died under suspicious circumstances, wrapped an eerie feeling around me.

"Let's hurry to the village."

Bridget didn't argue. In fact, I think after snatching off her falling mob cap, she moved even faster than I did until we were somehow racing as fast as we could, something no lady would ever be seen doing. With perspiration soaking our dresses and our hair awry, we were quite a sight. I paused for air, feeling a little ridiculous, but oddly exhilarated too. As if the sensation of danger just a breath away made me more alive than years of trudging though my daily routine. The notion was as unsettling as learning Helen had been murdered in the maze.

Bridget, with her cheeks flushed like bright new apples, her eyes shining, and her red hair flowing free, appeared more beautiful than ever. "Blimey, but that was fun." We stopped on the side of the road, hearing an approaching carriage. After just a week of working on reading she'd grown more confident as well as easier to understand. Next we'd work on her g's.

The carriage, sporting the Killdaren double dragon crest, flew past, steering purposely into a puddle near us. Mud splattered our skirts and raised my ire to a previously unknown level as I heard the occupants laugh. "That's twenty shillings," the driver called to the men.

"The bloody arses did that on purpose."

"Idiot buffoons." I brushed at my skirts. "Ladies aren't supposed to say bloody or arse. Who was it?"

"Not the Killdaren, I'll wager. And Lord Alexander always rides one of 'is fancy 'orses. So it 'ad to be either the earl and Sir Warwick, or someone visiting Dragon's Cove." Anger had made her drop her h's again. I didn't say anything this time.

"I thought no one ever visited the Killdarens."

"No one proper. But the viscount 'as been known to—" Bridget's voice died as a man on a white horse raced up. He slowed as he passed and I saw with surprise that it was Stuart Frye. He rode like a gentleman to the manner born, but when he saw us, he became so distracted for some reason he almost fell from the saddle when his horse leaped forward.

Bridget grabbed my arm as if needing support. When I glanced her way, I found her face had blanched white.

"What is it, Bridget?"

"Nothing. The man races as if the devil's on 'is arse, don't 'e?"

"Stuart?"

"Who else? Rides around like 'e's the bloody Killdaren or the viscount."

"The viscount would be Sean Killdaren's brother, right?" Though I knew that, I wanted to hear what Bridget had to say about him.

"Aye, Lord Alexander, the Viscount of Blackmoor. 'e lives on the other side of the forest in Dragon's Cove in a larger castle, as 'e's, h-he's the heir to the title. Earl of Dartraven he'll be someday, since he was birthed first. Heard it said they came out of the womb with their 'ands, uh, h-hands around each other's throats. Alexander feet first and Sean headfirst, killed their mama in the birthin' of 'em."

"Good Lord. Is there nothing but tragedy upon the Killdarens' doorstep?" I was pleased to see Bridget remember to correct her own speech.

"It's the curse, mind ya."

"All their wealth, and yet they're poorer than you or me when it comes to what really matters."

Bridget gave me a puzzled look. "Ye have an odd way of thinkin'. Ha! The Killdarens poor."

"Think about it, Bridget. Would you want to have all that they possess if it meant that your mother died in childbirth? If it meant you would either kill your sister or she would kill you?"

"Aye. I would." Bridget sighed. "No, and ya knew it afor ya asked. Ack, what are you doin' to me mind, Cassie? Me mother would cosh me had she heard, giving up all that wealth, just to have me family." She giggled and grabbed my arm, urging us into town.

We stopped on the street to part. "Can't wait to see me mum and little brother. We're havin' meat pies and sweet cake for my birthday."

"You didn't tell me. When is your birthday?"

"This Friday. I'll be eighteen. Old enough to be kissed, right?"

"Well, yes. If the gentleman had honorable intentions and asked your permission, I suppose it would be all right." I was shocked to learn that she was no older than Gemini.

"Blimey, all of that has to happen first? Have you ever been kissed, Cassie?"

Heat plastered my cheeks. "No." I'd been too busy writing my proper advice column to associate with gentlemen enough to reach the kissing point in a relationship. "Why?"

Bridget sighed. "Just wondering what it was like. Ye've a funny notion about yerself, what with always bathin' and no snorin' and no kissin' unless it's all proper. It all seems so complicated." She pointed down the street. "Remember to meet me at the church right there on time. Mrs. Frye will have our hides if we're late."

As I watched Bridget leave, I found myself wondering what a kiss would be like. Sean intruded into my thoughts and I imagined him kissing me. Shock rippled up my spine. Good lord. The man was a stranger and a dangerous one at that. What was wrong with me? I dashed to Seafarer's Inn as if the devil was on my heels.

The carriage with the Killdaren's double dragon crest on it pulled away from the entrance of the inn as I approached. As I watched it disappear in the direction of the village, an eerie warning crept over me. Who from the Killdaren household had come to the inn? And why?

I considered going to Constable Poole to see if he'd made any more inquiries into Mary's disappearance, but decided to keep my presence at Killdaren's Castle a secret for now and just have Aunt Lavinia call on him later in the week.

Easing around to the servants' entrance, I stole quietly through the downstairs of the inn. The guest parlors were empty and the dining area full. I didn't see anyone I recognized and gave up my search for who had come to the inn. Taking care not to be seen, I went to the apartments my family had rented. Just as I was about to knock on the door, I heard several maids coming down the corridor, and I quickly let myself inside.

Ensconced in the sitting room lounged my Aunt Lavinia and my sisters, all teary-eyed and clutching pastel handkerchiefs that wafted so heavily of perfume it made my nose itch. Tea sat untouched on the marble-topped rosewood table between them.

Andromeda stared at me as she dabbed at her tears. I came to a sudden stop. Their state didn't shock me. Mine did.

I'd had tea every day of my life since I could remember, yet in the time I'd been at Killdaren's Castle, which seemed tremendously longer than a week, I'd never even thought once of a scone or clotted cream or tea. My mouth watered and my stomach twisted.

"My word, but I am ravenous. You'd think I'd not eaten in a fortnight." Striding forward, I slipped some scones from the tray and popped one into my mouth, ashamedly not even bothering to use one of the dainty china plates delicately painted with miniature roses.

"What do you think you're doing?" Andromeda shouted and stood, an angry flush staining her cheeks.

I quickly swallowed the bite of scone. "Andrie? Whatever is the matter with you?"

"Cassie?" she gasped her mouth falling agape.

"Oh, oh, oh," Aunt Lavinia waved her kerchief as if she were about to faint.

"Good Lord, Cassie. But you're a sight! You've mud on your skirts." Andromeda shook her head. "And your face as well."

"What skirts?" Gemini dabbed her eyes dry and gave me a slight grin. "She's all but wearing sackcloth. She's a fallen woman!"

"You've a mob cap on, Cassie! I thought you were the cleaning maid!" Andromeda piped in an unusually high-pitched voice, her eyes wide with shock.

"Since that's what I am masquerading as, I'll take that as a compliment." Raising my hand to my cheek, I indeed found a bit of mud. A frantic feeling swept over me. "Good Lord, but I need a bath! You do have heated water, don't you?"

"You're masquerading. Just like a spy for the Crown! How intriguing," Gemini said. "Why we could all go there and—"

I choked on the last of the scone I'd stuffed into my mouth and coughed until tears fell. "Absolutely not," I said as soon as I could speak. "Not one of you will come near Killdaren's Castle, and there is nothing the least intriguing about scrubbing yourself blind from dawn to dusk, with no bath, and having rough wool itch you horribly everywhere."

Andromeda gasped again and grabbed my fingers, looking at the reddened skin and blisters. "You're hurt!"

Gemini jumped up and then both of them hugged me, muttering at how awful the situation was.

"I'm not hurt. I just want a bath. Please tell me you have hot water ready." Surely they would have thought to do so. Nobody seemed to hear me.

"Oh, Cassie, this is dreadful. I'll not have you harming yourself for this," Aunt Lavinia said. "You mustn't go back. We'll find out what happened to Mary another way. I've already written a letter to the magistrate in Dartmouth and I'm sure he'll be able to coerce Constable Poole to make a more in-depth inquiry into Mary's drowning."

Gemini pressed her handkerchief to her nose and backed away from me. "You smell very odd." She furrowed her brow.

"More than odd, rather ripe," Andromeda said.

"Worse," Gemini added. "Like a wet dog hiding in a rose garden on a hot day."

I stared at them, wanting to cry and laugh at the same time. An itch in the middle of my back seemed to spread. "A bath. All I want is a bath. I would give a fortune to have a hot bath. Servants don't have the same privileges as we often enjoy, it seems." I wanted to soak away the dirt and the aches more than I wanted to breathe.

"I'm sorry. The maids just emptied all the bath water and carried the tub away. We've water basins in our rooms—"

Tears stung and I shook my head. The town's clock rang the time and I realized it would take too long to order a bath and still have time to speak with my sisters as needed. At home, I never once considered where, when or how our servants tended to their own personal needs. My disappointment and frustration came with a humble and bitter draught.

Gemini must have sensed my upset and pressed a cup of tea into my hands, then shoved a chair behind me. "Rest a minute," she said.

"I'm all right." But I sat anyway and gulped the sweetened creamed tea, trying to bite back my emotions and gather myself. "There is much I need to tell you. First, Aunt Lavinia, I need to know if you've received any of Mary's belongings?"

"They informed me at the castle that they'd sent Mary's things to my address in Brighton before I arrived here."

"Mary always kept a diary when we were little, do you know if she still did?"

"I would think so, especially since she was so far from home." Tears filled Aunt Lavinia's reddened eyes.

"It would help to telegram your housekeeper to see if Mary's diary is amongst her things and have it sent to you here. Knowing Mary's thoughts about the people in Killdaren's castle would be invaluable." I then told them what I'd learned so far, omitting my encounter with Sean, the possibility that Mary might have been romantically involved with Stuart Frye, and the fact that Lady Helen's murder may have happened in the Killdaren's maze. Those were matters were too upsetting to disclose just yet. Not until I knew more. But I did tell them of Bridget's story about Mary possibly drowning while saving Rebecca.

"Oh dear," Aunt Lavinia wept, dabbing furiously at more tears. "Mary would have sacrificed her last breath to keep a child from harm. Why did they not inform me of this?"

"I suspect it is because they are very protective of Rebecca and feared you'd wish to speak with her. I've never even seen or heard the child yet. Bridget did say that the child screams for days if anyone mentions Mary's name."

Aunt Lavinia dabbed at her eyes. "My heart still cries that Mary would never have let the girl close enough to the sea to require saving in the first place, and even more so because of the child's blindness."

"I thought the same thing myself. Mary wouldn't have let Rebecca out of her sight for a minute."

Andromeda frowned. "What if something more sinister was afoot? The child couldn't see if anything untoward happened. What if someone else had been with them and harmed Mary? Are you sure the constable won't make a further inquiry into the matter?"

I shook my head. "Not until we have something more than suppositions. Still, Aunt Lavinia, you should visit the constable every few days, but please don't tell him I'm at the castle. While I am searching for the truth, I want him to be reminded frequently that we are not accepting his assessment of Mary's disappearance."

Andromeda jumped up. "Cassie, dear me, but I almost forgot to tell you. I overheard some maids talking yesterday. There are two gentlemen from London staying here at the Inn. They have spent every summer here with the Killdaren brothers since their youth, but haven't stayed with the family since the death of Lady Helen."

"Do you know the names of the men?" I asked, realizing they might have been the occupants of the carriage who had laughed at the mud splattered on me and Bridget. I didn't like the fact that men in close association with the Killdarens were under the same roof as my family.

Andromeda shook her head. "No, the maids didn't mention names. But I shall learn who they are." Determined purpose narrowed my sister's eyes, an emotion akin to the one that had me sneaking into Killdaren's Castle. I grew more alarmed.

"No. Don't make any inquiries, Andrie. Asking too many questions from intimates of the Killdarens might jeopardize my investigations. I'll learn who the men are from the servants at the castle. Besides, one of the men might interpret your curiosity as a familiarity and question your respectability. In fact, you, Gemini and Aunt Lavinia should go back to Oxford and wait for Mother and Father's return there."

"Good Lord, Cassie! Have you lost your wits completely? Not only should you have never taken on the post of maid, possibly endangering yourself, but how could you ever think we'd leave you here alone!" Andromeda's incensed words hit me in the face. She was right, and the burden weighing on my shoulders grew heavier. My decisions for us to come to Cornwall and to masquerade as a maid had set us all upon a path from which there was no turning back, unless I wanted to abandon my investigation into Mary's death.

I wasn't ready to do that.

I reached the church later than our arranged time, just as the town clock chimed the half-hour. At the last minute I had decided to gather a few things to give to Bridget for her birthday on Friday and that delayed me. I found her pacing in front of the stone and stain-glassed building.

"Sorry, I'm late," I called out, rushing to her with my package tucked under my arm.

"Wherever 'ave ya been? Gone through the 'ole village, I 'ave."

"I went to the dock near the inn. The fishing boats are so much fun to observe."

"Ya been watching boats?" she cried, her eyes rolling with disbelief. "Lord, but what am I going to do with you? We need to hurry fast. Iffen Mrs. Frye catches us coming in late, we'll be scrubbing every floor in the castle day and night till it's done, I tell ya."

I pulled a piece of straw from Bridget's hair and realized she wasn't upset with just me. "What happened?"

Panicked, Bridget patted her air. "Is there more?"

"I'll look as we hurry back. What happened?"

"When I was walking by the livery, Tom tried to force a birthday kiss on me."

I nearly tripped. "He did?"

"He tried. Made us both go tumbling into the hay. He wasn't too happy when I left 'im."

"Did he hurt you?" I asked.

"No, I hurt him, though." She grabbed my hand. "I may want to know what a kiss is like, but not from 'im."

"Who then?"

She didn't answer, but raced up the rise and I hurried after her. Running downhill to the village had been much more exhilarating than running uphill while juggling a package. Halfway, I had to slow to a gasping walk. The afternoon sun was hot on our backs and a lull in the tangy sea breeze made it even hotter. My muscles were heavy, as if they couldn't make another step, and my lungs ached as if I couldn't take another breath. I ached everywhere. Cleaning was not as easy a job as I supposed.

Whatever energy I had possessed this morning had abandoned me and left a pervasive lethargy behind. I itched from head to toe and I smelled awful. I wanted a bath, and I wanted to crawl into my bed at home and sleep without dreaming for a week. I wanted Mary back, too. For a brief moment, I stopped in my tracks, hesitant to return to Killdaren's Castle, for I saw nothing but trouble ahead.

Mary wasn't coming back though, and I couldn't turn away from finding out why. The mysteries cloaked within the heavy stone walls of Killdaren's castle drew me. Mysteries surrounding Mary and whether I wanted to admit it or not, the mysteries surrounded Sean, too.

I put myself in motion and kept climbing the hill to catch up with Bridget. She and I were a good distance from the village, walking the path near the forest, when a branch snapped loudly from the thick foliage. Someone was there, just beyond our sight.

Startled, we both jumped and increased our pace. But the person hiding behind the shadowed boughs of the maritime forest followed. We ran. Whoever it was cried out, angry, their heavy breathing crawled over me like spiders.

"Wait," Bridget gasped, pulling on my arm as she dug in her heels. "Jamie Frye," she yelled. "Come out of there, ya fool! What are ya don' a spyin' and a frightenin' us so?"

Her shout was met with another scalp-tingling cry and the crash of brush as Jamie Frye emerged from the forest. He had tears in his eyes and bloody scratches on his face, as if he'd run without blocking the scraping branches.

"M-m...ary." He looked at me. "Sh-h...e gone."

Though my pulse pounded as if I still ran for my life, I forced myself to draw a deep breath and steady my voice. I didn't know what to make of this giant of a man with the emotions of a child. "I'm sorry that she's gone."

He stood there, gasping, making me feel as if I should do something, to make the impossible happen and bring Mary back.

Bridget had no such notion. She planted her hands on her hips and fussed at him. "Jamie, ya get back and do your chores before your mama finds out ya left."

"Noo," Jamie yelled, his eyes narrowing to angry, stubborn slits as his fists smacked his thick thighs. I took a step back in case he decided to use one of the massive fists on us. Bridget did too.

Hoof beats, muted by sand, preceded the appearance of a rider approaching us on a stormy black horse. The bright sun behind him blinded me, casting him into dark shadows, and I thought for sure I was about to encounter Alexander Killdaren.

Horse and rider came to a thunderous halt so close that flying bits of sod would have splattered me and Bridget if we hadn't moved to the side. Stuart Frye swung down.

"Miss Bridget, Miss Cassie." He nodded our way. Then he glared at his brother. "Jamie, go back home."

"Mary." Jamie shook his head then pointed at me. "She'll die. Not an accident."

"Why?" I looked Jamie in the eye. "What wasn't an accident?"

He grabbed me, his ham-like hands digging into my shoulders. "Mary! I'll help you."

Stuart put his face in front of Jamie's. "I'm sorry, Miss Cassie," Stuart said loudly, very forcefully, and slowly, his gaze boring into his brother's. "Jamie is a little confused right now.

He is going to go home and we are all going to forget what he just said, right? I'll escort the ladies back just to make sure that is exactly what happens. Do you understand, Jamie?"

Jamie and Stuart stared at each other. Finally, Jamie released me, and after sending an angry glare in Stuart's direction, he left. Stuart had a white-knuckled hold of the horse's reins and his riding crop. I rubbed my stinging shoulders and watched him take a number of deep breaths as he waited until his brother was well ahead on the path home. Then he turned our way and gestured for us to precede him.

"Ladies, I apologize for my brother's confusion. Sometimes it is difficult for him to understand things that happen and he is having a hard time right now. If you will permit me, I will escort you." He spoke as cultured as any gentleman, making me wonder just exactly who he was. Not that I doubted he was Stuart Frye, but that he'd had more education and training than an ordinary groomsman.

"He is confused about the...the teacher that died." I hoped to get more information with my question.

"Yes, but I think he's finally understanding that Mary won't be coming back. He wants to help her, and has connected you to her because of your hair, which is like sunshine and silk in the sun. Very beautiful, so I can't blame him for following you." Stuart peered closer at me, too close. I looked away, and let the subject of Mary drop before he became suspicious.

Bridget turned her nose up. "Don't be flirting with Cassie, Stuart Frye. I'll not let her be fooled by your wiles, that's for sure. And I'll not be speakin to ya myself, iffen' ya don't stop yer flirtin' ways."

Stuart wasn't the least bit bothered by Bridget's set down. He grinned at me. "Tell Lady Bridget she'd best remove the straw from her skirts before she condemns another."

Bridget gasped, ruffling her skirts and indeed sending several straws of hay flying. The sudden change from fear over having Jamie stalking us and predicting my death to this left me giddy. I tried to muffle my laugh, but didn't quite succeed. Bridget glared at me, then at Stuart. She opened her mouth as if to admonish him for another infraction and he shook his finger.

"I'd hold my tongue, Miss Bridget. My mother sent me out to discover why it was taking you two so long. As it is, I'll be able to ease her ire by mentioning Jamie's upset. At this point I see no need to let her know that my brother only delayed you for a few minutes, but I could change my mind."

"Hmmph." Bridget closed her mouth and hurried her step.

The huge black horse reared up, and Stuart settled the beast effortlessly, speaking low and soft in words I couldn't discern. It was as if he wove some sort of spell over the animal, for it followed us meekly, not even flicking its tail in dissent.

"What did you say to the beast?" I asked.

"Just a few ancient words from the Celts," he replied mysteriously.

Though I doubted simple words could have procured such immediate results.

"Weren't you on a white horse earlier?"

"Such is the lot of a groomsman. Can't be true to one because I have to see to the needs of so many."

Bridget huffed at his remark and picked up her irritated pace, staying ahead of us.

Though he flirted with me as we walked, Stuart watched Bridget's back with an interest I hadn't notice him give her before. Despite the tensions between them, I had to admit his escort had a soothing effect on me, especially when we passed the dark hedges of the towering maze. My encounter with Jamie had scraped over my emotions, leaving them raw.

In the gardens, Bridget turned to Stuart. "No matter what trouble ya cause me, Stuart Frye, I'll not be letting ya take advantage of Cassie."

"Then we're on the same side. I plan to see that nothing happens to her either." He directed his gaze toward me. "You should go though. You should leave here and never come back."

I had the distinct feeling that he knew more about me than I wanted him to. "I can't do that."

"God help us all." He walked away then, leading the horse with softly spoken words of an unknown language. Bridget and I watched him go.

"Who is he?"

"The Earl of Dartraven's bastard son."

Though I'd suspected as much, I still found myself recoiling from the harshness of Bridget's tone.

"Is that why you don't like him? He had the misfortune to be born out of wedlock?"

"Ack no. A man's born where God wills, and there's naught he can do about it."

"Then why the animosity?"

She stiffened her spine. "No amimosness about it. Just keepin' 'is flirtin' ways clean. Thanks to the Killdaren, he's been educated and all. He's livin' here now, but he won't for long."

"What about Jamie? Is he the earl's son as well?"

"No. From what I 'eard, he's a Frye, the man the earl foisted Stuart's mum on when he found out she was pregnant with Stuart."

# Chapter Six

After assessing us with a suspicious eye that surely would have caught the least bit of dangling straw, Mrs. Frye gave us a lecture about tardiness and put us to work helping Mrs. Murphy in the steamy kitchens. My discomfort from the heat and no bath became an unbearable itch. I had to do something about my situation tonight or die.

Ever since I learned about Stuart, I found myself looking at Mrs. Frye with a different eye. I could see how at one time she might have been pretty enough to have attracted the earl's attention, but I still couldn't imagine her stern nature ever permitting herself to have an affair. Perhaps my growing itch kept me from empathizing with her. I almost couldn't sit still, and I greatly resented the fact that I couldn't go strip all my clothes off and ease myself into a soothing bath.

Around here, it would have been tantamount to treason and would have cost me my post. My growing sense of how unrelenting and unfair the rules that bound our society and those less fortunate burrowed deeper.

Soon the flavorful aroma of mutton stew, onions and baking bread teased my palate to a hunger as sharp as my itch and made it harder for me to concentrate on anything. My thoughts raced from Lady Helen's murder in the maze, to Mary's disappearance, to Jamie's volatile emotions, to my unforgettable encounter with Sean. After a week, my investigation had only garnered scattered pieces of information with no real connection other than their disturbing impact and the fact that everything revolved around those within the Killdaren household.

Suddenly piercing screams rent the air, making my slice into a meat pie go awry. Mrs. Murphy dropped the pan she held, and a tearful Bridget jumped up from her seat at the table where she chopped onions.

"It's the wee one again." Bridget raced to the door.

"Sounds even worse than before," Mrs. Murphy cried, wiping her hands on her apron as she hurried after Bridget. I followed. We all came to a skittering halt in the palatial center hall as a rotund woman with gray hair, fiery cheeks and a grim expression came barreling into the room.

"Where is the little termagant?" the woman muttered, looking about almost frantically as she gasped for air. "I left her at her nap for only a few minutes and she ups and disappears. The child is impossible to teach, even more so ever since that highfalutin teacher showed up, changed everything, then killed herself."

Grabbing the stair rail, I held on as I bit back a wrenching denial.

Oblivious to my shock, the woman carried on. "That child has most likely gotten herself lost again. Needs to have bread and water for a week to teach her to never wander about alone. She's nigh given me the vapors."

Cries kept punctuating the air, and I turned in a circle, trying to tell from which direction they came, but the rounded dome ceiling of the center hall echoed the sound as if from every direction. I didn't know which way to run.

"I'll check the library." Bridget ran in that direction.

"I feel faint," the nurse said.

"Here, here, Nurse Tolley." Mrs. Murphy grabbed the woman's arm. "Can't 'ave any of that now. You come sit over here while we look for the lass."

"I'll look this way," I called then scurried down the corridor I'd ventured to the night I'd met Sean. Though the child's cries suddenly ceased, I kept looking into every room down the corridor. The room where I'd overheard the earl and Sir

Warwick turned out to be a gentleman's lounge that smelled heavily of tobacco. The game room across from there, where Sean had pulled me that night, was empty, too. It grabbed at my senses, making me remember his exotic scent and the heat of his body pressing against mine. My skin tingled anew with the remembrance of his leather-gloved hand touching me more intimately than any man ever had.

I slammed the door shut and hurried down the corridor. My head spun from the number of rooms I looked into, each of them appeared to have but a single purpose. One was clearly meant to showcase a strange assortment of antiquities from an Egyptian crypt, including a wall of tiny tiles scandalously depicting men *and* women in a Turkish bath. Together. I quickly averted my gaze from the scandalous scene, even though I dearly wished to join them. I was to the point that I'd give two fortunes for a tub of hot water.

Another room held statues, dozens of them, and all of them at first glance were as exquisite and as blatantly unclothed as Michelangelo's *David*. When I reached the end of the corridor, I came to a set of double doors and my hand tingled as I grabbed the large brass handle in the shape of a dragon. On the doors were two carved dragons. My pulse raced as fast as my thoughts scrambled. This was his lair.

Sean's private wing. And now that I'd thought about it, this was the direction the round room with the glass dome had to be as well.

"Cassie, don't!" Bridget's emphatic hiss came from behind me.

I could hear her frantic steps grow closer and I sucked in a disappointed breath. I'd hesitated too long and missed my chance to innocently explore beyond where the lower servants were permitted to go. Still, I couldn't seem to release my hold on the dragon handle.

Suddenly, the door jerked inward, pulling me forward, and burying my face into the naked chest of man—a hairy naked chest that tickled my nose.

"Well, if it isn't the rose on the prowl again." Sean caught my arm in his firm grip, keeping me from falling to my knees.

I was so off balance that I had to brace my hand against his chest to right myself. The heat of his bare skin sent such an acute flash of fire up my nerves that I flexed my fingers, pressing them into the supple muscle and brushing the silkiness of his dark hair. Before I could even stop and think, I drew an unseemly deep breath, taking in the full effect of his exotic scent.

"Find what you're looking for, lass?" he whispered. His hand slipped from my arm and brushed along the side of my breast before moving to my waist.

"My Lord!" I cried, rearing back, my heart thudding at the burning intimacy as everything feminine within me flared to life. He appeared as if he'd just rolled from bed. His broad naked chest tapered to slim hips that were hugged by scandalously half buttoned black pants. His dark hair was awry and his firm jaw was shadowed with stubble.

"Wrong man. That title belongs to my brother." The fire in his green eyes turned to ice. He directed his gaze over the top of my head.

"Forgive us, Mr. Killdaren," came Bridget's breathless, almost terrified whisper. "The child is—"

"Right here," Sean said. "Rebecca, come." He held out his hand and a young girl walked tentatively forward with her hand stretched searchingly before her. She clutched a worn rag doll in her other arm. Her raven hair, as black as Sean's, hung in wavy tresses all the way to her hips. Tears fell from emerald green eyes, streaking her face.

Kneeling down, I reached my arms out toward her. "Don't be frightened, poppet. It's all right. You've had a fright, but you're safe now."

Pulling her forward, Sean placed the child's hand in mine. When he did, his fingers lingered against mine, making me look up. His green gaze bored intently, as if trying to see through a heavy fog. Then he shook his head. "This is Cassie, Becca. She'll take you to your mother."

He then narrowed his gaze so sharply that I felt the lash of it deep inside of me and I stood to face him on a more equal level.

He spoke before I could. "Tell the nurse I found Rebecca lost on the bell tower stairs. If the child wanders again, the woman will be looking for a new post."

Frightened by his anger, Rebecca burrowed against my skirts and I tightened my hold on her hand.

Sean stepped back and snapped the door shut. I stood there blinking with the door just inches from my nose, wondering if I'd imagined everything that had happened. The child clinging to my skirts and Bridget grabbing my arm told me it had all been real.

Rebecca stared sightlessly, her hand clutching mine tightly. Only then did I remember that she was blind. She was also the spitting image of Sean, leaving me to wonder if he really was her father.

Bridget dug her fingers into my arm. "He knew who ya were," she whispered. "It's all true. He knows everything. He's a blimey vamp-oh!" She clamped her hand over her mouth.

"Shh, don't say such things," I nodded toward the child.

"Sorry. Never expected to see 'im much less speak to 'im. Blimey, though, I can't believe he knew ya."

I opened my mouth to set Bridget straight about how Sean knew who I was then I shut it. Mrs. Frye and Mrs. Murphy followed by an entourage of people bore down on us, and I really didn't want anyone to know about last week anyway.

Mrs. Murphy pulled the nurse along as the nurse repeatedly excused herself from blame to a dark-haired woman next to her. Extremely petite, the woman wore the most elaborate lace and satin day dress I'd ever seen. She didn't appear to be listening to the nurse's excuses; instead, the woman's eyes were anxiously searching over the child. The Earl of Dartraven, whose expression seemed to be one of worry and something akin to fear or pain, kept looking at the woman then at the child then back to the woman. From the droll look on Sir Warwick's face, I gathered he'd followed the group out of boredom rather than concern.

Mrs. Frye had fire and brimstone sparking in her eyes ready to condemn Bridget and me to an everlasting punishment for disturbing the Killdaren. I nipped any lectures in the bud and spoke before she could find her tongue. Quite a feat considering her sharp words were always on the tip of her tongue.

"Mr. Killdaren found Rebecca and brought her to us. He said she was on the stairs to the bell tower."

"Cassie, this is Miss Prudence, Rebecca's mother." Mrs. Frye's stern glare reminded me of my lowly position.

"My lady." I made a proper curtsy to Prudence.

"The tower! She was in the tower!" Smaller than I, and as pale and delicate looking as a lily, the woman was almost too beautiful to be real. Everything about her glowed, the pearl of her skin, the black silk of her hair, the ruby of her mouth, the gold of her eyes, to the tears on her cheeks. I had to blink to assure myself that I'd seen correctly. She knelt before Rebecca and pulled the child into her arms. "Oh, my little dear!"

"The stairs leading to the tower," I clarified. "Mr. Killdaren said to tell the nurse that if the child is left unsupervised again, she'll be relieved of her post."

"Well, I never!" gasped the nurse, her face growing impossibly redder.

The Earl of Dartraven cleared his throat. Glancing his way, I thought his blue eyes appeared more watery than before, but decided I was imagining things because when he spoke, his voice was cold. "At least the chit is unharmed."

Prudence gave the earl a sharp look. "Her name is Rebecca."

I wondered if the tension between them was because the earl had refused to accept Rebecca as being his granddaughter. I didn't even know what the etiquette in regards to illegitimate descendants was. But I was certain Prudence's presence in the Killdaren household was completely improper.

Prudence turned her back on the earl and spoke to Rebecca. "Darling, how did you ever wander so far from your room all by yourself? That's almost across the whole castle."

"D-d-didn't." The little girl said. "H-h-help." Rebecca didn't say anything more and Prudence bundled Rebecca into her embrace again.

A strange feeling swept over me, making me want to take hold of Rebecca's hand again. No one seemed to notice any oddity in the child's choice of words.

"Well, now that everything is settled, we can all get back to the day." The earl sounded deliberately loud and jovial as he planted his finger in Sir Warwick's chest. "You, sir, are getting slack in your old age. Our appointment for whist was set to begin thirty minutes ago. You're late."

"*Au contraire.*" Sir Warwick looked as if he'd just come in from riding. "I'm a fashionable twenty minutes late and our appointment was for billiards." He nodded toward the billiard room. "Shall we? There's a hundred pounds at stake, I believe."

"Fifty, you reprobate." The earl and Sir Warwick walked away arguing.

I ignored the rest of their barbed banter to study Rebecca. She didn't seem to be screaming for help. Was I interpreting her words wrongly? I appeared to be the only one concerned. The crowd quickly dispersed, but my unease lingered.

A short while after Mrs. Murphy, Bridget and I returned to the kitchens, I went in search of Mrs. Frye, looking longingly as I passed a storage room where a discarded hip-bath sat. Mrs. Frye spent the late afternoons in the housekeeper's office just beyond the butler's pantry. The door to her room stood ajar, so I didn't have to knock. Inside I found Mrs. Frye with her nose barely an inch away from a ledger that she painstakingly wrote in. I quickly backed away from the door, knowing she'd not want me to know that she had difficulty seeing. I'd be scrubbing for a month of Sundays.

It would take her hours to log in the stack of bills sitting on her desk without spectacles. This time as I approached her door, I scraped my shoe against the floor. She looked up as I knocked.

"Mrs. Frye, I wondered if I might have a word with you."

"Don't ask me for any special favors, miss."

Heat flooded my face, though I had nothing to feel guilty for. Had I the notion to ask for use of the hip-bath, she'd answered my question.

"It's about the child, Rebecca. I have a concern. When her mother asked how she'd gotten to the tower stairs alone, the child said she didn't. I thought she also said help. Could someone have left her there?"

"Nonsense. You haven't been here long enough to know, so I'll inform you. Rebecca is a difficult child who never does as she's told. She wanders about, even at night, and has to be watched constantly. I wasn't surprised she wandered to the tower, though she never has before."

I still didn't feel comfortable with her answer, but was in no position to press my concerns, so I bit my tongue, and nodded at the ledger she wrote in. "I know you are very busy and I won't keep you, but should you ever need help with the ledgers, I am very familiar with keeping accounts."

She eyed me suspiciously. "I'll keep that in mind. We'll see how trustworthy you are with your work first."

"Yes, ma'am." I backed from her office. I had three things on my mind as I returned to the kitchens. A bath. Mary. And my unease about Rebecca.

Any intruding thoughts about *him*, his bare chest, his warm skin and his intoxicating scent I ignored, hoping desperately that if I didn't acknowledge them they'd go away.

Dinner that night proved to be a quiet affair, almost anti-climactic after the tensions that had brewed to the surface during the day. Jamie was present for the first time since he'd stormed out last week, but he didn't speak and he didn't look my way. Stuart Frye was more mischievous than ever. He'd reverted back to the role of outrageously flirtatious groomsman, leaving me to wonder if I'd imagined the cultured, gentlemanly demeanor earlier. Tonight, he flirted with everyone but Bridget and kept his gaze on the Oak sisters' bosoms. Bridget appeared as if she wanted to skewer him for it.

My thoughts of Sean had grown insufferably persistent,

and it wasn't until I was pushing the vegetables around in my bowl that I honed in on what was bothering me. Was Prudence currently his mistress?

In my opinion, Sean had he made advances on me. His search of my person that first night had been personal as had his murmured notion to meet him in the library one evening. Today, he'd been even more familiar. So had I.

As soon as Bridget and I reached our room the question burst from me. "What is Lady Prudence's relationship to the Killdaren? Is he going to marry her?"

"What's that, you said? Lady Prudence? Ack, it's Miss Prudence. Though now educated, she's a cropper's daughter, and he's the legitimate albeit second son of the Earl of Dartraven. He could never marry her. Should anything happen to the viscount, then the Killdaren would be heir to the title. He'll have to marry well, most likely a daughter of an earl or a duke."

"Did he father the child? It's not right that he continues to besmirch her reputation by having her live here in his home." I paced across the room, fueled by the injustice.

Bridget looked puzzled a moment. "She don't want to be living where she grew up at, that's for sure. A bad place, I tell ya. Besides, Prudence has never said who the wee one's father is. Could be the viscount at that, but it was the Killdaren who sent Prudence off to be educated and lets her and the wee one live here. So I'm thinking she's his." She lowered her voice. "But I hear the viscount's not to be trusted with the ladies. Why, he's worse than Stuart Frye ever thought of bein'."

Every question surrounding the Killdarens only seemed to lead to more questions.

Bridget diligently worked at learning to read every night. She'd progressed to reading all simple words without assistance and insisted on reading the first page of the story over and over until she knew every word. Then we spent part of the evening working on her speech, remembering to pronounce *h*'s and *g*'s and correcting *you* and *your* for *ya* and *yer*. Once we finished, Bridget went right to sleep, leaving me alone with thoughts of *him.*

I turned to the vampire book again for help, thinking it was time for me to learn what happened to the woman who had wandered into the bowels of the church to meet a man she never should have gone to meet.

*Instead of sinking his fangs into the woman's neck, the vampire brushed his lips over her throbbing pulse and lightly teased her skin with the tip of his fangs. "I can feel the heat of your blood, my lady. I can almost taste your richness. You make my blood surge for the pleasure of the hunt and the need for a mate," the vampire said, pulling her into his velvet bed until she knelt between his legs.*

*She could feel him too, the heat of him, the lure of his desire for her. She'd only known the scorn of her plainness, the brunt of rejection, and the cut of her loneliness. He looked at her as if she were Venus. His want was greater than anything she'd ever known and more frightening than anything she'd ever experienced.*

*She turned away, trying to fight his pull, knowing instinctively that her soul hung in the balance. But he wouldn't let her go.*

*"Look at me," he demanded.*

*The growing surge of her own want forced her to meet his demand. She lifted her gaze to his, and he smiled as he stared deeply into her eyes, entering her soul.*

*"You're mine, my beauty." He reached up and pulled loose the tie of her cloak, letting it fall from her shoulders. Then he slid open the buttons of her gown, discarding her fichu and her modesty.*

*"Who are you?" she whispered.*

*"Call me Armand. As Solomon feasted upon his love, so I shall you for eternity." He tugged her gown from her shoulders, exposing her bosom and the pounding of her heart. Then he bent to taste the creamy silk of her flesh.*

Heat swept through me, sending everything inside me into a jumble. Good heavens! I jumped up and threw the book under my cot, stripping off my dress and underclothes to take yet another meager bath in the wash basin.

The ewer and the basin were empty. I couldn't believe it. My first response was to call our housekeeper and make a gentle complaint about the oversight. I'd made it across the room and had my hand on the doorknob when it hit me that I wasn't at home. There was no housekeeper here to fill my basin at this late hour, because filling my basin was my responsibility to take care of, in and amongst the many hours that I spent laboring. Tears stung my eyes.

I knew I'd find water in the kitchens. A lot of water. I could even have heated water. There was also that discarded hip-bath in the storeroom. Perhaps for just a short while I could make use of it. Blissful relief and heavenly cleanliness was but a daring stairwell's descent away.

Without giving myself a chance to think twice, I hurriedly slipped on my soft cotton nightdress along with my light robe, grabbed soap, milk and rose cream, and quietly left my room. At the moment I didn't care if Mrs. Frye discovered me, or if the whole of the castle saw me naked.

Tonight, very little moonlight filtered through the windows. The small candle I held only let me see my next step. My ears strained to catch the slightest sound, but I heard nothing. In fact, for an old castle, it was unnaturally quiet. By the time I reached the kitchens, my nerves were scraped raw by the folly of my own imagination about what might be lurking in the dark shadows around me.

Upon second consideration, spending any more time than absolutely necessary in the kitchens alone was not a good idea. So my dream to slip into a hot bath in the discarded tub quickly changed to gathering a ewer of water and going back to my room, though I didn't know how I would manage to carry the water, my things, and a candle.

I'd just filled the ewer and reached for my soap and cream when the voices of gentlemen and booted footsteps grew louder, as if coming my way. In my haste to blow out the candle, I spilled water down the front of my gown and on the floor. I set the ewer on the counter, looking for a rag to clean up the mess so no one would slip on the spill.

"When are you going to free yourself from this elaborate crypt you've buried yourself in?" The unfamiliar man's voice came on the heels of booted steps as several men entered the kitchens.

Good Lord! I ducked instantly down, searching for an escape before I could be caught.

"I'm content," Sean answered, the deep richness of his lilting voice unmistakable. Light flooded the room, and I slid beneath the counter.

"Good God. You and Blackmoor both!" another man exclaimed. "It's a bloody shame. This rift between you has got to end."

"It will end when one or both of us are dead, Colin. If you and Ashton wish to persist in discussing this topic, then you'd best leave now."

"Bloody hell, but you're a cold bastard. Your brother said to tell you—"

"Nothing. Alex said nothing. I meant what I said, Colin."

The chilling slice of Sean's tone pierced right to the center of my stomach, leaving me feeling queasy. I huddled deeper into the corner under the counter.

"He's right, Drayson. There's no point in resurrecting Lady Helen's murder—"

"No bloody point? Good God, man. This whole situation is my fault. In eight years I've yet to forget. Every time I shut my eyes at night, I see her battered face, and every night I suffer the regret of the damned. If I hadn't told the constable that I'd seen you or Blackmoor exit the maze, none of this would have ever—"

"Enough!"

Steps grew closer and the sight of black boots tucked into black pants that molded themselves intriguingly to muscular legs moved in front of me, and I nearly gasped aloud. Instead of the sure-footed, predatory pace I expected, he had to make use of a cane. Not heavy use, but enough to show me his need of the dragon headed cane was necessary and not an affectation.

In the echoing wake of his shout, I heard Sean sigh. Then he spoke softly, but still faced the wall, leaving his back to the men in the room. "Colin, what you don't understand is there is nothing you or anyone could have done to stop what happened, nor what is to come. I've lost my appetite tonight. Why don't you and Ashton come back tomorrow? It will be a better night for hunting anyway."

His voice held such despair that I had to squeeze my hands into fists to keep from trying to soothe anything within reach, even if it was the tightness in my own chest. Then his last sentence filtered through. Hunting? What sort of hunting occurred at night? A flash of the vampire pulling the woman into his velvet crypt blazed before my eyes.

"Bloody hell, I've—"

"Said more than you should have, Colin. Let's go to the pub and come back tomorrow."

"Novel idea, Ashton," Sean said dryly. "I'll see you both then. But make it a little later. Around midnight."

"But—"

"Bloody hell, Colin, shut up. If there's more, save it for the pub. Sorry, we'll be back tomorrow at midnight and be hungrier for the treat. She's as bright as Venus you say?"

"A beauty. I'll see you then."

My thoughts rioted. Hunt? Venus? Beauty? Good Lord!

Another deep sigh echoed softly followed by receding steps told me the men had left. I kept my breaths shallow, doing my best not to make the slightest noise, waiting for Sean to leave, but he didn't. He stood facing the wall for what seemed like forever.

When he turned, he walked directly to the counter I hid beneath. Then he knelt, grabbed my arm, and hauled me out into the light like a sack of potatoes. Potatoes that had turned completely to mush.

My pulse pounded to such a deafening sound I couldn't hear a single thought other than I knew I was done for. I squeezed my eyes tightly shut, irrationally feeling that if I couldn't see him then maybe he'd just disappear.

"Well, what excuse do you hav—" His voice died into a hiss.

Silence pressed so heavily upon me that I thought it had suffocated me until I realized I'd forgotten to breathe. Sucking in air, I opened my eyes, surprised to find Sean staring at me as if frozen as well. I followed the direction of his gaze, looking downward. My robe had fallen open and the water I'd spilt on my nightdress had rendered it transparent. My breasts might as well have been completely uncovered.

"Oh, God!" I cried.

"From what I see, you ought to be praising Him rather than lamenting." His green gaze feasted hungrily on my breasts, much as the vampire in the book had feasted upon the woman.

Don't bite me, I thought as my vision went dark; a roar much like that of sea deafened me as a black tide tried to swallow me completely.

# Chapter Seven

I reeled and saw the cold hard stone of the floor rise to meet me. Just before I collided with it, a rough jerk pulled me back and I landed with my head propped against Sean's hard thighs. He'd caught me, cushioning my fall by easing me and himself to the floor.

"Fainting won't save you." His dark brows drew to an exasperated frown over eyes narrowed with suspicion.

I didn't care what the consequences were. I would not succumb to this man as the woman in the vampire book had. I glared at Sean and tried to muster a formidable outrage. "Who needs to faint? I'm certain that any moment now, your chivalrous impulses will reassert themselves, and you'll apologize for dragging me across the floor like a barbarian."

It was the best I could manage at the moment because every muscle inside me had the substance of drifting sand.

The corners of his mouth lifted slightly, and I stared at them, wondering at the deceptively soft fullness of his lips. Were his teeth a little pointed?

Good Lord. I had to be losing my mind. There were no such things as vampires. My grandfather's impossible stories of Celtic lore and Druid magic had apparently seeded a wild imagination inside of me after all.

"She speaks like the most proper of ladies, but her eyes sing a different tune. Your fascination with my mouth isn't going to save you either. What is the wandering rose doing here dressed like this?" He sniffed the air then frowned. "Well, not quite a rose tonight, I'm afraid. I want an answer. What are you doing here?"

I blinked, shocked. "You...you...dare to tell me I smell?" I was incensed. "I'll have you know that if *you* had *proper* bathing facilities for your employees and clean uniforms, then I wouldn't have been down here looking for bathing water. I wouldn't have spilt water on myself when I heard you and your friends, and my indelicate smell and improper dress would have never been brought to your attention. This whole incident is *your* fault."

"Indeed. Servants now require bathing facilities in addition to free use of my library? Are there any other grievances that need addressing, or undressing, in your opinion?" he asked, glancing back at my breasts, which felt oddly on fire and still exposed at the moment despite my concealing robe.

"Yes, since you've asked. Fresh uniforms daily. Higher wages. More time than just a half-day Sunday to see family. And hope. Hope of a future." I shoved my elbow back so that I could angle up from his lap and face him with some measure of dignity.

"Bloody hell," he muttered, dumping me off him.

I landed with a thud on the floor. Now free of his grasp, I quickly got to my feet, still clutching my robe closed, and started to run from the room. He groaned and I peeked over my shoulder. When I saw that he still sat on the floor, I skittered to a stop. He had his eyes shut and appeared to be taking deep breaths.

"Are you ill?" I said, taking a cautious step toward him.

"I'll live." His voice rasped deeply. He still didn't open his eyes.

Surely, I hadn't harmed him. All I did was sit up. And I was so little compared to his size. "You've not a very stalwart constitution." I stepped closer and frowned down at him.

He opened his eyes then, a direct, hard stare that slammed into me like a desert wind. He didn't have to say a word to tell me very little separated me from finding out just how stalwart his constitution was. "Perhaps that was a hasty assessment." I backed away.

"Very. Not to mention erroneous as well." He grabbed his cane and swiftly stood in a very stalwart, healthy way.

"Perhaps that too." I moved around so that the counter was between us and the servants' stairs were right behind me. He arched at brow at me, his keen gaze raking down my body, making me feel as if I wore only my wet gown, if anything at all.

"Do you need proof?" He stepped toward me, his lips curving into a very sensual smile that wrapped around me, urging me closer to him.

"No," I yelped, louder than I meant. His draw upon me was so strong that I had to back to the stairs to feel proper.

His expression changed suddenly as if pained and he turned from me, his free hand clenching into a fist at his side. "Good night." His voice turned harsh, so unlike the teasing amusement just moments ago.

"But—" I bit my lip. I felt as if I'd hurt him in some way, and I couldn't leave.

"Leave me." He spoke so loudly, so forcefully that something akin to fear snaked down my spine.

I turned and dashed up the servants' stairs blindly. Somehow I reached the safety of my room without falling. Once again I stood with my back to my locked door, gasping for air. I didn't move for a very long time. Finally, when I could stand no longer and had heard no odd noises, no steps in the corridor, and no tap of a cane against stone or wood, I crawled into bed. Once my head hit the pillow, I curled myself into a ball, pheasant shell in hand, and cried.

I cried for a bath. I cried because I smelled and my skin itched. I cried for home and my family, but most of all I cried for Mary.


A sharp rap on our door brought me and Bridget stumbling quickly to our feet, fearful that we were late, then confused, for the darkness of the night had yet to be softened by the predawn light.

"Blimey," Bridget muttered, stumbling to the door. "Who's

there?"

"It's Janet and Adele."

Bridget opened the door, yawning. "What's a matter with ya?"

The Oak sisters wore matching expressions of worry. "We were 'oping you'd know. Mrs. Frye wants us all downstairs in the laundry room immediately."

"It's three in the mornin'," Janet said. "Shameful the way she works us so 'ard."

"Worse than that, I tell ya," Adele added.

Bridget grabbed her dress and slid it over her head. Wincing, I did the same and nearly choked on the smell of my uniform. As I put on my stockings and my shoes, I quickly came to the conclusion that if I didn't get a bath soon, I just might expire. At least my discomfort kept me from dwelling on what had happened after I'd fallen asleep late into the night.

I had dreamed about Mary for the second time. I heard her calling to me as if she needed my help. This time we weren't in the sea. We were in the castle. I caught sight of her in a corridor, but when I ran toward her, I could never get close enough to touch her. Her white gown billowed from her slight form like a ghostly cloud as she led me to the marbled center hall then up the winding stairs to the second floor. At the third set of double doors on the left, she stopped, fell to her knees and begged me not to—

I don't know what she wanted from me, for that was the exact moment Janet and Adele had knocked. A heaviness settled inside me as I puzzled over and over what I had dreamed. I wanted to know the significance of it, and I definitely wanted to know if there were double doors on the second floor, and whose room was third on the left?

After Bridget and I dressed, the four of us hurried downstairs, surprised to find Mrs. Murphy hard at work in the kitchens. Fires blazed in the stone hearths where iron cauldrons bubbled. She wiped her hands on her apron then set them on her ample hips. "I've never seen the likes of this in all of my days, I tell you. The Killdaren has gone completely mad, he has."

"What is it?" Janet whispered.

"What are ye boiling?" Adele asked as she peered into one of the pots, wincing at the rising steam.

"Ourselves it seems, lass." Mrs. Murphy threw her hands in the air.

Bridget, Janet, and Adele gasped, taking frightened steps backward. "Ye cannot mean that," Bridget cried, her freckles blanching white and her blue eyes huge with horror.

"A Mrs. Turnbill did that over in Derry. 'eard about it last year. Boiled her maid and sold the broth she did." Janet grabbed Adele's hand and they took several more steps to the door.

Bridget stamped her foot. "Ack, this is nonsense. He's a vampire, I tell ya. They drink yer blood, not boil yer bones." She glared at Mrs. Murphy. "Now tell us the truth, ma'am."

Mrs. Murphy burst into laughter. "A vampire?" Mrs. Murphy gasped and laughed more. "The Killdaren has you believing those rumors, does he?" She shook her head. "The lad wants every one of us to take a bath! He's filled half the laundry with tubs. You'd have thought the world had come to an end, the way he had my Murphy and Stuart and Jamie rearranging everything in the middle of the night as if the Queen herself had made a decree."

"A bath!" Bridget, Janet and Adele's gasps rang twice as loud as mine, and their wide-eyed expressions were more horrified than they'd been at the notion of being boiled alive. I laughed so hard that tears brimmed my eyes.

Mrs. Murphy shooed us toward the laundry room. "Best hurry up. Mrs. Frye will be inspecting the results before the morning meal."

Bridget, Janet and Adele all groaned as if in pain. Meanwhile my heart sang as if I'd just been handed the crown jewels.

"There isn't any point in complaining and ye lasses best accustom yourself to the notion. Yer to bathe every Friday, more often if ye've the want. Now hurry up with it. I've a number of chores that need doing."

I led the way to the laundry, dragging the others with me. Entering the room, I stood a moment amazed at its transformation. Along the back wall in four barn-like stalls sat three hip-baths and one tub, each with its own privacy curtain pulled to the side. Steam rose from the tubs in a blessedly welcoming mist.

*He did this*, I thought with wonder.

Rushing over to the full tub, I dipped my fingers into the water and sighed. On a table beside the tub someone had placed a large bar of soap and a soft cotton cloth and my bath things I'd left on the counter in the kitchen last night. In seconds I had my shoes and stockings off, and had started on the buttons of my dress when I remembered the curtain. Turning to reach for it, I found Bridget, Janet and Adele still standing at the doorway, staring at me is if I'd gone insane.

Having had to round my younger sisters up for their baths when they were little and had yet to covet the comfort of cleanliness, I knew just what to do. "Come along with you now. We've much to do to pass Mrs. Frye's inspection and very little time left."

Grabbing Bridget's arm, I pulled her to one hip-bath, and shooed Janet and Adele to the others. "Now off with your clothes. I'll have Mrs. Murphy go gather fresh uniforms for all of us from Mrs. Frye, so she can't find a blemish." I'd have to wear mine pinned so as to fit well enough to stay on, but nothing was going to stop me from being wonderfully clean.

By the time I managed to get the three maids in the hip-baths and had put them through the horrifying experience of ducking their heads under the water and scrubbing their hair, I had very little time left for my own bath. The water had cooled considerably in the tub, but not even that could lessen my ecstasy as I sank beneath the water. I hurriedly subjected every inch of my being to soothing suds and a soft cloth.

I'd been given a new life.

"This 'ill be the death o' us," Bridget said as she helped me dry my hair with a soft towel.

"'twill be the making of you, Bridget. Once you've accustomed yourself to the exhilaration of being clean, all of life will be brighter. Think about it. Remember how you felt racing down the hill to the village yesterday? Don't you feel a little like that now?"

She frowned. "Perhaps, though running and bathing don't have much to do with each other iffen ya ask me." She narrowed her eyes and lowered her voice so that Janet and Adele, who were across the room couldn't hear. "Cassie, I don't know how, but ya did this, didn't ya?" Then she immediately shook her head and answered before I could. "No, how could ya?"

Suddenly, she grabbed my shoulders, a mixture of surprise and excitement on her face. "Blimey!" she hissed, still whispering, but more forcefully. "The Killdaren saw ya just yesterday and now he has us bathin'! He wants ya, that's what. Yer not going to have to scrub much longer, ya aren't. Be wearin' dresses and drinkin' tea with Miss Prudence. She was an upstairs maid until he took a fancy to her, dressed her up and had her educated he did." She clamped her hand over her mouth, looked about and lowered her voice even more. "Best keep this as quiet as we can, now. No use in setting tongues wagging before there's a need to. Miss Prudence didn't say a word to anyone about it until she couldn't hide that she was with a bairn. Ya might be right about this bathin' stuff after all, Cassie."

Bridget turned around and did a little dance on her way to the kitchens.

I stood, so flabbergasted that I couldn't even speak. Good heavens. She truly thought being a man's mistress was some sort of salvation.

During the morning meal, I still couldn't find the words to express my shock, partly because of Bridget's mercenary notions, and partly because I feared she was right. After last night's debacle, Sean most likely thought I'd deliberately exposed my breasts to his view and had arranged the employee bathing with an eye to furthering his acquaintance with me, a very upsetting matter in itself. But not as horrifying as the idea of involving myself intimately with a man in order to escape doing chores. It was most likely the only way a woman in Bridget's position in life could better her circumstances, and that realization disturbed me the most.

As the meal ended and the women gathered up the plates to be washed, I slipped a knife into my pocket, deciding any weapon would be better than no weapon. Bridget and I received the task of cleaning and polishing the music room after passing Mrs. Frye's cleanliness inspection. Amazingly, she informed us she'd be hiring two scullery maids and a laundress. Then, starting tomorrow, a fresh uniform would be readied every other day for each member of her staff. They were to wear it the next morning, having their person in just as clean a state. Every Sunday, half the servants would be off the entire day. Then the next Sunday, the other half would have the day free.

I wondered less about Sean's motives in providing a bathing facility then, and my heart warmed over the fact he'd heard and acted on what I'd said.

Bridget didn't say a word until she shut the ornately carved, gold-leafed double doors, closing us inside the music room, then she started dancing another jig, bursting with joy. "I'll not be scrubbing any more dishes or slavin' over any more pots! And two whole days a month with my family! It's a miracle, I say."

I could barely hear, for I stood in awe. The room wasn't just a receptacle for musical instruments, but boasted a theater as well. Elaborate chairs with cream brocade seats and gold accents faced a stage framed in rich, snowy damask curtains fringed with gold. A grand piano and a huge golden harp sat center stage and were backed by the gleaming gold pipes of a pipe organ. Lining the cream and gold walls in beautifully carved mahogany and glass cases lay exquisite musical instruments of wood, gold, and silver. Some encrusted with jewels, others so rustic and frail in appearance that they had to be as old as the Druids themselves.

"This is unbelievable. Who plays these instruments?"

"It's a right shame, it is, but no one does, though Mary was working with my sister Flora, teaching her to sing, she was." Bridget handed me a dusting cloth and moved to the first glass case.

I followed her, peering closer at the odd black flute-like instruments wrapped with gold dragons, thankful to see a printed card explaining its use, for I'd never seen such an instruments in my life. "Tartoelen Dragon Shawms," I read. "'Differently pitched wind instruments that imitate the human voice. These shawms were used by a young actress in Vienna during a performance for Emperor Maximilian the First. He became so enchanted that he claimed this golden haired actress, Anna Breisua, for his lover. Jealous and fearful of losing their power over the Emperor, certain court nobles accused Anna of witchcraft, of casting a spell over the Emperor through the Dragon Shawms—'"

"She...was burned at the stake for her sinful deed." Bridget finished the last sentence for me.

"Excellent." I focused on Bridget's improvement and avoided the pall the story cast over the pristine glow of the room.

Bridget frowned, more fiercely than ever before. "What do ya mean? That was horrible. The poor woman."

"I meant your reading was excellent, Bridget. The events told were indeed horrible. Thank God the world has moved past such barbaric practices."

"What do ya mean?"

"Parliament dispensed with that punishment about a hundred years ago, but if you ask me that was a couple of hundred years too late. After Bloody Mary's reign, few men were burned at the stake, but they continued to burn women to death for the crimes of murder and counterfeiting until 1790."

"Blimey. How'd you learn all that?"

"Reading. Books can tell you anything and take you anywhere in the world you want to go, Bridget."

Her eyes misted. "And I'm learning how. You know, you're like Flora's friend Miss Mary, you are. She was always helping and a teaching the wee one, and teaching Flora to speak proper, and learning us all about the world. She read us the papers every day, she did."

A huge lump of emotion caught in my throat. I nodded my head and scrubbed the glass harder, paying close attention to a blur that didn't disappear until I blinked. My cousin had left a legacy behind, one of care and love.

"We'd better hurry. We'll need to be further along before Mrs. Frye checks on us."

Bridget laughed. "You're learning too, Cassie." She smiled and I smiled back.

We quickly moved through a number of glass cases. As we did, I silently read the captions for each of the instruments, but didn't bring them to Bridget's attention. By the fifth case I had an ill feeling in the pit of my stomach.

As wonderful as this room was, each of the captions beside the musical instruments explained the instrument—a lyre, a lute, a cittern, a spinnettino, a viola—its time period, and how that instrument played a part in the demise of the woman who used it. Instruments that now lay silent as death, entombed in glass. The macabre research and expense to purchase musical instruments that had direct correlation to death cast a sinister cloud over the whole room for me, which I wasn't quite ready to expose to Bridget, so I kept my discovery to myself.

Mrs. Frye made her usual inspection. After she left, Bridget heaved a sigh of relief and chattered. I nodded my head appropriately as she talked about how beautiful the diamond and silver lyre resting on the cream satin. I kept seeing the poor maiden who'd plucked the wrong note, displeasing her Roman master, and died for it. Though her story didn't end there. The lyre played itself until the Roman master went mad.

"Do ya know how, Cassie?" Bridget's question caught me unawares.

"I'm sorry. What did you say?"

"Can ya play any of them?" She swept her hand out to encompass the instruments.

"Only the piano."

"Then ya must play me a song." She caught my hand and pulled me toward the stage.

"Well...I..."

"Please. Ack, just one. I've dreamed of hearing it played. Mrs. Frye won't be back for a while."

"All right."

Bridget and I hurried up the marble steps to the stage. I felt a little like I had yesterday when I'd run down the hill. From the pink flush staining Bridget's cheeks, I got the idea that she felt the same. What was it about doing something forbidden that made life more real? At least it did until the deed was done, then often life felt worse.

The piano was like a cream cloud of luxury, the keys were wonderfully light to my fingertips and the sound of the notes could only be described as heavenly. Brahm's "Lullaby" came first, bringing treasured remembrances of hearing my mother softly sing my sisters and me to sleep. Then the haunting tones of a Chopin Nocturne followed by many beloved songs eased from my heart and fingers to fill the hall, but when I hit the last high note, a muted clink sounded.

Frowning, I stood and peered into the piano bed, surprised to see a puddle of silk material bunched over the hammers. I pulled the material loose, discovering it to be a red scarf.

"That's my sister's," Bridget cried out and grabbed my arm. "She had it on the day she left, she did, a present from Jack it was. What's it doin' here?"

For a moment, my heart skipped with fear until common sense thankfully stepped in. "I daresay there's more than one red silk scarf. And it could be that your sister accidentally left it behind, which would make it yours." I handed the scarf to Bridget.

She stared at the red silk for a few minutes then slowly brushed her fingers over it before clutching it to her cheek. My heart went out to Bridget at that moment more than ever because I could see in the bare emotion shadowing her eyes how much she missed her sister.

"Is it all right if I run the scarf to our room? I might ruin it by stuffing it into my pocket."

I wanted to tell her that wouldn't be likely, but from the reverent awe in her blue eyes, I knew the scarf was too much of a valued treasure to ever be stuck into a pocket. "Go. I'll wait here."

Bridget didn't hesitate. She dashed quietly away.

After inspecting the inside of the piano for anything else obstructive, I sat again and replayed the song the scarf had interrupted. I played another, this one a lively Hungarian dance that reminded me of gypsies, bonfires and nights when the moon brushed the world with silver-star dust, creating a beautiful painting that perhaps only God could fully see.

Suddenly a suspicion that I was no longer alone in the room crept over me, along with the very chilling realization that I did not want to be alone with whoever had taken something so beautiful as music and made it so horrible. A curtain at the opposite end of the stage rustled, as if touched by a breeze...or a hand.

My fingers crashed to the keys, making a sharp discordant jumble, and I stood. "Who is it?" I demanded, determined not to give into the fear jumping onto my heart.

No answer, but I heard faint breathing that the stage amplified even more. Goose bumps pricked my skin.

Run! My mind shouted at me. The curtain rustled again and I stepped away from the piano, my hand sliding to the knife in my pocket as I hurried across the stage. Two steps from the stairs a sneeze echoed through the room. I'd expected any sound to be from a man, not the soft sneeze of a child.

Pulse beating less wildly, I turned and tiptoed across the stage to the curtains. Snatching them back, I found Rebecca huddling there, clutching her rag doll.

She cried out, moving away from me, her hand searching all around, as if she were terrified and needed to escape. She wore a pink lace dress over what had to have been a dozen petticoats considering how fully her dress flounced about her ankles. Pretty stockings and dainty slippers with pink bows that matched the tiny bows in her coifed hair completed her attire. She looked as if she were a lady about to meet the Queen, rather than a child at midday play. She'd apparently escaped the incompetent watch of her nurse again.

"It's all right," I said softly. "It's Cassie? Remember, I held your hand yesterday?"

She didn't respond. She kept backing away, uncannily moving in the right direction to escape. I thought about reaching out to her, but feared I would only frighten her more. I wondered how she'd gotten here without me and Bridget seeing her and I wondered why she'd come.

*The music. Play the music.*

Before I could question the thought, I went to the piano. "Would you like to hear more music?" I asked the child. She stopped moving away the moment my fingers hit the keys and the soothing tones of *Moonlight Sonata* filled the room.

After a few minutes, she moved toward me, sweeping her hand and foot in tiny, graceful arcs before her, making her look like a ballerina warming up for a performance.

"How old are you?"

She faced a point off to my right and held up seven fingers very methodically. Given her petite size, I had thought her to be five.

"Seven then." Hearing my voice, she turned in my direction. "Just the age I started to learn how to play the piano. Can you play?"

"N-n-no," she stuttered.

Was she still afraid? "Would you like to play?"

"C-c-can't, can't see."

"I know," I said softly, realizing that her speech pattern didn't stem from fear. "But you can still learn to play."

She shook her head and backed away.

"Well, then, perhaps you can just listen. Would you like to sit where you can best hear the song?" I meant for her to join me on the bench, but when she reached the piano, she sat on the floor, leaning against its leg as if she'd done it many times before. Adding that observance to Bridget's remark that no one ever played the instruments in this room, and the finding of the red silk scarf, made a puzzle just as unsettling as the histories of the glass-encased instruments.

"Blimey." Bridget rushed into the room. "I barely missed Mrs. Frye in the center hall."

Rebecca jumped up, holding her doll tightly to her.

"Oh!" Bridget came to a halt. "How did you get in here, wee one?"

Rebecca shook her head.

"Well, no mind. Come along with ya. I'll see ya back safe to ya room." Marching up, Bridget caught hold of the child's hand, and helped her down the stairs. "I suppose Nurse Tolley is up in your room snoozin' away, thinking you're at your nap."

Rebecca remained silent, but bowed her head. Bridget didn't seem to think it odd that Rebecca didn't say anything.

"I'll come with you." I hurried down from the stage. "It'll be good to know where Rebecca's room is so that I can take her back there should the need arise in the future." Bridget nodded and we all left the music room.

Reaching the center hall, Bridget turned up the expansive curved stair leading to the second floor. Our steps on the carpeted runners were silent and hushed, making almost every movement one of reverence, which happened to be very appropriate. Presiding on the walls from great heights were full portraits of what I assumed were dark-haired Killdaren ancestors. In the oldest painting, the style of dress dated from a generation or two prior to King Henry the VIII, and surprisingly enough, one painting showed a dark-haired gentleman with a man who appeared to be that King and his second wife, a smiling Anne Boleyn. Obviously she had no idea a beheading awaited her. It made me wonder if we all walked through life utterly unsuspecting of horrors lurking ahead of us.

That thought brought Mary to mind as the three of us reached the landing for the second floor, Bridget leading Rebecca with me following, and my scalp began to tingle as a queasy feeling roiled inside of me. I'd seen this rich corridor before. I'd seen the sets of double doors situated just like the ones we passed, and I knew we'd stop at the third set of double doors on the left, just as I had seen in my dream of Mary last night.

Mary had led me to these doors, to Rebecca's room, and had begged for me to...what? As desperately as I'd wanted a bath, I wished Janet and Adele had been a few minutes later waking Bridget and me this morning.

Nurse Tolley answered Bridget's knock. The moment the nurse saw Rebecca with us, she let out screech of frustration that sent Rebecca diving back behind me, clutching her doll to her heart.

"How dare you frighten her like that!" I admonished the woman as I steadied Rebecca with a comforting arm. Rebecca pressed against my skirts, like a toddler seeking comfort.

"How dare you, a scullery maid, speak to me like that! I'll have you know this child is the spawn of the devil. I put her in her bed an hour ago and she has not come through these doors because I've been in the sitting area the entire time."

Bridget shuffled in front of me and put her face in front of the nurse's. "Cassie ain't no scullery maid. And unlessen you pay her close attention and show her the respect due a highly educated person, then I'm a thinking we needs to let Mrs. Frye and Mr. Killdaren know the wee one was wanderin' about unsupervised again."

"Well, I never!"

"Then you had best learn or you'll be seeking a new post."

Since Bridget had done a rather admirable job of explaining things, I stood silently as the nurse huffed and puffed.

Part of me hoped she'd ignore Bridget completely, so that there would be justification in notifying Mrs. Frye of the nurse's lapse. I slid my hand down and clasped Rebecca's. Even if the child had a tendency to wander, there was no cause for the woman's attitude toward her. I thought the entire situation unhealthy and wanted to inform Rebecca's mother of that.

While growing up, my sisters and I had spent a tremendous amount of time in the care of nurses and servants because of my parents' archeological and academic pursuits, but in every memory of my childhood, only kind and loving people had filled our world. And I wasn't about to leave Rebecca with this woman if the child didn't want to go.

I bent down and whispered softly. "Rebecca, do you want to go with Nurse Tolley and finish your rest, or do you want me and Bridget to take you to your mother?"

"Go M-m-momma." She stepped forward, looking in the general direction of where the nurse stood. "C-c-cane. Please."

The nurse looked as if she were about to say something, then changed her mind. Leaving the door open, she went back into the room.

Even though I'd already stepped far past the boundaries of a downstairs maid, I moved inside the room, wanting to see what Rebecca's world was like. The large area held almost every toy imaginable to delight a little girl—rocking horses, doll houses, a silver tea set with even a child-sized table and chairs. And all of them appeared hardly used, silent and lonely, not the well-worn usage to which everything in the Andrews household had been subjected. Rebecca didn't lack for things, but I had no doubt that she starved for people.

The thought of growing up in a black void, where neither light nor color filled the world, was bad enough. But the thought of missing all of the wonderful, chaotic noise my sisters and I made was the worst of all. The laughter and the fun had in many ways been the heart of our home and I wanted to bundle up Rebecca and cart her to the inn to stay with my sisters.

I doubted her shyness and stuttering would last very long if she were plunged into the Andrews world. At the very least, Rebecca would be laughing rather than crying.

Nurse Tolley returned, surprisingly holding a cane that seemed to me to be a miniature of Sean's, complete with the carved dragon wrapping its silver, long handle.

Rebecca clutched the cane in one hand and her doll in the other, then sent the walking stick in arcs about her as she moved forward, miraculously missing the collection of toys.

"Let's go down the hall to your mum." Bridget let Rebecca

lead the way.

"I'll be right behind you," I told Bridget. As soon as she and Rebecca left the room, I turned to the nurse. "Calling her a devil's spawn is not only cruel, but also completely inappropriate. I suggest you watch what you say to Rebecca. Should Bridget and I hear anything untoward spoken again, we will indeed take the situation directly to Mr. Killdaren."

I left her sputtering and caught up with Bridget and Rebecca in the hall before another set of double doors.

Bridget knocked and a maid answered. "What d'ya want?' she asked lifting her nose as if Bridget should be looked over.

"We are here with Rebecca to see Miss Prudence," I said. "Would you please let her know?"

The maid scowled then went back into the room.

"Blimey, Cassie," Bridget whispered. "Whatever are you doing?"

"Wait." I bent down to Rebecca. "Poppet, would you like to come hear me play music again?"

"Y-y-yess."

"Good." I stood and whispered to Bridget. "We're going to fix things so we can keep a closer eye on Rebecca and the nurse."

Prudence appeared at the door and immediately reached for Rebecca. "What is it precious?"

Rebecca tucked her face into her mother's lace skirts. I cleared my throat. "Milady, I wondered if I might arrange it with Mrs. Frye to play the piano for Rebecca on occasion. She enjoyed the music so much today and I thought it would be good for her."

"You can do that?" Prudence's soft eyes widened with awe.

"I've had some musical training, ma'am. Would that be all right?"

She smiled. "Yes, but don't worry about speaking to Mrs. Frye. I'll make the request myself and leave the time up for you and her to arrange."

"Thank you, ma'am." After a short curtsy, I knelt to Rebecca's level. "I'll see you soon, poppet."

She nodded. Bridget and I left after Prudence and Rebecca disappeared into Prudence's room. Just before we reached the stairwell, I stopped. "What room did the teacher have, Bridget?"

Bridget frowned at me. "Blimey. What makes you ask?"

"Just curious about her." I wished now that I hadn't asked.

"She stayed up here with Miss Prudence, Rebecca and the nurse in the green room across the hall. It faces the ocean. She often would watch it and paint it. Odd that it took her life, ya know."

"Can...can we see it? Her room?"

Bridget looked about and shrugged before moving down the hall to a set of double doors across from Rebecca's. "Don't know what ya expect to see." She opened the door.

I stepped inside the pastel-hued room, easily picturing Mary sitting in the sun, painting the sea. "Just wanted to see the ocean from this side of the castle," I whispered to Bridget. Walking to the window, I gazed out over the sand and sea and slipped the pheasant shell from my pocket, running my finger over the carved M.

"We'd best hurry," Bridget said.

"Yes." I turned, scanning the room quickly for any sign of Mary in it. Other than the softness of the colors in the room and the darkness of the ocean stretching as far as I could see from the window, there was nothing of Mary there, and a sadness followed me from the room. Stepping into the hall, we found Rebecca's nurse standing in the doorway, watching us. Bridget nodded to her importantly, "We best finish this errand for Mrs. Frye. It doesn't appear that the maids have been dusting as well as they should, does it Cassie?" Bridget said, managing to bring a slight smile to my lips at her quick thinking. At least the nurse didn't challenge our presence in the room.

On our return to the music room, I realized that Rebecca and Prudence's rooms appeared to be situated directly over the stage portion of the theater. My playing the piano had enticed Rebecca from her bed, and she'd managed to slip past the nurse, who'd most likely fallen asleep and didn't want to admit it.

Bridget and I had just finished the cleaning and polishing when Mrs. Frye made an appearance and surprisingly declared our chores for the day finished. She'd hired the new scullery maids, and our help wasn't needed in the kitchen. Bridget went back to our room to rest and I decided to spend my spare moments outside.

The garden drew me the minute I saw the sun sparkling through it. I knew I shouldn't, but I wandered that way, thinking no one would see me steal a few moments of pleasure there. I seemed to have lost any sense of propriety. Servants didn't go for strolls in their master's gardens, but the thought of doing what I shouldn't didn't seem as important as it once had, not at the moment. I knew the flowers would have lured Mary into the garden, and I wanted to feel close to her, walk where she might have, and to see what she would have. I had no answers to Mary's disappearance, only more questions. The lives of those she was involved with revealed themselves to me like a growing fog upon a forbidding moor.

The extravagant wealth, exquisite design, and host of antiquities characterizing the inside of the castle spilled to its grounds. Each section of the formal gardens was a work of art. Queen Anne's lace and gladiolas trumpeted a marble statue of some goddess, while across hedges sculptured like sea waves and dripping with frothy blue blooms, Poseidon reined in his team of racing sea horses. Seven women danced around what appeared to be Zeus sitting resplendently naked on an elaborate throne. Each of the women were embedded in a beautiful display of seven different patches of delicate flowers and Zeus, of course, had a bed of roses beneath him. I paused a moment, drawn to the bold lines of his sculpted muscles, the impressive breadth of his shoulders, and the authoritative angle of his chin.

Sean came immediately to mind, for his stature and bearing seemed to have similarities with the marble god. Something urged me closer to the statue and it wasn't until I brushed my fingers along the hard, smooth stone of his thigh that I realized the sculptor continued his larger than life glorification of the Greek god to all areas of Zeus's anatomy.

Heat rushed to my cheeks and I immediately averted my gaze.

My word. Seeing such a sculpture was quite different than the insignificant depictions I'd seen before in art, and tremendously more intrusive than my study of anatomy books had led me to believe.

Last night's incident in the kitchen with Sean played over in my mind and my gaze riveted back to Zeus's maleness as a shocking realization burned through me. When I had pushed up from Sean's lap, he'd been, well, hard all over too. Now that I thought about it, much hotter and more supple than the marble, but just as hard. If the Killdaren was as big as this Zeus was, no wonder I'd hurt him. *Oh my!*

Glancing back over my shoulder toward the castle, I made sure I hadn't been caught studying Zeus so closely and hurried on. This time I kept closer to the castle and studied the sculpted hedges and the beauty of the flowers, chastising myself for letting my guard down. I'd been so bowled over by my discovery that anyone could have approached and I wouldn't have known.

Unless I stayed vigilant about what might be lurking around the most innocent of corners, I too could meet with an ill end. My walk in the garden reminded me of Rebecca's playroom, everything so beautiful, but so alone. A matching note struck inside me. I wanted something I couldn't put a definition to. I missed my sisters, but I didn't necessarily want them filling the void with drama or chatter about the next tea party. I didn't even want Bridget telling me the latest gossip. But I wanted to share the beauty of the garden with another, a man perhaps. I found the notion completely unsettling.

Walking farther, I came to the outcroppings of the round room and studied the building a moment. Were one to erase the effects of the gargoyle and eliminate the shrouded windows, the room with its glassed dome would actually be very nice, although unusual. Lured, I kept walking, wondering what lay around its other side, wondering what lay behind its dark windows.

Dragon's Cove, home of the Viscount of Blackmoor, lay

farther down the coast, beyond the forest. I stared off in that direction, thinking about Sean's refusal to hear anything his brother had said, and his resignation, that nothing could have changed what had happened between them and what would happen in the future. The death of one or both of them. I shuddered.

For a moment I tried to feel what Sean Killdaren must feel, but I couldn't. I dearly loved my sisters and couldn't imagine ever being so angry at them that I wouldn't listen to them or that I'd wish them dead.

"You look as if you belong here, lass. Though I'd dress you in silk rather than wool, and I'd replace the mob cap with flowers."

I knew the voice wasn't Sean's, still I whipped around and for a moment thought he was there. But as my eyes adjusted, I found the Earl of Dartraven standing in the shadows of a willowy-like tree on the edge the garden. Dressed in London's best finery, he sported a handsomeness that defied age. Were it not for the gray at his temples and what appeared to now be a great sadness in his blue eyes, he could easily pass for a younger man—one who looked very similar to his sons, I thought.

"I apologize," I said. "I shouldn't be here. If I'd known the gardens were in use, I wouldn't have intruded."

"No intrusion. I assure you. The Killdarens pride themselves on thwarting ceremony, so having a servant wander the gardens is a nice addition. And a welcome one. I can't be left alone with my thoughts for too long here. Too many memories."

"In the garden, you mean?"

"Everywhere in Cornwall, but especially here. This estate belonged to my wife. She turned the castle from a lonely stone manor to a place of incomparable beauty. She had such a lust for life that she transformed everything around her."

"You miss her." I couldn't ignore the sadness in his voice.

"No. Miss is too light a word for the anger I feel." He walked toward me, his eyes now cold enough to send a chill stabbing through me. "God's cursed everything I loved. But I showed him. I'll leave you to enjoy what I can't anymore." He nodded as he passed and moved toward the castle.

"Wait." I whispered. I didn't want to know, but I had to. "How? How did you show God?"

He turned back, smiling. "I stopped loving."

He stood there, waiting a moment or two for me to respond, but I didn't and he left.

I wanted to ask, *How? How can you stop loving?* But my question stuck in my throat, tangled in the emotion there. It didn't seem as far-fetched as it should that someone might mistake the earl for one of his sons, especially in the moonlight.

The garden's glory dimmed and I left it for the call of the sea with Mary on my mind. I walked to the front of the castle and crested a dune to gaze down at the churning water kissing the land. I wasn't alone there. Stuart Frye and Prudence were walking along the shore just a little ahead of me, their arguing voices carrying on the wind.

I started to call out and wave to them, but Stuart stopped and shockingly grabbed Prudence's shoulders, shaking her. "Do you honestly think it is going to get any better for you and Rebecca by staying here, Pru? You need to go find a better life."

She pressed against his chest, as if trying to free herself. "Let me go! You don't know what you're talking about. You've always had the best of everything and never had to go hungry or cold. I don't regret for a minute what I did to change my life and I won't ever let Rebecca do without either. No matter what I have to suffer to assure that. The Killdaren has done right by you and he's doing right by Rebecca, too."

"For what?" Stuart shouted. "So she'll never have a world into which she belongs? She'll always be the outcast. If you're hoping she'll marry a man with wealth, forget it. Bastard children aren't welcomed in society. I know."

Prudence slapped him and he released her. She turned and buried her face in her hands, weeping.

"Bloody hell, Pru. I didn't mean it that way. You know that." Stuart put his hand on her shoulders but she pulled away from him. He looked up then and saw me, and must have said something to Prudence, because she cried out and ran farther down the beach, away from the castle.

My stomach knotted. I didn't want to see her going off by herself. All I could think about at that moment was Mary and how she had just disappeared.

Stuart marched toward me. Dressed handsomely in a peasant shirt and brown riding breeches, his skin darkly tanned and his hair windblown by the salty sea breeze, he looked like an angry pirate. I stepped back, sensing that the force of his ire unchecked could be twice that of his brother Jamie's. No amusement or flirtation lay in his gaze now.

"Miss Cassie, have you ever the occasion to study the writings of Augustine?" His voice was tightly controlled.

I blinked in surprise at the odd subject. "No, I can't say that I have. I know he wrote a number of things about the church, God and himself, but not in detail. Why?"

"Augustine once asked himself, 'What was God doing before he created the universe?' Do you know what he answered?"

I shook my head, fairly certain that I didn't want to know.

"'Creating hell for the curious,'" he said. "I'd be very careful if I were you."

# Chapter Eight

I waited on the crest of the dune until I saw Prudence making her way back to the castle then I slipped into the shadows of a vine-covered arbor stretching across a terrace and waited for her to pass. I couldn't go back without knowing she returned safely. The change in Stuart gave me pause. At least with Jamie, he didn't hide a dark side beneath smiling eyes. Jamie let you know exactly what he thought and what he felt, even though it was intense and frightening.

As I stood there, the sound of a door opening behind me drew my attention. Turning, I stared wide-eyed as the French doors swung open with no one standing at a threshold. Only black curtains rustled in the breeze.

"Who's there?"

"Dare you venture where angels fear to tread, wandering rose?"

Sean. Before my feet could run, before my heart could race, before my mind could think, I walked his way. "Come where I can see you?"

"You must come to me, if you dare."

I stepped closer, parting the black velvet curtain so that I could see into the room. A hand wrapped around my wrist and pulled me inside, firmly, not roughly. The curtain fell into place, drenching the room into darkness. For a long moment I couldn't see, and I almost panicked at his hold on me. It was as if I was living the dream of my own demise as I disappeared into darkness.

"I hoped I'd see you." He released my wrist. My eyes adjusted to the dimness to see books, a table and a desk, but not him. My relief at being freed from his all-too-disturbing touch was short lived as he stepped up behind me, his breath warm against my neck, and his body hot behind my back. He didn't press himself to me. He didn't need to. Just knowing he was so close set me afire.

"You did?" My voice was but a whisper.

"I dreamed of roses, and couldn't sleep. Found myself even tasting them, lass." He inhaled deeply, making the tendrils of hair at my nape tickle me. My toes curled, and I went dizzy from the sensations stealing though me. I closed my eyes and must have either lost my balance or his magnetism gained control of my body, for I fell back against him.

"Careful." He grasped my shoulders; his hands were hot, burning through my dress all the way to my senses. I tried to straighten and he held me back, pressing the solid fire of his chest to me. "I imagine your skin is much like the petal of a rose; soft, seductive and fragrant, just right to taste, to sink myself into." He slid his hand to my neck, brushing my hair aside, readying my skin for him. My lips parted as I waited. My heart thundered for I knew his mouth was about to connect with my neck much as a vampire would feast—

"Good Lord! What is this madness?" I jerked away to face him, searching for my outrage, which seemed to have lost itself in yearning. The man, dressed again in black, loomed more dangerously than before, because today there was a smile to his lips and humor in his green eyes. At the moment, I would have preferred threatening. "If you dreamed of roses, then I suggest you check your bed for thorns."

He laughed. "I'm sure there aren't any there. You're spitting them from your glare."

"As you deserve. You take liberties, sir."

"You'll disappoint me if you cannot be honest. You fell into my arms today. You have to admit that, lass."

His Irish lilt in my ear, so deeply sensual, could have made me admit to treason. "Yes, but it wouldn't have happened if you hadn't pulled me into here and frightened me so. Where am I?"

"You don't know? I thought perhaps you were lurking outside my doors for a chance to peek inside."

"I wasn't," I gasped. "I was...just stepping into the shade of the arbor for a moment." I couldn't tell him the truth, for he'd ask too many more probing questions, and I'd be telling him more than I should. My thoughts grew muddy whenever he was near.

He lifted a disbelieving brow, which seemed to have the same effect on me as his voice whispering in my ear. Perhaps Andromeda had serious cause to question my sanity. I seemed to be truly losing my mind.

He moved to me. "I don't think it was fright that melted you against me, lass."

I slipped around the table to face him. "Yes. Yes, it was. Didn't you hear my heart pounding?"

"I felt the heat of your blood racing beneath my fingertips. But considering the way your lips opened as if just waiting for mine, I don't think you had fear on your mind. Shall we investigate that?"

I'd be lost in a heartbeat, was already lost. I glanced at the curtained doorway, thinking that perhaps I should have told him I was waiting for Prudence to safely return. This sensual interrogation was much more disturbing than having to admit my fears. I had to go. His spell over me was too great. I dashed to the door, but stopped to look back at him as I parted the curtain. "Why do you live in darkness this way, all alone?"

His arm went up to shield his face and he moaned, turning from the light. "Because I must," he said harshly. "Shut the curtain, or leave. Do it now."

I left. Too afraid to stay. More because of my need of him than his sensual advances or his reaction to the light.

The kitchens, bubbling with fragrant stew and lively chatter, were a welcome relief, making me feel almost normal, and I lingered there, helping cut potatoes and listening to Mrs. Murphy's stories of when Sean and his brother Alexander were little and the havoc they caused every where they went. It was hard to imagine that they were the same two men. Sunlight apparently hadn't had ill effects for Sean as a child. The opportunity to ask Mrs. Murphy why it did now never presented itself. Besides, I couldn't bring myself to ask the question, for it was laughable. Vampires didn't exist.

That night I dragged a fussing Bridget back to the new bathing room, where after much laboring with carrying water buckets, I luxuriated in a hot bath. Bridget did too, once I convinced her that her skin wouldn't rot from taking two baths in one day, though I think it was the rose bath salts that actually lured her to take a quick dip. Returning to our room, I helped her read more *of Powerful Vampires and Their Lovers* until late into the night. The first story ended on the page after the vampire feasted upon the woman's breasts. She gave herself over to him, forsaking all of life as she knew it, and promised to stay with him forever. He promised her an eternity of pleasure. I kept thinking of Sean and the power he seemed to hold over me, almost against my will.

Bridget closed the book and lay back upon her cot with a blissful sigh. "Oh, how bloody wonderful."

"Ladies don't say bloody," I reminded, though I felt like saying it myself, but for a different reason. *How bloody awful.* Rising, I marched the three steps across the room to the window, opened it and glared out at the night, anger scraping my nerves. "What makes it so wonderful to you? He's ruined her." I kept thinking about Sean and how much of a hold he had on me in so short a time.

"Ack, Cassie, there you go again with your notions and all. How has he ruined her? He wants her to be sure, but that's the way of passion. The wantin's what makes it wonderful." Bridget picked up the red silk scarf she thought to be her sister's and brushed her cheek.

"She can never go back to her life." I was angry inside.

"And what sort of life do you think it was?" Bridget asked. "A lonely and a cold one, I tell you." She scowled, somehow irritated with me now. "She was so unhappy that she was a-praying for someone, just anyone, to love her and he did. You people with all your educating don't understand something as simple as that. So she'll have to stay in a stone crypt with him. Beats scrubbing her hands to the bone till she gets ill and can't scrub anymore. Then who's goin' ta feed her, I ask you? You think about that, Cassie. Meanwhile, I'm goin' ta go to sleep before you ruin the fun of hoping a vampire will take a liking to me and give me a velvet bed of comfort forever." Lying back, she covered herself with her blanket and faced the wall, the red silk scarf on her pillow next to her cheek.

For a moment, I stood by the window, stunned. There was so much about the lives of the people around me that I didn't understand. How would I think and feel if I was imprisoned in their worlds, with no hope? Maybe Bridget thought I was condemning her sister for reaching for a better life by going with a man to a city to sing. Walking over to Bridget, I set my hand on her shoulder. "I'm sorry."

Her shoulder shuddered a bit, and I knew she was crying. "Nuthin' to be sorry for." Her voice was thick with emotion. "Good night."

She didn't move or face me and I realized that she didn't want me to see her tears. I slipped back to the window, feeling very out of sorts with myself and with life. The moon hung huge and bright, and a steady wind from the sea kept the sky clear as it chased ghost-like clouds inland. Even in the full moonlight the maze and the dense forest remained inky blots staining the graceful lay of the gardens and the grassy hills. I couldn't see Seafarer's Inn where my sisters and aunt were most likely all cuddled in soft beds on scented sheets. I missed them terribly, and felt that if I were just to see them for a few minutes, I'd regain my sensibilities and would be able to dismiss from my mind the feel of Sean's breath on my neck.

The thundering hooves of approaching riders from the village caught my attention. I quickly snuffed the candle so I could watch unobserved from my window. Two riders on dark horses and wearing capes that billowed out from their gentleman-like bearing raced down the land toward the stables. It had to be midnight, and the men had to be the two men who'd been with Sean Killdaren last night. The two men who were coming back to hunt? I watched them hand the horses off to another man that I determined to be Stuart Frye by the white of his shirt and the faint sound of his voice carrying through the night air.

The men disappeared into the house, and soon the dome of the round room glowed. And just like the last time I'd seen the dome lit, a screeching moan rent through the quiet, keening like a woman grieved or pained. My skin crawled, urging me to do something to end it. How could I have fallen so completely under his sensual spell today? I had melted back against him. I had parted my lips in anticipation of him. And tonight, I wanted to scream *What are you doing?* I reached the point that I was about to march down there and demand to know, when the noise abruptly stopped.

Now what? I wanted so badly to sneak downstairs again to eavesdrop that I readied myself to go before my common sense gained an upper hand, and I made myself think about what the consequences could be if I were caught. Taking into consideration the dismal failures of my nighttime excursions thus far, it would be best for me to stay put tonight and give Sean Killdaren a few days to forget me. I'd have to look for the opportunity to peek inside the round room during the daytime, since he slept then. Well, usually. Today was likely an exception. One I seemed to have inadvertently caused.

Besides, the men did have plans to "hunt" tonight. Until I knew exactly what they were hunting, I'd best stay in my room. Before I climbed onto my cot, I locked the window and the door and kept my hands off the vampire book, but still couldn't relax enough to sleep. Frustration wrung tight knots of tension inside me and my neck tingled, just where Sean had touched it. I'd thought it an easy plan to come here, bide my time, and ask subtle questions about Mary until I discovered the truth. Yet that plan was much harder than I ever imagined it being. I was desperately impatient. Someone I loved had disappeared and I wanted everyone to stand up and take notice.

My gaze settled on the suspect list I'd written, and I

snatched it up. Reading over it, I realized I'd gathered a lot of information. I pulled out my journal, which I'd neglected of late, and on a clean page rewrote my suspect list and began logging facts, impressions and events.

With each word, I felt better, as if I'd accomplished a great deal since arriving at Killdaren's Castle. Then I included my concerns for Rebecca, my dream about Mary, and my questions about Sean Killdaren and his brother, Jamie, Stuart, the earl, and Bridget's sister Flora's silk scarf, along with the gruesome facts in the music room.

As I read back through them, several questions stood out in my mind. What "wasn't an accident" according to Jamie? Why did Sean Killdaren never go into the daylight? Why did Stuart want Prudence and Rebecca to leave Killdaren's Castle? Why was Flora's scarf in a piano no one used? Why had Rebecca seemed so familiar with the music room? How had the earl proven to God he'd stopped loving? And more importantly, why had Mary led me to Rebecca's door in a dream?

The rest of the week I kept to my room at night and away from Sean's rooms during the day. Bridget and I worked diligently, cleaning sitting rooms and solariums and drawing rooms and bedchambers and rooms that I couldn't even fathom a reason to have. All for the sake of maintaining what hadn't been used in years and would most likely go unused for years to come. It was a waste of beauty and time to have so much and no one with whom to share it.

More and more, I came to realize the solitary existence of those who lived in Killdaren's Castle—a stone fortress, richly appointed and without bars, but no less a prison. There were no family gatherings, no meals together and no celebrations of any kind.

Though my knowledge of the family's activities was limited to that of a downstairs maid, who rarely heard the gossip of the upper servants since they dined separately from the lower servants, I'd learned the only time Rebecca had left her room this week had been when Bridget and I had brought her to the music room to listen to the piano. I'd wanted to take her every day, but had only managed convince Mrs. Frye to let us go once.

Maybe it was my dream of Mary pleading for me to do something for Rebecca, or maybe it was my own heart that wrapped itself around the lonely child, but I had a need to see her. Today I'd take Rebecca to the music room even if I had to thwart Mrs. Frye's authority to do it.

Miss Prudence's situation bothered me, too. What did the woman do, all alone at the castle? She didn't oversee the castle's housekeeping. She never went to the village. No one ever came to visit her. She seemed terribly sad.

But the one person who consumed most of my thoughts was Sean. What caused a man to spend his life living as he did? Every night I'd hear the screeching from the domed room and knew he was awake, and every day I knew he slept as others lived.

Whether it was me and my frustration over not learning more about Mary or my presence affecting those about me, but tension seemed to be thickening the air with each passing day, like a fog that kept moving in from the sea, becoming more and more dense with every passing hour.

Bridget didn't mention the vampire story again, and had claimed to be too tired at night to practice reading. I felt responsible somehow, as if I'd failed her or hurt her in some way, and I was now anxious over how she'd accept my birthday gift to her. Friday had dawned, and I hesitantly set the package on her bed. I'd never given someone a present that wasn't something new or just made, but I hadn't had time to shop on Sunday. Yet, giving Bridget things I rarely used but couldn't seem to part with before made me feel as if I were giving a bit of myself. I woke early and dressed, wanting us to have a few minutes before we had to start the day.

"Bridget." I shook her shoulder. "Wake up."

"What is it? Am I late?" She sat up quickly, brushing her burnished hair from her eyes.

"No, but you are eighteen. Happy Birthday." I pushed the brown papered package toward her. "I didn't have fancy wrapping, so you'll have to pretend that there are lots of ribbons and bows on it."

She blinked several times then looked at me puzzled. "Blimey, yer giving me a present for my birthday?"

"Yes, silly. Today is your birthday, right?"

"Yes, but..." Her eyes filled with tears. "I've never had a birthday present before. Only at Christmas, we'd have puddin' and a present. I...I don' know what to say to ya."

I drew a breath and swallowed. "Everyone deserves one birthday present in their life I should think. It's not much and they are not new, but they are favorites of mine that I wanted you to have."

"I'm sorry I've been out of sorts. Ye've just given me so many things to think different about that sometimes, I don't know what to think."

I laughed. "You know what? You've made me feel the same way."

"I have. Really?"

I nodded and she laughed. "We're good for each other then."

Smiling, Bridget reached for the package and reverently unwrapped it as if the paper were precious gold. When she found the silver brush and comb inside on top of a soft blue shawl, she burst into tears.

"Good lord. It's not supposed to make you cry."

"Can't bloody help it. I've never owned anything so beautiful. And don't you dare tell me ladies don't say bloody. There are certain times when no other word will do."

I smiled. "We'll discuss that later. Hurry and try on the shawl before we have to get ready to go downstairs."

She slid the shawl over her chemise and ran to the tiny mirror on the washstand, preening until she saw every inch of the shawl that she could. The blue of it matched the soft brightness of her eyes as I'd known it would, but I hadn't realized that it would make her red hair come even more alive with fire. She really did look beautiful in it, and really rather mature, like a woman blossoming to life from a girl, ready to give life herself. No wonder the livery boy had chased her for a kiss.

"I feel grown up now," she said, using the silver brush.

"And you look wonderful."

"I'm going to wear it down to breakfast. I don't care how unseemly Mrs. Frye will think it is."

I laughed, wishing I had brought another shawl for me to wear as well. Mrs. Frye needed something to shake her from her rigid routine.

At breakfast everyone was thrilled with Bridget's new shawl, except Stuart. He glared angrily at Bridget and demanded to know where she'd gotten the shawl.

Bridget lifted her chin to a stubborn angle. "Not that it is any of your business, but it's a birthday present from a very good friend." She turned her back on him.

"Don't wear it." He grabbed a biscuit out of the bread basket and stomped out the door, declining to eat the meal.

I saw Bridget blink back tears. Incensed, I marched out after Stuart, who was headed toward the stables. "You had no right to ruin her present," I shouted at his back.

He turned, glaring at me. "Did you give it to her?"

"Yes, what of it? Don't you think she deserves something pretty?"

He came back at me, anger flaring his nostrils and turning his face red. "I don't know what your game is, but Mary had a shawl that exact color. Would you know that?"

I blinked, shock draining the blood from my face as I scrambled to remember where the shawl had come from. I'd had it so long, I couldn't remember, but it was possible that Aunt Lavinia had made it for me, and she could have made Mary one as well. Mouth dry, I forced my voice to work. "Why would I know that? How many blue shawls do you think exist in England?"

He didn't say anything, but whipped around and went on to the stables, casting a dark shadow over the pink glow of the dawn.

The other servants were jovially teasing Bridget that Stuart must be jealous. She laughed at their remarks, but I could still see the hurt in her eyes. Suddenly, I saw something that had to have been in front of my face all along. Bridget harbored very strong feelings for Stuart.

I finished the drawing room in record time, but rather than going to the library to see if Bridget needed help, I located Mrs. Frye in the kitchens with Mrs. Murphy. They appeared to be working on the household accounts. "Ma'am, I'm finished early. I would like to take Rebecca to the music room for a short while, if I may?"

"We haven't time for nonsense today."

I stared at her a moment as I bit back hot emotion. Why was she so angry all the time? How she could be so hard?

"Now, Clara," Mrs. Murphy interjected, "it's not the wee one's fault that things are they way they are, and a little music will do the lass well. Lord knows she needs a few joys in her dark world."

"It's doing nothing but teachin' her to want to be what she can't. That's what comes of highfalutin ways. Thirty minutes," Mrs. Frye said. "I expect you back here in thirty minutes. Then I'll show ya how to work on the ledgers and the doors downstairs need polishing, too."

"Yes, ma'am." I hurried out, not wanting to waste a minute. I told Bridget where to find me when she finished, and went for Rebecca.

Nurse Tolley answered my knock, barely cracking the door open to speak. "What do you want?"

"To take Rebecca for music. I've thirty minutes to play for her."

"She's not dressed yet." She tried to close the door.

Considering it was almost noon, I doubted her excuse. I pressed my toe against the door. "I'm sure that whatever she is wearing will be fine for her to wear to the music room. Either you let me take her now or I will have to see Miss Prudence about this."

"You're just like that teacher, coming here and taking things over, thinking you're better than anyone else. It'll lead you to an ill end as well."

"What do you mean by that?"

"Happens all the time to women who stick their neck above their station in life—they end up with it broken." She left the door before I could respond. If eyes could bore holes, the woman's back would have become a sieve. I couldn't decide if she meant to shock me or if there was ill intent behind her words.

"Rebecca. It's time for music."

"She's h-h-here!" Rebecca's voice sounded like Christmas morning. I heard her careful, cane-sweeping steps and appeared at the door, wearing an emerald pinafore with a cream and lace under dress and her rag doll tucked under her arm.

I took her hand. "Ready, poppet?"

"Y-y-yes, please."

"You look very pretty today." I flicked a glance at the nurse. She smiled sweetly, her florid complexion like soured wine.

Dismissing the nurse, I turned my attention toward making the next thirty minutes the most fun that I could.

"What's your most favorite thing to do, poppet?" I asked after we had situated ourselves at the piano. Rebecca had yet to join me on the bench, choosing to sit at her favorite spot near the piano leg with her doll in her lap.

"S-s-stories."

"Then today we'll have the musical story of Humpty Dumpty. I'll tell the tale except for some very important parts. When I make this sound, you have to say 'Humpty Dumpty', and when I play this, you say 'All the Kings horses' and say 'All the King's men' when you hear this. Can you do that?"

She shook her head.

"I think you can. Try it once and I'll help you." By the time we'd played it twice, Rebecca laughed as I made the sound of "All the King's horses" racing over the piano keys. It was the first I'd heard her laugh and the sound made me silently vow to spend more time with her. I knew Mary had loved her, for I already did in so short a time.

My time with Rebecca passed too quickly. When I returned to Mrs. Frye, I learned Bridget had gone to the village to buy Miss Prudence some ribbons, leaving me to work alone on the ledgers and to polish the downstairs doors. I'd almost finished both tasks when I realized Fortune had been wagging her finger in my face for hours and I hadn't seen it. I could easily peek into Sean's wing under the pretense of scrubbing his doors.

Making sure I had the kitchen knife wrapped in cloth and secreted in my boot rather than my pocket, I ventured to the dragon-handled doors before I could change my mind. Once there I quietly slipped inside. The first thing I noticed was the aroma of his exotic spice lingering in the air. The corridor was dark and silent, filled with weaponry: swords and maces, pistols and lances that made the little knife in my pocket completely insignificant. At least I knew where to run should I ever have need for something deadlier.

Heavy carpets patterned with the Killdarens' coat of arms, two fire breathing dragons facing each other, muffled my steps. I'd seen the dragon emblem in the portrait of Sean and on the carriage, and now wondered at his uncanny likeness to the strange creatures—gleaming green eyes, fire in every breath, and a fondness for dark lairs.

Wood paneled the walls and heavy, ebony curtains blocked most of the sun's light from filtering in. Praying I wouldn't be caught, I slowly made my way in the direction of the round room, barely breathing as I clutched my polishing rag and beeswax.

Within minutes I reached massive black doors, and my heart thumped loudly in my ears. My courage fled as I eased one of the doors open. Rather than blindly dashing into the room, I pulled out my polishing rag, dipped a little beeswax on it, and started to rub on the door while trying to peek inside. I made two swipes before my eyes adjusted to the brightness of the room. Then my mouth gaped. There had to be thousands of books, filling the floor to ceiling shelves that were only interrupted by the black, velvet-draped curtains and a wrought iron spiral staircase. In the center of the room sat a huge black-shrouded lump.

Good Lord! Was it a crypt? I squinted to see better. The light had to be coming from the glass-domed ceiling above and down through the huge hole in the center of the second floor, which was made of iron, too. Pushing the door wider, I craned my neck out more, now only polishing the air instead of the door.

"Found what you are looking for yet, lass?"

Turning back, I found Sean standing in front of me. I was inches away from polishing his male anatomy. My eyes went wide as a very clear picture of the stone Zeus flashed in my mind. "Good Lord."

"I suppose you could thank Him." He grabbed my wrist, his hand branding hot, and without so much as a by-your-leave, he hauled me up, imprisoning me in his arms. His green gaze glittered as he stared into my eyes and a sardonic smile slowly curved his lips. The hard muscles of his chest and thighs pressed tightly to mine, setting every nerve in my body immediately on fire. I found myself thirsting for more of his heat rather than less. "What are you doing here?"

My mouth was so dry I could hardly speak. I bit my lip and his gaze fell to my mouth. "Polishing."

"The air?"

"The wood."

"Almost, but not quite." He tightened my breasts against his chest and something rigid press into my stomach. His dark hair laid brushed back from the sharp planes of his chiseled features. His eyes, though squinting hard against the sun, gleamed with fire.

"It's daylight," I whispered.

"And today is one of my best days. Why are you here?" he

asked again, almost appearing disappointed in me. "As much as I've done for you, you could at least be truthful with me. These are my private quarters, and you are intruding upon my privacy without an invitation. It's one thing if I open a door for you, lass, and another for you steal in here like a thief."

I sucked in a breath, feeling as if he'd taken every ounce of air from me as I looked into his eyes. How would I feel if someone stole into my secrets? Intruded into the dreams I kept hidden from the world? I touched his cheek, staring into the darkness in his eyes, somehow seeing myself there. "I'm sorry. You're right. I'm repaying your kindness with unkindness. I...was...curious." Somehow while meeting his gaze, I couldn't force out the other questions that lingered in my mind, both the important ones and the fanciful ones. *Did you harm Mary? Did you kill Helen Kennedy? Is Prudence your mistress? Is Rebecca your child?*

He blinked as if surprised by my answer.

"Then let me satisfy your curiosity." His gaze dropped to my mouth, completely absorbing itself there. My pulse leapt wildly and anticipation of something I'd yet to taste but had constantly dreamed about since I'd met him gripped my entire being. I could no more stop my lips from parting than I could have kept my blood from rushing.

I expected the soft brush of his lips and the warmth of his breath. Instead, firm lips claimed mine so passionately, I had to yield and respond or be lost. His tongue swept over mine, dueling with need, searching as if he thirsted for my very soul. Groaning, he pulled me impossibly closer, and more fire erupted between us when I met and matched the stroke of his tongue, sliding my hand from his grasp and burying my fingers into the silk of his hair.

His scent, exotically heady, filled my senses like a drugging elixir. He tore off my mob cap and slid his hand to the nape of my neck, devouring my mouth. I'd gone from knowing nothing to feeling everything in a few overwhelming moments. I pressed to him, needing more, needing to feel the hard warmth of him against me. He ran his hands up my sides and slid them over my breasts, burning them with the heat of his skin. I groaned, kissing him harder. "Please," I whispered, desperate beneath this torture of pleasure.

Suddenly, he reared back and released me. Breathing heavily, he fisted his hands at his side so tightly his muscles shook. "Go. Leave now. I'm not my father." His voice was low, and so desperately harsh, that I didn't hesitate or question him, though I didn't understand at all. I ran.

That I never once thought of the knife in my boot when Sean had been kissing me so...so passionately told me more than anything else, that I didn't fear him, at least not when it came to my life. I had yet to determine the safety of other people's lives. I knew without a doubt he was lethal to anything proper or decorous, for I would have let him satisfy my every curiosity at that moment.

Hearing voices in the kitchen, I skittered to a stop, taking a moment to calm myself and adjust my appearance.

Mrs. Murphy looked up from kneading dough as I dashed into the kitchen. Janet and Adele worked with her. "What ails ye, lass? Where's yer cap?"

"I must have lost it outside. I'll go look for it!" I said. "I've finished polishing the doors."

"Ye need any help?"

I shook my head.

"Take your time. In fact, if ye can bring me several sprigs of rosemary from the spice garden nearest to the stables, I'd appreciate it."

"Thank you." Relieved to have a legitimate reason for being outside, I exited and dashed down the steps, fleeing away from the garden. I went in the direction of the sand dunes to the right and front of the castle. The sound of the waves crashing against the shore suited my tumultuous mood. Every nerve within me tingled with life and heat. I could feel his touch, his kiss, as if he still had me in his arms. I clutched the pheasant shell in my pocket and held onto it for dear life as I fought for breath.

Cresting a dune, I stared at the sea, drinking in the

saltiness of its spray, feeling the wildness of it match the racing of my heart. The wind rushed at me, sending my mussed hair even more askew, pressing my dress tight to me, and caressing my body as softly and as firmly as Sean had. He reminded me of the sea, so powerful, so dark, I knew I'd be lost were I to enter his depths. Yet he was so beautiful, so intriguing, I couldn't turn away.

Before I had wondered why a woman such as Miss Prudence would have let herself be compromised. Now I had no question.

I should be horrified with myself for wanting him and responding to him. I should be outraged by his cavalier handling of my person. He'd given me no warning, nor asked for permission.

Hearing the sound of hooves, I looked back then swung around, shocked to see Sean charging up the hillside, astride a mammoth-sized stallion. He'd done little to change his appearance, only buttoned his stark white shirt to a barely decent point. The wind whipped at his hair and his clothes, defining his muscular frame.

I wrapped my hair up in my fist to keep it from my eyes and met his gaze.

"I owe you an apology. Do you accept?"

I couldn't seem to speak, but I did manage a slight nod, not sure I wanted to accept his apology, but unable to deny him.

"Should you enter my quarters again, uninvited, be prepared to share more than a kiss, Cassie." He raked his gaze down my body, fueling the fire he'd kindled. Then whipping his horse around, he charged down to the sea and went flying along the beach, making me envy his headlong pace and the wild freedom that seemed to pour off of him. I wanted to fly from here as well, to flee what was happening inside of me.

Shedding my prim, proper gowns for the loosely woven dress of a maid had unbound things within me that I never knew were there. A dark part of me wanted to return to his quarters uninvited to find out what would come next.

"Mar-ry!"

Before I could turn, Jamie's huge arms wrapped around my chest from behind, jerked me up, and crushed me against his chest. The smell of soil and soured perspiration assaulted me. With my arms clamped to my sides, I couldn't fight him or reach the knife in my boot, and he carried me like a rag doll away from the sea.

"Stop!" I kicked and squirmed, but nothing I did made any difference. "Help!" The wind seemed to swallow my cry and spurred his pace.

"Hu-urt you." He sounded as if he were crying. He ran faster, as if trying to whisk me away before anyone could see. He passed the stables and ran farther on to where I saw an opening in the forest, a dark path leading to God only knew what.

"Put me down!" His hold kept me from breathing enough air, making me feel faint. Real panic welled inside of me. "Help," I screamed, but I feared my voice had been reduced to a squeak.

He dragged me into the dense trees. The branches and sky overhead blurred. I struggled against his hold until I thought my bones would crack from the ferocity of his strength. Then he broke into a bright clearing and the sun blinded me. I heard a heavy thundering beat and thought it was the pounding of my heart until my vision adjusted and I saw Stuart charging toward us astride a dark horse.

"Jamie! Stop!" Stuart yelled.

Jamie turned and ran, nearly crushing me with the strength in his arms.

Whatever doubts I harbored about Stuart, I was never more thankful to see a man in my life.

"No...hurt...her!" Jamie yelled, rendering my breathing nearly impossible. I realized that I could die right there with help not more than ten feet away. I tried to reach out, to speak, but could only croak. The world around me turned into a blur of dark colors growing closer to black with every second that passed.

"Let her go!" I heard Stuart yell as if from a long distance away. Then suddenly Jamie fell to his knees. His hold loosened and I sucked in air, gasping desperately.

My vision cleared and I fought myself from Jamie's grip, but it wasn't hard to do at all. He didn't try to hold me any longer. He lay on his side, crying like a small child, who'd been left desolate and abandoned.

"Hurt...her," he cried. "Some...one...hurt...her."

When I looked at Stuart, I gasped and stumbled back several steps. He held the butt end of a long leather whip stretched taut. He'd wrapped the painful tip around Jamie's legs, forcing him to stop.

I didn't know what to say. I couldn't decide if Jamie wanted to hurt me or hurt Mary. Or if he was saying someone was going to hurt me or had hurt Mary.

"Bloody hell." Stuart turned to me with anger slashing the handsome lines of his face. "Why don't you just leave! Get off this cursed land and go."

He turned from me and went to his brother. "Jamie, it's all right. Do you hear me? This isn't Mary." After touching his brother's shoulder, he slipped the whip from around his brother's legs, expertly rolled it up, and slung it over his shoulder.

"Is he all right?" I asked.

"What do you care?" Stuart shouted. "What did you do to him?"

"Nothing. He found me on the dunes, grabbed me, and carried me here." I glanced about me for the first time and realized I stood in the middle of a circle of ancient carved stones. The stones faced the center of the circle, pagan in design with the curved figure of a woman on each of them. I swung around and found myself nearly at the foot of a huge center stone. The figure hewn upon it was decidedly male and played a harp made to look like a woman bent unnaturally backward, welcoming the musician with open arms. An eerie feeling swept over me, one that made me feel I had trespassed into a place no human should ever go. "What is this?"

"The Circle of the Stone Virgins," Stuart said.

Just then the sound of pounding of hooves beat their way down the path and Sean charged into the clearing. Seeing us, he veered sharply and rode up.

"Good God! Killdaren out during the day? What in the bloody hell is going on?" Stuart stared at Sean, sounding as if he'd just seen the unbelievable.

The way Sean slid so expertly and fluidly from his horse evoked a feeling inside of me that made me want to do nothing but watch the man in motion. He seemed to be coming to my rescue. The horse heaved as if he'd been ridden hard and a dark trail of sweat drenched its sides.

"What is the problem here?"

"No problem, sir. Just showing Cassie the Stone Virgins," Stuart answered, his tone sarcastic, much like sugar laced with arsenic. "Jamie tripped and Cassie and I were trying to help him up."

"He—" I began.

"Is he hurt?" Sean cut off my denial of Stuart's explanation.

I gasped. Well, I'd obviously mistaken his intentions. He seemed to be deliberately ignoring me.

"I don't think so, sir," Stuart said.

"Don't you have duties to attend to, miss?" Sean turned and looked at me for the first time. Whatever warmth or fire I'd seen in his eyes earlier had fled, leaving cold green glass behind with edges jagged enough to slice a woman bare.

I couldn't take it. I turned from him and stared hard at Stuart a moment. He met my gaze with one that told me I had better not say anything to Sean about Jamie, and I decided I wouldn't. Jamie could have thought he was protecting me. He might have killed me in the process, but it was possible that his motives were honorable.

What would Sean do if I told the truth? Send Jamie away? Punish Stuart for lying? Somehow I felt that Jamie was part of the key in learning what had happened to Mary.

Sean looked doubtful, but he didn't question Stuart any further, and the way they stared at each other sent even more shivers down my spine.

All was not well between Sean and his illegitimate brother.

"Please excuse me." I backed away. Turning on rubbery legs, I ran down the path, past the stables and garden maze, heading directly for the castle. I slid inside, closing the huge door behind me. Then I shut my eyes and tried to breathe. My sides hurt and most likely had bruises.

"Where is your mob cap? Your hair is completely indecent. I'll have a word with you immediately in my office." Mrs. Frye clanged her teacup on the counter from where she stood next to Mrs. Murphy and left the room. Scones scented the air along with cinnamon.

"Yes, ma'am." I followed her back to her desk, which seemed even more buried beneath papers and bills.

"I'll not tolerate my staff being improper at any time!"

Outrage and heat flooded me. "I wasn't."

"Your unbound hair is telling enough. Tomorrow, there will be no meals and you will scrub every floor downstairs."

I cringed at the thought, but didn't argue. "I am sincerely sorry, ma'am. I meant no harm."

She studied my face. "You are looking very pale. Are you having a bairn?"

"What?" I cried out.

"Are you pregnant? Has Seamus gotten hold of you, girl?" She shook her head. "No, you can't be. You haven't been here that long. So what is your ailment then?"

"I think you work her too hard, Ma." Stuart spoke from just behind me.

Startled, I jerked to the side so I could see him.

"You don't need to be interfering into my affairs, Stuart Frye."

"Then don't punish her for what God gave her. It would be no different than punishing Jamie for what God didn't give him."

Mrs. Frye gasped and turned as white as her stark collar.

Stuart ignored his mother's reaction. "Cassie gets her meals and all of the maids will scrub the floors and have it done in an hour, rather than a day. That's if they need scrubbing at all. And since her punishment is settled, I need to speak with Cassie about Jamie a moment."

Mrs. Frye glared at her son. "Stuart Frye, I'll not have you turning into your fa—"

"Don't you dare say it." He slapped the doorframe with the palm of his hand. "Cassie, would you mind waiting for me in the kitchen?"

I glanced at Mrs. Frye and she gave me a tight-lipped nod. Stuart stepped aside and I hurried out, but I didn't go all the way to the kitchens, I stopped in the corridor, just out of sight and pressed my back against the wall, hoping I could hear more.

"It's Mary again," Stuart said.

"What do you mean, again?" Mrs. Frye cried out. "She's gone, and good riddance. She almost killed him."

I bit my lip and dug my nails into my palm. The anger and hate I heard in Mrs. Frye's voice gave me a chill.

Stuart sighed. "She tried to help him. Tried to teach him to read and write."

"No! What she did was made him think that he was normal. That he deserved more in life. She knew he loved her, and she made him believe that he could...he could..."

"Be a man?" Stuart said harshly. "Unfortunately, Mother, he is one, and you're going to have to stop hating us because of it. Jamie is confusing Cassie with Mary. He just dragged her from the beach to the Stone Virgins."

"Dear God. I'll dismiss her! She'll be gone in minutes."

"And is that what you're going to do the next time, and the next? Keep sending women away rather than fix the problem? I think with Cassie's help, we can get Jamie over this."

"What makes you think she'll help us?"

"Two reasons. After being attacked herself, she worried about Jamie being hurt. And she didn't tell the Killdaren."

"What did ya say?"

"You heard me. The Killdaren was up and out riding in

broad daylight."

"But that's impossible—"

"Apparently not. I'll have Cass—"

I didn't wait to hear anymore, but scurried quickly to the kitchens and had just planted my bottom in a chair by the fire when Stuart walked into the room. Mrs. Murphy raised her brows at me but didn't say a word.

Stuart came and stood by the fire. Feet spread apart as if manning the helm of a ship, he held his hands out, warming them. "Fire's an interesting thing, don't you think, Miss Cassie?"

"What do you mean?"

"One can't help but watch it, to stare into its depths and wonder at its power. It fascinates us. We can't live without it. And it will kill in a flash. Like water you might say. Come walk with me a moment, and I'll have you back safely before the evening meal."

With both his mother and Mrs. Murphy aware that I was with him, I didn't fear for my life. And I was more than curious about what Stuart had to say about Mary.

I knew my cousin well; there wasn't a malicious grain of sand between her toes. So how could she have done anything to garner so much hatred from a rational person?

I stood. "The evening meal will start shortly." I suddenly realized I hadn't seen Bridget in a long time. My stomach knotted as I remembered Jamie following us from the village last time. "Mrs. Murphy, has Bridget returned from the village yet?"

She frowned. "No, lass. I haven't seen her. She's late."

Stuart sighed, as if too burdened to carry another potato in his sack. "I'm sure she's fine. I'll check with my mother about Bridget's expected return while you make sure she isn't in your room. Meet me in the garden as soon as you are done."

Swallowing the sudden lump in my throat, I nodded and hurried up to the room I shared with Bridget. Everything was as we had left it that morning. After splashing water on my face and gathering another mob cap, I found Stuart waiting outside the kitchens, just before the entrance to the formal gardens.

"My mother expected Bridget back an hour ago. I don't think there is any cause for worry, but we'll walk toward the village as we talk."

"Why did Jamie drag me to the woods?"

Stuart didn't answer immediately. He seemed to be thinking of what to say so I scanned the area, searching thoroughly as we passed the stables, even though it was unlikely Bridget was there. It wasn't until I didn't see Sean astride his horse that I realized I'd been looking for him. My anticipation irritated me, and I thought of Stuart's assessment of fire and water. Sean was the same for me.

"I'm sure you've heard about Mary," Stuart finally said.

I drew a deep breath. "Yes. She was a teacher here."

"Teacher, mentor, rebel. Mary came and wanted to change everyone's lives. For a time I think we believed she could, and that makes her senseless death even more painful."

"You were involved with her, then?" My hand fisted as I waited for his answer.

He searched my face intently. "We weren't lovers. So you can disregard anything Bridget has told you otherwise. Mary was a friend to all, and she brought...hope. Mary *was* hope, especially to my brother Jamie. As you heard my mother say when you eavesdropped on our conversation, Jamie loved Mary in the way a mortal man might love an untouchable angel."

"I didn't—"

He lifted a questioning brow. His dark eyes held a challenge to tell the truth as well as a hint of humor. "I would have in your position. And I would think it insulting if I didn't credit you with as much intelligence as God gave me."

"Very well." That was as much of a confession as I was willing to make. I found myself liking him, despite my desire not to. "You said Mary's death was senseless. What happened to her?"

He caught my elbow, bringing us to a halt. Looking me dead in the eye, he spoke very succinctly. "I know nothing more than what you have already heard, I'm sure. Gossip runs more rampant amongst the servants in a household than sewers run in London. Mary went on a picnic with Rebecca. Rebecca returned without Mary and I found their picnic basket, blanket and Mary's boots on the beach. She drowned."

I blinked then searched the area ahead for Bridget, giving myself the needed moment to rein back my automatic denial. As much as I didn't want to accept the fact that Mary was lost forever to us, I prayed that it was as simple as Stuart said. "Given those facts, that would be a logical assumption. So what does all of this have to do with Jamie and me?"

"He can't accept that Mary is dead. It may be that in his heart he wants you to be Mary, and it upsets him that his mind tells him you're not. He most likely saw you on the dunes this afternoon and had an overwhelming desperation to save Mary from harm."

"Then why drag me into the woods and not to the castle?"

"For some reason Jamie feels safe in the Circle of the Stone Virgins."

For a long moment I wondered why. The place felt far from safe to me, almost eerily evil. "Where did the stones come from?"

"It's been here for centuries. Most likely it's an ancient worship site for the Druids, or even a pagan temple for warring Romans when they conquered the Celts."

I pushed the stones aside to think about later and focused on Jamie. Could his actions be explained so simply? Was he trying to protect me in some odd way? I could easily understand Jamie's feelings, if that were truly the case. After each of my dreams, I'd felt the panic, the desperation to do anything to keep a loved one from harm.

Drawing another breath, I slipped my elbow from Stuart's grasp, realizing once again that I'd completely forgotten that he'd touched me. His touch held none of the fire that Sean's did. I started walking again. "So, how can I help Jamie?"

"That would be the dilemma. Should you show him kindness and spend time with him like Mary did, or do I ask you to show him no kindness, so that he knows without a doubt you are not Mary?"

"I would think only kindness can heal."

"And that makes you like Mary. I have to confess there has been a moment or two when the sun hits the shine of your hair that I almost think you are Mary. It might help if you bound your hair tightly back and covered it completely with your mob cap."

"What was Mary teaching him?"

"The alphabet. How to write, and hopefully how to read."

"I've already been working with Bridget." A wild idea hit me, one I wasn't sure would be very welcome in some schools of thought. But after seeing the unchanging horizon of the servants' lives, I knew I now firmly believed in educating the masses. Everyone deserved the gift of reading and writing. It would be one step that would give them more of a choice in the future. "I suggest we have a class for all of the servants who want to learn after the evening meal one night a week. That way, everyone can benefit, and Jamie will see that while it seems I am similar to this Mary, I am different."

A gust of wind whipped a strand of hair across my face. Before I could brush it back, Stuart did. My breath caught at the sudden action and its familiarity, but my heart didn't pound. "You didn't happen to be suddenly born in May of this year?" he asked.

"What?" I shook my head, thinking I'd heard wrong.

"You are so like Mary that reincarnation would explain a lot. Unfortunately, I think there's a more logical explanation. Since I know Mary didn't have any sisters, you must be one of her cousins of which she was so fond. If you're here to find answers other than the ones given, you're wasting your time."

"I don't know what you're talking about." I promptly tripped because my knees were rubbery. I would have fallen had he not caught my elbow. I'm not sure what else I would have said to convince him because the harsh sound of a woman weeping cut into my shock. Stuart heard, too, and turned from me.

"Wait here," he said tersely then ran ahead to the bend in the path.

I decided that I'd much rather have Stuart's dubious character in sight rather than stand alone with the dark of the forest at my back. I hurried after him, even though he didn't follow the path but turned toward the sand dunes, increasing his pace.

Following close at his heels, I felt my insides hurdle over a cliff when I saw Bridget on the ground, head bent as she huddled protectively against the rise of the dune and the whipping wind. She had the blue shawl I'd given her clutched tightly about her, as if seeking comfort.

# Chapter Nine

"Bridget! Good Lord! What happened? Who hurt you?" I asked, running to her.

Stuart gave me a sharp look, but I ignored it as I fell to my knees in the warm sand. I didn't care if I was jumping to conclusions. Jamie's supposedly protective attack on my person weighed heavily on my mind, and I had yet to decide his intent. If Jamie were trying to protect me, then why did Stuart lie to Sean? Why not just tell the Killdaren the truth? But I didn't dare ask more questions so soon. If Stuart had a suspicion of who I was and why I'd come, how long before someone else made the connection?

Bridget, teary-eyed and pale, looked up from where she'd been crying into her mob cap. She saw me and cried harder. "Oh, Cassie, what am I ta do?"

I wrapped my arm around her shoulders. "While I'm thanking God you're alive, can you tell me what has happened to you?"

"Not me," Bridget said. "It's me mum. She has the consumption. Won't live another year, they're sayin', and she'll need tending to before too long. Me brother Tim's just six, and I've not gotten a note from Flora yet, either. I can't even tell her about our mum."

Part of me sighed with relief that nothing untoward had happened to Bridget. Since coming to Killdaren's Castle, my imagination had grown almost to the point of the ridiculous, but then, there'd been enough incidents to provide ample fuel for my imaginings.

Another part of me empathized with Bridget's pain. Here she'd been given plenty of warning of a loved one's death, and yet was as powerless as I had been to stop Mary's or my grandparents' deaths. "We'll sort this out." I squeezed her shoulder. "You'll see, there is an answer. We just have to find it."

Bridget nodded her head, trying to stifle her sobs.

"Which doctor did she see?" Stuart asked.

Bridget's eyes widened. "Couldn't afford ta 'ave a doctor come. Old Mrs. Compton does most the doctorin' for village folks like us."

"I understand," Stuart said. "But you should have—"

"Should've what? How can you understand anything?" Bridget shouted, sounding almost bitter. "You pretend to know our troubles Stuart Frye, but you can't. You don't know what it's like ta see your mum and your brother a hurting, and you can't do anything else but go and scrub fancy floors that never get used just to barely keep your family from starving."

"I do know." Stuart straightened, coldly stepping back from Bridget, his jaw taut, his eyes bleak. "I know what it's like to have someone's life in my hands, and I know what it's like to make bitter choices. If you can walk, I suggest we get back to the castle. I've already pushed my mother as far as I can for the day." He held out his hand to Bridget, but she ignored his offer of help, and struggled to her feet alone.

"Don't need ya to talk to your mum on my account neither." Bridget started marching down the path, her anger at Stuart apparently bolstering her as she pulled the blue shawl tighter around her.

From the clenched set of Stuart's jaw as he stared at Bridget's back, I determined now would not be a good time to ferret out more information. Given all of the factors of my situation at Killdaren's Castle, there never seemed to be a good time for asking questions.

Stuart turned to me when we neared the stables. The storm raging in his dark eyes made me shiver, and told me a lot more lay hidden inside him than what I'd seen. "Whatever your reasons for being here, I'll keep silent for now," he said. "Don't make me regret it."

He stalked off then, leaving me feel as if he'd raised an axe and I had best tread carefully or he'd let it fall.

Bridget and I spent most of the evening after dinner talking about her family. Though less teary-eyed, she had no hope that her mother would live through another Cornish winter, and she despaired about what she could do. I tried to reassure her and thought I could do a number of things to help her, even bring her and her family back to Oxford with me when I left Killdaren's Castle, though I doubted an Oxford winter would be any milder. But I couldn't tell Bridget any of that yet.

Exhausted, Bridget fell asleep early, deciding to delay reading the next story in the vampire book—a decision I was thankful for. The title of the next story, "Forbidden Fruit," didn't sound as if it was anything I needed to delve into. Not if I wanted to have any peace of mind whatsoever. The forbidden fruit of my attraction to Sean and the heated memory of his kiss didn't need anything more to fuel them.

I took out my journal and added today's events, then reread the entries, frustrated with how slowly the secrets at Killdaren's Castle were unraveling. I wanted to grasp the end of that yarn and jerk hard, even if it sent the ball spinning out of control.

One thing I could do was research the history and legend behind the Circle of the Stone Virgins. Stuart had said that the stones might have had their origins in Druid lore, and I recalled that the library downstairs had several books on the subject.

Lighting a candle, I stole downstairs, listening very carefully for any whisper of sound as I went directly to the library. I slipped inside, taking care to be very quiet. Knowing Sean's picture hung in the shadows made me feel as if I'd entered his bedchamber. I tiptoed across the thick rug, smelling the lemon and beeswax scent lingering from the cleaning Bridget and I had given the room earlier. I also detected a hint of something else, and sniffed the air as I pulled from the shelf several of the Druid books that were mixed in with the vampire books. *Mastery of Druid Magic. The Sacred and Profane Rites and Rituals of the Druids and their Children. The Druids' Thirst for Humans.*

"You surprise me. I thought it would take longer for you to meet me."

"Oh!" I jumped in fright, sending the books flying as I juggled the candle. "Meet you?" Turning fast, I found myself face to face with Sean, or face to chest to be more accurate. This time the casual cotton of a white shirt lay soft and inviting across his broad shoulders and supple flesh. Warmth and mystery emanated from him, and I clenched my fist to keep from reaching out to touch him.

To see his face, I had to tilt my head and retreat a step, which brought my back against the bookcase. Leaning toward me, he planted his hands on the shelf behind me, trapping me between his arms, blocking my escape. An escape I am sure I would have made, had my mind been capable of thought.

It wasn't, just at present.

The dampness of his hair and the smooth line of his jaw, combined with the fresh scent of soap and spice, told me he'd just come from his bath. We stood so close I could count the flecks of green and gold in the irises of his eyes. Having all of his dangerous male appeal so unexpectedly close disconcerted me to the point that all I did was stare at him. The only thing keeping his body from pressing into mine as it had during his kiss was the flickering candle in my unsteady hand.

He blew the candle out.

"Oh!" I stood in the dark, desperate for my eyes to adjust to the moonlight.

"Can't have us catching on fire, can we?" He must have been able to see in the dark because he took the candle from my tingling fingers.

"No, fire is good," I gasped, already burning. For a moment I stood there, waiting helplessly for him to kiss me, until I realized what I was doing. Good Lord, had I lost all sense of myself? "Cassiopeia's Corner" would have advised any woman finding herself in such circumstances to take drastic measures and gain a proper footing. Only, I didn't want to stamp on his foot and flee, but I did want to learn more about him, and I would have to compromise my notions of propriety to do so. I planted my palm in the center of his too tempting chest and pushed. He only took one step back, which gave me some breathing room, but not much.

I narrowed my eyes. "What are you doing here?" I demanded.

"Since it is my library, I think I'll ask you that question."

"Oh." I winced. "Forgive me, I forgot myself."

He studied my face a moment. "You're forgiven, but first satisfy my curiosity," he said. "What is a pretty maid such as yourself looking for in books about Druid magic and powers?"

I arched a brow. "Perhaps I'm looking for spells to make odious men keep a respectable distance. You took enough liberties with my person earlier today, sir."

He laughed, making me feel like a mouse cornered by a hungry cat. "I recall a mutual liberty taking, lass. But considering you were trespassing into my private quarters, I had the right to not only know why you were there, but also could have viewed your intrusion as an invitation to take more from you than the kiss I did. In fact, as much as I've tried to fight my attraction, I regret not doing so." His gaze dropped, seemingly studying my mouth, then moved lower.

My breasts tingled.

"I suggest you answer my question, Cassie. Or I might be moved to coerce the answer from you." His gaze slid over me. "In a mutual way, of course."

Deep inside me, I knew I shouldn't find his threat exciting. I shouldn't wonder what a mutual coercing entailed, but the notion intrigued me in an utterly improper way, that I blurted out the truth before I *could* entice him into a coercive action. "I wanted to research the Circle of the Stone Virgins that I saw today. Mr. Frye mentioned they might have a Druid origin."

After studying me a moment, despite the darkness, he pushed back from the bookcase, freeing me. I didn't run or move, but waited to see what he would do. He lit the candle, flooding a dim light about us. Surely my sigh was one of relief and not disappointment. Using his cane for balance, he nimbly picked up the books I'd dropped.

"Do you and Stuart spend a lot of time together? I saw you walking toward the village this afternoon as well." He spoke casually, yet I sensed an underlying tension.

He didn't glance my way. After setting all but one of the books on a table, he tucked his cane under his arm, then opened the book and thumbed through the chapters.

"I barely know the man." Did he think my association with the groomsman inappropriate? Then I remembered I was but a downstairs maid. My insolence to him, even though provoked, was shameful. "Today, we met by...accident at the stone circle." I didn't have an explanation for keeping silent about Jamie's attack, other than to keep my own council until I determined friend from foe. "And when Bridget was late returning from the village, he escorted me to find her."

He glanced up from the book, his eyes narrowed. "You sound as if you had reason for worry. Why?"

I shrugged, unwilling to divulge my concerns about Mary's death yet, because anything I could have said would have made him even more suspicious of me. "Bridget was...uh, upset. Her mother is ill. The consumption. Bridget is at a loss of how to care for her and her young brother."

He handed me the book, *The Sacred and Profane Rites and Rituals of the Druids and Their Children* opened to a chapter with an alarming title. "The Seduction of the Innocent." I nearly dropped the book.

"From what I've been able to piece together, the Stone Virgins have their roots in a local legend about Daghdha. Are you familiar with him?"

"He was an imaginary king of the fairies, was he not?"

"Imaginary?" he asked, quirking his brow.

"Surely you don't believe in such musings as dancing fairies and vam—er, leprechauns?" I asked, heat flaming my cheeks.

Turning from me before I could read his expression to know if he'd heard my slip, he walked across the room and lit the fire. There was a part of me that winced to see so magnificent a man hindered by the need of a cane, even though he used it so gracefully. I wanted to ask how he'd been injured, but couldn't. Not yet. Flames licked their way over the kindling, enticing me closer to him and the fire. Though summer, the late night dampness of the castle-like manor called for the extra warmth, as if every degree of heat was necessary to fight lurking chills, and perhaps to chase the shadows from the owner himself. In the dark of the night he appeared as mysterious as his portrait looming on the wall behind him.

I watched as he placed a log on the fire then settled into a leather- and brass-winged chair, motioning me to the matching, opposite seat. "If you're asking if I believe in miniature winged creatures flitting about, then the answer is no. If you're asking if I believe in nonmortals, then the answer is yes."

He spoke with such assuredness that a lump of questions settled into the pit of my stomach. Did he speak of spirits or something more sinister? Weren't vampires considered to be nonmortals?

Like Pandora, I was urged forward by curiosity until I found myself perching on the edge of the chair with the Druid book clutched to my breasts. Though unwise, I wanted to open this forbidden box of knowledge more than I wanted to be safe. Or was it the man himself drawing me to the forbidden? No proper woman would pursue such subjects, nor would she remain alone in a room with a man in the middle of the night, but then, nothing I had done since coming to Killdaren Castle had been proper. I tried to tell myself that any information I could glean would aid my investigation of Mary's death. Inside, however, I knew the truth. I wanted to know more about Sean, who he was, and what he thought almost as much as I wanted to know the truth about Mary.

"Nonmortals?" I asked tentatively, afraid to know what he meant.

"I hear the scandalous imaginings of all things dammed in

your voice." He laughed, the rich sound as warm and beckoning as the fire. And probably just as devouring, I reminded myself. "Human nature is an odd thing, is it not?" he asked softly. "Always tempting man to his demise. Though I'd love to oblige your fancies, I fear my answer is more mundane. Let me ask you a question first. Do you believe in God?"

"Of course."

"Is God mortal, then?"

"No." I bit my lip in chagrin.

"So there is a spirit world, where things exist that man cannot explain, correct?"

I nodded, my throat too tight to speak. I knew all too well about the unexplainable. In my mind, my dreams of death were forewarnings from the spirit realm, but something never spoken of beyond the circle of my family, for fear of condemnation from those who did not understand.

"Then imagine with me a moment that God is not alone. It is possible that He presides over more than just man? There are a number of archeological wonders about the world leading one to believe that more than just mortal man and beast have walked this earth. Where the notion came from that the *Tuatha de Danaan*, the fairy folk, are diminutive creatures, I don't know, but from all reports, they are giants capable of magic for good or for ill."

"You say 'are' rather than 'were'. Why?"

"You listen well. Are you sure you want to hear about the Stone Virgins, lass? For they didn't die virgins," he said softly, his tone deep and luring.

I shivered. Pleasurably. We'd already obliterated any lines of propriety. "Yes," I said, slightly breathless. "You can't leave the story there."

He smiled, slowly, making me feel like a morsel about to be eaten. "The legend centers around Daghdha's insatiable appetite for women and his jealous wife, the queen of the fairies. Being the god of fertility, his powers and actions were generally believed to be good, and the harp he played, magical, capable of controlling the minds of mortals. He commanded the seasons and the emotions of man with his music, a note for sorrow, a note for joy, and a note for dreams. And whenever the opportunity arose, Daghdha didn't deny himself sport with mortal women." He paused, sliding his gaze over me, making me flush.

"And?" I prompted, wanting to escape the fire he licked over me.

"Well, given Daghdha's odious description of a huge-bellied giant, naked below the waist, and our local legend of the Stone Virgins, I'm of the opinion he could also seduce with the Uaithne, his harp made of living oak. He could play one note and any woman would come to him, willing to give herself to him."

"He sounds like an unconscionable, uncouth beast."

Sean smiled. "Perhaps. Here in Dartmoor's Forest, on the eve of Beltane, away from the eagle eye of his queen at Tara, Daghdha lured seven of the most beautiful mortal virgins into the forest with his harp and seduced them with his prowess, showing them each the high pleasure of immortal relations. Then he turned their earthly bodies to stone before they could tell anyone of his deed or before his queen learned of his indulgence."

"That's horrible," I cried.

He laughed. "Well, it is rumored that he only put stone figures here to keep his queen from looking no further should she ever learn of his exploit. What really happened is that he fell in love with the women and chose them for his own. He gave them the knowledge of the gods and the gift of immortality, and took them to a secret lair to spend eternity pleasuring them."

"That's not any better."

"Isn't it, lass? The knowledge of the gods and an eternity of pleasure, never to know pain again?"

Snapping the Druid book shut, I stood and marched across the room, agitation stealing over me. "It doesn't matter what he gave them. It was criminal of him. He used magic to seduce them then took their lives from them. He gave them no choice."

He laughed again, seemingly enjoying my irritation.

"Perhaps. It could be that they wouldn't have chosen differently had they been given a choice. There are those who would pay any price for knowledge and eternal pleasure."

"You're missing the point. Those who would pay any price, though foolish, at least were able to choose. I cannot believe that you'd rationalize and condone what he did by saying they might not have chosen differently."

He rose and slowly walked toward me. I deliberately kept my gaze directed at his face and not on his infirmity. I almost had the feeling that his gaze was measuring my reaction to his use of the cane.

"What would you do?" he asked softly, "Given the offer of knowing the unknown of the universe, and great pleasure always, would you choose to leave this mortal life?"

I opened my mouth to assure him that I would never willingly forsake all that I held dear, but he pressed his finger to my lips, shocking me silent.

"Think on it a bit. Don't speak rashly, and make very sure that it isn't ignorance of what that knowledge and pleasure might be before you answer."

I nodded and he lowered his finger, letting it brush softly against my chin and neck as he stepped away. Before he could turn, I touched his arm. For a moment I'd seen pain in his eyes and I suddenly had to know. "Would you? Would you give up your life for that?"

"In a heartbeat, lass," he said.

I released his arm as if burned, but I needed to know more. "Why?"

His laugh was harsh. "I don't think you really would like hearing the answer to that question, for there are a number of reasons why I'd leave this godforsaken life. Take the Druid book and go back to your room and let fairytale dreams ease your sleep."

I watched as he poured a glass of amber liquid from a decanter on a side table, filling the room with a hint of scotch, similar in aroma to what my father drank on occasion. Then he moved slowly to the chair, stretching his legs before the fire.

"Is your injury one of the reasons you'd leave this life? Do you have a lot of pain?"

"You're not much different than me, Cassie. The wanting to know all, no matter the cost. Only you've not the courage to admit it. You'll let curiosity lead you a step at a time to your demise rather than just leap."

I sighed, exasperated. I had the feeling that he was deliberately trying to chase me away again, as he had in all of our other encounters, and I wasn't going to go running this time. "How were you hurt?"

Staring into the fire, he took another sip and my exasperation grew.

"What if it isn't me who would be choosing to leave this life out of ignorance, but you?" I suggested, challenging him.

"What?" His gaze snapped back to me and I nearly smiled at the shocked look on his face. I daresay few had ever accused him of being ignorant.

"As far as I can tell you've cut yourself off from everything worthwhile in life."

"Such as?"

Having come this far, I saw no reason not to blurt out the truth. "People. You wouldn't even listen to a message from your brother. You sleep all day, totally uninvolved with everyone, and then do God knows what at night alone in your round room. No wonder you have no affinity for this life. This house has people, but it has no life, no family, no love."

He laughed, but no real amusement filled the bitter sound. "I have my reasons for living the way I do. Besides, I know you've heard the rumors. Very few people would care to associate themselves with a cursed murderer."

I gasped, backing up a step, feeling the blood drain from my face. "Was that a confession?"

"It doesn't matter. If I told you I didn't murder Helen, you wouldn't know if I were lying or not, so anything I said would only ease *your* conscience at this point, not mine. Everything that happened was meant to happen and nothing could have stopped it." His harsh tone cut like jagged glass. It was full of pain and anger, and I wanted to reach out to him, to do something to ease the hurt I felt pouring out of him. But it was the hopelessness of his words that nearly undid me. "When it comes to destiny, nothing matters, not even truth."

"How can it not?" I asked. "As God lives, how can it not matter?"

"It doesn't."

"Why?" I stood for a long time, waiting for him to answer, but he didn't, giving me no choice but to leave. "As long as you believe that the truth doesn't matter, then nothing will ever be worthwhile," I said quietly, before I went.

Upon reaching my room, I dressed for bed and slid beneath the blanket, my mind too full of Sean to read anything more about the Stone Virgins.

# Chapter Ten

On Sunday morning, Bridget and I went to the village, she to see her family, and I to see my sisters and aunt, and as luck would have it, we weren't among the servants to have a full Sunday off this week. Our turn would come next week. The moment I slipped into the apartment, I knew something wasn't exactly right. It was all too early for Andromeda, and even more amazingly, Gemini, to be awake and outfitted in their best dresses.

"Did you learn anything new about Mary this week?" Andromeda asked before I could say a word.

Though I'd learned a number of things, from Sean's kiss to the Stone Virgins, none of it was fit for my sisters to know. I could readily see Andromeda leading an impromptu archeological expedition to The Stone Virgins. "No. It has been a very frustrating week." I spoke hesitantly, deciding that I hadn't really lied. "Are you going somewhere?"

"No. Not that we know," Andromeda said. "Just decided it would be proper to look our best on the Lord's Day."

Gemini giggled, almost guiltily.

I narrowed my gaze at her. "Is there something you need to tell me, Gemmi?"

She shook her head. "Not that I know of. Yet."

Andromeda jumped up from her decorous position. "We have a bath ready for you." She motioned me to a room.

"Yes, and I'll order tea to be sent up," Gemini said. "And I'll gather you a fresh packet of undergarments and things to take with you."

Though I didn't need a bath, I wasn't one to ever turn down a hot one. But the more I lay in the steamy water, the greater the sense that something was amiss with my sisters grew. Where was their usual chaotic chatter, their drama? I joined them and my aunt for tea, thinking that whole household seemed unusually organized this morning, as if they didn't need me to keep order as before. Was the difference and distance I felt between me and them because of the secrets I harbored? Or was it because my thoughts drifted to those at Killdaren Castle, who were growing in their importance to me? Bridget and her sick mother, her young brother and her absent sister. Little Rebecca with only her rag doll and nurse for company, rather than a life full of friends and affection. And mostly to Sean, a man who seemed to have no one and nothing but darkness and hopelessness. Ever since last night, his harshly rasped *it doesn't matter* kept echoing in my heart. How could he believe that?

"Did you hear, Cassie?" Aunt Lavinia asked.

I blinked. "I'm sorry. What did you say?"

"The housekeeper telegraphed that she couldn't find any journals or sketchbooks among Mary's things. Her paints were there, but no paintings."

"That can't be right." I set my tea cup into the saucer, hearing it rattle as my hand shook. "Mary would never be without a sketchbook or her paintings. I might have believed she didn't keep a journal, but her sketches and paintings were her life as much as teaching."

"Some of her things must still be at the castle then," Andromeda declared.

"I don't think any of her things were left in the room she used. I saw it," I said softly. "It is beautiful, pastel green with lots of satin and lace and a magnificent view of the sea. I could easily see her there, happy and painting. And little Rebecca, I know Mary must have grown to love her very much; she's such a lost child. One of the people at the castle, described Mary as hope. She'd brought hope into their lives."

"Thank you." Aunt Lavinia dabbed at her eyes. "I needed to hear that she was happy in her post. I mean she always wrote to me of such things, but I thought she did so to keep me from worrying about her."

"Letters! Why didn't I think of that?" I rose from my seat and paced the room. "What do you remember from her letters, Auntie?"

"Goodness. She always wrote so much. I don't know what to say."

"But you still have her letters, don't you?"

"Yes, at home."

"Can you have the housekeeper send them to us?"

"Of course. I'll telegraph for her to send them special delivery."

Andromeda sat up. "Was that the church bell already?"

"Yes, I think it was," Geimini added.

I frowned and shook my head, wondering if I had water in my ear. "I didn't hear it."

"I'm sure I did. You should take a few scones back with you." Gemini quickly wrapped scones into a napkin and handed me the package of fresh underclothes and the two older dresses I'd chosen to take with me.

It wasn't until I reached the church after a quick goodbye and heard the church bells just ringing that I knew for certain my sisters had deliberately hurried me along from the moment I'd arrived. Something was definitely amiss.

Turning around, I marched back to the inn, and entered the apartment. "Andrie, Gemmi, come here immediately." I don't think I'd spoken to them so since they were in nappers.

"What is it, dear?" Aunt Lavinia came hurrying from her room into the sitting area.

"Where are they?"

"Didn't they mention their trip to you earlier?"

"No."

"Must have been distracted with our talk of Mary. Andrie and Gemmi have gone on an excursion to some archeological site nearby. Something about stones and maidens, I believe. Is there anything wrong, dear?"

"No. Why didn't you go with them?"

"Having a difficult time with my gout lately. Walking any distance would have been out of the question. But I made sure they were well chaperoned."

"All right," I said, though nothing was right. The thought of my sisters going to that eerily strange place in the forest alone sent waves of panic crashing at me. Though what I thought could go wrong on such a seemingly innocent venture, I hadn't figured out. All I could think of was Jamie dragging me there. "Forgive me for rushing off, but it is suddenly getting late."

Hurrying from the inn, I encountered Bridget on the main street in town, her unmistakable red hair bouncing in long curly tresses over the blue shawl I gave her. That she wore it every moment she could, despite the summer's heat touched me deep inside. "Come on." I grabbed her arm. "We've a secret errand to run."

"What is it?" She asked, matching my hurried step.

"I want to see the Stone Virgins before we have to be back at the castle."

"What would have you in such a dither to see moldy stones in the forest?"

"I can't really explain. I just must. Will you come with me?"

"Blimey, Cassie. Sometimes you can be so strange. Well, if we're going to the Stone Virgins, then we best run as fast as we can, or we're going to be very late. We can take the village path. It'll be shorter." Turning to the right, she guided me up the street past the church.

"Do the villagers go to the stones often?" The path cutting up beside the church graveyard appeared well worn, but eerily isolated. Even though the main street was a stone's throw away from our path, the fact that the looming gravestones and black iron fencing stood between us and the church seemed to cut us away from the warmth of the living.

"Ack, only twice a year, much to the vicar's despair. May Eve and All Hallows' Eve has everyone a dancing and enjoying a pint or two and forgetting anything about who they are. I haven't been to the celebrations since working at the castle. Mrs. Frye won't let anyone go. If you do, you lose your post. Two maids went a year ago, and when they came stumbling back after midnight, she handed them their things and made them leave the castle that minute."

"She's a hard woman." The sound and flit of a starling chasing a robin skittered by, but failed to leave a sense of normalcy behind. Even the patches of bright pink and white rhododendron did little to ease the brooding air.

"She's had a hard life, and not exactly a fair one. She had the earl's bastard, but she didn't get sent to a fancy ladies school or have any life of ease like Miss Prudence. I think that's why she doesn't do the wee one any favors, either."

"What happened to her husband, the man the earl made her marry?"

"Heard Jamie's father, Phineas Frye, the earl's top groomsman, was shot in a hunting accident before Jamie was born. Maybe that's why Mrs. Frye's so bitter, havin' lost her husband afore her babe was even born. Then I imagine it would sweeten me none to have a son like Jamie, either. He can never be a man, and no longer a boy. Don't know how to treat him."

"I feel sorrier for Jamie and his frustrations than I do for Mrs. Frye. I think she'd have a better life if she wasn't so bitter. How is your mother?"

Bridget sighed. "Not good. She still has her strength, mind you. But I think her cough is worse. Tim, my little brother, is scared. And I am too. We've still no word from Flora. Makes me think that she had to have gone to Paris to sing. Make no mistake, I'm happy for her, but it's such a long way from here, and I keep worrying about what we're going to do."

"I'm sorry." I squeezed her hand. "I'm sure everything is going to work out all right. There's an answer. You'll see."

She squeezed my hand back. "I pray so."

We walked on in silence, lost in our thoughts. The trees lining the path thickened, diminishing the sun's light and warmth. I kept peering anxiously up the pathway, thinking that

I was searching for my sisters, but as the whole mood of the forest changed around me, becoming darker, more forbidding, and I realized that I was looking for danger. The thought of my sisters out in that danger shot cold anxiety through my heart.

After my encounter with Jamie, I'd thankfully put my stolen knife in my pocket within easy reach. I'd learned that I could have the deadliest weapon ever made, and it would do me little good if I couldn't get that weapon in my hand. When we reached a shadowed bend in the road, I instinctively slid my hand into my pocket, finding reassurance in the solid metal and the sharpness of the blade. The road steepened considerably, telling me the Stone Virgins concealed in the maritime forest were on an elevated knoll in comparison to the village, as if the eerie place secretly presided over the townspeople.

So much tension built inside of me that I was almost disappointed when Bridget and I broke from the forest, reaching the area of the Stone Virgins and its massive center stone statue of what I now knew had to be Daghdha and his Uthaine, the living oak harp he used to seduce the virgins. The clearing, sun-drenched and peaceful, held none of the sinister air I'd felt when Jamie had dragged me to it. Birds chirped merrily to each other, bees and flies droned about their business. All appeared well.

Or perhaps the great flood of relief I felt at not finding my sisters here, and thus nowhere near Killdaren's Castle, made the area seem benign.

"Now what?" Bridget crinkled her creamy brow into a frown.

"Let me look a minute and we'll go." Leaving an impatient Bridget, I took a quick turn around the Virgins, envisioning the beautiful women being led to their doom by the lure of sweet music. It suddenly gave me the same ill feeling that the music room did, and I shuddered. On my way back to Bridget, I crossed the middle of the circle and examined the giant stone there, surprised to discern from the time-eroded etching on the stone that Daghdha was indeed depicted as being naked below the waist, with an ample belly and even larger genitals. The huge, almost crypt-like base that he rose from in combination with his height brought that anatomy to my eye-level. Lord, I'd gone all of my life giving little more than a cursory thought to the male anatomy, but now I couldn't seem to escape it.

Irrationally, I stepped closer, studying the stone harp and its frame of a woman bent backward, realizing that to play the instrument, the god's hands would have to grip her breasts. I shivered at the thought, then cried out when a swarm of flies suddenly rose from the statue's base. I looked down and saw a dark stain, and leaned curiously closer. Terror stabbed me. I screamed and jumped back.

Blood.

A dark, congealed maggot-ridden puddle of blood lay at the god's feet.

Bridget ran to me, craning to see as she looked up at the statue. "Blimey, Cassie! What is it?"

I pointed at the ground. "Blood."

Round eyed and as starkly white-faced as I felt, Bridget grabbed my arm. "Let's go. Most likely the leavings of a hunter poaching on the Killdaren's land, but I ain't waiting to find out."

I didn't argue. We didn't speak until we broke through the forest to find Killdaren's Castle, stable, and gardens in sight.

"Who should we tell?" I asked, gasping for air.

"Stuart," Bridget said without question. "I'll tell him." She headed for the stables.

Not about to be left behind nor alone, I hurried after her, but paused just inside the stable doors to wipe the perspiration from my brow—then decided to stay there as Bridget approached Stuart. At the moment he was standing on a stump, adjusting harnesses hung there.

"There's blood on the ground up at the Virgins," she said.

"What?" Stuart swung around so quickly that he lost his balance and came tumbling right over on Bridget. In her attempt to move out of his way, she fell backward and Stuart landed on top, pressing her to the ground with his face buried in her bosom. Whether stunned or hurt I couldn't tell. He didn't move, except maybe to turn his head a bit.

"Get off of me this minute, Stuart Frye!" Bridget yanked his hair.

"Ouch," Stuart yelled, rearing back enough to look at Bridget. "Nice of you to cushion my fall." He grinned, looking so pointedly at Bridget's heaving bosom that I had to turn my back to them.

"You're getting my shawl dirty, you bloody arse. Get up!"

"Temper, temper, my lady."

I heard a considerable amount of shuffling and figured it was safe enough to turn around again, just in time to see Bridget smack Stuart on the arm. "Philandering buffoon," she said. "Stop lazing around. There's a puddle o' blood at the Stone Virgins. Best find out who's poaching on the Killdaren's land get them to stop afore there's trouble. Don't want to see anyone losing their life o'er a rabbit or such."

Stuart shook his head. "Blood at the Stone Virgins?"

"Yes. Haven't you heard anything I've said?"

"I think I'm starting to understand. What were you doing there anyway?"

"Cassie wanted to look around on our way back from the village."

Jerking his gaze up, I saw Stuart's surprise at finding me there. Either that or he found my going to the Stone Virgins shocking. I would have liked not having him know. He knew too much about me already.

"I think you should report it to Constable Poole," I said.

Stuart shook his head. "I'll handle it."

"No point in bringing the law into it," Bridget said. "Especially if someone is just trying to feed their family off of Killdaren land. Don't need to bring more trouble to folks already having hard times."

I wanted to argue, to ask them what if it was something more sinister afoot, but I had no evidence, and I could just see Constable Poole's mustached smirk. I'd let Stuart handle the problem for now, but asked him to let me know what he found out.

That night, after Bridget fell asleep, I dressed, still unsure what I would do. I couldn't get Sean's parting words out of my head. Had he ventured to the library again? Dare I go there myself? Before I could change my mind, I hurried from my room. Upon reaching the library door, I saw the warm glow of a fire flickering in the hearth. My heart pounded so loudly that I was sure it could be heard echoing through the whole castle.

"I hoped you'd be here." I stepped into the room. The dark-haired man who had his back to me turned from where he sat studying the flames, only then did I realize it was the earl. Fire scorched my cheeks.

"Indeed." He stared hard at me for a moment. "And what do I owe the pleasure of such hopes?"

I coughed as I tried to spit words out of my frozen lungs. "I...well...never had the opportunity to respond to your statement in the garden. Your words disturbed me so much that, well, I couldn't speak at the time."

The earl burst into laughter. "Lass, you lie well. Must be some Irish in your blood. It would seem you've met Sean other than when Rebecca wandered to the bell tower, then. Come have a seat." He motioned to the sofa by the fire and I took a step into the room, drawn to his fatherly demeanor, which reminded me a little of my grandfather. Then I hesitated. I didn't really know this man at all, and his emotions in the garden seemed to have changed as quickly as the wind.

"Don't be afraid, lass." He moved to the far side of the room and sat down in the same leather chair Sean had occupied last night. "You're bonnie enough to have any man be thinking what he shouldn't, but I think you've an eye for my son and I won't be trying to turn your head any other direction. He's entirely too alone in life."

"You'd approve of such an impropriety?" I asked before thinking about who I spoke too. Considering Stuart, this man had had his share of scandal.

He burst into laughter again, this time reaching for a drink I hadn't noticed on the table by the chair. A nearly empty decanter sat next to the glass. He was a bit into his cups again.

"I'll let you and my son discuss that matter, I think. Tell me about yourself, lass. From the stiffness to your skirts, I detect a bit of English in with that Irish. Am I right?"

The man was flagrantly improper, but I still found myself warming to him. Enough so to move a little farther into the room and perch on a small chair near the door.

"Maybe more than just of bit of English then," he said.

"Enough to see me through my Irish blood with few mishaps." I found myself laughing when he did. "At least that's what my English grandmother always told me."

"She did, hey. And what did your Irish grandmother tell you?"

"How did you know?"

"Never met either an Irish or an English who didn't have something to say about the other. Mixing the blood lines even stirs up more trouble, but what the bloody hell for, I haven't figured out because they're so muddied this day and age that there isn't a bit of difference between them, just a matter of the tongue these days. And the starch."

"Well, my Irish grandmother would always say that it was a good thing her daughter married into the Andrews family, otherwise the blood would have stopped running in their veins they were so stiff."

"Smart woman."

"You didn't mean what you said in the garden, did you?"

"Don't let a few laughs from a tongue loosened by drink fool you. I meant it. Job was a better man than me."

"But how can you stop loving? It isn't possible."

"Ah, lass. You young women are so alike. Mary would ask me the same question and say the same thing. She couldn't do a thing to save us Killdarens, and I fear you won't be able to, either. Cursed is cursed. You'd be surprised how easy it is to stop loving when you figure out that it's your loving that's killing everything about you."

Suddenly the warm fuzzy feeling, the one similar to what I'd feel listening to my grandfather's stories, froze in my breast.

"You'd best go on now before you're seen with me here, or the curse rubs off on to you."

I stood, half facing the door, unsure of what to do.

"Go on with, you now. I've a mind for quiet."

"I still don't believe you," I told him. "Not about the curse and not about the other, either." Then I left the room, just as unsettled as I had left Sean the night before. What was it with these men? And why in the devil did I let them upset me so with the talk of curses and doom?

Hearing something down the corridor, I glanced up to see what looked like a caped shadow disappear around the corner into the center hall.

Sean.

I ran toward him, skittering into the center hall, trying to look in every direction at once. It was empty. Then heart running almost faster than it could beat. I went to the corridor leading to Sean's wing, but it stood dark and silent. Yet, lingering in the air, I thought I detected a hint of the strange, but luring aroma of spice that clung to Sean and scented his rooms.

Was he there in the shadows? Was it my imagination?

Finally, I turned and went back to my room. If he'd been there and didn't reach out to me, it wouldn't do any good to go chasing down the corridor after him. I went to bed feeling worse than I had the night before. I much preferred Sean's harsh words to his silence.

Other than to comment that hunters used the stones as a cutting board on occasion and that the problem had been taken care of, Stuart didn't say anything else about the blood at the Stone Virgins when I asked him on Monday. I knew that whatever the cause, it wasn't a sight or a feeling I would ever forget.

The week seemed to be passing much too slowly, winding tension around me as tightly as a spider's web. I'd given thought to my sisters' odd behavior on Sunday but had come to the conclusion that if there was anything wrong, Aunt Lavinia would have contacted me. I'd couched my questions about where Mary's sketchbook and paintings might be under the guise of collecting material for the class I planned to teach for the servants. So far I had found no trace of Mary's artwork. Rebecca continued to worry me; I'd only been able to see her once since Friday, and she'd been very quiet, more withdrawn than usual.

Sean had made no contact with me and I didn't venture to the library again, fearing the silence more than whom I might see. Neither had I heard any noises from his round room. A misty fog had blown in from the sea and hovered over the castle, dampening the air, as well as the spirits of those in the castle.

On Wednesday evening I set up my classroom in the kitchens. None of the upper servants appeared, but slowly all those I ate the evening meal with every night came, with the exception of Stuart. He brought Jamie to the class, seated Jamie at the far end of the table from me, then left.

Jamie didn't look at all happy. He sat there glaring at me the entire hour. Between Mr. and Mrs. Murphy's laughs and the Oak sisters' giggles, I managed to set Jamie's antagonism from my mind. The fact that Bridget had already learned enough about reading and writing to be my assistant rather than my pupil impressed everyone. Bridget practically glowed with her growing confidence. The class went so well that I held one on Friday evening as well. Jamie came, but his demeanor hadn't changed. I approached him at the end of class, catching sight of a paper he'd written his name on.

"That's very good work," I said.

Holding the paper in his hand, he studied his name. "J-A-M-I-E." He said the letters out loud.

"Yes," I said softly, touched by his determined effort.

He held the paper out to me. "For you."

Unsure of what to do, I took the paper, trying to decide what to say. I felt compelled to at least bring up the subject of Mary, a thorn in this giant's hand. I'd wanted to speak to him about Mary since arriving at Killdaren's Castle, but feared seeking him out alone. "You are learning your letters quickly. Mary taught you well."

"No!" he shouted. Pulling his paper from my hands, he thrust me aside so hard that I fell back over a chair as he ran out the door.

"Blimey." Bridget rushed over and helping me up. "What happened?"

Mr. and Mrs. Murphy hurried over as well. "Are you all right, lass?"

"Yes." I gathered myself. "It...it was an accident. I tripped moving away from Jamie. He is still upset about Mary."

"He loved her," Mrs. Murphy said. "She treated him with a kindness most folks don't. Spoke to him like he was a normal person, she did."

"It was a sad day for us all when she drowned," Mr. Murphy said. "We loved the lass. Everyone did."

I swallowed, forcing back the emotion crowding over me. Perhaps my search for answers to Mary's death was truly a fruitless one. So why couldn't I seem to let it all go? Why had Mary come to me in a dream about Rebecca? The darkness hovering over me only seemed to grow more and more obscuring, like that of a cloud turning into a violent storm. I didn't think I would try and ask Jamie about Mary again. Had Mary said or done something to upset Jamie? If a mere question could turn him violent, what would he have done if Mary had rejected him in some way? What if Jamie had tried to show his affection for Mary physically? What would have happened then? Could her kindness to the giant have caused her death?

That night after Bridget fell asleep, I dressed and stole downstairs again, but the rooms lay silent and empty. I even ventured to the doors leading to Sean's rooms and pressed my hand to the wood, debating on whether to honor his privacy, or to force him to see how he was throwing his life away by believing what he did. The earl, too. I didn't understand it.

Then as I stood there, in the dark of the night, I found myself considering the impossible. With all of the earl's talk of being cursed and killing everything he loved, and Sean's nocturnal life, could they really be vampires? And dear God, could Mary be in a crypt beneath the black shrouds in the round room? I owed it to her and possibly in some twisted way to Sean, too, to discover the truth. But not tonight. I went back to my room. I didn't write a single word about my new thoughts in my journal, I couldn't—they were too fanciful. But neither could I dismiss them.

Saturday dawned and with it a sense of expectation that something would happen, a feeling I had little affinity for, given anything likely to happen wouldn't be good. But I'd had no warning dream, so I faced the day on edge.

Bridget and I were given the task of dusting the two rooms of eclectic art I'd discovered when looking for Rebecca a couple of weeks ago. We started with the statue room. After dusting off twenty nude figures then coming to a couple, nude and intimately entwined, I had to sit back and rest. Bridget had done as many statues as I, and we weren't finished yet.

I thought I would scream if I had to wipe another man's privates. At least these statues followed the miniscule precepts of the great masters when it came to such matters, but for whatever sophomoric reason, I couldn't seem to dismiss the anatomy from my mind. Having to dust so many kept me thinking about Zeus in the garden and Sean. And the entwined couple now had me thinking many things I shouldn't. "My word, but this is a bit much to take."

"Makes a person's arms ache, it does." Bridget swiped her sleeve across her forehead.

"Someone surely had an obsession with naked statues. It's almost obscene to have so many."

Bridget laughed. "Is that what you're so flustered and huffing about this morning? Ack, Cassie, don't you realize that all over the world males are male and females are female? Just like horses and pigs and cows and bulls and dogs. We got the same parts and are wanting to do the same thing. It's what God gave us the parts for. Nothing to be ashamed of."

"I'm not ashamed." Horses and pigs? Bulls and dogs? The same? Good Lord, I hoped not.

"If you're not ashamed, then you aren't very comfortable with the notion."

"Well, such things are not proper material for thought or discussion."

"If you can't think about it, and you can't talk about it, and you can't do it, then you might as well end the world tomorrow 'cause there won't be nobody around to be living in it. Now does that make any sense at all?"

I sat back and sighed. "No."

"My mum says it's what keeps the world going."

I nodded, thinking that Bridget and I truly had come from two different worlds. My mother would faint before saying something like that, and I think my sisters and I would have fainted to hear it. But in all honesty, Bridget was right, except for one thing. When it came to Sean, he didn't make the world go around. He stopped it in its tracks.

We finished the statue room and I went back to the kitchens to get more rags and lemon wax to tackle the next room, while Bridget made a head start.

Clutching clean clothes in my hands as I left the laundry, I heard voices coming from the second kitchen and moved closer to hear. Mrs. Murphy and Mrs. Frye were talking.

"Stuart says the Killdaren left for the village an hour ago. He hasn't been there in eight years. This is big trouble. I wonder if it has something to do with Mary's drowning. I didn't know the Killdaren was so well acquainted with her until the magistrate questioned everyone and he mentioned they'd had a number of conversations." Mrs. Frye sounded almost fearful, which puzzled me, until I realized that if Sean, Jamie or Stuart had had anything to do with Mary's disappearance and she knew about it, then she would be afraid.

"Whatever gave you that idea that he was seeing the magistrate again, Clara? I'm hoping that it's a lass that has him about. Something needs to change around here. The way the

Killdaren and the viscount are wastin' their lives is what ain't right."

My mind had latched on to one fact: Sean had spent time with Mary and he was presently out of the castle. Now might be the only chance for me to see what secrets he kept in the round room. And if, God forbid, my thoughts after midnight were true and Mary did lie in a vampire's crypt, well, maybe I would find that out, too.

"Bridget," I called, dashing into the art room. "Hurry. Take these and dust as fast as you can. I've got something to do that can't wait, and I don't want anyone to know that I'm not in here with you, all right?"

"Blimey, Cassie. What is it?"

"I can't talk now. I'll tell you later." I quit the room before she could ask any more questions. Looking carefully over my shoulder and taking a moment to make sure no one was about, I went directly to Sean's private door, grasped the dragon handle and ducked inside. In moments I was in the round room with my heart pounding and my palms perspiring. The books surrounding the room passed in a blur as I went right to the blinding swathe of sunshine centered on the huge, shrouded mass sitting in the middle of the room.

Once there, I froze a moment, almost fearful to know what lay beneath. Slowly, I reached out and set my fingers upon the black cloth. Heat radiated into my fingers and I snatched my hand back, remembering what had happened to the woman in the vampire book when she touched the crypt.

"Cassie, you fool. There are no such things as vampires." The whisper of my voice echoed upward, drawing my gaze in that direction. Through the grated iron floor above and the huge center hole, I could see the sky as if I lay upon a sunny hill on a picnic. Clouds drifted overhead and the graceful swoop of a raven passing over the glass dome left his shadow dancing over me. It was amazing. I knew as high as the round room went that if I were to climb the stairs to the top and walk the rim, I'd most likely be able to look out at the sea and the forest and be able to see almost everything for miles around. The only thing

165

that could keep me from that view was still sitting unknown before me.

I set my hand back upon the shroud, this time pressing down and feeling something very hard and warm beneath it. Fisting my fingers in the cloth, I pulled, but the material caught upon something underneath. Before I could tug hard, thick arms suddenly wrapped around me and a heavy hand covered mine. Sean. I could feel, smell and taste him immediately.

"Remember what I said I would do if I found you in my rooms again without an invitation? What price should you pay for your insatiable curiosity today?" He whispered softly into my ear as he pressed his hard body firmly against my bottom and into every curve and dip from my calves to the nape of my neck. Heat erupted everywhere as my pulse raced as fast as my mind ran *through* and *from* the consequences he intimated.

"Oh God," I whispered, dropping the cloth. "I'm sorry. They said you went to the village."

"And so I did. But I'm back and just in time, it would seem."

"Uh, perhaps a few minutes early. Do you think you could leave and come back in just a moment?"

"I don't think so."

"Would you shut your eyes and count to ten, then?"

"Not a chance, my wandering rose. You made a choice. Are you brave enough to see it through?"

I swallowed hard and squeezed my eyes shut. "Do your worst, and let's be done with it."

His chest heaved as his laughter rumbled. "Do you think that's how it's done, lass? Vampires have a much better way."

Embarrassment that he'd clearly heard my whispered comment moments ago added more flame to the fire raging inside of me. "There are no such things as vampires."

"Aren't there?" he whispered. "You make me think differently. There are many places I'd love to put my mouth on you, Cassie. I'm feeling very hungry for your flesh and the heat of your blood." His lips, then his teeth, brushed the side of my neck and gave a little nip to my skin. I shivered all the way to my toes.

I tried to ignore what he said, tried to ignore how he made me feel. Surely, practical logic would see me through this blunder. "No. There are no vampires. I said that because of the heat. When I touched the shroud it was hot just like the crypt in the book and I, well, it gave me pause."

"Book? Crypt?" He stepped away and swung me around to face him. I could tell he'd been out riding. His dark hair was windblown, issuing an invitation to touch and tame in much the same way the pain I'd seen and heard in him had urged me to soothe. But there was no soothing the fire that glittered in his green eyes, least none that a gentle hand could accomplish. "You're reading *Powerful Vampires and Their Lovers*?" He spoke very slowly and distinctly, making the deed sound so risqué that I couldn't own up to it alone.

"Certainly not. I'm teaching Bridget to read, and that's the book she chose."

"Indeed." He flashed a devilish smile and cocked a querying brow as he advanced toward me. Good Lord, my heart took flight at the predatory look in his eyes as my stomach fell into a bottomless pit, wrenching everything in between. "So, it was of little interest to you when Armand lured his woman to his crypt?"

Reaching out, he tugged off my cap then slid his finger down the side of my neck, spreading fire to places inside of me that I didn't even know existed. My breasts seemed to swell and grow heavy and wanting. My breath caught when he skimmed along my collarbone to the center of my chest and stopped at the buttons of my dress.

He deftly unbuttoned the top two. "You read how Armand wanted to feast upon his love as Solomon feasted, and you thought or felt...nothing?" A third button fell swiftly beneath his determined advanced.

I was sure that I would faint at any moment, or erupt in flames as he undid two more buttons. It seemed I was tied to a stake and burning. I couldn't breathe and I couldn't move. My dress gaped, leaving only my gossamer chemise to cover my heated breasts like a whisper of mist trying to hide the sun. I wavered on my feet.

"Breathe, Cassie. I'll not let you off so easily." He pulled the edges of my dress further apart. Grasping my hips, he drew me to him, looking down at what he'd uncovered. I sucked in air, desperate for it, and winced as I felt the silk of my chemise stretch tightly over the sensitive tips of my breasts.

"You make me hungrier than I have ever been." He stared deeply into my eyes.

Whatever fears this man generated, whatever doubts he fostered, disappeared as my desire coalesced into a dark, almost obsessive need for his kiss. My lips parted. He bent his head and I felt the fire of his mouth upon mine. The power of his want consumed me as each kiss went deeper, demanded more, and gave more. Then he left my lips, kissing his way down my throat and bending me over his arm. Stepping impossibly closer, he pressed the bulk of his leg between mine, holding me captive as his mouth closed over the tip of my breast through the silk of my chemise.

"Oh, God," I groaned, falling more into his arms as my knees gave way. Leaving one breast, he claimed the other, groaning deeply as he suckled until my breath rasped and my body shuddered with the need for more. Then suddenly he pulled back.

"What?" I whispered, trying to think, trying to remember why I shouldn't give myself over to this unbelievable pleasure.

"You're mine." His voice was fierce. He scooped me into his arms and walked determinedly out of the round room, despite his hitched stride. Cool air brushed over my dampened chemise, tingling my breasts, and sending an urgent warning to my mind.

"I think...we...need...to...talk about this." My speech lasted the length of a short corridor where armor and weapons passed in a blur. Then he backed his way through double doors and tossed me on to the biggest bed I'd ever seen, with the softest counterpane I'd ever felt. He followed me onto it, pinning me down before I could even bounce.

"You should have thought about that before you walked through the dragon doors, lass. No maid comes to a man's rooms without this crossing her mind. You've done it twice, almost three times since coming here, and I think it's time I help you find what you're looking for."

"What did you say?" Outrage wiped any fear or desire from me. "You think I deliberately entered the round room to entice my way to your bed?" I pushed against his shoulders, trying to escape, but made little progress. Finally, I looked him directly in the eye and planted my finger in the middle of his nose, pressing him back.

"Do you think you're the only reason a woman might be tempted to go where she shouldn't? You're no different from that odious fairy, prancing about seducing unsuspecting virgins. Let me up immediately!"

Staring at me, as if confused, his green eyes shadowed with want and something deeper, a loneliness I didn't want to see. He slid to the side, letting me go. I rolled from the bed and stood staring at him a moment, oddly feeling as if I didn't want to go.

"I'm sorry." I ran for the door.

"Cassie!"

I halted with my fingers wrapped around the dragon handle.

"You might want to button your dress before leaving. And if you're daring enough to come back at midnight tonight, I just might show you what I do in the round room."

My fingers fumbled on the buttons of my dress as my ire grew. "I know exactly what things you'd like to show me. Well, not exactly, but you've given me a pretty good idea today. Whatever you may think of me, Sean, I'm not that."

"Are you a virgin then?" he asked from just behind me.

Startled, I swung around, backing to the door, wondering how he could move so silently. My cheeks flamed at the serious question in his voice. It didn't matter I had intimated I'd run from a scandal. It didn't matter that I had been brazen enough to intrude into his privacy. And it didn't matter that I'd shamefully responded to his advances. What mattered was the sting of his question against my character. Then I recalled his answer to my honest question before regarding his character.

"It doesn't matter." I cocked my brow at him. "You barely know me so you wouldn't believe me if I told you the truth, and at this point it would only ease your conscience, not mine. Besides truth isn't really that important, is it?"

He stepped back as if I'd hit him. I took the opportunity to duck out the door, thinking that maybe I'd stretched way too far to make a weak point and now everything would come crashing down. Thankfully, I found my mob cap on the floor of the round room and thought I would escape from this investigative disaster without further harm. But when I slid open Sean's door to make sure the corridor to the art room was clear, I came nose to nose with Sir Warwick.

He stared at me a moment, then a slow grin spread across his face. "A skirt." He grabbed my arm and pulled me down the corridor.

"Sir, begging your pardon. Is there a problem that I can help you with?" I hissed, trying to slow his pace by stumbling. Dragging my heels would have been too overtly disobedient. At the door to the gentlemen's lounge he stopped.

"I win. I told you it was a skirt that had the boy up and about during the day, Dartraven. Just caught the wench slipping from his quarters. That'll be a hundred pounds."

I thought I'd already suffered the worst fires embarrassment had to offer. I was wrong. This was so bad that my face and body went completely numb with shock.

The Earl of Dartraven stared at me for a long moment, looking far from the amused man the other night. Then he glared at his crony. "My apologies for a so-called gentleman's inexcusable and unbelievably cruel behavior. Please leave us, miss."

I barely managed a curtsy without falling before I stumbled my way across the hall and into the art room where Bridget worked.

She took one look at me, dropped her rag, and came running.

"Blimey, Cassie, whatever is wrong? Are ye ill?"

All I could do was nod and sit on the floor just inside the door. And truthfully, I did feel as if my insides had turned themselves wrong side out. Sir Warwick was clearly no gentleman, and it made me ill to think he had something he could hold over my head. I would have preferred an axe.

# Chapter Eleven

Sunday brought a heavy fog that the morning sun was just starting to dissipate. Bridget and I huddled together, clinging to the forested edge of the path, each thankful of the other's presence as we hurried to the village. This was our first full Sunday off. I should have been smiling instead of having my heart so full of the troubles at Killdaren Castle and guilt that I hadn't worried more about my sisters' archeological expedition last Sunday. It occurred to me, in hindsight, that I should have been worried enough to sneak back to the village to see them. But my mind had been consumed by those at the castle.

Even now, I couldn't walk away from them. In fact, even if I had discovered the truth about Mary's fate, I wouldn't be able to leave. Not yet. Bridget was part of that. Rebecca was part of that. But Sean was the center of it. My thoughts of him were like the waves of the sea tossing to and fro at the whim of the wind, so caught up in the current, there was no escape other than to see the storm through.

After overhearing the conversation between the Earl of Dartraven and Sir Warwick, I told Bridget that I'd gone to the round room to discover what Sean did there at night. Then I lied. I told her I'd become frightened over a noise and left before discovering the secrets of the round room, and that Sir Warwick had caught me leaving Sean's quarters, and assumed I'd been in the Killdaren's bed. She commiserated with me over the situation and thought it best to keep quiet and see if the whole thing would just disappear. The discussion left me feeling worse. It seemed as if more and more lies were making the cloud over my head bigger and darker.

And Sean made it harder for me to think with any semblance of propriety. I hadn't taken him up on his offer to join him in the round room last night, and he'd deliberately goaded me by spending the entire night in the round room, making the awful screeching noises a number of times. I'd had as little sleep as he. I yawned heavily several times before I parted with Bridget on the outskirts of town with plans to meet her that evening.

The humid breath of morning had dampened my skin, dress and cap, making me appear as unkempt as a wet alley cat, a condition that would most likely send my sisters into another fit of worry when they saw me.

Upon my approach to Seafarer's Inn, I thought I heard my sisters' laughter tinkling in the wind, and I shook my head at how easily the mind could conjure things held dear, making them seem so real. Passing an overflowing patch of sea pinks near the dunes and craggy rocks of Seafarer's Point, I snatched two handfuls to take to my sisters and became distracted arranging the bouquets as I walked. So it wasn't until I nearly stumbled upon the party breakfasting on the terrace of the inn that I realized the laughter I'd heard *was* my sisters'.

My sisters and three men! I ducked behind a potted tree before being seen.

"Colin, what say you? Is this not the most divine breakfast beverage imaginable?"

"It is indeed, Ashton. Sets a glow upon these ladies that rivals the beauty of this morning's sunrise."

"And such an extraordinary sunrise, too, Mr. Drayson." Andromeda laughed rather oddly, as if she couldn't help herself.

"Most beautiful," Gemini said.

Then she and Andromeda giggled, unusually loudly. Whatever was wrong with them?

"What did you call this juice, Lord Ashton? I'm having trouble remembering the odd name."

"A cocktail, Miss Andrews. It's an American invention. A Professor Jerry Thomas wrote an entire book of such concoctions."

"I'd love to try every one of them," Gemini said.

"This one is quite enough," Andromeda said. "In fact, I don't think we should do any more sampling of the juice. Cassie is coming today, and I'm not exactly sure she'd approve of our sunrise adventure."

"I remember you mentioning at dinner last night that you had an older sister. She isn't staying with you at the inn?"

"Well, yes and no," Andromeda said. "She's a journalist working on an important story."

I barely heard Andromeda's declaration. The blood drained from my face as I popped out from the side of the tree. That deep toned voice. That slight Irish burr. God in heaven, it couldn't be!

I gasped as I stared right at Sean. He looked my way and smiled.

"Don't be shy, maid." He called out to me. "I'll pay you for the flowers if you've enough for these lovely ladies this morning."

I stood frozen in place, stooped over and twisted around the potted tree. My back wrenched and I had to bite my lip to keep from crying out in pain.

"Come along." He motioned me over.

"Whoever are you speaking to, Viscount Blackmoor?" Andromeda asked, leaning heavily to the side to see.

Viscount Blackmoor!

The moment Andromeda caught sight of me, she gasped, started to rise, but tangled her foot up in between the table cloth and fell to the ground.

"Miss Andrews!" The men all shouted simultaneously as they jumped from their seat and rushed over to Andromeda.

In seconds I saw my whole investigation unravel and I couldn't let that happened. I forced my feet to move, then my mouth to follow suit. "Oh, milady! Are ye hurt? Beggin' ya pardon, milord. 'ere ya can 'ave the flowers, ya can. Just don't go *tellin'* anyone. I canna loose my job, I just canna! Please don't tell!"

Andromeda sat straight up, mouth hanging open as she stared at me. The three men knelt at her side.

Gemini stood, turning over her teacup. "Why Ca—"

"I'm all right," Andromeda shouted loudly. "Flowers! Do get some flowers, Gemmi."

I blinked, forcing my mouth to stay shut. They were both going to get more than a piece of my mind. Cavorting with men at sunrise, drinking spirits! God in heaven, my sisters were as near to ruin as I! Where was Aunt Lavinia? Why hadn't she called a halt to such a shenanigan?

Gemini caught on and must have seen the murderous glint in my eye as well. She didn't say a word but walked unsteadily over to me. "These are beautiful," she said, her eyes doing their best to apologize. I couldn't say anything to her, for the viscount walked up, causing a storm to whirl inside of me. He was so like Sean, yet I knew he couldn't be Sean. So part of me responded, my heart sped, my stomach tightened, but another part of me yearned for the familiarity of Sean's gait, or a hint of Sean's unique scent. When I took the pound note the viscount pressed into my hand, I felt some heat, but not a raging fire.

"I believe in honest pay for honest work," he said. "Keep that and we'll not mention this incident to your employer."

"I think Miss Andrews has turned her ankle, Blackmoor. Why don't you carry her inside while James and I send for the doctor?" one of the men said.

The viscount frowned. "She barely fell, Colin. Let me take a look." He returned to Andromeda.

Gemini stood, glancing warily back and forth from me to Andromeda, who had completely forgotten me. She was looking at the viscount touching her ankle as if he were, well, Zeus! I jolted, unable to believe she'd let a stranger touch her, even to check an injury. Her gift of touch had forced her to keep others at arm's length for years.

"Perhaps you shouldn't walk on it until the doctor sees it." The viscount scooped Andromeda up into his arms before I could form a protest. "We should have returned these ladies to their aunt a long time ago."

"I hope Dr. Luden doesn't have a dyspeptic attack when he finds me suddenly on his doorstep again. A grim reminder of the past, I'd say," one of the men said, then laughed uncomfortably.

The look on the viscount's face changed from irritation to stark pain, maybe anger. The intense emotion drained the blood from his face. "If that was meant as a joke, it isn't remotely humorous." Then he turned on his heel and stalked inside with Andromeda in his arms.

I thought I would swoon. In public, in broad daylight, the man planned to carry my sister to her room? Andromeda didn't seem the least bit unsettled by the situation. In fact, she had her arms wrapped around the viscount's neck, and had this awed look about her that had remained undaunted by the viscount's fierceness.

Gemini looked at me, as if asking what to do.

"Go with her!" I said shortly, forgetting that one of the other men was still near. He turned sharply as Gemini dashed for the inn.

I cleared my throat. "Should I get more flowers fer the lady?"

The man shook his head. "Not today, but I daresay the way Mr. Drayson has been conspiring to put Blackmoor and the ladies together, I think there will be a number of opportunities to sell flowers in the future."

"Don't be setting the onus for this venture completely on my back, Ashton," the other man said as they walked to the door. "You agreed with me that Blackmoor wouldn't be able to walk away and I think we may have been right. Now, if we could only get Sean here and interested in the other sister, they'd eventually *have* to speak to each other."

"I don't know. I'm beginning to think it was a mistake. The chits may all be too much like Lady Helen. Their golden hair, their lovely blue eyes, their laughter and innocence. It is almost uncanny to find them here..."

The men went inside, cutting off the rest of their

conversation. Heart pounding, I dashed for the servants' entrance with a whole nest of bees under my mop cap. God in heaven, what had my sisters gotten into?

Instead of confronting them immediately, I had to huddle in a dark corner for nearly a quarter hour until the viscount exited my family's rooms. Then I slipped inside to find Aunt Lavinia in an uproar, Gemini chattering excitedly, and Andromeda propped like a queen on the settee in the sitting room.

Aunt Lavinia flapped around like a wet hen. "Has anyone seen my smelling salts? That man just carried you in his arms in public! My sister will never forgive me for allowing you to engage in such a familiarity with that kind of man."

"He's a viscount, Auntie. Whatever can you possibly think is wrong with him?" Gemini asked.

"Why, he's soooo...male! Nothing like the refined gentlemen in London or Oxford. It's utterly unseemly."

Andromeda saw me standing in the doorway and jumped up, running across the room to grab my arm. "Cassie, quick, go hide. The viscount will be back in just a moment."

Andromeda sounded as if God was expected. Since when had any sort of a title impressed her? Gemini was the one caught up in such nonsense.

"You're not hurt," I accused.

Her rosy cheeks went nearly purple. "Well, I might be just a little. Now hurry." She shooed me toward a room and then ran back to the settee. A sharp knock on the door made me duck into the closest room.

"Miss Andrews?" the viscount called out. "May I come in?"

"Yes," Andromeda said.

The door opened. "Dr. Luden will be here shortly. Perhaps a cool cloth on your ankle will help."

"I'll get it," I heard Gemini say.

Biting my lip, I kept my ear pressed to the door.

"So, you say you and your sisters are from Oxford?" he asked.

"Yes," Andromeda's voice sounded breathless.

"And your older sister—"

"Cassie."

"Is a journalist?"

"A very important one."

"I see. And your father?"

"A professor of Greek history. He's close to discovering the temple to Apollo that Alexander the Great had built during his march to conquer the world. Currently, I am cataloging all of his finds."

"Something my father and mother should have hired someone to do. There are several family estates filled with things and nobody knows all that is there. They traveled extensively before her death."

"I'm sorry to hear of your loss."

"I never knew her. She died birthing my brother and me."

The door opened. "This makes twice in as many days you've called me, Killdaren. Though this patient looks a great deal healthier than yesterday's."

"I beg your pardon?" the viscount said. "What are you—?"

"My apologies, your lordship. The resemblance between you and your bother has grown over the years. I've not seen you in a long time."

"May I speak to you a moment over here?" the viscount's voice sounded ominous. "How is my brother? Has his condition improved?" They had moved near the door I listened from and had lowered their voices.

"Remarkably," said the doctor. "I couldn't believe it when I saw him yesterday. He can only be out for a short time, but it is more than we ever expected."

"And his leg?"

"That will never change, but you can't blame yourself for it."

There was a long pause before the viscount answered. "I'll always blame myself. I'll wait outside for a report about the lady's ankle and will take care of your fee." I shivered at the cold dismissal in his voice, even as I wondered what had happened between Sean and his brother.

I heard the doctor sigh as the viscount left the room. "Well, milady, let's see what the problem is?"

Andromeda cleared her throat. "Since resting, my discomfort has improved greatly, so I might not be in dire need of your services."

"Yes, we all thought Andrie was more injured at first," Gemini added.

"Ah. No amputation needed then," the doctor said.

"What?" Andromeda squeaked.

The doctor chuckled. "I think I can make you more comfortable with a bandage. It wouldn't hurt the viscount to feel compelled to inquire about your condition for a day or two, now would it?"

I'd have been more scandalized about the doctor's suggestion, except I kept thinking that if the viscount were around, I'd learn more about Sean Killdaren, his condition and why the viscount held himself responsible for it.

"This is utterly unbelievable." I marched across the floor after hearing my sisters' explanation for their scandalous breakfast, as well as a number of other activities. They'd been gadding about with the viscount, Lord Ashton and Mr. Colin Drayson. A picnic. Dinner at the inn. And an archeological excursion to see the Merry Maids, another circle of druid stones with a less lurid legend behind it than the Stone Virgins.

"How can you accuse us of being scandalous, Cassie? We've dressed and conducted ourselves as ladies. Having breakfast on the dining terrace can hardly be called scandalous."

"I'm referring to your inebriation. Cocktails?"

Aunt Lavinia sank into the nearest chair. "Good Lord! I definitely need my smelling salts."

Andromeda bit her lip and winced. "Well, that was a slight miscalculation. Have you ever had one?"

"Certainly not. Did you not know they're made with strong

spirits?"

"Mr. Drayson mentioned that, but I told him we were quite used to strong spirits."

"You lied?"

"It wasn't exactly a lie. All Andrews are known for their lively spirits and stubborn traits. I just simply applied another meaning to his words."

"Whatever for?"

"Well, Gemmi and I have discussed this and consider it our duty to help you in this investigation. Establishing an acquaintance with the gentlemen seemed the best way to ferret out important information. A venture that I daresay has already proved most useful."

"How so?"

"Well. For one thing, I know that the accusations against the viscount in the murder eight years ago are completely false. His brother must have done it."

"He didn't." My passionate denial was met by a bevy of arched brows. I even managed to shock myself over how strongly I felt about the matter. Andromeda must have discovered the viscount innocent when he touched her, which implied Sean guilty by default. My heart thumped. "He didn't kill Helen Kennedy. I know it." My cheeks burned.

Aunt Lavinia fanned herself. "Good Lord."

Andromeda set her chin to a stubborn angle. "Cassie, listen to yourself. You've known this man a short time and suddenly you are one hundred percent sure he's innocent of murdering a woman eight years ago?"

"Don't ask me how, I just know," I said stubbornly.

"Why?" Andromeda persisted.

"I just don't...think the Killdaren is guilty. Because he's..." I shook my head, unsure of how I knew Sean was innocent.

"See. You're not thinking clearly," she accused. "You're going to have to admit, Cassie, that you need us. You aren't the only intelligent person about. The investigation Gemmi and I are conducting by our innocent acquaintance with the viscount,

Lord Ashton, and Mr. Drayson is just as important as yours, and a great deal safer. Besides, the experience has been rather liberating. I think I have spent too much time with books and antiquities. And speaking of time, you need to stop wasting what little we have by lecturing us, and tell us what you've discovered."

Andromeda faced me fiercely and, I feared, rightly. But no matter how justified her argument, the situation sat ill with me. I could see no solution at this point, but wasn't willing to concede just yet. "First. You'll have no more cocktails at sunrise. Aunt Lavinia must be present at all occasions, and no there will be no more excursions to archeological sites, since Aunt Lavinia can't accompany you every minute. You'll all stay safely at the inn together."

Andromeda planted her hands on her hips. "But, Cassie, that isn't fair."

"Your promise, or we pack and leave immediately for home."

"And what about you? What about your safety? Are you willing to leave your post as a cleaning maid?"

Visions of Sean's deft hands sliding open the buttons of my dress brought a strangling heat to my face. "I'll not venture from the castle alone." I guiltily knew that my greatest danger lay within the stone walls. Well, that wasn't precisely true. I'd been alone when Jamie had taken me into the forest to the Stone Virgins.

"Andrie, I think you're being a bit unfair about this," Gemini interjected, surprising us both. "Cassie is scrubbing blisters onto her hands and living through untold hardships. She doesn't need to be worried about us here as well. The least we can do is promise to stay together and stay at the inn. Now let's not waste any more time."

Glad to leave the subject of my activities in the castle behind, I settled into a chair. "We have more time today. I don't have to be back until this evening."

"Good. Then we'll order lunch and a bath," Andromeda said. I started to tell Andromeda that the bath wasn't needed, but then decided the changes at the castle were too complicated to explain. It was easier to take the offered bath.

"Mary's letters arrived," Aunt Lavinia said. "I haven't been able to open the box, though." Her voice was tight with pain that I saw shadowed itself in my sisters' eyes. I realized that, although everyone was putting on a brave front, inside we all deeply felt the loss of Mary.

"I'll read them," I said softly. "I know it will be hard, but we need to learn of Mary's thoughts before she disappeared."

Aunt Lavinia sighed. "I know. So much of me hopes that there has been some strange mistake or accident, and that she'll reappear at any moment, even though I know that isn't possible. Not after this long. I also keep wondering why we stay on here. What more can be accomplished?" Aunt Lavinia buried her face into a handkerchief.

"We're still here because none of us are ready to leave Mary behind." Reaching over, I hugged my aunt, for I understood what she meant. Without a body, it was difficult to truly grieve for Mary. For no matter how much time passed, there was this irrational hope that somehow Mary would miraculously appear. Perhaps it was that hope that drove me and my sisters toward doing what we shouldn't. Or was it our way of grieving? Were we sifting through the remnants of Mary's life as she last lived it because we had no body to grieve over? More questions with no answers. The time with my sisters passed too quickly, and it was with an uneasy heart that I embraced everyone before leaving.

I found Bridget on her knees inside the church, praying fervently at the altar, and knew her mother must be worse. My heart wrenched. Walking up the aisle, I knelt beside her. I expected to see tears of sadness in her eyes as she looked toward me.

"Oh, Cassie," she whispered. "You won't believe it. The most wonderful thing has happened." She grabbed my arm and pulled me up, dragging me from the church as she chattered. "It's a miracle, I tell you."

"What? Is your mother better?"

She shook her head. "Don't know exactly about me mum just yet. There's a doctor seeing her and he's giving her some medicine that is helping. He isn't sure if she has the consumption or if it's another lung ailment and won't know for a week or two, I think, but there's a chance she might be all right and I'm going to pray for that and hope for that with all of my heart."

"Me too," I said.

"I'm going to have to thank Stuart, as well. It goes against my grain to think kindly about him for anything, but I don't have a choice."

"Did Stuart hire the doctor?"

"Must have. He's the only one beside you who knew. My mum was sure the doctor mentioned something about the Killdaren's man. So I'm figuring he meant the Killdaren's groomsman."

As we walked back to the castle, Bridget and I fell silent, each lost in our thoughts. As always the sound of the sea brought Mary to my mind, reminding me that I carried her letters with me. I was anxious to find a quiet moment to read them, hoping I'd learn more about those within the castle's stone walls.

Thundering up from the dunes as if he'd been waiting for us to appear along the village path raced Stuart on different horse. Though smaller than the black stallion he'd ridden before, the copper colored one ran faster and more gracefully than the other.

"Ladies." He dismounted. Trailing the horse behind him, he joined us on the path.

"Are you hanging around waiting for me to thank you proper?" The edge in Bridget's voice made me wince.

"You're so ornery you wouldn't know a proper thank-you even if the Queen herself introduced you to one."

"I do too."

"Prove it."

"Fine." Bridget grabbed Stuart's arm, turning him toward her. "Stuart Frye, I thank you for sending a doctor to care for my mum." Then she leaned up and pressed a plucky kiss to his cheek that surprised us all.

Stuart caught Bridget's arm before she could move away. "Do that again. I wasn't expecting it. Therefore, it wasn't a proper thank-you."

Bridget huffed, but relented. Her thank-you was a good bit shorter this time, and when she went to peck Stuart on the cheek, he turned his head at the last minute and Bridget's kiss landed on his mouth. He kissed her back. Embarrassed, I turned away to watch the pelicans swoop over the dunes. I wasn't sure what Stuart did, but I heard Bridget moan then almost screech.

Turning, I saw her smack Stuart on his shoulder then she jumped back, clearly nowhere near as outraged as she wanted to be.

"You're no proper gentleman," she huffed.

Grinning, he went back to his horse. "That's a title no bastard can lay claim to." He swung into the saddle, a cynical smile on his face. "But I am man enough to admit the truth. It wasn't me who hired a doctor to see your mother. I thought about doing so, but by the time I rode into the village to do it, the deed had already been done."

I burst into laughter. Bridget screeched again as if she'd run him through with a sword.

Stuart was man enough all right. Man enough to face Bridget's wrath from the top of a horse. I laughed harder.

Bridget glared at me then at Stuart. "You let me kiss you twice knowing that! How dare you!"

Stuart laughed. "Just because I'm not a gentleman doesn't mean I'm stupid, woman."

"Stuart Frye, it'll be a cold day in hell afore I kiss you again."

"Better fetch yourself a good winter coat, Bridget. Now that the deed is done and I know how much you like it, hell is about to freeze over."

# Chapter Twelve

After dinner that night, Bridget and I read the next story in the *Powerful Vampires and Their Lovers* book, "Forbidden Fruit". A story that confused us with every unfolding word.

*The deed was done.*

*Mary's head had rolled and the blood of her cousin stained her hands. Tears fell unchecked from the queen's eyes. She lay alone in her bed, feeling the fate of the world pressing in on her. There was no one she could trust. No one she could turn to. She'd known nothing but coldness and treachery her whole life, and in a tiny corner of her heart, kept hidden from the world, she longed for a moment, a single moment of love from someone who wanted nothing but herself.*

*"I am at your service, my queen."*

*Rolling to her side, knife from beneath her pillow clutched in her hand, she lashed out at the man, who had to be an assassin. Even from the grave, Mary's treachery reached to destroy. The man, the most darkly handsome she'd ever seen, laughed. Rather than jumping back from her blade, he stepped into harm's way and grasped her wrist, stopping her stab, a bare inch from his heart.*

*"Would you wound the man whom you've just cried out for? Did you not just wish to be loved?"*

*"I've no wish but for your death, knave!" She drew a breath. "G—"*

*Her scream for help was snuffed by the press of his hand. "Watch carefully, my queen," he said. Using his grip on her wrist* to guide the knife, he moved the blade from hovering over his heart to the very sensitive hollow of his throat. She'd never felt such strength as the man had. He pressed the knife to his throat, cutting into his vibrant flesh. A tiny trickle of blood appeared then disappeared. When he removed the blade, the cut healed over immediately.

The queen stared, disbelieving.

He moved the blade back to his heart and released her wrist. "Do your worst, if you must. It will not matter, I shall heal. But the wound to your heart this day will never heal. I feel your pain, for once, long ago, I too, had to kill in order to survive." Sliding his hand from her mouth, he placed his hand upon her breast, over her heart that beat so wildly. No man had ever touched her so, and the heat of his touch burned a fire through her breast that eased the pain that had been wrenching her apart.

"Who are you?"

He smiled, showing his fangs.

"Draco, a vampire who needs no nation, nor wealth, but only the love of a woman. A woman who would love me for me and not for the immortality that burdens my days." He slowly slid his hand away from her breast, leaving her aching for another touch. "There are those who are not fit to live a day, much less forever. So, my queen, do you call for your guards? Or would you care to share some wine and cheese? I'm curious as to why a woman who commands a nation can be so lonely that her cry reaches across centuries of time?"

"I must dress."

"Pity, I was about to ask you to undress."

"Only a virgin queen can call her heart fit to rule."

He smiled. "There is more than one way to pleasure. Perhaps, I'll show you."

"Perhaps I will call my guards after all."

He walked to the wine and poured two glasses. Then drinking from each, he brought one to her. She didn't call her guards. She didn't dress either.

"Blimey, what do you think he means by 'more than one

way to pleasure'?" Bridget asked, setting down the book.

"I'm certain it must have something to do with vampire lore." I stood and went to the wash basin. I felt the need of a cool cloth, and definitely had to occupy my hands. The urge to read more was almost overwhelming. Out of the corner of my eye, I saw Bridget close the book and lay back on her cot with a sigh.

"Is it really like that, do you think? Queen of a whole bloody nation and as lonely as a street urchin?"

"Yes. Look at the castle here. Don't you think Sean Killdaren, with all of his riches, is just as lonely?"

Bridget nodded and by some unspoken agreement, we both readied for bed and turned the lights out. Earlier I'd placed the box of Mary's letters under my bed and planned to read them as soon as Bridget fell asleep. Meanwhile, I lay back on the lumpy cot, running my finger over the ridges of the pheasant shell and its carved M, wondering if cries of the soul could be heard across time and distance, for surely, I had felt Mary's cry to me.

Turning to my side, I thought I detected a hint of Sean Killdaren's exotic scent. Surely my imagination had gone wild, but then the edge of an envelope cut into my cheek. Pulse racing ahead of the anticipation filling me, I searched inside my pillow case and found the letter.

It was blank on the outside, but I knew it was meant for me and I knew from whom it had come.

Sean.

My hands trembled as I lit a candle stub, thankful to hear Bridget's soft snore, for I don't think I would have been able to delay reading the note, even if it meant having the whole world read it, too. It didn't escape my notice that he'd placed the note intimately inside my pillow, rather than on it or beneath it, and that made heat curl inside me as hotly as if he'd slid into my bed. I'd invaded his privacy and now he'd intruded into mine, unexpectedly turning the tables.

He'd sealed the letter with a dragon imprinted upon gold wax. Inside, the card read:

*For tonight only, this card assures safe passage to the round room.*

*Upon my honor,*
*Sean Killdaren*

My heart caught then hammered. I'd expected flowery words, a proper apology for the liberties he'd taken. How dare he plague me with such a ludicrous, utterly scandalous temptation? I threw the invitation to the floor and plopped back into the bed. Then, deciding I needed to hide it, I stuffed it under my pillow and blew out the candle. Ha! Surely, he had to think I was about the most unintelligent being that ever set foot upon the earth.

Safe passage! Ha! Upon his honor! Ha! It was more likely to be a sinful passage, upon his bed.

I shifted, uncomfortable on the lumpy cot. Then I turned to my left side and tried to forget everything about Sean Killdaren. Instead I found myself recalling the way I had left him in the library. Then I heard the loud screeching from the round room. I could not spend another night with the noise and not know what it was. I had to go. Go to him or go insane. I dressed in one of the older gowns I'd brought with me without even lighting a candle. I didn't want to shed any light on the action I was taking. If I had, I might have let propriety raise a ruling hand.

Heat tingled my palms again as I opened the door to his wing. It gave me but a moment's pause, as did the remnants of his exotic scent lingering in the corridor. My heart pounded, determined to make every moment of my journey beyond any safe practical boundary fraught with apprehension. And I realized with an almost dismal sense of fatalism that Sean was right on more accounts than I ever wanted him to be.

Like Sean had accused in the library, I'd not the honesty to immediately give up this life for all knowledge and pleasure. Instead, I ventured out only a step at a time, but just as assuredly going to my own demise. This wasn't only about Mary anymore. Not when it came to Sean, the lonely man in the darkness of the night. This was about me, and what he made me feel. It didn't mean I wouldn't keep searching for an answer to what happened, but in that search, I was now looking for myself. The true Cassie that lay beneath all the prim and proper advice I'd been writing for years.

I expected, *wanted*, to find Sean waiting for my arrival, perhaps pacing the corridor, wondering if I'd come. It was the least he could have done after torturing me so. He wasn't. The only indication that he might be expecting me was that the door to the round room hung ajar, but the recesses beyond lay dark and now quiet.

I cleared my throat as I peeked into the room, my mind scrambling as to what to call him in person. I knew him more intimately than I should, and yet I barely knew him at all.

"Uh, Mr. Killdaren? Are you here?" Even I could hear the squeak of apprehension wobbling my voice.

His deep laugh came from somewhere up above. "Welcome to my lair where vampires feed and dragons breed. Enter if you dare."

I stopped and didn't even breathe.

He laughed again. "Surely you have more gumption than to let a few words frighten you away, lass."

"Where are you?" I moved inside the room, craning my neck to see beyond the shadows.

"My name is Sean. Take the iron stairs to the top. Light a candle if you must, but hurry and you'll be one of the few women in history to see the Great Nebula in Orion."

Nebula? I wasn't sure exactly what that was, other than it sounded similar to Dracula. I did know that Orion was a star constellation, but that was little consolation. Choosing not to light a candle, for I was still hiding in the dark from myself, I groped my way to the stairs and began to climb. Once I reached the second floor landing, I discovered another grated iron floor above where the night sky made the glass dome an invisible barrier from the wind.

Reaching the third floor landing, I tried to absorb what I found Sean doing and stay calm. Not an easy feat when I wanted to stamp my foot and rail at him.

Seated and engrossed in his task, the infuriating man didn't even bother to look my way as I approached.

"You're an astronomer?" My voice was ripe with accusation. "That's all! That's what you do all night that leaves the world whispering horrid stories of nefarious dealings? Why on earth don't you tell someone the truth?"

He motioned toward the monstrous telescope. "People deserve the tortures they let their own ignorance imagine themselves into. I've more important things to do than soothe the world. Come look at the nebula before I lose sight of it. The moon is wreaking havoc with my hunt tonight."

Hunt! Ha! If I hadn't been such a ninny with my head filled with vampire stories, I surely would have been able to figure this out. It was the only practical answer. A huge telescope had lurked under the black shroud in the middle of the room. Clamping my mouth shut as I desperately tried to swallow my outrage, I crossed to him. I had no doubt I deserved every tortuous moment I'd spent wondering what transpired in this room.

To learn what he did at night was something as innocuous as stargazing seemed to make a lamb out of a lion. Well, not exactly, I mused, setting my gaze on him. The shadows and the starlight intensified his dark power. Just as my hand tingled whenever I touched the dragon handles to his room, so did my body whenever near him—as if some magnetic force kept pulling little parts of me and attaching them to him.

"Come," he demanded. Leaning from the lone seat behind the telescope, he grabbed my hand and hauled me to the cushion he quickly abandoned. Then moving behind me, he urged me forward with a gentle nudge. "Look right here and tell me what you see."

Adjusting the tilt of my chin, I tried to peer into the glass. How I managed to formulate a sentence with the heat of his body pricking every nervous inch of my back, I held as miraculous as my first up close view of the heavens. "I see a misty cloud. I didn't know there were clouds so far away."

"There aren't. What you are seeing is a collection of gases in space that may very well be the womb from which future stars will be born."

"Good heavens." I peered again at the fiery mists. "I suppose stars have to be born too. I just never really thought about it. This is an odd telescope." Sitting beneath the huge tube was more than daunting. I felt like an ant peering into a tunnel the length of the Thames.

"Currently, it's the largest refracting telescope in existence. Thomas Grubbs in Dublin designed and built it for me a number of years ago."

"Then you've been studying the stars for a long time?"

"Continuously for the past eight years and on occasion before then."

Since Lady Helen's murder, I thought. I bit my lip, deciding it was now or never. "What happened eight years ago?"

His green eyes narrowed, grew cooler and distant. I felt the chill.

"I invited you here to see the stars," he said. "Not to talk about the past."

"And I want to see as many stars as you can show me. I never expected to have the heavens at my fingertips. I just have some questions that need answers."

"Don't you know that answering questions is like eating honey from a bee's nest? Every sweet answer you extract stirs up more stinging trouble. Some things are better left alone."

I sighed.

"I'll make you a deal. We stargaze first then I'll answer two questions."

"What if two aren't enough?"

He slid a finger down my sleeve and over my hand, then brushed his thumb against my palm, making me ache inside. "We could negotiate for more," he said softly. "I'll satisfy your curiosity if you'll satisfy mine. Your wit, your mind, your beauty urge me to explore you as I would the stars. In infinite detail." He leaned down, his mouth a breath away from kissing me.

All I could think about was how he'd sent me past all thoughts propriety, past all caring of anything but my desire to satisfy my want of him. And how little I really knew of him. I turned my head to feel his breath caress my ear as he sighed. "That doesn't sound like a promise of safe conduct to me."

He stepped back and laughed before answering. "Eliminating hostile advances doesn't exclude friendly, mutual interaction."

The feeling akin to having a fire lit beneath the iron grate at my feet grew hotter, roasting me alive. I wet my lips. "I believe the stars await us."

"Coward." He softly teased, as he stepped behind me and I shivered with pleasure.

I stiffened my spine a number of degrees, saving me from becoming a puddle at his feet again. "I'll have you know there is nothing cowardly about prudence."

"That would depend on your objective, I should think, but if the lady wants stars, I'll gladly satisfy her. We'll start in the east and work across the horizon to some new discoveries I think I've made."

"New discoveries?"

"I'll explain later."

More than an hour flew by as my mind fed on the wealth of information he shared, and my body's awareness of him multiplied. From the way his voice deepened and the increasing accidental brushings of his hands and body against mine as he positioned the telescope, I thought he suffered a similar affliction. I never knew a man's hands could be so...stimulating. The strength of them and their adeptness and care at manipulating the dials and knobs was as mesmerizing as his voice. It showed a side of him that stood in contrast to the harshness, as if beneath the rough barrier he held up against the world there was a man who deeply cared, a man who'd arranged a bath in the middle of the night for me, a man who'd...seen to Bridget's family, I thought, suddenly realizing that was why he'd gone into the village Saturday. The doctor's comment to the viscount when mistaking him for Sean, about meeting him twice in as many days and the health of the patients, fell into place.

"You arranged for Bridget's mother's care," I said softly.

He stilled a second then shrugged, keeping his attention focused on the lens. "Are you interested in learning more about the stars?"

I promised myself to return to the subject another time and followed his lead. "I had no idea there was so much to learn."

Looking up from the scope, he smiled slowly, somehow able to run his gaze over my whole person though we were tightly cramped in the space of one seat. Over the past hour we had progressed from him standing behind me to him sitting beside me. It had been a practical progression that suddenly seemed utterly impractical. Every nerve within me throbbed to the rhythm of his voice and the stroke of his touch.

"There are few subjects that I find as fascinating as the study of the stars," he said.

"And what would those be?"

"Curious Cassie. Are you sure you want to know? Philosophy and religion aren't on the list."

"Then what? Science?"

His gaze dropped to my mouth, lingered, then dropped further, making my breasts ache from the fire in his gaze. My eyes widened, as my mind followed his unspoken lead and the space we were in shrank. "That's not a study," I said as hotly as my body flushed.

"Oh, it most certainly is. One that is as ancient as the study of the stars. Over the centuries there have been a multitude of books written on the subject."

"I've never heard of them."

He stood. "Not surprising, given our present culture. If you need proof, I can direct you to the bookcase downstairs that they fill. You might find some interesting reading there."

I swallowed. A whole bookcase? Not just a shelf? Good Lord. Standing, I slid from behind the telescope and moved away. "No. Thank you. I will accept your word on the matter and I will stay with the study of the stars, please. Given that my sisters and I are named after them, I should have taken more interest in them before."

Instead of letting me gain the distance I sought, he followed me. "Cassie? Cassandra?"

"Cassiopeia."

He laughed. "The queen. How fitting. You've a queenly nature. You move and speak in such a way as to command others to follow. You're demanding."

"Cassiopeia was a vain, selfish queen who caused a great deal of trouble." I frowned. I'd decided my name was a fluke that had nothing to do with me, an oddity I'd had no choice but to forgive my parents for giving to me.

He stepped closer to me, almost too close, and continued as if he hadn't heard me. "And you're beautiful," he said softly.

I opened my mouth to deny that, too, but something inside of me wanted to absorb his wooing words, even though I knew them to be false. The resulting conflict must have left my mouth agape. He reached over and tapped my chin up. "Hasn't anyone ever told you that before?"

Meeting his gaze, I shook my head.

"Very remiss of them." He studied me a moment then moved past me, going to the railing. "What stars are your sisters named after?"

Was that all he was going to say? Remiss of them? As if the subject was of little import? When a gentleman told a lady she was beautiful, didn't he expound upon it a little more? Or at least kiss her? It took a moment for my mind to function as it should.

"Actually, I think it was more because of my parents' fascination with all things Greek that led to our names, rather than the stars. I'm the oldest; Andromeda is next, and finally Gemini."

"I hear fondness in your voice. It must have been an awful scandal to drive you from your family. What happened?"

Caught in my lie, my stomach flipped, making me feel as if he'd focused his telescope on me and had turned up the magnification to a burning acuity. I couldn't seem to force the necessary lies from my mouth. I shook my finger at him. "Very clever, Mr. Killdaren, but I'm not going to let you get away with it."

"What?"

"Distract me from asking the two questions you promised in our bargain. I've stargazed with you. Now it's your turn to truth-gaze with me."

"I'd hoped you'd forgotten." Rather than look at me, he stared out into the night and I joined him at the railing, seeing the night blanket the sleepy countryside and the darkened gardens below. Only the blackness of the maze was discernable from the rest, as if it could never really belong.

"Tell me what happened, with Lady Helen. With your brother."

"That's two questions."

I counted it as one and wanted to protest, but decided to argue later. "Agreed."

He hesitated, gazing out at the night. "There isn't much to tell other than all of life can change in the twinkling of an eye, or a star for that matter. Eight years ago my brother, two close friends of ours, and I had plans to join the local festivities celebrating Samhain, and then watch a meteor shower the night of October thirty-first. Along the shore, south of here, is a very prominent cliff near Dragon's Cove called Dragon's Point. It is perfect for stargazing without the accoutrements of an observatory. Tensions between my brother and I had stretched to the breaking point. We were fool enough to fall in love with the same woman, and even more foolish for believing either of us could walk away unscathed, or escape the curse than had been laid upon us from birth. We'd thought it simple to let the lady choose, and both of us wooed her relentlessly."

My mind boggled at the thought. One Killdaren was more than I could handle. Two would leave a woman senseless.

"Unfortunately, Helen couldn't make a choice. Until that night, that is."

Silence followed and stretched to the point where I

snapped.

"Surely, the tale doesn't end there."

"I wish it did. But you are right, it doesn't."

"Then who did she choose?"

"Neither of us. She sent Alex and me a note, separately, asking us to meet her at the center of the maze. Alex at ten that night. Me at eleven. Neither Alex nor I told the other, thinking that we'd been the chosen one. When she told me that she couldn't marry either of us because she loved both of us and had decided she was running away to a convent so her father couldn't force her to marry anyone else, I stormed away angry, hating Alex for what he'd done. I'd been the one to pursue Helen first, and thought he'd now ruined all of our lives. The villagers were drinking heavily at the Samhain celebrations, and I joined them before going to Dragon's Point to see the meteor shower."

"And?"

"At midnight Helen was found in the center of the maze murdered. Alex found me at Dragon's Point and accused me of the deed. I'd been seen leaving the maze last, which of course was true since I'd met with her last. I accused Alex. We'd both been drinking and we fought bitterly, seemingly trying to kill each other. We fought to the edge of the cliff. I fell over."

This time, when he didn't say more, I went to him, touching his arm. "I'm sorry."

"Me too. Alex should have let me die. The curse would have been done with, and I'd have no pain." He pulled away from my touch and began walking. I hardly noticed his limp, for I had eyes only for his heart.

"Come, I'll escort you to the stairs in the kitchens, then I'll return and lower the telescope back into place. These pulleys are deafening."

I'd learned the source of the wild screeching and didn't care. "You can't leave it there."

He turned, folding his arms across his chest. "Is there something wrong with the telescope where it is?"

I blinked. "What? Who cares about the telescope! You can't leave the story there. If your brother saved you, then why don't you speak to him?"

"Your two questions are up."

"Then I'll negotiate for another."

He walked right up to me, pressing himself to me. "Would you?"

"Yes," I said, breathless.

"What are you offering?"

I looked at his mouth, thinking of how his lips had felt against mine, of the power and the passion with which he'd branded me. "A kiss?"

"I've already tasted your kiss. And while worth almost any price, I'm of the mind to experience what I've yet to know. Just as you must have lain abed every night aching to know about this room and me, I have lain abed and dreamt of you. Dreamt of making love to you, of feasting on the lushness of your breasts, licking the cream of your skin, and tasting the very essence of your desire. I ache to know you as deeply and as painfully as I ache to move. Tonight particularly so. I offered you safe conduct and I am a man of my word, but I have limits and we've reached them. My bed or the stairs, Cassie?"

# Chapter Thirteen

*I chose his bed and he knelt before me, his gaze burning through my clothes. "I offer all that I am and all that I have to you."*

*Sliding my fingers from his, I cupped his cheek in my hand, feeling the rough texture of his evening beard, absorbing the warmth of his skin. "I fell in love with you the moment I saw your picture. I cannot deny you."*

*He surged to his feet, sweeping me into his arms. "You're mine. No excuses this time." As before, he carried me swiftly down the short corridor to his bedchamber, but this time he set me gently upon his bed. Leaning down, he set his lips on mine. Reverently at first, then more demanding as the heady desire between us ignited and flamed to a scorching fire of need.*

*I pressed to him, wanting more, restless for things I'd never known. Groaning, he pulled at my buttons, impatiently pushing aside the rough wool to expose the wispy chemise that covered my breasts.*

*Sitting back, he gazed down at me, running his finger across my lips, down my neck, then splayed his hand against my chest. I felt branded by the heat of his touch and the potency of his gaze. "You are so beautiful. I must see all of you now."*

*I groaned. My desire pulsed so hotly within me that I had to be afire.*

*The tiny pearl buttons of my chemise flew as he ripped open the delicate cotton and—*

"Cassie! Wake up."

"What?" I reared up, blinking in confusion in the dark. "What's wrong?"

"Ack, that's what I was going to ask you. You're moaning in your sleep as if you were burning alive. Do you have a fever?" Bridget sat on the edge of my cot.

Gathering my wits, I realized where I was. My room. My bed. I hadn't taken Sean up on his challenge. I'd chosen the stairs rather than his bed, but I had dreamed otherwise.

I grabbed Bridget's arm, awed. "I had a dream again!" I'd counted the one of Sean as a vampire a fluke. Now that I'd dreamed of him twice, I felt this warming sense of being normal for the first time in my life. Well, as normal as a woman could feel, having dreamt of being ravished!

"Must have been a bad one."

"Oh, no. It was, well, wonderful." And Good heavens, so utterly scandalous that I could barely think straight. I knew my cheeks had to be scarlet, perhaps permanently so.

Bridget laughed. "You dreamed about the Killdaren, didn't you."

"No, I...yes. Have you ever done that? Dream about a...well..."

"A man and all those things you think aren't proper to talk or think about?" She sighed. "Nearly every night since coming here."

"Three years? You've been dreaming about Stuart that long?"

"Who said anything about Stuart?" She sounded irritated as she stood and moved back to her own cot. "We'd better sleep more now. The sun's going to be rising soon."

I wasn't about to let Bridget escape my question so easily. "Then is it Mr. Killdaren, or any of the other men?"

She sounded as if she hit her pillow a couple of times. "No. It's Stuart. And you can just wipe that grin off your face. Even if I can't exactly see it, I know it's there."

Smiling, I laid back down. "Why are you so prickly to him?"

"He has this education and all. What would he want with me besides getting beneath my skirt? One of these days he's going to go back to the city and he'd leave me behind, so it's better I don't like him at all than to be left with a broken heart. Now let's get back to sleep." She yawned, though I thought it a pretense to end our conversation rather than sleepiness.

Once comfortable on the cot, my mind drifted back over last night and the choice Sean had issued in an almost pain-filled voice. "My bed or the stairs, Cassie?"

It had taken every fiber of my being to choose the stairs. How could he be so attracted to a woman as simple as myself, a woman he thought to be a downstairs maid! How I could ache so deeply for him? Inside, I was still poised on that moment of wanting to forsake everything just to be with him, do anything to soothe my burning and to ease his pain. Marriage between us was out of the question.

What man would marry a woman who dreamed of other people's death? Then there was the matter of my station in life. Though not the immediate heir to an earldom, if Sean did marry, he would need to marry a woman far above me, a woman with a dowry worthy of the Killdaren's wealth.

There were some proprieties in society that were unchangeable, and status was one that few ever broke free from. Besides position, there was Sean's belief in the curse itself. Though I gave little countenance to it, for I truly thought curses in the same realm as vampires and fairies, I knew Sean didn't take the curse as lightly.

He believed, and as long as he did, it would stand in his way of ever having a future.

Even so, all of me wanted to experience those things with Sean Killdaren that were utterly improper for an unmarried woman to think about, much less want with every beat of her heart. He was like a dark prince from a strange world that I couldn't resist, and didn't want to either.

I woke early, my eyes scratchy from the lack of sleep. My body protested, wanting more rest, but I knew that if I didn't at least try and read one of Mary's letters this morning before Bridget woke, I wouldn't be able to until late that night. Even then, so much of me hoped there would be another invitation for stargazing in my pillow case.

Pulling out the box, I found Mary's letters weren't organized at all. It would have taken too long to put them in chronological order this morning, so I closed my eyes and pulled one out. Opening it, I first noted the date. Almost seven months ago. January of this year.

*Dear Mother,*

*As much as I long for your company, and the comfort of your smile, I know that my decision to come to Rebecca a right one. She's a bright child that I hope one day will gain the confidence to live beyond the walls of her room. I've hesitated to write of the others here at the castle except to give you brief captions of them, but even more so than Rebecca, those that live here live in a world of darkness.*

*The light of life that so filled my childhood doesn't shine into this corner of the world. I hope that I can change that. Sometimes I wish I could bring all of my family here and let them fill the rooms with their zest.*

*I'm painting the sea in my spare time, capturing moments of golden light and crashing waves for a special friend who hasn't been able to see sunlight for a very long time.*

I thought I had a good idea who the friend she spoke of was. Sean. What I didn't know was why he couldn't see the light, for I knew he could see, and how special did special mean?

The rest of the letter spoke of family matters, inquiring about my mother and father, and me and my sisters. That Mary had asked about me, at a time I'd been so involved in answering the letters of strangers for my column, stung my heart and brought tears to my eyes. I'd let something precious slip through my fingers because I'd been too caught up in the proper and practical. I'd never be able to go back and recapture that moment, when I could have written to Mary, could have discovered what joys and worries filled her life. Folding the letter, I returned it to the box, and slid it back safely beneath my cot.

Reading Mary's letters was going to be harder than I ever imagined it would be. I determined that, somehow, I would bring about all those things that Mary had hoped for.

"Did you like the happy tune, poppet?" I asked, stretching my fingers against the ivory keys.

Rebecca shifted on the piano bench next to me, nodding her head, her rag doll clasped tightly in her arms. It was the first time she'd joined me on the bench. "More, p-p-please, Miss C-c-cass."

"Certainly. I've a rhyming song that my sisters and I used to play all the time when we were little. I want you to sing it with me."

She shook her head, hunching her shoulders and wrenching my heart at how little she believed she could do. "After you learn the words, I'll teach you the game. It's very easy and I daresay one that you could win better than anyone else in the castle."

Scrunching her brow in doubt, she sat silent for so long a moment that I feared she would back away from the progress we'd made. Finally, she whispered, as if she didn't want anyone but me to hear. Odd, for we were alone in the music room, a place that I still was unable to relax in. "I c-c-could w-w-win?"

"Yes," I whispered back. "In the game, whoever reaches the ground first wins, and since you're the littlest person around, you can do that better than anyone else. This used to be my sister Gemini's favorite game to play, since she was the youngest of us all."

"Can I m-meet your s-s-sisters?"

"I hope someday, poppet." My heart squeezed painfully. How could I leave those at Killdaren's Castle and never come back? "I truly hope that someday you can. And then you can play this game and even have a real tea party.

"This is how it goes: Ring around the rosie, A pocket full of posies. Ashes, Ashes, we all fall down." I played the lively tune, which in my mind had little to do with the death it sang of and more to do with fun, though I doubted the children of London thought that when the black death had raged. "Now sing the first word with me—Ring."

"R-r-ring," Rebecca parroted.

"Ring around," I sang.

"R-r-ring around."

I nearly stopped playing the tune as I absorbed the fact that Rebecca hadn't stuttered on her second word. "Ring around the rosie." I watched her carefully.

"R-r-ring around the rosie."

Tears bit my eyes. I was sure Rebecca herself didn't realize that she hadn't stuttered. "You sing beautifully."

Rebecca shook her head.

I stopped playing and put my arm around her. "You do. You sing like the littlest angel in the world."

"M-m-mary," Rebecca suddenly cried out, shocking me. My heart skipped a beat then thundered. She flung herself from my arms and cried out again. "M-m-mary!"

I reached for her, catching hold of her hand. "Rebecca, stop. It's all right poppet. Don't be afraid."

She shook her head, trying to pull away from me as she clutched her doll so tightly I thought she'd break her fingers. I wouldn't let her go. I didn't want her to hurt herself and whatever was causing her this deep pain, I didn't want her to be alone in it.

Her breaths came in sharp gasps and she trembled horribly.

I sat on the ground, pulling her into my lap, and wrapped my arms tightly around her and her rag doll. She struggled, screaming for Mary over and over. I wondered if I were doing the right thing and decided to hold her closer, tighter, and to sing softly. A lullaby my mother had used to comfort me when I had dreamed of my grandmother's death came to mind and I sang softly.

I was about to give up when Rebecca stopped thrashing and pressed herself to me. Crying tears, but no longer screaming.

"You've wrought a miracle."

The soft whisper came from behind me, toward the back of the stage.

Turning slightly, I found Prudence there, her hands fisted, worry and pain etched deeply upon her face. How did she get there?

"I didn't see you come in."

"I've been here since I heard her cry out. There are stairs backstage that lead up to my and Rebecca's wing."

I wanted to gasp, wondering why someone hadn't seen fit to tell me that, but then bit my tongue. Exactly who was I? A mere maid, and unless there was a particular reason I would need to know about the staircase in order to perform my duties, no one would ever mention it to me. Learning of the staircase would go a long way toward explaining how Rebecca had appeared that first day when Bridget and I were cleaning the music room. I wondered if it might not also explain how Rebecca was getting past her nurse to wander alone.

"May I hold her now?" Prudence asked, surprising me with her polite and gentle tone.

I started to rise. "Of course."

"Stay there," Prudence knelt beside me, kissed Rebecca's head. I saw tears fill the mother's eyes, seeing her daughter so wrenched her painfully. "It's Mum, precious. Can you hear me?"

Hiccupping, Rebecca nodded.

Prudence held out her arms. "There now, come to Mum, and I'll make it all right."

Rebecca plunged herself into her mother's arms. Prudence pulled her tightly against her bosom and kissed the child's head again. "She's never quieted this quickly before. It's always taken at least a day and the sleeping medicine the doctor prescribed for her to calm her down."

Prudence rocked Rebecca a few minutes, humming off-tune to her. "I heard you sing, dumpling. The lady is right, you sing beautifully."

We both looked down at Rebecca, only to find she'd fallen asleep, having likely exhausted herself.

"Can I help you get her to her room?" I whispered.

"Yes, thank you. If you'll help me rise, I can carry her up."

When Prudence was upright and Rebecca safely tucked into her mother's arms, she turned to me. "Please, will you come see me? Have tea in my room? I'd like to speak to you about Rebecca."

"Yes, of course."

"I'll send for you this afternoon." Then she smiled softly, "It will most likely put Mrs. Frye into a complete dither."

I grinned. "Imagine that."


Though in any ordinary household, the housekeeper would in no way ever deny the request of a person in a higher position than herself, when it came to Mrs. Frye, I had no assurance she wouldn't find a way to stop me from going to tea. My back ached and my mind spun. The center hall of Killdaren's Castle, though not as vast as the Hall of Mirrors at Versailles, was just as daunting to clean. I polished the marble floor like a whirlwind, determined to finish it before teatime. Bridget had joined me in the almost impossible task. She'd never failed to help me ever since I arrived at Killdaren's Castle, and it made my heart squeeze. Even though she'd not get tea herself, Bridget worked harder than I to remove any excuse Mrs. Frye might have to keep me from meeting with Rebecca's mother. As we cleaned, I swore that someday soon I'd make sure Bridget had tea every day.

Meanwhile, I puzzled over Rebecca's situation. Prudence was so loving to Rebecca that I couldn't reconcile her keeping the nurse to care for Rebecca. Nor could I understand why Rebecca, even though blind, was so frightened.

Bridget and I were just finishing the floor when Mrs. Frye

appeared.

Knees currently numb, I stood, pressing my hand to my aching back and surveying the perfection of the floor.

"Humph. Miss Prudence has requested that you come to her." Mrs. Frye eyed me as if I'd stolen the silverware.

"Then it appears I've finished just in time."

"You're to go to her quarters."

I started untying the apron I'd soiled.

"Don't think you're done for the day," Mrs. Frye harped in. "There are more chores that need doing and you missed a spot by the banister."

"I'll take care of that, Mrs. Frye," Bridget said.

"No. I've other chores for you. She can finish it after seeing Miss Prudence. I don't think she'll be but a minute."

I opened my mouth to protest. Bridget and I had done everything we were supposed to have done for the day. Bridget caught my eye and sent me a silent warning not to argue. I bit my lip, feeling outraged and frustrated.

I moved toward the stairs that would take me to the second floor. "Then if you will excuse me, I won't be long."

"Where do you think you're going?" Mrs. Frye shouted.

Turning, I blinked at her with surprise.

"The backstairs, missy. I warned you that I'd not tolerate you putting on any airs, and you've done nothing but that since you came here. Be careful or you'll not have a job."

Anger burned the back of my throat, partly because of Mrs. Frye's inflexible harshness, and partly because I'd given her the opportunity to reprimand me.

Servants used the servants' stairs even if it wasn't convenient, even if it cost them twice as much labor. I would have expounded on the propriety of that at length in "Cassiopeia's Corner", advising that all rules had to be followed to preserve order. As I hurried to the backstairs in the kitchen, I determined that if I ever were in charge of such a vast holding as a castle, I'd toss propriety on its ear and set rules that made sense.

"Come in," Prudence called out after my knock.

From the richly elaborate dresses Prudence and Rebecca wore, I expected to see such ostentation in their surroundings. I didn't. Their living quarters on the second floor were highly simple compared the rest of the castle and the fashionable decors of the day. Like the pastel hues of the room Mary used across the hallway, this room carried a theme of soft blues. Elegant and peaceful were the words that came to my mind.

Prudence motioned me to a chair across from her then sat herself.

"Thank you for inviting me." The numbness in my knees had turned into a throb and I thankfully sank into the heavenly cushions of a buttoned wing chair.

On a marble topped table between us an elaborate array of goodies was set, and the mouth-watering scent of brewed tea and fresh scones filled the air. Prudence asked about my day, then after pouring us both a cup and handing me a plate piled with almond-speckled scones, she went directly to the heart of the matter. "I've appreciated the time you've taken with Rebecca. I think it is helping her."

"I have grown to care a great deal for Rebecca, and I have some concerns about her situation here."

Prudence set her teacup down, her cheeks flushing. "I have little care for what the villagers or anyone else thinks about my presence in the Killdarens' lives. All I care about is that Rebecca has the best of everything, and all the mean gossip and judgmental busybodies in the world aren't going to change that."

I choked on my scone. "Good heavens, you completely misunderstood me, Miss Prudence. I meant Rebecca's crying today, and uh, if I may say so, the harshness of her nurse."

Prudence drew a deep breath then picked up her teacup. "My apologies. I had a horrifying experience with the villagers and I am overly sensitive to criticism in regards to my living here."

"I am so sorry to hear of it. Not to pry where I shouldn't, but what happened in the village?"

"If the Killdaren hadn't saved me, I think they would have burned me alive or stoned me to death."

I set my teacup down with a rattle this time. "You're serious aren't you?"

"Unfortunately, yes. The world does not take kindly to unmarried women being with child."

"So, Mr. Killdaren stopped the villagers from harming you?"

"He and Stuart stood against a mob of raging villagers. They rode up on horses with pistols cocked and the Killdaren told the villagers he'd killed before and would have no qualms killing again. The first man or woman who harmed me was dead. They all ran."

I wanted to say a word or a phrase that would lead her into telling me if Sean was Rebecca's father, but I couldn't force the words from my lips. Deep inside of me hid the irrational notion that if I didn't know for a fact that Sean had fathered Rebecca, then I could blame it on his brother, Viscount Blackmoor.

"How long has Rebecca had difficulty with her speech?" I said, picking up my teacup and abruptly changing the subject before my habit of seeking out the truth at all costs could exercise itself.

"Just recently. She went through the traumatic experience of having someone she deeply cared for die. I think you playing music for her has helped her grief."

For a moment I wondered if the china I held would snap. "Mary? The person she cries for?"

"Yes." Prudence's eyes widened with surprise.

"I'd guess as much from what I've heard others say. What happened?"

"She drowned while on a picnic with my daughter. Exactly what happened, no one knows for sure, but it must have been awful. Rebecca hasn't been able to speak of it. She only cries inconsolably whenever something reminds her of it. Mary used to call Rebecca a little angel. I think you said that to her when you spoke of her singing."

"Yes." I was incapable of saying anything more at that moment.

"When Rebecca sang today, I noticed she didn't stutter as much."

"I noticed, too."

"An amazing surprise, and one that gives me hope she will recover from what happened."

"Yes." I had to force myself to breathe. "I think the music distracts her mind from the fear that has her in its grip."

"I would like for you to play for her every day and encourage her to sing, if you would. Perhaps this will help Rebecca recover faster."

I nodded, not trusting myself to speak. I deeply wanted Rebecca to heal, and a part of me couldn't help but wonder that if Rebecca overcame her fear, she might be able to tell me what happened to Mary.

"Good. I'll speak to Mrs. Frye about the matter. Now what do you have to say about Rebecca's nurse?"

"I feel that Rebecca's nurse is unnecessarily harsh, and at times speaks to Rebecca in what I would consider to be a less than nurturing manner. You obviously love your daughter greatly, and I wondered if you were aware of the situation."

Prudence sat forward, nearly at the edge of her seat, a frown cut deep into the perfection of her features. "I am aware that the nurse can be stern on occasion, but I've never witnessed her treating my daughter harshly. Do you speak of a specific incident?"

"Well, yes. A few weeks ago, when Rebecca heard me playing the piano, she must have slipped down the stairs to the theater without her nurse knowing. Bridget and I brought Rebecca back to Nurse Tolley and the woman screamed at Rebecca, frightening her."

"I shall have a word with her then. I haven't spoken to Nurse Tolley about her rigid demeanor because the nuns at the convent school who educated me were by far much harder task masters."

"Thank you." I didn't know what else I could say. I had to be satisfied with the situation for now. Being able to play for Rebecca every day would put me into more contact with Nurse

Tolley. At least I could report to Rebecca's mother if I saw any more incidents of ill treatment.

"Whatever are you doing here?" Prudence demanded, looking at me as acutely as Stuart had. "You're an educated, accomplished woman. Why are you here as a maid, and not teaching as a governess?"

"I needed the job, and no governess positions were available." I stood. "Mrs. Frye wanted me back quickly. Thank you for inviting me."

Prudence blinked with surprise and I saw a flash of disappointment cross her face, making me sorry for my hasty retreat. She stood. "Yes, thank you for coming."

I had to bite my tongue to keep from suggesting we have tea again. I'd hurt Prudence by rudely cutting the tea short, and as I walked from Prudence's room, I had the same feeling as I'd experienced over Mary's letter that morning—as if I were once again allowing fear and caution to rule my life.

# Chapter Fourteen

That night after the evening meal of a savory fish stew, Bridget helped me again in teaching the servants to read and write. It was the last thing I wanted to be doing. I still ached from scrubbing the center hall, and all I wanted was a bath and bed. I refused to think about stargazing again.

I doubted Sean would issue any more safe passages, and I didn't dare go without one.

The tables, counters and chairs in the kitchens provided ample space to teach the servants and the room soon filled. As in our previous classes, everyone appeared, tired but eager. Jamie still sat as far from me as possible and kept his angry gaze focused on me continually, an unnerving situation I had yet to be able to change, though there'd be no more explosions from him since I'd mentioned Mary's name last week.

Jamie resented me, as if I was responsible for Mary's death. He clearly didn't want to be here, but he couldn't stay away from me, either. In some odd way, I understood. As I'd grown closer to those around me, I found myself questioning if anyone had really killed Mary, and it became more and more a possibility to me that my cousin had accidentally drowned. That still left the mystery of Lady Helen's murder, for I couldn't believe Sean was guilty. If Andromeda had read the viscount's mind correctly, then someone else in Lady Helen's life had killed her.

Leaving my thoughts, I started the class writing the alphabet again, everyone taking turns with the few materials we had, when Stuart entered, carrying a huge sack.

"What are you doing here?" Bridget demanded under her breath when Stuart reached us.

I winced at the antagonism barbing her voice. Stuart only grinned and lifted a brow, whispering back. "Your increasing irritation proves that your affection for me grows every day, so I forgive your rudeness."

I had to cough to cover my laugh or Bridget would have never forgiven me.

She glared at Stuart. "Why you...you...there aren't words to describe your...your..."

"Stop blabbering rubbish and come help me pass out these supplies the Killdaren ordered," he said softly. "Your hands are not the only helping hands in the world."

My fake cough turned into a real one as I choked over the questions stuck in my throat. Learning that Sean not only knew about the classes, but had also helped with the supplies, reached deeply inside me. By the time Stuart and Bridget had emptied the sack, everyone had paper, writing implements, a Bible, and a primary book showing both the alphabet and numbers. Seeing tears gather in their eyes as they ran their work-roughened hands over their new belongings tightened the emotion welling inside me.

Sean was not the man he, and the rumors about him, would have the world to believe.

Stuart proved his helping hands by staying to assist others with the reading and writing after giving out the supplies. He also proved his point about Bridget's affection. Her irritation grew by the minute.

The class lasted an hour, and then another twenty minutes passed as everyone shared some conversation before leaving. Stuart was the last to go, and Bridget's temper had built to an explosive point by then. After he left, she stomped across the room, setting the kitchens back to rights.

"Ack, if that man thinks being here is going to change my opinion of his womanizing ways, he's in for a mighty disappointment."

"I think he came because he genuinely wants to help. I also think he's the one who let Sean Killdaren know we needed supplies. And if he is wooing you by doing so, what's wrong with that? You're the one who defended the vampire luring the lady from her loneliness in the story."

"Humph. That story doesn't have anything to do with Stuart and me. Besides, the man didn't take his gaze off me the whole time he was here. It's enough to make a woman insane, it is."

I understood, as being with Sean made me feel that way. "You'll feel better once we soak in the tub with some rose bath salts."

"You and your baths. You think they're an answer to the world's woes."

I hid a grin and headed for the laundry area where Mrs. Murphy had left steamy water waiting for us. Bridget might bluster about bathing every night, but she no longer balked. We filled the tubs and as I undressed she put the rose bath salts in my tub then went to scent hers.

"We're out," she declared.

Holding my robe up for modesty's sake, I slid the curtains open to find Bridget pouting over the empty jar.

"Don't worry. There are more in our room on the desk."

"I'll be right back." She dashed out.

Humming to myself, I slid into the steamy water, feeling the aches and pains ease and my eyelids close. But there were tensions inside me that no amount of warm water could ease. My desire for Sean and the mystery about Mary were uppermost in my mind. My other concern was the fact that someday soon I would have to leave. I couldn't masquerade as a maid forever. I had a life and a family and a future I would eventually have to face. At that moment, I couldn't reconcile the person I had now become since arriving at Killdaren's Castle with the me I'd been most of my life.

I stood on a precipice, and any direction I might choose, I would lose that which I could not live without.

A loud crash brought my eyes wide open to find Jamie

standing in the laundry room. A bucket that he'd obviously dropped rested at his feet. He stared at me, mouth agape.

Shrinking deeper into the water, I crossed my arms over my breasts, gasping for air enough to scream but only croaked like a dead toad.

"Ma-a...ry," he called, moving a step closer. Then another step, reaching his hands out for me. "Mary hurt you."

In an instant I envisioned him dragging me naked to the stone virgins. Horror ripped away my paralysis and added a sharpness to my voice that made Mrs. Frye at her worst seem like a lamb. "Stop immediately! Mary's dead! Do you hear me! Get out of here now!"

"Mary!" he shouted, his cry of anguish reverberating in the room. I held my breath as he slammed a fisted hand to his heart then ran from the room.

I would have immediately left the tub, but my legs wouldn't work and a black haze covered my vision. I buried my face in my palms and drew deep breaths, determined not to faint and drown.

Another clattering of the bucket and breaking glass made me scream. A scream that died the second I saw Bridget sprawled on the floor with a broken blue vase before her and soft pink roses scattered everywhere. She gasped then burst into tears.

My bath had turned into a circus. Dragging myself from the water and donning a robe, I hurried on shaky legs and put an arm around Bridget.

"It's all right."

"No, it's not. He gave me flowers. Nobody's ever given me flowers and now I've broken them."

"Who—" I cut off my question, staring at the roses Stuart had to have given Bridget. A soft smile settled in my heart.

I patted Bridget's back. "Not to worry. You climb into the tub and calm yourself while I find something to put these beautiful roses in. Our room will smell like a garden for days and then I'll show you how to dry them so that you can keep them forever."

Sniffing, Bridget turned a tearful, hopeful gaze my way. "He really likes me, doesn't he? Even though I don't have a lick of education."

"Yes. And don't belittle yourself, Bridget McGowan. You've a tremendous amount of wit, a big heart, and as far as education goes, that's something that changes for the better every day. So it doesn't matter, now does it?"

"No," Bridget said, as we both rose to our feet. She went to the tub and I dressed in fresh clothes then looked for a vase and a broom.

Once I had things cleaned, I brought the flowers to Bridget, having found a small stone urn that I didn't think would be missed. Bridget finished dressing and pulled the flowers into her arms, breathing deeply of the roses, her cheeks as pink as the blooms.

"There's something very special about you, Cassie. No matter what happens, there is this light inside you that chases away the darkness."

Smiling, I turned from Bridget and gathered up our belongings. I walked into our room first, hanging our clothes over the chair and accidentally dropping a mob cap. When I bent to pick it up, I saw a gold sealed envelope on the floor by the desk. Sean. My heart raced as an odd, ill feeling settled inside me.

What if Stuart hadn't sent Bridget the roses? What if they'd been for me? I tucked the envelope into my pocket, feeling it burn there as I helped Bridget arrange the flowers on the table by her bed.

"I almost don't want to read the rest of the queen's story tonight. I could sit here and look at these all night long." Bridget took another deep whiff of the roses. "Where do you think he got them from?"

"The village. We can wait to read about the queen," I said, eager for us to retire so that I could read the note.

"No. I've been thinking about her."

I sighed, resigned to wait, realizing that if he'd written asking me to come, I shouldn't go. That maybe I should pretend

I hadn't even found the note. "I have too."

"Let's read then," Bridget said, and I nodded. We were cohorts in this naughty venture I'm sure neither of us would have been brave enough to do alone. And part of my wanting to read tonight was to delay learning what Sean had written to me. I doubt he'd issue any more safe passages. That meant I had to decide if I was willing to go without one.

*"We have to stop seeing each other. You have to stop coming to me. This week has been more than I can bear. The loneliness will be harder now. But I'll never forget the pleasure you've given me."*

"Wait," Bridget said. "Did we miss a page? What pleasure? Are they not going to tell us about the week the queen spent with Draco?"

I turned the page back. "I guess not."

"But they can't do that," Bridget said.

"They did. Do you want to skip this story and go to another one?"

"No. I want that the author should have written this one right."

"What would you have had them write?"

"All of the things that people do when they fall in love. All of the things that girls like me never know. Dinner and dances and operas and balls."

I shut the book. "Do you want to write our own story then?"

"What?" Her eyes boggled.

"Write things the way we want them to be. We can tell it anyway we want to."

"Blimey. I never thought about it like that before. Maybe. But not tonight. I want to know about the queen they way the story is now."

"All right." I opened the book.

*The young queen turned, wrenching painfully away from Draco, the man who would take her from her burdened, virgin life and give her immortality and the only love she would ever be sure was true.*

*All others would want her for another reason, for power, for wealth, or to be king of a nation. Only he could love her for herself.*

*"Go, please. There can never be happiness between us. I am bound to this life and you to another."*

*"Seven nights, my virgin queen. One more week to convince you that my love is worth all that you would leave behind."* Draco *smiled sadly, unable to walk away.*

*"The fruit you offer is one that I would give my soul to know, but it is forbidden, for I cannot sacrifice my nation. I would cease to be queen then, and that is all I am."*

*Draco crossed the room and caught the queen in his arms. "Don't say that. It isn't true. You're a woman, a beautiful woman. My woman."*

*Tears flowing, she pressed her fingers to his lips and he gently nipped her fingertip with his fang, careful not to break her skin and draw the blood he so desperately wanted to join with his. He could force her to be his, press his thirsty lips to her throat and make her his. But to do so would destroy the very part of him that enabled him to love.*

*She buried herself against his chest. "Were I any other woman in the world, in any other nation in the world that would be true. But it is not. I'll reign and I'll die, and if there is mercy in this world, then one day we will share the love burning so deeply within us."*

*Wrapping his arms around her, he blinked back his own tears. "Seven more nights?" he whispered.*

*"Yes." Her cry muffled with a sob.*

"Blimey." Bridge pulled the book from my hands and tossed it onto the bed before dashing at the tears in her eyes. "I can't read any more of it tonight."

Neither could I, but I didn't say so. I didn't want to think about wrenching sadness when my feelings for Sean were such a bubbling caldron of doubt. I could foresee no ending different than that of the virgin queen and her secret, dark lover.

"It is a sad story." The note in my pocket pulled upon my heart as deeply as the queen's denial. If he'd asked for me to come, how could I not go? But how could I go and forsake all that I knew was proper?

"Why doesn't she just love him?" Bridget demanded.

Tears stung my eyes. "She does."

"But she won't be with him, and he loves her. Her fear of losing him is too great to let herself love while she can." Bridget shoved the book aside and plopped onto her bed. "It's just a story," she said. "It has nothing whatsoever to do with me and Stuart."

I blinked. Stuart? I'd thought only of Sean. "You're absolutely right." I marched to my cot and slipped off my boots. The story had nothing to do with either of us.

"I'm right?" Bridget frowned as if she expected that I would argue with her.

"Yes. You are." I snuffed out the candle. "I suggest we get some sleep."

Had I honestly believed that, I might have been able to shut my eyes and drift off rather than to feign sleep for an eternity as Bridget tossed and turned. I thought I would scream with impatience before she started to snore. I waited a few more agonizing moments to make sure she wasn't going to awaken, then I lit a candle stub and ripped open the envelope. Two cards fell out. Written in his bold script were two short notes.

*I hope these blooms bring you as much pleasure as your soft, fragrant skin brings me.*

*This ticket entitles the bearer to a trip to the stars and beyond.*

There was no mention of a safe passage.

I also knew that I would go.

When I opened the dragon-handled doors, I found him standing there, waiting. He seemed unsettled, his hair askew, his expression worried. I suddenly wondered if he'd been in pain.

But that wasn't what brought me to a standstill. It was his attire, or lack of it. Gone were the traditional accoutrements of pants and shirt. In their stead he wore an open, black-silk robe embroidered with a silver dragon breathing fire over his left breast. The open neck of the robe exposed an indecent amount of his fascinating chest.

He had on pants, but they weren't normal restrictive pants. They were silky and moved fluidly with the muscles beneath. My heart felt as if it reached him before he reached me.

"I'm glad you came." He slid the door from my grasp and urged me into the corridor enough to close the door behind me.

Mindful of the thorns, I clutched a pink rose I'd taken from the bouquet before leaving my room.

He smiled, setting his cane aside. "They are beautiful, are they not?" He took the rose from me and trailed the bloom along my cheek.

"Most beautiful," I whispered, taking a step back as I tried to absorb the intensity of his gaze and the power of his presence. He made every part of me tingle with awareness.

"As are you." He stepped closer, letting the rose slide down my neck and across the exposed skin of my chest. Then, setting his palms on the door behind me, he brushed a kiss to my lips. "Will it be the stars again tonight? Or shall I take you beyond?"

"The stars," I said, desperately hoping that I could keep control of the overwhelming temptation to be with him. I forced my hands to my sides to keep from touching him. He was so close, and I knew if I even brushed my hand against the silk of his robe, I would be lost.

He dropped his forehead to mine. "God help me, Cassie. I don't know how strong I can be."

"First," I whispered, not sure how the word escaped my lips, but everything within me cried to be with him. He snapped his gaze to mine, intensely searching. I dampened my lips, "Stars first...then..."

"Last," he groaned as if in pain. "Stars last." He kissed me then, hard and deep, pressing me up against the door, molding his body to mine. The fire of his touch only made me thirst for more.

"Last," I whispered in defeat, wanting him so much that I

could no longer stand on the propriety upon which I had built my life. Tears stung my eyes. He stopped trailing kisses across my jaw and gazed into my eyes, then drew a deep breath and stepped back.

"I'm rushing you. I'm sorry. Come with me." He held out his hand and I put mine in his. I knew he wasn't taking me to the observatory in the round room and I didn't protest.

Surprisingly, he didn't go down the long corridor leading to his bedchamber. He led me to the first room on the right, revealing the study I had seen briefly before. This time a comfortable fire-lit hearth and a candlelit table brought a warm glow to the darkness. The black curtains were open now, revealing the sea and the stars. Tempting bites of cheeses and fruits and sweet confections filled silver platters on the table where goblets and wine stood ready next to another bouquet of roses that enticingly scented the air.

"This is...this is wonderful. Thank you." I drew a breath, feeling the angst inside me ease. He'd shown as much care for me, a mere maid, as he would have a queen.

"Sean," he said. "You haven't said my name, Cassie. I want to hear it."

"Sean."

He closed his eyes a moment as if he wanted to commit the sound to memory.

Moving to the table, he pulled out a chair for me and set the pink rose on the table. I sat and he took the seat to my right, reaching for the wine. The seating was so close, so intimate that I could feel the heat of his arm next to mine. After pouring two glasses, he gestured to the food. "What is your favorite?"

I studied the delicacies a moment, biting my lip. "They all look delicious."

He laughed. "You can have them all, but which do you want *first?*"

His emphasis on the word brought his kiss at the door tingling back to my mind, drawing my gaze to his lips.

He smiled, leaned over, and brushed his lips against mine.

"That can come first. You choose."

I picked up my wine goblet and sipped, surprised at its exotic sweet taste and warmth, and took another long drink, enjoying the feel. "This is unusual."

"It's spiced, a blend of Asian delicacies and clove, ginger and nutmeg. It is meant to please the palate and heighten your senses."

*Meant to seduce.* I pushed the thought away and took another sip, though not as much as before. With no safe passage mentioned, I had known his intent before I came, and had agreed to it at the door. It was too late for second thoughts. I also knew in my heart that if I really wanted to leave, he'd let me go without question.

"Since you don't have a preference, we'll save *all* of the sweets for last." Placing an assortment of cheese and grapes on both plates, he motioned for me to eat, and started himself.

I bit into the cheese. Fresh and soft, it nearly melted in my mouth.

"So your family lives in Oxford?"

I nearly choked on the cheese, realizing that conversation could be even more detrimental than kisses. "Yes."

"Mrs. Frye said your father lost his post."

"Well, yes. He is currently looking for something else," I said, rationalizing that searching for Apollo's temple would make the essence of that statement true. I continued to eat and drink, hoping he'd let the conversation drop.

"And you had to take a position of a maid because there was a scandal, involving you?" he asked a few minutes later.

"Yes, one that would make references difficult. I didn't try for any other position."

"You brought a gun with you here. Were you somehow forced in this scandal?"

Heat stole up my cheeks, and I grabbed for my wine, surprised to find it mostly gone. I finished it in one swallow. "In a manner of speaking."

"Did the bastard pay?"

I jumped at the ferocity in his voice, and my pulse raced at the anger barely veiled in his green eyes. "Yes." I looked away. When I found whoever harmed Mary, they would pay. "Can we speak of something else? If you haven't traveled in recent years, who collected all of the art that fills the castle, and the instruments in the music room?"

"A gruesome collection, isn't it? I'm not sure if my father or Sir Warwick collected the artifacts and their unique histories, as they both have a morbid sense of humor. I know my mother had the theater built with the piano, organ and harp. She loved music and invited a number of world-famous musicians here to play. As for the other collections, some came from past generations, but a number of things my father and mother collected before she died."

"I'm sorry."

He shrugged. "I never knew her and my father never spoke of her."

"His grief was too great?"

"I couldn't say. Except for occasional hunting parties and to escape the city heat during the summer, he spent most of our youth in London while we were raised by servants here on the coast until attending the university in Cambridge."

"That's where you met your friends?"

"Ashton and Drayson? How did you know? Ah, in the kitchen that night. A memorable moment and not exactly all pleasant."

Heat flooded my face. "I hadn't meant to hurt you, hadn't realized what...well...happened."

"I survived." Smiling, he poured more wine for us both and picked up a confection. He held a sweet cake up to my lips. "Taste."

Feeling odd at being fed, but unable to resist, I drew the morsel into my mouth. His fingers brushed my lips, making me tingle deep inside. "Fig," I whispered, naming the fruit.

He smiled and held up another. "Now this one."

"It should be my turn." I bit into the treat. "Cinnamon and..."

"Honey, the nectar of the gods." Leaning back, he drank some of his wine.

"The confections are not all the same."

"No. I like a variety of flavors."

"I wouldn't have guessed that." I offered him one.

"Why?" he asked first, before tasting the morsel.

"Your life appears so uneventful in a conventional way. The solitude. The..." My thoughts scattered as he shook my world from its foundation. Instead of taking the sweet into his mouth, he wrapped his hand around my wrist, holding mine still, and took two bites of the treat before finishing it off, brushing the sugar from my fingertips with his tongue. His gaze never left mine. Thoughts of uneventful and conventional vanished.

I didn't remember to breathe until he let go of my wrist. Whether it was the wine or his burning sensuality, I was on fire.

"You read a lot." I stood and went over to the book cases next to the fire. A mistake. I was already too hot, so I moved to the French doors, and gasped, thankfully finding some relief from my burning desire in the sight of sea. Beyond a stone terrace stretched the moonlit water with splashes of silver cresting the waves, making a masterpiece of fluid beauty.

"A breathtaking view," he said. "Would you care for music?"

I turned from the sea. He'd risen from the table, cane in hand, and stood in the middle of the room as if unsure of what to do.

My abrupt departure from the table had to have been less than reassuring. But I didn't know what to say. I felt so torn between wanting him and doing what I knew a proper woman should. "Do you play an instrument?"

"Not in a long time. I've a collection of music boxes, though. Come choose your song." He led me to the back of the study where along one wall were ten large music boxes. Each had glass-encased dancers—some of them had elaborately dressed couples in miniature ballrooms, others were of a man and a woman alone, in a room, in a garden. One of the couples appeared to be standing in a black void; I bent closer to see why, and saw tiny jewels pinpointed the black velvet.

"Now why did I know you would be drawn to 'Moonlight Sonata'?" He turned a crank. The couple began to swirl around the box to Beethoven's haunting tune. Then he set his cane aside, lit a match, and bent beneath the music box. Suddenly the couple was swirling amid hundreds of tiny stars as light set the jewels aglow.

I knelt next to him so that I could see. "Oh, how beautiful."

He leaned closer. "All the constellations are there. Leo. Sagittarius." Directing me with his finger he pointed them out.

"Orion," I said, finding another.

"Cassiopeia." His voice deepened as he spoke, and on the glass he traced the star pattern with his finger, making me feel as if he had brushed me with his touch instead. The fire inside me spread to every unmentionable place. My breasts tingled; my chemise shrank, everything else heated.

"I love this. Who made it?" I asked, forcing my mind to function.

"I commissioned a jeweler. The stars are diamonds." I glanced at him, as I heard a note of yearning in his voice. His gaze was intent on the dancers. I then realized that the couple dancing beneath the stars, so free and graceful, was something he would never truly be able to do.

"Would you like to dance?" I asked, before sanity and propriety could stop my heart from speaking.

He stood abruptly, grabbing his cane. "You know that's impossible."

I rose and put my hand on his arm before he could turn away. "Why?"

He didn't answer, just glared at me, telling me that the reason was self-evident. When he tried to ease from my touch, I tightened my grasp. "What if I wanted to sing, but didn't have a perfect voice? Should I never sing? Should I never let my heart feel the joyfulness of song?"

"Of course not."

"Then I ask you again. Would you like to dance?"

He stared at me for a long moment, his green gaze

searching. I held my breath waiting, realizing that more than anything else I wanted to dance with him. I wanted all of those things Bridget and I had wanted the author to write about the queen and her vampire.

Turning toward me, he slid a hand behind my back and I drew a hopeful breath. I moved my hand from his arm to his shoulder and set my other hand atop his that held the cane. Then I smiled up at him. "I should think swaying back and forth—"

He leaned down and kissed me deeply then eased my head against his chest. "Cassie," he whispered as he drew me closer to him then began to turn slowly. After a few steps, he dropped the cane and wrapped his arms tighter around me. I stepped into the embrace, turning my cheek to press closely to his heart, hearing its beat echo in mine.

His steps were halting, but the movement made my heart sing and my soul dance.

"Sean." I tiptoed and softly pressed a kiss to his lips. At the last second, I realized I wasn't tall enough and pushed up onto my tip-toes. I must have misjudged my balance, or the wine might have had a hand in the matter. Whatever the reason, I fell against him with all of my weight when he was in mid step.

"Damn." He struggled to regain the balance that completely crumbled from beneath us. We landed on the study floor with a thud. Him below. Me on top.

"Good heavens. Are you hurt?" I reached up to feel the back of his head.

Whatever I said or did ignited him. His hands grasped my bottom and shifted me up to where his mouth could cover mine, and all thought ceased as my world exploded into a universe of sensation and pleasure.

Kisses melded with caresses until my breaths grew ragged and my body ached. He rolled to his side then moved on top of me, sliding his legs intimately between mine.

Leaning on one elbow, he kissed me again, leaving me gasping for air, fueling my want to a fevered state. My tongue sought thirstily for his. My hands went to his chest, but instead of pushing him back, I slid them along the warm silk until I felt the supple heat of his skin. That wasn't enough; I moved further, burying my fingers into the soft texture of his dark hair, growing delirious on his drugging scent.

I thought of my dream, the scandalous sensations that had heated me then, and found little comparison to the true fire Sean made me feel. I gave myself up to the forbidden passion, to know him in a way I would never be able to once I left the castle and went back to my staid life of advising other women to never do what I did now.

Running my fingers through the silken hair of his left temple, I felt the long ridge of a scar across his scalp, and pulled him closer to me, feeling with all of my heart what he must have suffered. Before I could say anything about it, he spoke.

"Roses will never be the same. You've burned the fragrance into my soul," he rasped, dragging his lips from my mouth to kiss his way down my throat, stealing away my thoughts. His fingers deftly unfastened the buttons of my dress then pulled down my chemise, freeing more and more of me to the hot pleasure of his tongue.

His hand slid beneath my skirts, between my legs, and caressed me intimately, ripping all thought from my mind. All I could do was feel as he suckled the aching tips of my breasts, like nipping lush berries before they could disappear. My hips pressed willfully to the heat of his muscled thigh and the stroke of his hand.

I groaned at unbelievable pleasure.

He moved to the side, loosening my drawers and pulling them down then his as well. My heart thundered even harder as the silk of his pants and the burning heat of his flesh slid up the insides of my thighs and his rigid arousal pressed against me, seeking entry. I froze at the sensation.

"Shh." He brought his lips back to mine and drank deeply. "What happened before doesn't matter. I won't hurt you." He slid his fingers along my sensitive flesh, finding one spot that sent lightning through me and mercilessly rubbing his fingers over and over no matter how my hips arched to him. Just as I thought I would scream, he brought his mouth to my breast and suckled hard. I cried out, shuddering with pleasure as stars blazed before my eyes.

"That's only the beginning of pleasure, Cassie." He leaned over me, covering me with his body. His hips thrust and his arousal pressed to me, sliding along my intimate parts rather than inside of me. I pressed to him when the hard heat of him touched that so sensitive place. Then he froze as the murmur of voices filtered into the room.

"He'll come tomorrow night, Ashton, if we have to drag him along."

"He can't deny us one party. He doesn't have to know about the women."

The faint voices were followed by a sharp rap on the French doors, the French doors on the other side of the table we lay in front of. "Lights are on. He has to be in his study. Hey, Killdaren!"

"Oh. My. God." I tried to move.

"Don't move," Sean rasped harshly. "The table is between us. They can't see us. Not unless you move."

"I can't just lay here like this and pray that two men who are less than a dozen feet away are going to miraculously disappear."

Another knock, this time hard enough to rattle the door. "I say, Ashton. Is that roses on the table?"

I was perilously close to panic.

"And two goblets of wine. Warwick is right, he's got a wench."

"A cleaning maid."

"When you've been alone as long as he, any wench will do."

"Let's go find one ourselves." Their voices faded with their footsteps.

Sean groaned. "I am going to kill them."

"I won't know. I'll have already expired."

"It's not true. That's not why I am here with you. I have

been alone for a long time, but that isn't why I want you. There is something very special about you, and it's not just your beauty, Cassie, or my attraction. It's deeper. I can't explain it and I can't stay away from you. Believe me, I've tried. I want you and need you more than I want life itself." The raw need in his voice brought my embarrassed gaze to him, and I felt the depth of his desire all the way to my soul. Yet, my heart and mind were in so much turmoil, and shame had me in a choking grip.

"Please. This isn't right. I have to go. I'm sorry." To my embarrassment, tears filled my eyes and kept coming.

"Shh. All is well." I felt him turn. "They're gone. Come on." I'm not sure how, but within minutes I was upright and dressed, his deft fingers accomplishing the miracle. "I'll take you to the stairs."

"No. Please. Just let me go. I need to be alone." I still couldn't meet his gaze again.

He stepped back and I hurried to the door and left. I ran down the corridor, leaving his wing. Tears blinded me. I made it to the kitchens, but couldn't go up the stairs yet. I couldn't let Bridget see me like this. I turned to the laundry room and ran into one of the bathing stalls Sean had had built for us, for me. And gave in to my tears as I huddled in the dark, so confused that I didn't even know why I was crying, or for what I was crying.

Dim light flooded the room. Glancing up, I saw Sean set a candle on the edge of the tub. Then he pulled me into his arms and held me tightly. "Cassie. Please, don't do this to yourself. There is no shame in beauty, and tonight was beautiful. More than I ever believed possible. Don't let whatever you are feeling take that away from us."

Drawing deep breaths, I clung to his words, calming myself. "I'm sorry. I don't understand what is happening to me."

"Nothing to be sorry for. Go to bed and in the morning you'll be able to think clearer."

I nodded, finally able to meet his gaze.

He smiled gently, but in his eyes I saw a stark pain.

"I've hurt you," I said.

"No. They hurt you, but I'm not sorry for the interruption. I can't marry you, and I wrongly let my desires convince me that I could disregard consequences and feelings and take what I so desperately wanted."

Considering his place in society and mine, I'd known marriage wasn't possible, but the heavy weight of that reality still pressed painfully upon my heart. I, too, had wrongly thought that I could abandon what I knew to be right. "I don't want it to be this way."

"There is no other way. I live in the shadow of a curse. And it will die with me."

"What do you mean?"

"You've heard the rumors. The Dragon's Curse. When twins are born into the Killdaren line, one will kill the other."

"That can't be real. It's just...a legend...like that of a vampire."

"No. It's not. Eight years ago I would have agreed with you, nothing could have made me believe I'd kill my brother. But during that fight I wanted Alex to die. And he wanted me dead as well. The murderous seed inside us will never be visited upon the next generation."

"That was just drink and...and grief. He saved your life."

"The fight was fate. And he should have let me die. Just as it was fate tonight that things between us should end before going too far."

Taking my hand, he urged me to the door. "Go to sleep. There is nothing else to say."

Tears were blurring my eyes again. I wanted, needed to argue against what he'd said, but I couldn't put the words together. I needed to think, so I left. He didn't follow me from the room. Reaching the stairs, I stood there for a few minutes, unable to leave, not until I told him that it was the most beautiful night of my life and that I didn't believe in curses. Turning back, I went to the door of the laundry to tell him, but my voice died in my throat.

He stood naked in the tub, pouring what had to be ewers of

cold water over himself. The flickering light of the candle revealed rivulets of water streaming over his head and broad shoulders, running down through the mat of hair on his chest and following a tapering dark line to his groin, which still burgeoned with arousal. He wasn't much different from Zeus anywhere. Once I absorbed that, I saw the jagged scar on his left hip and thigh, and winced at the pain he'd suffered, and from the agonized groan he emitted, still suffered.

I left before he saw me. I wanted to go to him, but I wouldn't again. Not until I knew that, no matter what, I wouldn't leave him.

# Chapter Fifteen

"What's the matter with ya today, Cassie? Ack, I know the queen's story is a sad one, but it's just a story. Nothing we need to upset ourselves over."

Leaning forward, I let my forehead rest on the cabinet I was polishing, even though I knew I'd have to polish the spot again. "For some reason, I'm extraordinarily fatigued today."

A result from not having slept a wink all night, I was sure, but I couldn't tell Bridget that. She'd want to know why, and that was something I could never tell a soul. How could I go back to my life and pretend last night never happened?

My whole life before was a lie, and my whole life now was a lie.

I couldn't go back and I couldn't walk away. Not from Sean. Not from Rebecca. Not from Bridget. Yet how could I stay and spend my life as a maid and a mistress? I couldn't do that either.

And how could he believe so strongly in a curse that he'd sacrifice his whole life to thwart it?

Mrs. Frye entered the room. "Bridget! Cassie!" She didn't inspect the room, looking for fault, but had a worried look on her face. "Have you seen my Jamie today?"

"No, ma'am," Bridget said.

I shook my head. She nodded then left. Bridget met my gaze and I shrugged. Something wasn't right.

Mid-swipe I remembered what happened last night while I was at my bath. Good Lord! I dropped my rag, knocking the tin of polish across the floor as I jumped up.

Bridget rose. "What's wrong?"

"Stay here. I forgot something." Leaving Bridget, I ran all the way to the stable. Inside I found one of the stable hands.

"Where's Mr. Frye?" I asked.

"Don't know. Everyone's a looking for him. Been missing all day."

"I mean Stuart. Not Jamie."

"I'm right here," a deep voice sounded behind me.

Turning, I found Stuart standing in the doorway. The sun glinted off his hair and shone partly on his unshaven jaw, giving a warm appeal to his rugged looks.

"I need to speak to you alone," I said.

"I'll go check on the flowers in the garden to see how fast they're growing," the stable hand said with a knowing grin, then ducked out.

I glared at his back, then at Stuart for not disabusing the man of his assumptions.

Stuart leaned against a stall. "What can I do for you, Miss Cassie?"

"I may know something about Jamie."

"What?"

"Last night, during my bath he walked in. I think he was returning a mopping pail. He saw me and started crying 'Mary' and 'hurt' again. He moved toward me, frightening me, and I screamed at him to leave and that Mary was dead."

Stuart winced. "And you're just now thinking to tell someone?"

"I'm sorry. So many things happened. Bridget came with the roses, all excited, and fell and cried, and I honestly didn't think he would go anywhere but to bed. I had no idea he would be upset enough to leave."

Stuart sighed. "I understand." Then he frowned as if just hearing what I'd said. "What roses are you talking about?"

I swallowed hard, meeting his puzzled gaze dead on. "The big bouquet of pink roses you will swear until the day you die that you left in our room for her."

His brows lifted. "And who would have put those roses in your room for me?"

A hot flush covered my face. "Mr. Killdaren."

Stuart's gaze bore into mine. "If the Killdaren is sending you roses, you're in serious trouble. More trouble than Mary ever thought of being in."

"What do you mean?" I asked. He started to turn away as if he'd said too much. I grabbed his arm. "You have to tell me!"

"There's nothing to it really. As I told you before, Mary wasn't one to leave others in their misery. She came here and she changed things. From what I can piece together from our conversations, her friendship with the Killdaren helped bring about his ability to be in the sun now. She told him that after his injuries, he'd needed time to heal. But over the years he'd grown so accustomed to the dark that full light would bring nothing but pain. She told him he had to take his exposure to full sunlight a minute at a time, adding a minute each day until he could see in the sun. She said she was learning that about her own fear and the water. She painted pictures of the sea for him, pictures with lots of light, because he couldn't see the sea during the day."

My throat squeezed tight, for that was so like Mary, and another choking thought slipped into my heart, filling me with dread. I reeled on my feet, and fell back against a stall door with a thump. Pieces of loose hay showered down on me. "Was he...was he in love with her?"

He caught my shoulders. "I don't know. She may have had feelings for him. She didn't say. But it is obvious you are entangled with him. And it's obvious the Killdaren is following in his father's footsteps. Just be careful he doesn't force you to marry a stable hand when you get pregnant with his bastard."

"I'd heard the earl married your mother to his top groomsman."

"Nothing so mild. The earl forced her to marry Frye, and after I was born, Frye beat my mother where nobody could see his handiwork. She wouldn't leave because staying here bought me privileges I wouldn't have anywhere else. Frye beat her when she was pregnant with Jamie. That is why he is the way he is. Is that the road you want to take, Cassie?"

The horror of such a thing wrenched my heart. No wonder Mrs. Frye was such a harsh woman. No wonder she resented Rebecca and Miss Prudence.

"Then, the hunting accident that killed Frye..."

"Wasn't an accident. The earl found out what Frye had done and killed Frye without a trial. When you live in the wilds, men take justice into their own hands rather than wait for the law."

I turned away, suddenly desperate to leave. I couldn't stay here and hear more.

I couldn't face the questions Stuart asked.

"Wait, Cassie. I didn't mean to hurt you."

I didn't stop. I hurried blindly from the stable and ran right into Sean.

"What?" He righted me then pulled hay from my hair, looking at me with a cloud of confusion in his green eyes that darkened with anger.

"It's not what you think," I said softly.

His glare over my shoulder at Stuart was icy.

Sean turned his back on me, his fists were clenched as he moved toward a waiting saddled horse. "It doesn't matter, lass. Your favors are yours to give." His voice was tight with pain.

Tears flooded my eyes.

"The hell it doesn't matter," Stuart yelled. He grabbed Sean's shoulder, shoving him about to face me. "Look at her. But before you walk off another cliff, why don't you open your eyes and really look. Do you see a woman who just tumbled in a haystack, or a woman haunted because you're no better than our father?"

In one swift, violent move, Sean grabbed Stuart's shirt and pinned him to the stable door. "Were you any other man, I'd kill you for that."

Stuart didn't fight back, but just stared Sean in the eye.

"Were I any other man, I wouldn't be here."

Sean sighed and released Stuart. "Let's go find Jamie." Sean turned to me. "It was the realization that you'll belong to another someday, not that you were with Stuart. I meant what I said last night about destiny. That's why it doesn't matter."

Stuart gave me a puzzled look, but I couldn't answer his silent question. Emotion choking me, I turned to the castle, feeling as if my heart was being trampled under the hooves of Sean's horse. Inside, I went back to Bridget.

"Blimey, Cassie. What's happened to you? Are you ill?" She gently checked my forehead with her fingers then put a comforting hand to my shoulder.

I burst into tears and she wrapped her arms around me. "There now, it can't be as bad as all that. You've shown me there's an answer to almost everything." She gave me a clean rag to mop my tears and held me comfortingly.

Gulping, I rested my head on Bridget's shoulder, thinking that for the first time since I was little, somebody was bolstering me. And perhaps, I'd gained my first true friend ever, other than my sisters. When my tears had spent themselves, Bridget eased back.

"Now what has you so upset?"

"I..." My voice died. I'd either told too many lies, or kept too many secrets to tell anyone the whole truth. I sighed.

Turning away, Bridget shrugged and picked up the lemon polish and a rag. "Well, ya can tell me later if you can't now."

I'd hurt her feelings. It occurred to me then that no matter what my good intentions, I was living a lie that, when revealed, would hurt all who had become dear to me at Killdaren's Castle.


Thoughts of Sean, my desire to go to him, Jamie's disappearance, and the growing cloud of my lies shadowed my day. But I forced myself to put on a front of lightness. Rebecca already had too much darkness in her life.

"Ring around the rosie, A pocket full of posies. Ashes,

ashes, we all fall down." Rebecca tumbled to the ground before I could even bend my knees. Bridget just shook her head and smiled.

"You win, poppet." I laughed. After teaching Rebecca the rest of the song on the piano this afternoon, I decided to take her outside, and had brought Bridget with us. No one had told me I couldn't, though I don't think Mrs. Frye would see that frolicking on the hillside was teaching music to Rebecca.

"I d-d-did? N-n-never won be-f-f-fore." Her smile brought a deeper glow to her flushed cheeks. Sunshine glinted brightly on her dark locks and turned her eyes to emerald jewels so bright they had to be the most precious in the world. Even if I had to bear Mrs. Frye's disapproval, seeing Rebecca happy in the sun was worth the price. Though, with Jamie still missing, Mrs. Frye wasn't exactly keeping close tabs on what we did today.

"You're faster than my little brother, you are," Bridget said.

That really impressed Rebecca, making her smile bigger.

I wanted to ask her about Mary and what happened the day Mary disappeared, but I couldn't. Not yet. And I had little hope that Rebecca would be able to tell me or anyone anytime soon.

"P-p-play again?"

"Absolutely."

"Blimey, but I'd forgotten how much fun this was. Makes me wish my brother was here."

"I wish he were here to play too." I stood and squeezed Bridget's hand. Had I been in charge of Rebecca's care, proper or not, I'd have all the village children over to play with her.

We took Rebecca's hands in ours and helped her to her feet. "Now hold on tight and let's spin around as fast as we can."

She giggled and then burst into song. "Roses we all fall down."

"No! Not fair. It doesn't count unless you sing it all."

"Roses," she sang, but before she could finish the verse, I tripped and sent us both tumbling over. I hit the ground and she fell on top of me.

Bridget caught her balance and stayed standing. "You two look very silly."

"I won." I laughed and tried to catch my breath.

"No. D-d-didn't sing all."

"You're right, poppet."

"P-p-play again."

"Let me rest a minute."

"Are you sure you're not ill?" Bridget asked.

Ill at heart. "No, I'm fine. Can you hear the wind and the sea talking to each other, poppet?"

Rebecca laughed. "Don't talk."

My heart hammered. She'd spoken without stuttering for the first time since she started singing without stuttering. "Yes, they do. You just have to listen. They're arguing over who has more power."

"*Listen to me break upon the shore. Wind, you have no might,*" says the sea.

"*Watch me whip away the sand. Wave, you have no flight,*" says the wind.

"*Who needs flight when I can sweep from sea to sea with my tide?*" scoffs the sea.

"*And who needs might when I'm free to circle the world wide!*" cries the wind.

Before I could say more, the sound of approaching horses thundering over the dunes intruded.

Rebecca cried out, blindly searching for me as if panicked.

Sitting up, I pulled her to me. "What is it, poppet? What's wrong?"

"M-m-mary," she cried. "H-h-he t-t-took Mary. H-horse man h-h-hurt Mary."

Bridget gasped. My heart pounded painfully. Sean and Stuart appeared from around the corner of the castle on two huge stallions. The closer they came, the louder Rebecca screamed.

"Tell them what she said," I told Bridget. Gathering Rebecca tighter, I ran for the castle. "Can you tell me more, poppet?"

Rebecca was too hysterical to hear my soft spoken question, but she'd said enough. In a blink of an eye, she'd changed my world. Circumventing Nurse Tolley, I took Rebecca right to her mother and told her what had happened. Wrapping Rebecca in her arms, she settled into a nearby rocking chair, and hummed sweetly to the child, soon easing her screams to small cries.

I turned to leave.

"Don't tell anyone what she said," Prudence whispered, shocking me even more.

"Why not?" I asked.

"She is just starting to recover. We are not well liked here, and a hounding of questions about Mary will only traumatize her more."

Though I understood her concern, now that I had a reason to support my suspicions, I thought the dangers of there being an unknown murderer lurking in the shadows more harmful. "It's too late," I said. "Bridget, Stuart and the Killdaren already know."

"There's no worry then. They'll do anything to protect Rebecca."

"Doesn't it bother you at all that something bad may have happened to Mary?" I'd started to believe my suspicions of Mary's death false, and now knew more than ever that they weren't. Someone had killed Mary, and I wanted to shout my suspicions aloud at everyone in the castle.

Prudence frowned. "Yes, but I can't help her. You have to understand. My daughter is all I have. She is more important than anything else."

"I understand, but sometimes the best thing we can do for the people we love is to find the truth."


Dinner at the servants' table was unnaturally silent, with those present barely touching the rich stew Mrs. Murphy and the new scullery maid had prepared. Stuart kept his gaze on Bridget. Bridget kept her gaze on her stew, separating the vegetables into piles on her plate. Janet and Adele kept whispering, looking at Stuart with fearful faces. I was more interested in observing what changes had been brought about by Rebecca's cry about Mary. The word had spread to everyone.

"Enough." Mrs. Murphy stood up from the table. "This silence isn't going to send my hard day's work to the slop pile."

"Then maybe we should all talk about what is happening. What did happen to Mary. And where Jamie might be," I said.

"We know where he is," Stuart said, surprising me and everyone. "He's in the forest, hiding. I'm sure after another night alone, he'll come back, or let the Killdaren and me find him tomorrow."

Mrs. Murphy drew a deep breath. "The lass is right. We need to speak of Mary's death, and Rebecca. Mrs. Frye thinks we're taking what Rebecca said too seriously, and I happen to agree with her."

I blinked. I had expected Mrs. Murphy to believe in Rebecca.

"You wouldn't be saying that if you'd been the one to hear her," Bridget said.

"She's a delicate lass with a wild imagination. How can we know for sure that a man on horseback took Mary just because the horses frightened Rebecca today?" Mrs. Murphy asked.

"Wouldn't it be better to ask how and who might have harmed Mary first, before discounting the child's fear?" I asked, fighting to keep the emotion out of my voice.

Stuart sent me a hard and knowing look that I chose to ignore. From everyone else's stares, my interest must have hit them as unusual.

"Let's humor the lass," Mr. Murphy said. "Once we talk about all of those who'd be on horseback, we'll see how little truth there can be in the wee one's cry. Who rides on Killdaren land?"

"The Killdaren. The viscount and me," Stuart said harshly.

Not Sean, my heart cried.

Bridget gasped, sounding the way I felt. "That's not all.

There are...there are others."

Mr. Murphy agreed. "Right you are, lass. Ya might add the earl and Sir Warwick, on occasion."

Bridget shook her head. "There are more. There are those friends of the Killdaren's who come every summer. They'd arrived before Mary disappeared. Maybe someone from the village, and the constable, now and again, while looking for smugglers in the caves."

"I think we should tell the constable what Rebecca said," I added, now that he'd been mentioned.

"No," Stuart shouted, unnecessarily loud. "We are absolutely not bringing Constable Poole into this matter. Not on a blind child's hearsay, who is so frightened she can barely speak. He'd laugh in our faces."

That was a statement I could readily believe.

"Add Jamie to the list of riders too," Bridget whispered.

Stuart sat back in disgust. "He never chooses to ride anywhere."

"Not always," Bridget said. "He rode up and down the beach looking for Mary for days, and he rode like a man who could handle a horse."

Mrs. Murphy cleared her throat. "Well, there haven't been any strangers around. And everyone else we know wouldn't have harmed Mary. So there's no sense in believing what Rebecca said. She's blind and delicate and must be confusing the sound of the sea with that of the horses."

Bridget and Stuart glared at each other. Everyone added their agreement, and I swallowed my denial. Nothing more would be accomplished by arguing tonight. Part of me wanted to accuse Stuart or the viscount or the earl or Sir Warwick or even a stranger, just so I could remove any doubt that shadowed Sean from other people's minds. For I knew with my whole heart he was innocent. His kindnesses didn't stem from any guilt, but from a pure heart.

But then I found a tiny burr under the smoothness of that thought. I found myself wondering, why? Why did Sean want me, a mere maid? Mary had called him a special friend, and they'd obviously shared more than a conversation or two for Mary to paint the sea for him. Was he attracted to me because I reminded him of Mary? Did people ever really know each other? And could the person who harmed Mary be sitting here at the table? I had to answer yes to that. No one could ever really truly know another. I'd lived among these people for over a month, but none of them really knew me. I'd learned that I didn't even know myself.

Exhausted, Bridget and I skipped reading the end of "Forbidden Fruit" and went to bed early, but neither of us could sleep.

There was no note from Sean. I looked everywhere before going to bed. On the floor, under the bed, in my pillowcase and under it. But there had been nothing. I listened for the screeching sound of him hoisting his telescope into place, but only heard the sea and wind. His silence this night told me as deeply as his words that he meant what he'd said about the Dragon's Curse and fate.

He'd made a pact with his brother that there'd be no future generations of Killdarens to suffer the curse.

I huffed and tossed and turned myself, fighting the urge to go to him.

"Cassie," Bridget whispered.

"Yes."

"Do you think Flora is all right?"

I hesitated. It seemed to me that Bridget's sister would have surely been able to write or send a telegram by now. But could I tell Bridget that yet? It was still possible that a post was delayed. The red scarf wasn't necessarily Bridget's sister's. "If she went to Paris, I daresay it might take a bit longer for her to send a regular post, especially if she had any difficulty getting there or settling in. I wouldn't worry just yet," I said, though I felt the niggling worry within me. I think that had more to do with my concerns about Mary's disappearance, though.

Bridget sighed. "You're right. Perhaps by the time I hear from her, the doctor will know exactly what ailment my mother has and I'll know what I need to do."

"Yes, don't worry. Whatever needs to be done, we'll make it happen."

"Blimey, but I believe you, Cassie. You give me hope." She paused. "What do you think about what Rebecca said? That a man on a horse took Mary?"

"I think she's telling what she knows. I think there was a man on a horse."

"Blimey," Bridget said. "Almost makes you wonder if you should go to sleep at night."

Bridget didn't say more and I soon heard her soft snore.

I felt as if I would explode from the thoughts of Mary and Sean swirling around inside, building my frustration and my hopelessness to the point that I wanted to scream. I fervently wished that I could find hope for myself.

Unable to sleep, I finally rose and pulled out the box of Mary's letters to read.

They all started with Mary's thoughts of her mother and my sisters and me, wrenching me with the care and hopes that she had for us. In them she told about everyone in Killdaren's castle. Her care for Rebecca and Prudence and Flora and Bridget and Stuart and Jamie and Mrs. Frye and, finally, Sean.

I'd almost reached the end of the letters, my eyes drooping, when I read a passage that gave me pause.

*Our secret is out, my training Flora to sing. He found us in the music room today, upset that a mere maid was making use of the beautiful room with so many tragic and horrible stories. I fear I wasn't the lady you raised me to be, Mother, for when he insisted that we leave, I quite rudely told him what I thought of his highhandedness. I find I have little use for the injustices social classes impose on one another.*

Who was he?

I read the letter twice more, but didn't find the mention of a name. In her haste or upset, she'd forgotten to name the man.

After perusing the last four letters and learning nothing new, I set them in the box and pushed it beneath my bed, then found the pheasant shell on the desk. I'd neglected to carry it with me lately. Holding it, I thought about Mary, of her life here, and of the sea, and what must have happened to her. Tears filled my eyes and fell unheeded. I cried for her, for myself and for Sean.

Mary had been harmed in some terrible way. I hurt for her. Sean believed he could never be free from the shadow of a curse and would live his life alone in darkness. I ached for him. And I was bound by...propriety? The thought of allowing such a thing as society's dictates to keep me from following my heart struck me deeply as being very wrong. But I had my sisters to think of, and I could not bring such a scandal upon them. I was bound and torn by my love.

I must have drifted off to sleep hearing Bridget's soft breathing and the sound of the waves relentlessly crashing ashore, because I heard Mary calling to me again.

*"Cass. Cass, wake up. I must talk to you."*

*"Mary? Where are you? It's so dark. I can't see you."*

*"No one can see me. I'm in a dark, dark place. Nothing but stone now."*

*"What happened?"*

*"It doesn't matter. What matters is what is happening now. Come with me. Hurry. It's almost too late."*

*"Where?"*

*Mary didn't answer. I scrambled around in the dark, searching desperately. "Mary! Answer me!" I saw a light in the far distance and ran toward it as hard as I could. My breath rasped, my legs and chest hurt with the effort to reach the light before it disappeared. Just before stepping into the room, the light blinded me. I moved forward anyway and found myself falling, as if I had stepped off a cliff. Suddenly, I could see. I saw Killdaren's Castle from above, as if I were a gull swooping down. Moonlight and mist bathed its stone walls an eerie blue, deepening its shadows. A keen sense of evil reached out to me, tried to grab hold of me. I escaped by flying higher. I would have flown away, but on a ripple of wind passing me I heard a tiny cry and looked back.*

*Rebecca clung to the roof. I dove back toward the castle, fighting the sense of evil trying to stop me. Before I could reach the child, I saw her slipping, screaming, calling for help.*

No! I tried to scream as I woke from the dream, but I couldn't. I couldn't breathe either. A gloved hand had covered my mouth.

# Chapter Sixteen

I realized two things simultaneously. I'd been dreaming about Rebecca falling to her death, and I wasn't dreaming about the hand over my mouth. Before I could fight or try and really scream, a voice whispered in my ear.

"Cassie, don't scream. I'm sorry to frighten you. I need to speak to you, please." Sean's voice sounded tight with pain.

I nodded and he slid his gloved hand from my mouth. "I'll wait outside your door."

Scrambling up, I rose, but felt as if my stomach fell into a bottomless pit. Rebecca. The same sense of dread that had haunted me after my first dream of Mary, and those of my grandparents, sat coldly in my chest. Grabbing my robe and slippers, I rushed to the door then turned back and shook Bridget awake. "Get Stuart and go to the roof, now. Don't ask why. Hurry."

Sean stood in the hall with a small lantern. "I had to see you. I have—"

"There's something wrong. We can't talk now. It's Rebecca. We have to hurry." I pulled him down the corridor.

He grabbed my shoulder, stopping me. "What are you talking about?"

"I can't explain. We must get to the roof. Rebecca is on the roof somewhere."

He shook me. "Good God, woman. Have you lost your mind?"

"I pray so. But please, just take me to the roof. There's no time. It may already be too late. It always has been before." My voice broke as wrenching pain tore through me. "Please," I whispered, desperately.

My panic got through to him. "Follow me." He turned, but instead of going to the stairs, he went the opposite way, his cane-aided stride so fast that I had to run. At the end of the corridor was a tiny, padlocked door.

I groaned with frustration. "Key?"

"No need." A swift kick splintered the door open.

The entry and passageway weren't meant for a man of Sean's height and he had to stoop to an almost unbearable angle. Even I had to duck my head. "Where does this go?"

"A back way to the bell tower at the other end of the castle."

"Hurry."

"Why?"

"My dream. I saw Rebecca falling from the roof in my dream."

He stopped.

I ran into him and pushed him out of frustration. "Go," I said. "If I'm wrong you can throw me from the roof."

He didn't comment, but moved ahead. Reaching the bell tower, I passed four large bells with roping and ran to the opening, peering into the darkness. "Rebecca!" I screamed. "Rebecca!"

The wind seemed to take my cry and run away with it, leaving my hair ruffled and my heart crying with frustration. "Rebecca!" I yelled louder, determined to beat the wind.

Sean's hands settled on my shoulders. "Cassie. This is ridiculous. Calm down and tell me what this is about."

"I can't. Not until I'm sure what I saw isn't real." I shut my eyes trying to remember where I'd seen Rebecca on the roof in my dream. It was the other side. She'd been opposite the side of the sea. Turning, I found the opening on the other side of the silent bells, boarded up. I ran to it, pushing against the wood.

Sean grabbed my hands. "Cassie!"

"Take it down," I cried. "Please."

"It's boarded up because the stone is crumbling. It's not safe."

"Please. Oh, God, please." I tore at the wood, breaking my nails.

"Move." Sean slammed his palm through the wood, pulling it aside.

"Rebecca! Rebecca!" I leaned forward and Sean jerked me back as pieces of stone crumbled away. I heard them skitter against the roof and then nothing but the wash of the sea upon the shore and the low whip of the wind through the tower. I prayed that I was wrong, but I couldn't let go of the feeling that Rebecca was in danger.

"Rebecca! Please!"

Sean shook my shoulders. He looked wild, as windblown and desperate as I. "Cassie. This is far enough. What in the bloody hell is going on?"

A weak squeaking cry, like that of a wounded bird sounded. Rebecca.

Sean whipped around to the opening, carefully holding the lantern out as he looked. "Good God! Hold that out and for God's sake whatever you do, don't lean against the stone."

Cane in hand, Sean went to the other opening and climbed out.

I held the lantern and saw a little patch of white on the roof not far away. My breath caught and suddenly I was back in my dream seeing Rebecca, feeling the evil, hearing her cry for help and seeing her fall. The wind gusted upward just as Sean came into view, crawling slowly along the edge of the steep pitch. He hadn't quite reached the patch of white when I heard Rebecca scream as she had in the dream, and I knew she was sliding.

"Rebecca!" Sean shouted. My heart dropped as he lunged forward and caught hold of the patch of white. I died inside as they both slid downward. Surely they were going to plunge to their death. But rather than just moving closer to the edge of the roof, Sean wrapped his arm around Rebecca and rolled sideways, hooking the end of his cane on a chimney and stopping their fall. My muscles hurt as I watched him painfully strain his every tendon to its limit as he pulled himself and Rebecca up enough to rest against the chimney.

*Thank you, God!* I whirled around looking for another miracle. I needed something to reach them with. In three steps, I saw the ropes hanging from the bells and went for one of them. Only I couldn't reach high enough, nor did I have strength enough to unknot the rope from the bell. Jerking on the rope sent the bell clanging horribly loudly.

Frustrated to the point of tears, I was about to run back into the castle when I spied a knife on the floor. Grabbing the knife, I cut two of the ropes from the bells, tied them together and then tied the end to the rope still attached to one of the heavy bells. I tested the knot as well as I could and then hurried to the crumbled opening.

Sean and Rebecca were still against the chimney, but more securely situated than before.

"Sean." I held out the rope. "I've attached the bell ropes together. I don't know if it is strong enough to hold you yet. Test it."

"Be careful. The stone will crumble. Throw the rope here."

My toss slid the rope close to them. Sean hooked it with his cane, and as he pulled on it, snapping it tight, more of the opening broke away, sending a shower of large stones down on them.

"Wait," I shouted. Retrieving the knife, I carved a groove in the mortar at the most solid section of the opening and slid the rope into it. "Try that. Wrap it around both of you and tie it, so you'll be safe."

After maneuvering the rope around, Sean pulled hard on it. Dust fell, but no stone.

"Good," he said. "We're coming up." He drew closer and I saw blood covering the left side of his face. One of the crumbling rocks had to have hit him. He moved up the side of the roof, nearly flattened against it, with Rebecca between him and the roof. He pulled himself and the child, who clung to his neck, up in an agonizingly slow process of gripping the rope then adjusting his footing and anchoring the cane on the tile.

I was surprised and grateful to realized that a jagged knife blade jutted from the cane, puncturing the roof.

He was going to need more help. Swallowing my fear, I went to the sturdy opening and gingerly slipped onto the roof. The wind caught at me, my knees shook, and my heart jolted at the sight of how far away the ground was. I closed my eyes a moment, focusing on Sean, then inched my way around the bell tower until I could see him.

Closer than before, I saw that blood streamed down his face and had soaked his shirt. My stomach wrenched. He was breathing heavy, his muscles stretched beyond strength.

"Sean. I'm here."

"Bloody hell. Go back."

"No. Not without you and Rebecca."

He wrenched on the rope. Only then did I realize he didn't have the rope tied around himself, but around Rebecca, who held onto him. Just his grip kept him from falling to his death.

My heart railed at him. For the next eons of minutes, my heart only beat with every pull that brought him closer to safety. Had the man no regard for his life?

*No. Remember, he'd give it up in a heartbeat. It doesn't matter.*

Something happened inside me, something that told me I couldn't let that happen, ever, no matter what the cost.

*Everything mattered.*

He stopped, dug the cane into the tile, tested it then let loose of the rope, and pushed Rebecca up. "Get her. I need to rest a minute."

"Why don't you have the rope around yourself?" I cried when I got Rebecca into my arms.

"I would have crushed her if I fell. Get to the tower."

I held Rebecca tightly. "Everything's all right now, poppet. Just hold on to me."

With no rope, Sean hung onto the side of the roof with only his quivering muscles and his cane between him and death.

"Go." Sean's voice was weak, blood was everywhere.

I prayed harder than I'd ever prayed and I glared at him determined not to lose him. "Not without you."

Balancing against the bell tower, I untied Rebecca and slid the rope back down to Sean. Whether I was delusional or not, I felt balanced enough on my perch to hold Rebecca a moment until I was sure Sean was safe.

"Blimey, Cassie! Don't move."

Looking up, I saw Bridget in the opening and heard Stuart coming around on the roof.

"Give me, your hand," Stuart said.

"No. Get Sean up first."

"Bloody hell."

Stuart and Sean spoke at the same time.

Anchoring himself on the roof with his body and holding the rope, Stuart reached down and grabbed Sean's wrist. This gave Sean enough leverage to grasp the rope. Moments later, both men were up on the ledge with me.

"Now get them inside," Sean said to Stuart.

I didn't argue. Minutes later I was handing a whimpering Rebecca to Bridget.

Bridget gathered Rebecca to her, comforting the child with soft words and secure arms.

Turning with tears in my eyes, I watched Sean limp back into the tower, blood on his face and shirt and so weak he had to lean against the wall to stand. His cane no longer sported the deadly blade.

The fool. I loved him. Had likely loved him from the moment I saw the man beneath the myth, but now could no longer hide from the truth of it.

I turned to Sean, wanting put my arms around him, to touch him in some way, just to feel for myself that he was alive. "You're hurt."

"Not so hurt that I can't hear what in the bloody hell is going on." His angry tone brought me to a halt.

Stuart handed Sean a handkerchief and Sean pressed it to his head.

"Why do you have Jamie's knife?" Stuart asked, picking the knife from where I'd left it.

I stared at the knife as if it had turned into a cobra. "I wish I knew what in the bloody hell was going on too." I prayed I could find a place to sit before I fainted. "Rebecca, can you tell us how you got onto the roof?"

"Poppet? Can you help us?" Bridget added softly.

"H-h-horse-man," Rebecca said. "H-h-horse-man take me to heaven. W-w-want Mum. Not h-h-heaven."

"Who is the horseman?" I asked.

Rebecca started to cry again. As my gaze met everyone else's, I saw no answers, but only more doubt into Rebecca's story about Mary being taken be a horseman.

"I think someone put Rebecca on the roof because they want her dead."

From the look in Sean's eyes, I knew I had better start talking fast if I expected to live longer than the next minute. Fortunately, my ringing of the bell earlier had wakened those in the castle and I heard a rumbling of people coming, Mrs. Frye, the earl, Sir Warwick, the Murphys.

"It would be best continue this discussion in the library, privately," Stuart said.

Sean snapped his gaze to Stuart. "Do you know what's going on?"

Stuart looked hard at me. "She seems to know more than anybody."

I thought by the time I'd dressed and walked to the library, I would have decided what to say, but I entered the room without a clue. My biggest dilemma was how much of the truth I wanted to reveal, and what price was I willing to pay to tell it. I knew I loved Sean, but I didn't know what I would do about that. Sometimes loving meant leaving before you could hurt that person, or before he had to hurt you.

I expected there to be more than just Sean in the library. There wasn't.

He turned from where he stood in front of the lit hearth, a drink in his hand. He'd changed as well, and had a bandage in place on his left temple. His face was pale, his expression tight with pain.

"Stuart and Bridget are with Rebecca and Prudence." Sean accurately interpreted my panicked glance about the room. "If what you said is true, then I don't want the child alone, and Prudence is so petite, physically she'd only be a slight hindrance to a man bent on murder. I poured you a scotch, Cassie." He motioned to a side table that sat within warming distance of the fire. "I suggest you drink it."

"Thank you." I moved to the chair and quietly settled myself, but didn't touch the drink. My hands were shaking too badly.

He moved to the chair opposite me and eased himself slowly into it. His limp was more pronounced than before, his expression pained, his green eyes haunted. He had his dragon-headed cane with him, and must have noticed my staring at it.

"There's a release just under the handle that frees the blade."

I nodded. "How badly were you hurt tonight?"

"I'll heal. But what almost happened to Rebecca would have been irreparable. Start talking, Cassie."

I hesitated. Once he knew of my dreams, would he send me away?

"We won't leave this room until I have all the answers." His voice brooked no argument.

Deep down, I always feared that once a man knew I wasn't normal, he would turn away from me. Maybe that is why I always stayed safely within "Cassiopeia's Corner". "I had a dream of Rebecca falling from the roof and knew I had to get there fast."

He leaned forward, a muscle ticking in his tight jaw. "Tell me everything, Cassie. Don't make this harder than it has to be. I want all of it now. Nobody has a dream and wakes knowing it was real."

"I do. Ever since I was very little, but never like tonight." I told him about the few dreams I'd had growing up and of my grandparents' death. I didn't mention Mary.

"So how was tonight different than before?"

"I never saw how they died before. I would dream of them, know something was very wrong, and I would call to them, but I would never be able to reach them and they would never answer. They only disappeared into darkness. When I woke, I'd have this sense of dread deep inside me. Then the news of their death would come. But tonight, it was different, a...a lady called to me, told me to come with her. When I followed, I felt a dark evil and I saw Rebecca clinging to the roof before screaming and falling."

"No one was on the roof with her in your dream?"

"No."

"Did you see how she got there? What do you make of this horseman?"

"No. And I don't know what to think of the horseman, but I do think he is real, and I think he's trying to harm Rebecca."

"Other than setting up a guard for her, I can't do more to protect her unless she can tell us more. Or you can. Have you had other dreams that reveal things to you while you've been here?"

"Yes."

He narrowed his gaze at me, demanding an answer. "Cassie?"

"I've had three other dreams this past month, two about you that were what normal people must dream, and then another one with the lady who called to me tonight. She led me up the stairs from the center hall to a set of doors. I later learned the doors were to Rebecca's room."

"And from this you surmise someone is trying to kill Rebecca? For what bloody reason? She's a child without even an inheritance or a surname."

"She had a teacher recently."

Leaning back, he shut his eyes as if grieved. "Mary."

"Were you close to her?" My pulse waited for his answer

253

before racing on.

Sean's eyes opened and narrowed. "No, not in the way I am to you."

I swallowed, unsure of how to interpret his answer. He must have read the question in my heart. "Cassie, she was a friend who died in a drowning accident."

"Are you sure? I think she met a different end, and I think Rebecca may know something. And I think the murderer is trying to kill her before she recovers enough to tell what she knows."

"Good God, woman." He rubbed his bloodshot eyes. "This is too far-fetched. Your dreams I can relate to because just as I was getting ready to leave the castle tonight, a voice inside of my head kept demanding that I go to you first. But murder..." His voice broke. "Again?"

I knew he referred to Lady Helen.

"Who do you think is a killer?" he rasped harshly, his eyes burning with intensity.

"I don't know who. Someone who knew Mary. Someone who lives here. You tell me."

"Do you think it is me? I've been associated with the murder of a woman before. I knew Mary. I live here."

"No. Not you."

"I was awake and dressed. I could have left Rebecca on the roof. How can you be so sure?"

"I just am. I know it now, whether I knew if for sure before. You risked your life to save her."

He shrugged. "I could have done that to save myself from blame, once you knew Rebecca was on the roof, I'd have had no choice."

"No. You didn't do it, and you can't convince me otherwise."

He studied me a moment, his expression intense but unreadable. "Stuart, then?"

"I don't think so."

"Why?"

"I don't know. Perhaps I'm being foolish in thinking a

murderer would be recognizable. But I sense Stuart cares too deeply for Rebecca to harm her."

"Then what of the other servants?"

"The only one who shows any anxiety about Mary is Jamie."

"He wouldn't deliberately harm—"

"He is stronger than he realizes, and he could have killed Mary by accident. His behavior has been rash."

"That doesn't explain Rebecca. And he's been gone since yesterday."

"What if he doesn't want to hurt Rebecca himself, but make sure she has an accident? He wouldn't be responsible that way. Finding his knife in the bell tower has to mean something."

"The plot you suggest is too complicated for Jamie to reason out."

A noise in the corridor brought Sean to his feet. I'd left the door open.

"Who's there? Show yourself immediately!" Only the sound of muffled steps answered. I stood, thinking to go look, but Sean managed to make it to the door quickly, despite his injuries. A frustrated palm to the door jamb told me the corridor was empty.

He swung, advancing toward me. "Who are you, Cassie Andrews?"

I stepped back, then decided to hold my ground. I lifted my chin. "Just a woman escaping a scandal, a woman who happens to have odd dreams." I couldn't seem to force the truth out. Not like this.

He waited until he was nearly touching my body with his before he stopped and spoke. "I don't think so. Why weren't you afraid for me?" He brushed my cheek with the back of his finger, making my breath catch at the luring lilt and deeply sensual tone to his voice. It was such a change from the way he'd spoken moments ago.

"What?"

"Given your history of portentous dreams, why didn't you

warn me of danger if you dreamed about me?" He pressed closer, sending my pulse racing. I danced to the side and grabbed the drink he'd fixed for me. Taking a burning sip, I nearly choked as the fire swirled its way inside me, warming the flames he'd already fanned. Irrationally, I gulped some more, until I could delay no longer. "They were a different kind of dreams."

Moving closer again, he nudged my chin to meet his gaze. "How so?"

"I'd rather not say."

"I think I have a good idea," he said dryly, turning from me. "You also make me forget any and all resolves to stay away from you in a heartbeat. Go pack your things, Cassie."

I blinked with shock and gulped the last of the drink as my stomach wrenched itself into a knot. He was going to send me away.

"I'm not leaving," I said fiercely. "Not until I know Rebecca will be safe. No matter what you do." And I wasn't leaving until I discovered who'd murdered Mary and where she was buried. In the dream Mary had said she was in a dark place, nothing but stone now.

He turned toward me, eyes hauntingly sad.

"Send you away, lass? Though I should for your sake, I haven't the strength just yet. You can't leave here until I know you're safe. Whether it's an excuse to selfishly keep you just a little longer or not, you're not going anywhere." He didn't touch me, but his gaze stripped me bare. "You're like the wind, lass."

"What do you mean?"

He shook his head. "I'll explain later." His voice hardened. "There's an art to warfare, and until I know who I'm fighting, I'm closing my perimeters, propriety be dammed. You, Prudence and Rebecca will move into my wing tonight."

"Why me?"

"God knows what people will do once word spreads about your dreaming abilities. And if there is a murderer afoot, you put yourself in his path tonight." From the dagger sharp glint in his green eyes, I knew his intent to protect was deadly.

I could make everything easier. I could leave Killdaren's Castle, secretly take Prudence and Rebecca with me, and run with my sisters back to Oxford, where we'd all be safe. "Bridget," I accidentally said out loud, remembering to take her to Oxford, too.

He blinked and I did too.

"Bridget comes with me."

He nodded, but I found little reassurance in his accompanying smile.

"I must ask. Rebecca. Is she yours? Was Prudence once—"

He pressed a finger to my lips. "That you ask wounds me. My father could better answer that question. He has little regard for the consequences of his actions."

I knew my eyes grew wide, and I thought a man as elderly as the earl had to be utterly unconscionable to have seduced Prudence. Eight years ago, she'd have been younger than Gemini's tender eighteen.

# Chapter Seventeen

"Blimey, Cassie," Bridget whispered. "This has to be about the strangest night there's ever been. And I'm right not sure I'll ever be able to sleep in such finery. There's nary a lump to settle against, the bed is so soft."

The night's events had exhausted me to the point of immobility. So many things pressed on my heart and mind that I couldn't absorb them all. I wanted to rest for a minute. "Just shut my eyes a moment," I mumbled to Bridget. The bed was soft, the curtains, though open at the moment, hung decoratively from the bed post. Lavender and a hint of the sea scented the sheets. Antiquities from the orient stood in the shadowed corners of the room, giving it a personality and life that comforted me.

Bridget and I shared a room that connected with Prudence's, where she insisted Rebecca sleep. I wasn't sure if Prudence was going to let Rebecca out of her sight for the next twenty years.

In the chamber next to Prudence's was Sean. The windows were locked and the dragon-handled doors were locked as well. It was odd that I now found myself on the inside of the realm I'd been so curious to invade ever since arriving at Killdaren's Castle.

"There're so many dark things about the room," Bridget said. "And these curtains hanging over me... However do people sleep like this?"

I sighed. My eyes drooped and I mumbled something

comforting to Bridget, telling her that morning was almost here and that she needed to sleep. The next thing I knew it was morning, and Sean had once again filled my dreams with seduction. This time we'd danced beneath the stars with the moon lighting the sand to silver, before his kisses led us to a bed of silver and roses.

Judging by the light streaming through the window, it was late morning, and Prudence's maid entered the room with a breakfast tray. She plopped it down with a clatter on the table beside the bed. I didn't want to leave my dream. I didn't want to leave Sean alone beneath the stars.

"Blimey, what's that!" Bridget scrambled from the bed disoriented. I sat up, blinking.

"Your breakfast, miss."

"Where's Rebecca?" I asked.

"She's just waking, but Miss Prudence is still asleep. May I bring the child in? The Killdaren has dismissed Nurse Tolley."

The news about the nurse didn't surprise me, but her deference to me did. "Of course. Won't Mrs. Frye be—"

"No. Miss Prudence has requested that both of you be her and Rebecca's lady's companions. The Killdaren has already ordered Mrs. Frye to hire other maids for the downstairs."

"Imagine that." I looked at Bridget, rather pleased with the situation.

Bridget wavered on her feet then pitched forward in a dead faint.

Luckily she fell on the bed, where I could catch hold of the back of her sleeping gown to keep her from crumbling to the floor. She came to a few moments later when I pressed a cold, wet cloth to her face.

"Did I die?" she asked.

"No, but you did swoon. A rather inauspicious beginning to your career as a lady's companion. You must be stalwart enough in any situation so that you can care for the delicate sensibilities of a lady."

"What does bloody inauspicious mean?" She frowned as

she pushed up from the bed.

"It means not a very good start."

"Then what am I supposed to do?"

"Get back in bed. Eat your breakfast. Then after we dress, we'll go see if there is any correspondence Miss Prudence would like for us to attend, or she may wish for us to read to her. There are quite a number of duties she may need our assistance with."

Bridget's jaw went slack and I thought she would faint again. I patted the bed and reached for the silver tray, filled with delicate nibbles of fruit and cheese and bread and meat pies.

The maid led Rebecca into the room and brought her to the bed. My insides wrenched at how pale and wan she looked in her night rail with her black hair in wild tangle about her drawn features.

Taking Rebecca's hand, I helped her up. "Come on, poppet. We're having a morning tea party. Would you like some?"

"Y-y-yess."

"Good. I've got a wonderful tale to tell you about a tea party and a funny rabbit and a little girl who had a very scary adventure, but was all right when it was over."

Looking up, I was shocked to see Sean standing in the doorway. He wore the black silk robe and pants he'd worn before and his hair was mussed as if he'd just risen from his bed. Catching my gaze, he nodded then abruptly turned away, shutting the door behind him.

"Bridget, help Rebecca with her scones and I will be right back." Grabbing my robe, I raced out the door.

"Sean," I whispered, seeing him at the end of the dim hallway, about to enter his bedchamber. I went to him. He leaned against the door frame, as if needing the support. "You look as if your pain is worse. What is it?"

"Don't worry. Light induces headaches. Some days are worse than others. When I was first injured eight years ago, they were excruciating. The condition has been increasingly improving until this morning."

"It was the rocks last night, wasn't it?" I reached for him, but he pulled back and I fisted my hand. "What can I do to help?"

He sighed. "Stay with Prudence and Rebecca. Stay together and stay inside the castle until I'm well. Perhaps tomorrow."

"There's nothing else? I feel as if this is my fault."

"No. On the contrary, you kept tragedy from us. We'll talk later." Turning, he went into his room and shut the door. After a moment, I pressed my hand against the cold wood, promising myself that I wouldn't let propriety stand between us and I wouldn't let him shut me out again.

The day went by faster than imaginable, which is the only reason I stayed sane. My thoughts kept going to Sean, wanting to speak to him, wanting to be with him. After seeing him appear in my doorway that morning, I expected for him to return, but he didn't, and the barriers that separated our lives gave no leeway for me to steal away to see him.

But as bright as the new day dawned, a dark shadow hovered over me. Someone had taken Rebecca to the roof and left her to die, and that someone was in the castle. When I dressed, I made very sure I put the knife in my pocket, something I'd let myself grow lax at doing. I also determined to get my father's pistol back from Sean tonight as soon as I saw him.

Bridget, Prudence and I spent time in the music room as I taught Rebecca part of a song to sing and showed Prudence the repeating notes from A to G on the piano. Bridget kept walking about the room, taking the hem of her dress to polish a spot here and there on the glass or to straighten a chair. I finally had to insist that she come and sit with us on the piano bench and learn too.

Later, in the ladies' salon, Prudence had her maid bring out a number of trunks, which to my amazement contained the most exquisite tapestries I'd ever seen.

"Where did these come from?" I knelt, carefully going through them. Some were scenes of history. Others were like pages from a storybook, showing knights and battles and castles of medieval times.

"I did them," she said softly.

My eyes boggled. There had to be dozens. "But how?"

She blushed. "I can't paint, but I love color. It's what beauty I can make. And Rebecca can feel the things on the tapestries, so it makes us both happy."

I realized then that what made the tapestries so unique was that the images on them were raised above the backgrounds, giving them depth and character. Braille tapestries.

"H-h-horse, p-p-please," Rebecca said.

Prudence handed her a tapestry with several wild horses running and Rebecca traced her finger over them. "H-horses."

"How do you make them that way, Miss Prudence?"

"I can teach you and Bridget." She was excited. "Whatever you want to stand out you embroider over it four or five times, following the same stitches each time."

"Blimey," Bridget said, her mind seemingly incapable of thinking of any other words at the sudden change in her life.

"I would love to learn," I said.

The work would have made any tapestry take so much longer to complete, and Prudence had finished so many. I had more respect for Prudence, a cropper's daughter who'd had a child out of wedlock, than I did for a number of women I'd met in respectable society.

I could never go back to "Cassiopeia's Corner", and perhaps writing important articles wasn't what I was meant to do, for I suddenly felt that there was another story I would want to tell. A story of love, in which a mother had loved her blind child enough to figure out a way for her child to see.

The high spot of the day was seeing Bridget sit down to tea. After serving Prudence and Rebecca, I passed Bridget a plate of scones and sugared tea in a cup with a saucer. She sat completely still for a moment then looked at me, her blue eyes filling with tears. "Cassie. You have to help me write this down. Tonight I want to write every minute of today so I can go back and read it over and over again no matter what happens."

"I promise." Tears stung my eyes.

Out of the corner of my eye, I saw Prudence smile, and I realized that she'd reached down and brought Bridget and me out of the servants' realm on purpose. Not to ease her life, as most women in her position would, but to bring ease to ours, to thank us for helping to save her daughter.

"Miss Prudence?" Her maid came in. "You said to let you know when the doctor was leaving. He's doing so now."

"What doctor?" Was Sean more injured than he led me to believe?

"For the Killdaren. I'll be just a moment." She set her cup aside and hurried from the room. I stood to follow her, but the door shut and I realized I couldn't. I'd not the right, and it would always be that way should I stay on at the castle. The only time I could go to him, the only time I could let my heart be free, would be in the dark of the night, when the world lay silent as the grave. Not much different from the vampire story of Armand and the maid. The choice I could not understand before, I was almost ready to commit myself to now.

I went back to the tea table, carried the conversation, told Rebecca more about Alice at the tea party in *Through the Looking Glass*, and had to fight hard to keep my sentences coherent. Ten minutes into my story, Rebecca fell asleep in her chair, and I fell silent. Bridget was still agog at the treats.

Prudence returned with tears in her eyes.

My heart skipped then pounded. "What is it?"

She shook her head. "His headache is worse than this morning. The doctor thinks the Killdaren's injury last night has caused a relapse of the swelling in his head. It took him years to recover enough to be able to stand the sunlight again. I just don't know what he will do now." She started to cry. I handed her a napkin, trying and failing to stem my tears. Prudence didn't notice them. Bridget did. She gave me an odd look, telling me an explanation was due.

"What can be done?" I bit my lip to keep from crying aloud. I'd sent the rocks crashing down on him. It was my fault.

"Nothing. He won't let anyone near when he's in such pain. I'm sorry to do this, but I think I'll retire with Rebecca. She's so exhausted from last night. From now on, I don't care how improper anyone thinks it is for a mother to care for her child; she'll not leave my sight. I'm not a real lady anyway."

Reaching out, I touched Prudence's arm. "You're more of a lady than a number of ladies I've met."

She gave me a sad smile. "Only in my own little world here. Nowhere else." With her maid's help, she collected a sleepy Rebecca and left.

Bridget set her cup down. "Cassie? Tell me what has you so upset? I mean, it is sad, but he'll recover."

"It's my fault. I made the rocks fall and I...I...I love him."

"You were saving him and the wee one, Cassie. But blimey. In love with the Killdaren? How? Ah, love at first sight. Sorta happened the first time I saw Stuart when I was just fifteen. Mary often read a proper lady's column called 'Casopia', she did. I remember Mary telling us the advice for love at first sight, is to wait a year before letting the gentleman know, gives him time to prove himself worthy and makes him know she'll be a right proper wife. And I decided that was exactly what I wanted to be."

I laughed and cried harder at the same time. "Bridget, you're going to be the best proper wife ever, but don't follow that advice. Follow your heart."

"Do you think so?"

I nodded, and knew I would.

After Bridget and I bathed, I kept the door to our room slightly ajar, hoping by some miracle Sean would recover and pass by, or I'd hear news of him. The corridor remained empty and I knew I had to go to him tonight. I had to know what his condition was.

The moment Bridget fell asleep, I stole from the bed and dressed in the worn cotton dress of my own I'd brought with me. Dusk had fallen only a short while ago, and as I made my way to his doors, just a few steps away, my heart hammered as if I'd run all the way from Oxford.

I had my hand on the door handle when a man's hand settled over mine from behind me. It wasn't Sean's. I nearly screamed as I swung around to face Stuart.

"What are you doing here?" I asked.

"Odd. I was just about to ask you the same thing. I'm guarding the fortress as requested. Your turn."

"I must see him. I must know how badly he's hurt."

"Going to take the thorn from the lion's paw, little mouse?"

"If I can."

"I don't know what you expect the outcome of your venture will be, but I wouldn't go in there unless you're prepared to accept whatever it is."

"I don't have a choice. Not anymore."

"I don't think any of us have a choice anymore. You've set things into motion that will unravel this world. My biggest question is who is going to be around to knit it back together." Stuart left.

I felt odd entering Sean's room with Stuart knowing I was there, but I pushed that and Stuart's words to the back of my mind as I slipped inside. I'd run out of time and patience for propriety. All I had room for in my thoughts at that moment was Sean. I saw him the instant my eyes adjusted to the dark. He lay on his bed, his arm flung over his eyes, his fists clenched. I thought I heard a low moan coming from him. I ached for him.

I didn't want to frighten him, but I didn't want to give him the choice to send me away either. Moving as silently as possible, I went to the wash basin and poured some cool water into it. Then using a clean, rose-scented handkerchief from my pocket, I dipped it in the water and approached Sean.

"I told you I didn't want to be disturbed. Leave now."

"I can't. Let me set this cloth over your eyes. It will ease the pain some."

He stilled and sighed deeply. "Leave, Cassie. I don't want you here now. Never should have let myself want you at all."

"I can't leave." More daring than I'd ever been, I sat gently on his bed, near his head and slid the cloth against his forehead. "Please. Just a few moments, let me help."

He moved his arm and my cloth aside and glared at me from pain-narrowed eyes. "Anything you do will only cause more pain, believe me."

"Maybe not." I leaned down and I pressed my lips to his forehead, his bandaged temple, and then to his lips. He responded as if he were a dying man offered one last hope of reprieve. His tongue thrust against mine, seeking succor in the passion. His unshaven cheeks were rough beneath my palms, his hair soft and silky to my fingertips. I breathed deeply, drawing the essence of his unique scent deep inside of me.

Be it right or wrong, the barriers that had stood between us had fallen away in a blink of an eye on the roof last night, and all that stood between us now were my jumbled emotions, emotions that could only be eased by knowing him this way. I met his seeking tongue with mine and pressed the edges of his robe aside to feel the supple heat and strength of his muscled chest, the silk of his hair, the beat of his heart beneath my palm. I reveled in the contact of his hardness to my softness.

"Cassie," he whispered, pulling me closer until I half lay upon him. Reaching down, he eased my knees up until I found myself sitting on his stomach, looking down at his dark handsomeness, and intense gaze. The position made me feel heady, almost powerful, and nowhere near as vulnerable as I thought I would be in coming to him with my heart.

"I'll hurt you," I said.

"No. Let me look at you." He ran his finger through my hair, loosening it from the combs I'd put in. He slid his fingers beneath the collar of my dress, caressing the nape of my neck, then along my collarbone, and moving to the buttons of my dress. I bit my lip as he slipped the buttons free and stripped down my dress and chemise. I'd always thought that passion would have to completely sweep me away before I'd ever be so bold as to respond to a man's caress with such pleasure. I was wrong. Passion was sweeping me in a tide, but I wasn't drowning in it like last time. I was thoroughly enjoying its sea. Taking my time to taste his salty skin, feel his rippling strength, and to lose myself in the pleasure and the power of his touch.

He made me feel more alive than anything had ever made me feel. Arching my back, I pressed my breasts deeper into the cups of his hands, reveling in the sensations his fingers burned into me as he deftly rolled his thumbs over the sensitive tips until my hips matched the rhythm he stroked. He shifted his hips, bringing my feminine flesh intimately against his rigid male flesh, then he pressed harder, more insistently. Though separated by cotton and silk, nothing could mask the raw and urgent hunger of his need or my responding desire.

My eyes flew open to find him watching me, his gaze darkened with desire. This was the beauty of man, the beauty of woman, that they were created to be together. I responded by pressing myself to him, rubbing myself against his hardness. He moaned.

"You're like the wind to me," he whispered. "Fierce and passionate, gentle and moving. Always swirling within my mind, bringing fresh warmth every time you pass by me."

Emotion swelled inside me, squeezing my heart. I splayed my hands across his chest, recalling the protective heart that beat so surely inside him. I caressed his taut muscles, feeling his supple strength and the silk of his hair. His words, his touch, warmed me to the tips of my toes. "If I'm the wind then you're the sun that moves me," I told him.

He drew me down for a kiss that seemed to leisurely search the depths of my soul, and brought the sting of tender tears to my eyes. From our previous encounters, I expected wild, unthinking passion and found this gentle exploration so moving, so exquisitely touching, that my heart swelled and my soul sang.

Turning to his side, he nudged me off of him. Then slowly, deliberately, watching my every expression, he stripped away my clothing, leaving me naked, but strangely not vulnerable. He followed every exposure with the caress of his hand and the brush of his kiss, touching me intimately everywhere until I writhed from the fire burning in my loins. The pleasure in his gaze, the unspoken praise in his reverent touch, made me feel glorious, more woman than I'd ever known I could feel.

I pulled at his robe, needing, wanting, to see and touch all of him. He slid his robe off then his pants, standing before me as Adam had before Eve. The long jagged scar that I'd seen before cut across his left hip and down his thigh.

"I'm not a perfect man," he said.

Meeting his gaze, I saw the haunting edge of pain in his eyes and in his voice, and realized that his struggle with pain was why this exploration into the senses had moved so much more slowly than before. Was I only adding to his pain? I wanted to cry no, to reach out to him and pull him comfortingly into my arms. "Nor am I a perfect woman."

Though his jutting arousal, so Zeus-like to my mind, stood between us, I sat up and, leaning to the side, pressed a kiss to the scar.

Then, feeling bolder, I brought my mouth higher, kissing the ridges of his abdomen and then his chest, I reveled in the difference between us. I slid my hand over his scar, up his back, and down along the pattern of silky hair leading to his groin.

"You're beautiful everywhere." I brushed my fingers over his rigid arousal, feeling the burning heat of his need.

His breath hitched in a rasping, deep gasp. "Cassie." He caught me up in his arms as he fell back onto the bed, me beneath, him above, pinning me between exquisite hardness and softness. Then he kissed me and touched me everywhere all over again, molding my breasts to the shape of his palms and the heat of his mouth. Claiming my heart and soul with every nuance of his desire, he slid his hands over my stomach, then lower, spreading my legs open and caressing my intimate places, suckling my breasts until all of me wept for him to ease the fire burning within.

"Sean, please. Show me everything." I pulled his hips to mine, wanting the rigid heat of him intimately against me.

"Everything," he answered and drove himself inside me.

"Heavens!" Discomfort and pleasure and an intrusive, but intimate feeling filled me as he joined himself to me. Man to woman.

"Hell." He leaned back and glared fiercely at me. "*You* said there'd been a scandal! You're a virgin." He groaned deeply, roughly. "God help me. Were a virgin."

I wrapped my arms and legs around him, assuring he couldn't leave me. I couldn't lie to him, not here, not now, but neither could I tell him about Mary. Not like this. "Trust me. I had to come here. And I want you. I want you to show me what lies beyond the stars. Don't leave me in the dark, alone."

He hesitated but a moment, then slowly started to ease himself in and out of me, filling me with the driving force of his passion. Over and over he thrust into me as he kissed my lips, and caressed my breasts until I was on fire with desire. Then slid his fingers to where he joined his body with mine and found that spot of white heat where I ached for him the most.

My back arched and my hips thrust to meet him. "Sean," I cried, as he swept me into an indescribable realm of pleasure that left my body shuddering, and my mind exploding with bright stars.

# Chapter Eighteen

Still drifting in a fiery nebula of pleasure, I heard Sean groan deeply, his body pulling abruptly from mine then he shuddered his seed against me. I tightened my arms around him, feeling a strange mixture of gratitude and loss.

His weight pressed upon me, but I welcomed the heaviness of his body resting on mine. It felt so right, so natural, to cushion him with everything of me. Our breaths mingled and the rapid thundering of my heart beat in tandem with his. As the remnants of pleasure continued to echo through him into me, my spirit and soul seemed to mingle together with his in the hazy mist. I slid my hands up his back and eased my fingertips over the bandage on his temple.

"Tell me, about your injury and the darkness. Why does the light hurt?"

Rolling to his back, he pulled away from me. This time the exposure of my nakedness to the cool air left me vulnerable and bereft.

"Sean?" I reached for him.

He caught my hand before I could touch him. "Get dressed, Cassie. We have to talk."

All of my newfound misty pleasure dissipated, and I wanted to cry out against having it ripped so quickly away. My lies had caught up with me. I took a deep breath, determined that nothing was going to steal away this love, determined I wasn't going to let my virginity or propriety or any other thing such and the Dragon's Curse or society's mores keep me from loving him.

As soon as we'd dressed, Sean led me to a sitting area in a shadowed corner of his room. Moonlight spilled softly through the windows, but did little to soften the harshness of his features. He appeared darker and more dangerous than the night I'd first met him, for before me stood a man stripped bare of almost everything but pain.

Pain, it seemed I was only going to add to. For I had lied to him, and while my intent had been noble, I realized that I wouldn't have wanted to make love to a man and not know who he truly was. I'd not given him the same courtesy. Lowering my gaze, I was about to explain and apologize when I saw paintings stacked along the wall. Dozens and dozens of them. They were of the sea, beautiful and wild and full of light. They were Mary's.

Sean spoke before I could find my voice. He paced, as if deliberately causing himself pain. "I've given you the benefit of doubt for too long. Your father, who teaches at Oxford, is currently out of the country, and as far as my man has been able to discern, he still has his post, but I considered you only told Mrs. Frye that because you were too ashamed to speak of the scandal. Understandable, given the proper advice column you've written for years. You would have had to come and hide in Cornwall to escape. But it appears there was no scandal. So why are you here Cassie? No more lies." His green gaze cut deep, unrelenting in his demand.

I barely managed to close my mouth. "How...how...did you learn all of that?"

"I've an excellent factotum whom I trust implicitly to take care of my affairs. A man who lives as I must couldn't function without such an employee. When I fell over the cliff eight years ago, my injury made exposure to light excruciatingly painful. Only recently have I been able to tolerate the sunlight with a minimal amount of pain. After our first encounter, I sent him to investigate. I also wanted to know that whoever had harmed you had paid for doing so. You led me to believe you'd been forced."

"Good Lord. You knew all that and still...still..."

"Wanted you? You have no idea how badly I wanted you, Cassie. I think I would give and forgive almost anything. I want the truth now."

"It's Mary." Tears filled my eyes. "She was my cousin. I dreamed of her. She called to me and I could never reach her. I woke with that horrid dread curling inside of me and I knew she was dead. The telegram about Mary's drowning arrived from Aunt Lavinia that morning. My sisters and I came immediately. We all believed that something was wrong. Mary feared the sea. She never would have gone swimming. And your refusing to see my aunt made us even more—"

"What? I've never received a request."

"But she came here repeatedly."

"I'll look into it. Go on."

I winced. "I...started conducting my own investigation into Mary's drowning when I couldn't get Constable Poole to reopen his investigation into Mary's death. The rest you know. I came here to work as maid so that I could find out what happened to her." I hesitated. "You have all of her paintings."

"She gave them to me. She wanted me to have light in the darkness. So that's it?" He turned from me, hands fisted, voice haunted. "Everything you've done here has just been to learn about Mary? You've been looking for a murderer?"

I ran to him, grabbed his arms and pressed my cheek to his back. "No. A thousand times no. In coming here, I've lost my life within the lives of those here. Rebecca. Bridget. You. I can't live without all of you, yet I can't live with you all as I am now. And I am afraid now that I'll have lost everything. Sean, please believe me. I love you." Pain as great as the pleasure we shared ripped through me. "Please," I whispered. "Please don't turn away from me."

He bowed his head, pulling away from me, wrenching my heart apart. "You're damned, Cassie. Because there is no life here. Leave me now. I need to think. I'm sorry, but I didn't ask you to come here. Not tonight. And now what is done cannot be undone. I can't give you back your virginity, but I can send you on to a better life. There is no future for us, Cassie."

"It doesn't have to be that way. You only think it does because you won't let yourself see anything any different. You're choosing darkness over light."

"I am cursed, and doomed to live in darkness. There is nothing else. Now leave."

"Do you not love me?"

My heart waited in the following silence and broke on his harsh answer. "No."

Oh God. I couldn't take the pain. I couldn't stay and fight, not when my heart hurt so badly that he didn't love me enough to leave the darkness. I turned and left him in the dark, realizing how naïve I'd been. He may have needed me. Wanted me. But he didn't love me.

I rose the next morning, having not slept. My eyes were swollen, my throat was scratchy, and my heart so wounded that I could barely breathe. I told Bridget and Prudence that I was ill and asked to rest alone for a while.

Sean was everywhere in my mind. I couldn't escape him. He'd cast a spell over me that left me wanting and aching for him. I had to pull myself together, to put him from my mind and focus my efforts on discovering who murdered Mary. But I made little progress in the dark.

Bridget and Prudence left me inside until noon, then insisted I go to the gardens with them.

The sun hurt my eyes and I tried to stay in the shadows as Bridget and Prudence walked ahead, talking about the spring flowers. I followed, holding Rebecca's hand while she carried her rag doll with the other. She seemed to know of my hurt, even though she couldn't see me, because she kept squeezing my hand. As we strolled we neared Zeus; tears flooded my eyes, even though I chided myself for letting a reminder of Sean so move me. My love hadn't ceased because he didn't love me, but it had turned from pleasure to pain. I slowed my pace with Rebecca, letting Bridget and Prudence move farther ahead so they wouldn't see my tears. I could hardly see where we were going and didn't care. I blindly followed their blurry shapes.

A little while on, Rebecca tugged on my hand and I blinked down at her. She didn't say anything, and since I hadn't spoken, she didn't even have her face turned toward me. But she held her rag doll up to me. "H-h-hold dollie. Sh-h-he helps."

I came undone. "I love you, poppet." I sat down on the ground, pulled Rebecca and dollie into my arms and cried.

Suddenly someone grabbed me from behind, jerking me by the waist, tearing me away from Rebecca. I tried to cry out, but a large smelly hand covered my mouth.

"M-mary hurt you." Jamie pulled me backward. I tried to beat at him, to kick him, to free myself, but I couldn't. Terror cleared my tear-blurred vision and I saw the garden before me suddenly disappear behind a dark hedge. The maze! My mind screamed. The maze! He held me so tight I couldn't breathe.

As if from a faraway tunnel, I heard Rebecca scream. "C-c-c-caasss."

Jamie ran with me, faster than I would have ever thought he could move. Dark shadows and even blacker hedges whirled by. Fear, so paralyzing, so deafening that I could hardly think, gripped me by the throat. I'd made a fatal mistake. I had no weapon. In my sorrow, I'd blindly left my room without the knife, and I'd failed to get my father's pistol from Sean last night. I'd given no thought to what dangers might lurk during a walk in the gardens with Bridget and Prudence, and now I would pay the price.

I tried to fight harder.

"No, Mary," Jamie cried. "Hurt you."

Wrenching my head to the side, I finally could draw enough air to keep from fainting. I saw the broken remains of a gazebo looming ahead, so easily discernable by its half-rotted shape. Jamie went directly toward it, dragging me.

I drew enough air and screamed.

Jamie stopped and hit me across the cheek, knocking me to the ground. "Shh. Hurt you. Hurt you."

Stunning pain lashed through me. He grabbed my arm, wrenching it as he pulled me to the gazebo. Once upon its splintered floor, he dragged me to an open trap door and threw me into the yawning black pit. I screamed, reaching out for anything to save myself, and caught hold of the rung of a ladder. I managed to hold on long enough to break my fall to the bottom of the earthen room. Jamie jumped the distance effortlessly and pulled on a rope hanging down. The trap door shut, drenching us in the dark. I screamed again.

"Shh. Hurt you, Mary. Hide." He must have had the eyes of a bat, because I couldn't see, yet he grabbed my arm and started dragging me with him.

"Please, stop. Tell me about Mary." I tried to reason with him.

"Hide." He kept dragging me further. In the darkness, I started to see shadows and knew I was no longer in a room but a tunnel that went on for what felt like forever. Then the dank smell of wet earth changed to a putrid scent as he drew closer to a gray area ahead. That meant light. I focused on it, praying.

We reached a dimly lit room, and he pushed me down on a filthy cot. "Hide," he said again. "Hurt you."

I drew a deep breath, trying to think past my pain and fear. Was he trying to tell me to hide?

He walked across the room and lit a candle. I quickly recognize that we weren't in an earthen chamber now, but one of stone with primitive designs etched on the walls. Circling the room were carved stone statues as large as the one of Daghdha in the center of the Stone Virgins. They were placed closely against the stone walls, leaving small crevices draped with spider webs. The statues dwarfed Jamie. I suddenly recalled Stuart saying that Jamie felt comfortable in the circle of the Stone Virgins and I wondered if it was because they made him little again.

"Jamie," I said, hoping that I could reason with him if I calmed myself. "Help me. Take me to the castle. Help me."

He shook his head. "Hurt you." He pointed across the room, moving aside so that I could see.

The decomposing remains of a woman with blond hair lay on a cold stone slab. Mary.

I fought the retching and the dizziness that tried to rip my sanity from me. Hot and cold sweats gripped my body. I'd been searching for a loved one, but the reality and the horror of finding her dead devastated me. I crawled back on the cot until I hit the stone wall behind me. I could barely breathe, for I knew I, too, would die. I couldn't give up.

"What happened to Mary, Jamie?" I asked, hoping again to find reason in the giant.

He shook his head and yelled. "Hurt. Hurt you too." He paced about the room agitated. "Don't talk," he said.

I bit back my questions, deciding to be as invisible as I could, hoping that if I waited long enough, I would find an opportunity to escape. I knew running while he was awake was out of the question. He would have overpowered me in minutes. No loose stones or sticks or any other weapon lay close to me, but I didn't give up my search for an escape.

I wasn't sure how long I'd been there, a ball of numbness and terror, but I saw the shadows in the room grow, even though the candle remained lit. Only then did I realize that there had to be light coming from outside into this room. Light meant escape. I started studying the upper regions of the room, my heart shrinking in horror as I discerned the exit. It lay directly above the stone slab Mary lay on. I'd have to climb onto that, and even then I didn't think I was tall enough to reach the stone opening.

That meant the only way out was the way I had come in.

Jamie moved and I darted my gaze toward him and to where it appeared he was headed. A wooden table sat in the corner with only one thing on it, rather in it. A large knife stabbed into the wood. He reached for it, and I bit back a scream, wrenching myself from the wall and off the cot. I ran for the dark opening he'd brought me through.

"Nooo, Mary." Knife in hand, Jamie lunged in front of me. Screaming, I turned to the side, backing away from him until I hit the protruding arms of a Stone Virgin.

He stepped toward me. I desperately searched the room, edging around the Stone Virgin, hitting spider webs that I was too terrified to push away. Then I saw the dark crevice between the wall and the statue, so slight a place that a man like Jamie couldn't reach. Sucking in my stomach, I wedged into the space, turning my head sideways to fit. Cold stone scraped my cheek and jaw, and painfully pressed against my breasts, but I burrowed deeper into the crevice as Jamie screamed for me but couldn't reach me. I cried out in horror as a spider crawled along my neck. My arms were pinned to my sides. I could do nothing but stand wedged between the stone and suffer its roving, and I wondered if the quick blade of a knife might not be a better way to die.

"Cassie. Where are you?"

I thought I was dreaming, hearing the deep ferocity of Sean's voice because I so badly wanted to hear him, see him, touch him one last time.

"Cassie!"

Thundering steps and the flickering light of torches filled the chamber, telling me I wasn't dreaming.

"Sean!" I screamed as loud as I could.

"Nooo! Hurt you," Jamie yelled.

"He has a knife!"

"Drop the knife, Jamie, now!" Stuart yelled.

There was a loud scuffle and Jamie's deep sobbing filled the chamber.

"God, it's Mary." Sean voice rang with horror. "Bloody hell, Cassie. Where in God's name are you?"

"Here," I gasped. "Behind a Stone Virgin." I tried to move and couldn't, suddenly I couldn't breathe and my heart raced. "Oh God, I think I am stuck."

Scraping and heavy breathing sounded near the opening. I couldn't see Sean, but I knew he was there. The heat of him reached me before his voice. "Cassie? More scraping. "I can't reach you."

"Nor could Jamie," I said. "Where is he?"

"Stuart has tied him. He can't hurt you."

"He killed Mary," I said, nearly sobbing. "And kept her body in this room."

"Cassie. Come out, please. I need to see that you're all right."

I tried to move again and couldn't. "I can't," I cried, tears stinging my eyes. It was irrational to feel that I was going to die there, but I did. "I can't."

"Yes, you can. Just remember exactly how you held your body to get in there. Don't cry. Let your body relax. Close your eyes. Think. Be calm. Think of yourself as small and soft. Reach for me and I will be there."

Closing my eyes, I focused on his voice and listened to him as he repeated his words over and over again. Slowly, moving closer to him an inch at a time, I freed myself. The moment I reached the edge of the crevice, he pulled me out, into his arms. Warm and solid, I wanted to sink into him and never move again, but I pulled back instead. "Spiders. Please. Get them off me. Please."

Sean quickly brushed me off, using his coat to combat the webs as I scrubbed my fingers through my hair. I took his coat when he finished. My heart wept at the sight of Mary on the cold stone and I laid the coat over her.

I looked and saw Jamie, lying on the ground crying, his hands tied behind his back, his feet tied together. Stuart sat on the ground next to Jamie, his arm on Jamie's shoulder as tears ran unchecked.

"He must have killed her for some reason." Tears filled my eyes. "He loved her, but he must have killed her. Where are we?"

"A burial chamber beneath the Stone Virgins," Sean said gravely. "Do you think he became confused about the legend, Stuart? Wanted to keep the woman he loved forever?"

"Send for Constable Poole." Stuart's face was ravaged with pain.

"You're sure?" Sean whispered.

"Yes," Stuart rasped. "Jamie won't understand...being hanged, perhaps there'll be another way to end this for him..." His voice choked into a sob.

And more tears filled my eyes. Sean swung me into his

arms. "Shh. You're safe now, lass."

I shook my head and buried my face against him. I couldn't stem the flow of tears as he, limping without his cane, carried me from the room.

"Sean, you'll hurt yourself. I can walk."

"I'm fine." He pulled me tighter. Even in my distraught state, I could tell he was far from fine. Without his cane, his stride hitched too sharply to be balanced in carrying my weight. He stumbled a little and cursed.

I buried my face against his neck. "Please, Sean. Just having you with me helps more than anything. Let me walk beside you."

He sighed, letting my legs slide down to the dirt floor. Holding me a moment, he dropped his forehead to mine. "Cassie." Cupping my cheeks in his hands, he pressed his lips reverently to mine. "I'm sorry," he whispered.

A cry from Jamie echoed into the tunnel before I could speak. Sean stepped back and put his arm about my shoulder. "Come. We must hurry."

Drawing a breath, I nodded. And we hurried forward, helping each other. The tunnel now flickered with torchlight and the acrid scent of smoke filled the air. Several sharp turns ahead, we met the earl and Sir Warwick coming our way. They were armed with pistols and sported far from their usual bored countenances.

"You have the lass, thank God," the earl said.

"I thought these bloody tunnels were boarded up," Sean answered harshly.

"I thought they were too," said the earl. "Alex appears to be using the caves to sea for some bloody reason. We've just come from that way, having met Constable Poole on the beach investigating a report of smuggling."

Sir Warwick peered at me. "So you found the wench alive."

"Her name is Cassie," Sean said coldly. "Mary's cousin. Her suspicion that Mary's death wasn't an accident has proved true, so you might as well go back and get the constable. We need him." He turned an angry and disgusted look toward his father.

"I wouldn't go into the Stone Virgins' burial chamber, Father. Only more consequences to your sins lie there. You never should have passed your used goods onto a groomsman. Jamie would have never ended up as he is." Sean started walking away, pulling me with him.

"You don't know what in the bloody hell you're talking about," the earl yelled. I winced at the pain in his voice, and wanted to reach out to him, but Sean had pulled us too far away. "Until you've loved and lost, don't condemn another."

Sean stopped in his tracks, but he didn't turn around to face his father. He looked at me in the flickering light a moment then moved on. Silently, more determined than before, as if he were running from a greater tragedy than what we'd left in the burial chamber.

He didn't say anything as we reached the ladder leading from the caves, only urged me up ahead of him into the broken gazebo, then guided me through the shadowed maze. It wasn't even dark yet. I'd only been with Jamie a short time, but it seemed so much longer. Still, the hedges of the maze loomed so darkly that it felt as if night had descended, a starless, moonless night.

I shuddered as we emerged to see the sun, a bare sliver of fading hope on the horizon. Squinting, Sean flinched, holding his arm up to block the light as he turned his face from it.

"You're in pain." I pressed my hand to the rough warmth of his shadowed cheek and then to the bandage on his temple. He flinched away from my touch.

"No more than usual." His voice sounded strained.

I nodded toward the maze. "This is where Lady Helen died?"

"I've often thought about cutting it down."

"Why haven't you?"

"Destroying something my mother created for fun won't change what happened. So there'd be no point."

"Who killed Lady Helen? I don't believe you did and I have to wonder if your brother did, either. With the tunnel here, anyone could have killed her and not been seen. Why did only you and Alex fall under suspicion?" I drew a deep breath.

"Could Jamie have done it?"

"At sixteen? He was large enough then to have harmed someone, but even now it is difficult to believe he intentionally hurt Mary. Helen was beaten, brutally so. I don't think Jamie had anything to do with her death." He sighed. "She was an angel, and Alex and I were the only ones who would have had any reason to kill her."

"Are you sure? Isn't it possible someone else could have? There seems to be so many unanswered questions."

"Bloody hell, Cassie," Sean exploded. "Don't you understand? There isn't going to be any happy ending, with all the ribbons tied into pretty bows. Yes, another man could have murdered Helen. But it doesn't change things. The Dragon's Curse still stands for me and Alex, so it doesn't matter what suspicion clouds our lives. In fact, it's better this way for everyone." The growing darkness cast shadows on his stark features, revealing the hopelessness of his thoughts. "So, let it go. You can't change the past and you can't run away from fate."

"Only if you're blind, you can't." I turned from him. "And I don't think Lady Helen would agree with you. She deserves justice." Anger fueling me, I marched to the house.

"Cassie, wait." Sean caught up with me and grabbed my hand. For a moment I thought he would reach out to me, grasp hold of a future for us, and tell me that he loved me. "They know who you are," he said, and my heart seemed to break, tears filled my eyes, but I refused to let them fall. "Stuart told everyone you are Mary's cousin. I think he hoped to keep the men who were searching for you from shooting Jamie on sight. He tried to convince everyone that Jamie had only taken you because he was trying to protect Mary's cousin." His voice roughed with anger. "Mary's death may have been an accident, but harming Rebecca and you was unconscionable. Hanging Jamie would be like hanging a child, though. So I'm going to have Constable Poole assure me that he'll be locked up instead."

"Mary wouldn't want Jamie to hang either, but I want to

see the constable before he leaves."

"You'll never know how deeply I regret that any of this ever happened."

As I stared into his eyes, I realized that he spoke of more than just Mary's tragedy. He regretted knowing me as well. That hurt worse than his refusal to believe in a future. I bit down on the inside of my cheek, determined not to cry. I realized then that he truly did not love me as I loved him. For I would never regret, loving him, touching him, and knowing him with my mind, body, and soul.

The kitchen door opened and I turned away from what would never be mine to hold again.

Bridget came running out, tears pouring from reddened blue eyes filled with worry. She ran up and hugged me. "I should be spanking you for lying to us all. You're bloody proper Cassiopeia from the paper, who'd have believed it."

"I'm sorry."

Others poured out the kitchen door, the Murphys, Mrs. Frye and Prudence with Rebecca in her arms.

"You disappeared in a twinkling of the eye, you did. Was it Jamie?" Bridget asked.

"I'm afraid so," Sean said. "Mary's body was found in the chamber he took Cassie to. Apparently he's been hiding there."

"No! You can't hurt him." Mrs. Frye burst into tears. "You can't."

Mrs. Murphy reached for her. "Clara, I'm sorry but…"

"You don't understand. I…I did it! It was an accident," Mrs. Frye cried.

# Chapter Nineteen

My breath caught as shock rippled through me and, judging by the sounds of surprise and denial cutting through the evening air, stunned everyone. Blindly reaching for her husband, Mrs. Murphy stepped back from Mrs. Frye.

Mrs. Frye flinched.

"Is that why you never told me that Mary's mother wished to see me?" Sean asked harshly, his hands fisted.

"Yes." Mrs. Frye backed away from everyone, her eyes fearful and her body shaking.

"You took Rebecca to the roof and left her there?" Sean's voice lowered, becoming lethal in its roughness. The vibrating anger ripped through me.

Mrs. Frye shook her head, appearing confused. "N-n-no, n-n-no. Jamie must have been trying to protect me. I don't know. I haven't had time to figure it out. I really believed the child had wandered. He didn't hurt Mary. The child isn't hurt. They can't hurt him. He's been hurt enough, even before he was born."

"How did the accident happen?" Sean demanded.

Mrs. Frye blinked. "I...an argument. We argued about Jamie. I was angry that she was making him want things he could never have. I shook her by the shoulders. She stumbled back, fell down the...sand dune, rolling faster until she hit her head on a sharp rock. Then she...was...dead."

Sean moved closer to Mrs. Frye. "Why did you hide it? Why didn't you just tell everyone what happened?"

"I don't know," Mrs. Frye sobbed. "They can't hurt Jamie."

Sean shook his head, as if the world rested on his shoulders. "You're going to have to tell the authorities. They'll probably arrest you and Jamie both until they determine exactly what happened, and why you felt you had to hide what happened."

My head spun. The unfolding events were more than I could absorb. I must have wavered on my feet, for Bridget and Prudence reached for me at the same time.

"Cass," Rebecca called, holding her arms out to me.

"I'm here, poppet." I gave her a big hug.

"H-h-horseman g-g-gone? H-hurt no more?"

I looked over at Mrs. Frye, who was sobbing into her hands, and I wondered how Rebecca was confusing the sound of a horse with Mary's death in an argument with Mrs. Frye. It didn't even remotely match, but Rebecca desperately needed reassurance. "Yes," I told Rebecca. "There's nothing for you to worry about anymore."

After giving me salve for my scrapes, the doctor declared that all I needed was a bath, hot broth, a brandy and a good rest. Bridget and Prudence took the doctor's advice to heart. I delayed leaving Killdaren's Castle long enough to gather my wits, clean myself up and to speak to Constable Poole.

Word that he awaited me in the library finally came.

"Well, if it isn't the illustrious Miss Andrews," Constable Poole said as I walked into the room, his cold voice stealing any warmth the hearth fire had flickered into the room.

"I gather you two have met then," Sean said from off to my left. Jerking my head his way, I gasped and my heart raced, unable to free itself from his spell. I hadn't expected Sean would be present.

"Yes, we've met, and none too pleasantly, either," Constable Poole said. "On her arrival to Dartmoor's End, Miss Andrews was quite adamant of the Killdaren's involvement with her cousin's disappearance. Though the guilty party wasn't who you thought, I imagine you are quite pleased with yourself." He smiled.

"I beg your pardon." Fury whipped through me and any thought I had about bringing up the discrepancy in Rebecca's horseman's story and Mrs. Frye's testimony died. I didn't want this man anywhere near Rebecca, and now fully understood Prudence's reluctance to have Rebecca questioned about Mary. Before I could say more, Sean stepped forward.

"Constable Poole. If your callous rudeness to Miss Andrews is to express your loyalty to my family, then it is a highly misplaced endeavor, and not appreciated. Despite her deception in entering my home, Miss Andrews has my complete respect and support, and is grieving for a loved one. I suggest you keep that in mind, sir!"

The constable narrowed his eyes. "My apologies, Mr. Killdaren, Miss Andrews. I didn't mean to offend. What is it you wished to speak with me about? I've a number of details to attend in regards to settling your cousin's case, and will also have to speak to your aunt about her wishes for Mary's body."

I only nodded my head, unable to verbally accept this man's insincerity. I thought his handling of my cousin's death criminally inept. "Thank you, but there is no need for you to speak to my aunt. I will. I'd much rather give her the news myself, and we'll inform you of our plans for Mary's burial soon. I assume you will have the local coroner examine Mary's body and give a report?"

"Given her condition, I not sure exactly what that will accomplish," the constable said. "I think I can handle the details of my job well enough, Miss Andrews."

"Then you will see to a coroner's report as Miss Andrews has requested, correct?" Sean's tone brooked no argument.

"Of course, as I just said." Constable Poole stiffened, agitated with what he clearly saw as interference into his realm. "Is that all Miss Andrews?"

I glanced at Sean and dug my nails into my palm. "No. I think there should be a reinvestigation into Lady Helen Kennedy's murder."

"No!" Sean's voice cut so sharply I flinched.

The constable smirked and sent Sean an "I told you she

was trying to harm you".

I ignored them both and plunged ahead. "I believe a grave disservice was done to both Lady Helen and the Killdaren family, Constable Poole. And if you won't investigate the matter further, then I have contacts in journalism that would be very interested in what I have to say."

"If you won't mind leaving us now, Constable, I'll speak to you about this at another time." Sean moved to the door, closer to me. The moment Constable Poole exited the room, Sean grasped my elbow. "Miss Andrews, I think you need to take a seat."

"No, Mr. Killdaren. We're well beyond a polite conversation. What are you so afraid of?"

He faced the fire. "I told you earlier. Only Alex and I had motive. I'll not see him hanged."

"But what if your brother is innocent as well? Not just your life is being ruined."

"I have cause to believe Alex's anger the night Helen died was beyond his control. I met with Helen last, and the way she described his reaction...Besides, our lives were ruined from conception. Nothing can change that."

"Well, it certainly won't change if you won't ever allow yourself to see a different way," I said, devastated by his blindness. I loved him, and he didn't love me enough to see another way. The hopelessness of standing there in firelight with him, struggling in a churning sea of pain rather than holding him, cherishing that we both yet lived after coming so close to death, was more than I could bear. I had to leave Killdaren's Castle, and I had to tell my family that I'd found Mary.

I went to the door and he didn't stop me, didn't call me back. I wanted his touch with every fiber of my being, couldn't imagine never knowing its thrill again. I couldn't imagine not hearing the timbre of his voice or facing the piercing green of his gaze. Tears fell. I turned to look at him one last time, feeling as if my insides were being twisted into knots. I wished that I could have spent one more night in his arms, loving him as woman to man, burying my hand in the silk of his hair, pressing against the heat of his body, breathing his scent, and feeling the fire of his passion.

He still faced the flames of the fire. "We'll speak in the morning about taking you to your sisters and your aunt." His voice was jagged with cutting pain. His hands were fisted at his side and I knew he hurt, that he wasn't indifferent to me. But he didn't love enough to let himself live.

I didn't say anything more. I wouldn't be here come morning, but I didn't tell him that, because I didn't have the words to say goodbye.

I entered the bedchamber I shared with Bridget, dashing at my tears. She, Prudence and Rebecca were there.

"Blimey, Cassie, what is it?"

"I...I have to go now," I said, bolstering myself.

Prudence gasped, stricken. "Surely, the Killdaren isn't asking you to leave?"

I shook my head. "He mustn't know until after I'm gone, and I will leave a note explaining why I left for you to give to him in the morning. I have to go see my sisters and my aunt at Seafarer's Inn. I have to tell them about Mary." I couldn't see Sean again and still hold onto my resolve not to beg him to love me.

But that wasn't truly possible, and I'd always known it, though I'd forgotten it. Someday I would dream of death again, and what then? What if I dreamed of his death, or the death of our child? If my own mother could step away from me at a moment like that, how could I ask a man to share that burden?

Rebecca ran up to me and I pulled her into my arms for a tight hug.

"Horseman gone. Mary's in heaven," she said.

"Yes." I hugged her tighter, glancing at the surprise on both Prudence's and Bridget's faces.

Rebecca had made a huge step, but I had to ask just a little more. I brushed her cheek gently. "Can you tell us more about the horseman and Mary, Rebecca?"

She shook her head. "Horseman came from the sea and took Mary. She cried." Tears filled her eyes then and I feared she would revert back to her hysteria. "Mum!" she called.

"I'm here, precious." Prudence enveloped Rebecca in her arms. Rebecca sighed and placed her head on Prudence's shoulder instead of screaming. We knew then that whatever trauma Rebecca had suffered that day, she was recovering well, though we might never know exactly what happened.

I looked at Bridget and Prudence and Rebecca and my heart squeezed painfully again. How could I leave them? They'd all become so dear. Seemingly reading my mind, Bridget's eyes watered, and she started fussing with the furniture, speaking very fast, as if hurting and trying to cover it up. "I'll be leaving here myself, sometime. As soon as we hear from Flora, I'm going to take my mum and my brother there and tend to my mum. The doctor's still not sure what's wrong. He doesn't think it's the consumption, but she isn't improvin' as well as she should. I think it's because she's not restin' as she ought. Keeps taking sewing to help pay for things since Flora's gone."

"Well." I swallowed hard. "You have to let me know where...Oh Bridget...You have to come to Oxford! You, your mum and your brother! You and he can...you both can get an education!"

"Real schooling? Blimey, Cassie." Bridget's eyes were brighter than stars. She shook her head, and tears filled her eyes again. "I can't go. Not yet. I can't leave Stuart to face the arrest of his mum and his brother alone. I have to help him. And I have to wait on word from Flora too."

I nodded, understanding, but still feeling as something precious kept escaping me every attempt to hold on to it. "Then later. You must come as soon as you can."

She nodded.

"And you too, Prudence. You must come to Oxford to visit me and my family. And there are teachers there that could teach Rebecca so many things that she could do."

Prudence shook her head. "No, Cassie. This is our world.

Rebecca and I would be outcasts anywhere else. I know who I am and I'll not pretend to be different. Besides." She brushed a loving hand over Rebecca's head. "I don't dare leave. As long as Rebecca and I are here, he can't pretend we don't exist. He can pretend we don't matter, but he can't forget us."

I saw a sharp stab of pain in Prudence's eyes before she buried her face against Rebecca's soft hair. And I realized for the first time that all of her quiet ways, her dignity, and almost haunting beauty were because she loved a man who wouldn't return her affection.

"The earl," I whispered.

Prudence nodded.

"Casss, d-d-don't go," Rebecca cried, slipping back into her stutter.

"I have to, but I will see you again." I was determined to keep them a part of my life somehow. All of Mary's hopes for Rebecca had to come true and I wanted to see it happen, even if from afar. "I have a present for you," I told Rebecca and reached into my pocket.

Heart squeezing, I dug the pheasant shell out of my pocket and ran my finger over the M carved into its smoothness.

"Here, poppet." I took Rebecca's hand and pressed the shell into her palm.

"This is my promise that I will see you again. It is a very precious treasure and I'm going to let you keep it for me. It is a beautiful shell from the sea. And every time I see you, I'll give you another shell so that you can feel some of the wonders from the sea whenever you want to."

Coming over, Bridget looked down at the shell. "May I see it?"

Rebecca handed it to her. "Your cousin had a shell just like this, she did. Only it had a..." She looked at me, her eyes misty with sadness. "It had a C carved in it."

Bridget handed the shell back to Rebecca, who absorbed herself in running her tiny fingertips over it.

My smile trembled. "We found the shells while vacationing together when were ten and kept them all of these years to remind us of each other."

"Thank you," Prudence said. "I'll make sure she cares for it and I'll let her know how special it is when she is older."

"She'll have many more to her collection by then," I said. Though little, the pheasant shell was a big promise not to forget everyone here that Mary, and now I, held dear.

Prudence nodded. I could tell she didn't believe me, but I would prove her wrong. Maybe even one day convince her and Rebecca to come to Oxford for a visit.

"Do you need help getting your things together?" Bridget asked.

I shook my head. "I, uh, readied them earlier, after seeing the doctor. I don't have much." I was leaving with so much less than what I'd come to Killdaren's Castle with. My heart. "I do need a few minutes to write Mr. Killdaren a letter."

"And I need to get Rebecca to bed." Prudence's smile appeared forced.

"I made a promise." I hugged her and Rebecca.

"A s-s-seashell pw-w-womis-se." Rebecca held up the shell

"That's right. A thousand-shell promise."

Rebecca smiled. "T-h-h-housand."

Just as soon as Prudence and Rebecca left, Bridget pulled on her blue shawl. "I'll have Stuart ready the shopping buggy and I'll ride with you to the inn, if it is all right. It'll give me time to speak to him about his mum and his brother. I was wrong, you know, about him not knowing what it was like to have his mother and brother hurting and not be able to help. He's lived his whole life that way, and I didn't realize it. All I could see was the privileges he'd gotten in life."

"I'm glad you can see differently now."

"We've been good friends for each other." Bridget was teary eyed again.

I gave her a big hug. "The best of friends. And I expect you to keep your promise to come to Oxford."

"I will. In the meantime, I'm making Stuart continue with the classes we started. I want to learn and the others do too."

"You will learn." I drew a deep breath, realizing there were so many other things that I'd be leaving undone here. How could I bear it? It was almost as if my life in Oxford never existed. So much of my heart belonged here.

Bridget nodded and started to leave. At the door she turned back toward me. "If you love him, why are you leaving?"

"Sometimes loving means you have to leave. Both people have to want the same thing, and be willing to sacrifice for it, or they can never be together."

"Like queen and Draco?"

"Yes."

"I wish we could write this differently."

"I do too."

Bridget sighed then left, leaving me with no more excuses. I gathered the pen and paper and prayed for strength. I had to force myself to do the impossible, which was to tell Sean goodbye.

*Dear Sean,*

*Forgive me for fleeing, for leaving this letter to say what I must. But I knew I wouldn't be able to say goodbye any other way. I came here looking for the truth behind Mary's death and somehow found a different truth as well: the truth I've been hiding from in my own life. In coming here to Killdaren's Castle and seeing the struggles of those who live in its shadowed walls, I learned that the advice I'd been giving to so many isn't wholly true. There are more important things in life than etiquette and propriety, and they are not found in the dictates of society. Those things are compassion, love and hope, and are found within the heart. Knowing you has brought them painfully, and beautifully, into my life and into my heart.*

*I have compassion for your pain, and in the depths of the night my spirit will reach out to comfort you in your darkness. You'll feel me in the wind rushing in from the sea.*

*My love for you will endure as long as the stars fill the heavens, for it is not bound by even the frailty of my own heart. Even though you do not hold the same depth of affection for me*

291

*as I do for you, I know you felt the beauty of our union.*

*So this is my hope for you, which fills my heart. Don't spend your life forever beneath the shadow of a curse. Find the courage and the strength to love and to dance beneath the stars.*

*Eternally yours,*

*Cassie*

I slipped silently from Killdaren's Castle, with my belongings and Mary's letters in an old potato sack. It was an hour before midnight, and a light fog had eased in from the sea. Its misty fingers wrapped around me, tightening the pain in my heart.

The castle loomed behind me its gray walls dim and its corridors still haunted with silence, as if I'd never been there. The gardens and maze stood before me, dark reminders of things I didn't want to remember, but would never forget. I didn't dare look at the gargoyle guarded observatory or think of the stars and what had lain beyond them in Sean's arms. The tangy salt of sea air mingled with my falling tears, and the moon, a big bright ball of it, shone brightly down, trying to show me that all was not dark with the world at the moment. I didn't want to see. The stars would never the same as before, for in a twinkling, my life had changed and Sean would be forever imprinted in the heavens as surely as if he were a constellation as large as the universe.

I gave the maze's dark hedges a wide berth, and shuddered as I passed on my way to where Bridget and Stuart waited for me at the stable. I was so absorbed in my own troubles that I had almost entered the stable before I heard the raised voices.

"I refuse to walk away from you. You have to let me help," Bridget yelled.

"No, I bloody don't, Bridget. You know what the villagers are like. They're a superstitious mob. Once word of what Jamie and my mother have done gets out, I'll be reviled, and so will anyone associated with me."

"You can't stop me," Bridget said, her voice growing louder.

She stormed from the stables and nearly ran into me. Her red hair curled wildly about her face and her blue eyes were fiercely determined. "Bloody stubborn man. Can't see past his idiotic opinions, that's what. Who is he to decide what's best for me?"

I stopped and stared at Bridget a moment, wishing a little shouting could set my world aright.

Bridget smiled at me, dashing at the tears on her lashes. "Blimey, ladies don't say bloody."

I laughed a little. "Sometimes no other word will bloody well do."

Reaching Seafarer's Inn, I went up the stairs to the apartments only to find them alarmingly empty. All of my sisters and aunt's belongings were there, but they weren't. I immediately went down to the proprietor. A contrast of mussed hair and impeccably neat dress, he stood at the front desk, polishing its surface.

"Excuse me, Mr. Lloyd. Would you be able to tell me where my aunt and my sisters are at this evening? I seemed to have missed a communication with them."

"Why certainly, Miss Andrews. They are in the dining room. Viscount Blackmoor is having a private party." He looked down at my dress and cleared his throat. "Would you like for me to escort you in once you've, uh, refreshed your appearance?"

I blinked with surprise at his rudeness. Then I realized I still wore a maid's uniform. At least I didn't have on a mob cap, but I didn't dare delay to see what this private party was about. It was highly unseemly for them to be at a gentleman's private party this late. It was nearly midnight.

"No. I would like for you to escort me now."

I'm not sure what debacle I expected to intrude upon, but it wasn't a gaming den. Everyone looked up at my gasp of outrage, and there was a dead silence. I never in my life expected to see the Earl of Dartraven and Sir Warwick there with Sean's two friends, the viscount, my aunt and my sisters.

"What's your son's wench doing here?" Sir Warwick said to the earl, smiling nastily.

"So, that's the beauty Sean seduced—" Lord Ashton's sentence was cut by a jab to the ribs by Mr. Drayson.

"That's my sister," Andromeda declared, her cheeks flushed and her eyes over bright.

The blood drained from my face as the axe of a scandal fell on my head. From the shocked looks bouncing about the room, my reputation had been felled.

# Chapter Twenty

"Go ahead and spoil the surprise, Ashton." The deep voice came from behind me. Sean's luring lilt set my heart to racing, he wrapped his arm around my shoulders, ushering me into the room, as his scent and warmth washed over me. "This is the beauty I'm going to marry."

I turned toward him, shocked to have his dark and vibrant countenance truly beside me. Without the backdrop of the castle's large rooms, he cut a more imposing figure than ever. His black riding pants tapered sleekly down to leather boots. His white shirt lay casually open at the neck, and he'd flung his ebony cape across a broad shoulder. My knees shook. Seeing him set my heart to racing until I realized why he'd announced to the world that he was marrying a woman whom he'd told that he didn't love and couldn't marry.

If I hadn't already been on the verge of fainting before, I was sure that I now would, just as soon as I informed a bloody stubborn male that I refused to be his noble sacrifice on the altar of propriety. I'd rather live with the scandal than marry without love.

The room erupted in noise. My sisters squealed, hurrying toward me, their walk just a tad bit unsteady. The earl winked. Sir Warwick shook his head as if he were not seeing and hearing right. Sean's friends burst into laughter, and Aunt Lavinia, her cheeks scarlet, kept looking between Sean and the viscount, fanning herself.

"No," I whispered to Sean, gritting my teeth against the yes my heart wanted to shout.

"Yes," he whispered back, iron determination lacing his hiss, and narrowing his green gaze. "Since *you* didn't bloody stick around for me to *ask* you properly, you're just going to have to wait." He nudged me toward my sisters, and I pushed back.

How did the man have the audacity to sound peeved at me! "This is..."

"The way it is," he said firmly. "Talk to your family. I have some business to attend to."

Moving away from me, his hitched gait more pronounced, Sean strode determinedly toward the viscount, who, looking grim, quickly stood. Silence descended like a death knell as all eyes riveted to the two men who were mirror images of each other—except Sean was pale and the viscount as tan as a sailor might be.

The tension filling the room gripped me, made me feel that at any second Sean and his brother were going to explode. The men were so charismatic that there honestly wasn't room for the both of them in the small den. It was easy to see how their countenances had perpetuated the rumors of the curse. They were like warrior gods of legendary lore, preparing to battle for the world.

"I'm dissolving the pact." Sean voice was tight and sharp.

"I see," the viscount drawled, matching Sean's antagonism with a deceptive ease. "It wasn't my idea, so I am glad to see it end."

"As soon as I can arrange my affairs, I'll be leaving here with Cassie. If you and I never see each other, and live a country apart, perhaps we can change fate."

The viscount looked as if he flinched then nodded. "As you wish."

Sean turned to me, his gaze burning with a mixture of anger and desire. "I'll wait for you in the inn's parlor." He left the room, sucking all of the air from my lungs.

"Dear me." Aunt Lavinia fanned her flushed cheeks as she approached me. "Do you think it's safe to go? He looked a bit upset, dear."

"Oh, Cassie, this is wonderful!" Gemini clapped her hands. "We'll have a wedding fit for a queen!"

"My word, Cassie, he's exactly like the viscount, only more, more...dangerous. I think you had better stay here." Andromeda reached for my hand. The moment she touched me, her eyes widened and a hot blush rushed to her cheeks. "You love him."

I pulled my hand away before she could discern anything else, especially about Mary. It wasn't the time or the place to tell them about Mary tonight, and Sean and I had a great deal to discuss at the moment. "I'll be back in the morning and we'll talk about everything. I have much to tell you," I said. "Meanwhile, I suggest you ladies retire before everyone's reputation is ruined. You aren't drinking cocktails again?" I asked, studying their flushed states a little closer.

"Certainly not." Aunt Lavinia huffed out her generous bosom. "I'm chaperoning this venture. Surely that is acceptable."

"It's almost midnight and this looks to be as close to a gentleman's gaming hell as you will find outside of London. There are no other guests from the village present, and the men are all bachelors."

"Yes, I know dear," Aunt Lavinia blinked, as if agog at the thought. "Such manly ones too," she whispered. "But I wonder how it became so late? Why, we we're just having dinner a short time ago, then decided to play cards. It must have been the viscount's spiced wine that made me lose track of time."

"Spiced wine," I choked out. Good Lord. They were all slightly inebriated with an aphrodisiac!

"Yes, a most invigorating beverage you simply must try. Mustn't she, my lord?"

Turning, I found the viscount studying me very intently. "So, you're the absent sister who's been conducting an important investigation? On my brother, it would seem."

"I haven't time for explanations now. I'm sorry to be rude, but everything will have to be said later. For now, I must go. And my aunt and my sisters shall immediately retire to our apartment without any more *spiced* wine to guide their way."

After giving my aunt a pointed look, I ducked from the room with my sisters and my aunt gasping at my rudeness, to a viscount no less. But I had to call a halt to the evening's shenanigans and I couldn't wait another minute to see Sean, whom the viscount was not, no matter how much they looked alike.

I entered the parlor ready for battle. It was empty. "Sean." I searched the shadowed corners. Feeling a breeze, I saw the French doors stood ajar and I moved that way.

He stood in the moonlight at the end of the terrace, gazing out at the sea. The wind brushed his dark hair and ruffled his cape. He had one boot planted on a low stone wall, his hand resting on his bent knee, looking so haunted, so handsome, so alone. My heart tumbled over itself, reaching out to him before I could rein it in. My love for this man of shadows and the night ruled my every day.

"We have to talk, Sean." I moved to him. He kept his gaze on the sea, drawing mine to it as well.

"Yes, lass, we do. I received your note."

"You weren't supposed to until morning. I've barely left the castle. How?"

"I had to see you. I went to your room and found you and Bridget gone, and nearly leveled the castle with my fear that something had happened to you. Prudence enlightened me as to the letter and to your flight." He turned to me, a man who'd lured my heart into his darkness, and left me there alone. "I don't suppose you've been able to tell your family about Mary yet. Do you need to go see them before we talk?"

"No. I've decided to wait until morning. A few hours won't change anything and given their state of mind at the moment, it would be crueler to tell them now than to wait. They think I've returned to the castle, and those at the castle think I'm at the inn."

"Good. We have some time to be together, then. To talk. If you are well enough to do so?" His gaze searched mine as he reached out and brushed a strand of hair from my face. "I'm sorry about Mary. I know your heart grieves," he said softly

I drew a deep breath of the sea air. "She was a beautiful, giving woman. I cared for her deeply and shall miss her. But my heart is more at peace now than in great sorrow. Since dreaming of her death, I've had time to accept that she's gone. Staying so busy at the castle, becoming involved with everyone there that Mary cared about, has taken away a lot of the pain. I fear my aunt and sisters haven't fared as well."

"They didn't appear stricken this evening."

"No. I think they are inside, though, and are desperately latching on to any reason not to think about Mary. Your friends and your brother are giving them ample fodder to fuel their escape. Both times that I've seen my sisters in the gentlemen's company, they've been in their cups so to speak, cocktails at breakfast and spiced wine for dinner."

"Spiced wine for all of them?" Sean's chest heaved a little as he choked back a laugh.

"It's not amusing," I said. "Considering its...its stimulating properties, I would think you'd be outraged on my behalf that men in your association are practically seducing my entire family."

"I fear I have a confession to make. The wine is no more stimulating than gingerbread cookies or flavored candy. In fact, it is even less inebriating than regular wine. You only feel its effects because it is sweeter and you tend to drink more."

Surely not, I thought. Just the memory of that night, the flushed warmth and tingling need stealing through me, captured my senses again. "Then why did you infer otherwise?"

Leaning closer, he whispered in my ear. "The power of suggestion has a tremendous effect on the mind and the senses, and I was bent on seducing you. Kissing you. Touching you. Making love to you."

My breath caught, my breasts grew heavy, my flesh damp. "Why?" I whispered, wanting to know his heart, wanting to hear him say that he loved me, just as I had told him.

He cupped my cheek then slid his hand down to press against my breast, over my thudding heart. "Can you honestly not know? Lord woman. What you have done to my life!" He brushed his lips over mine, lightly, so unexpectedly that I didn't have time to respond before he pulled me into his tight embrace, speaking softly into my ear. "I want to dance beneath the stars now, and nothing less will do. You've turned my world upside down, taken everything I believed to be irrevocable and ripped it apart. You came to me last night, gave me your heart and soul, and though I selfishly took that moment, I knew I had no right to more. No right to bring you into the darkness of my world. I still don't have the right."

"Yes, you do." I lifted my head from the solid warmth of his chest to gaze into the moonlit sea of his eyes. "I—"

He brushed another kiss to my lips. "Shh, let me finish."

"After you left me in the library earlier, I went back to my rooms, determined that my life would go on as before. I'd built a world over the past eight years in which I could content myself, to some measure, until my days in this godforsaken life should end. But there you were, in my bed. You were in my study. You were in the music room. You were in the castle, so I went outside to escape you and walked to the edge of the sea and you were there as well, in the stars, in the caressing wind. In my mind. I once told you that I would give up this life in a heartbeat. That is no longer true. I cling to every heartbeat now, Cassie, because you are in my heart as well."

"You mean, you weren't just being noble and trying to save me from scandal?"

He grabbed my shoulders. "God no. Noble would be to send you away. Noble would be to never let you decide if you wish to live your life during the hours of the night. Noble would be never to subject you and future generations to the Dragon's Curse. I am being wholly selfish in wanting you with me, wanting you to share my life, such as it is. I will do everything in my power to escape fate, yet I can't demand that you share it. I love you. I want you to marry me, but I won't accept your answer until morning."

My heart swelled with the passion pouring from him to me. "There's no need to wait. My answer—"

He pressed his finger to my lips. "Not until morning." He stepped back, taking my hand in his. "Come let me show you of my love until then. We've had little time together. Tonight will be our night." He urged me down the steps. His horse waited at the back of the inn. He mounted, then pulled me into his lap to sit side saddle before leading the horse down to the shore.

Once on the sand, he came to a stop. "If we're going to do this often, you're going to have to give up sitting properly."

"What do you mean?"

"Too much pressure on my hip." Sliding his arm about my middle, he lifted me off his lap a little. "Move one leg to the other side of the horse to sit astride."

"But—"

He pulled my skirts up, exposing my stockings and drawers from the thighs down. "You're covered completely and no one will see."

I slid my leg over, feeling very strange as my thighs settled against his and my bottom pressed intimately to his body and the saddle pressed against me. He groaned softly in my ear, pushing harder against me. "I want you."

I gasped, as fire spread through me.

Keeping one hand under my breasts, about my waist, he urged the horse on until we were racing across the sand. Salty wind and humid mist buffeted us as my body melded to his and the freedom of the flight filled me, making me want to dance and laugh and sing all at the same time.

"This is how being with you makes me feel, lass." The need vibrating in his voice shivered down my spine.

"You do the same for me." I leaned my head back against his shoulder and angled my face to press a kiss to his neck. He turned his lips to mine and covered my mouth with his. His lips and tongue were hot and demanding as he tangled his passion with mine then set us both on fire by sliding his hand to cup my breast, kneading its softness to an aching point. Breathing raggedly, he brought the horse to a stop.

"I want you in the moonlight." He slid from the horse and reached for me.

Unsure, I placed my hand in his, feeling his warmth and his strength in his grip, and the fire gleaming in his eyes. He led me up from the water's edge and the damp shoreline until we reached the soft powder of sun-warmed sand where the moon made a silver bed of light.

"First, dance with me beneath the stars. Let me feel you move against me, with me, to the music in our minds."

I walked into his embrace and wrapped my arms around his neck, pulling his body as close to me as I had the strength to do. He began to hum as he swayed with me beneath the stars, the wind and the salty breeze caressing me as his deep voice and the feel of his supple flesh against mine enlivened me until I nearly burst with the need for more. "Touch me," I whispered. "Kiss me. Make me yours."

He laughed. "Oh, I will. There's no doubt of it. I want to see the cream of your skin set aglow by the moon. I have a number of things in mind to experience with you tonight." Stepping back, he slid his cape off and spread it on the ground.

Then he kissed me deeply, his deft fingers undoing the buttons of my dress to touch me. "I want you naked beneath the stars." With skilled determination, he set out to satisfy his want. Soon my dress fell to the sand, then my chemise, my drawers and boots, leaving only my dark stockings and garters. "Lay down for me, Cassie."

Moving to the black cape, I lay back against the silk lining, smelling his scent and that of worn leather. Kneeling beside me, he threaded his finger through my hair, spreading it out about me. "Your hair is the sun that I can see without pain."

Then he moved my arms up, sliding my fingers behind my neck, bringing my breasts higher. He kissed me, groaning so deeply that my stomach clenched in anticipation. Leaving my lips, he nipped my neck with a tingling bite.

"How much have you read of *Powerful Vampires and Their Lovers*?" he asked.

I blinked, trying to think past the pleasure rippling through me and the luring almost fearful tension of being naked outside and making love beneath a full moon. "What?"

"The book you are reading, remember?" He smiled.

"Not...not past 'Forbidden Fruit'."

"Good. Then tonight will be a surprise." He nipped my neck and breasts again with tiny, almost stinging but pleasure-inducing bites that tingled as the coolness of the air replaced the heat of his mouth. "Don't move." Sliding his hands down from my breasts, he brushed over my stomach and eased off each stocking, spreading my legs far apart as he finished.

"Sean, this feels—"

"Sensual, Cassie. Don't mistake the excitement God meant for a man and a woman to share for something wrong or sinful. It is what we were created to be." He stood at my feet, between my legs, looking down at me, and stripped off his clothes as I watched. Like velvet covered marble, his body gleamed in the moonlight, a mixture of light skin and dark hair, hard need and supple muscle. He was beautiful and powerful in an elemental way, and his desire for me, so evident in his arousal, filled me with a hungering satisfaction that only making love to him could satiate.

He fell to his knees between my legs and planted his hands on either side of me so that he could lean over me. Once again he nipped at my skin, starting with my breasts until they throbbed with pleasure, their tips hard and wanting. I tried to reach for him, but he pressed my arms back down as he rose to his knees to look at me. "For now, just feel the pleasure I want to give you."

In a swift move, he slid his hands beneath my hips, lifting me until only my shoulders rested against the ground and his face was...

"Heavens," I cried. "Whatever are you doin—"

"Feasting." His mouth covered my femininity, nipping and laving until I wept from the fiery pleasure, but he never nipped just the right place. My breaths grew short and raspy, my skin became fevered, my pulse raced until my body throbbed. "Sean. Sean...please." I arched to him, and his kiss finally centered on the very heart of my burning flesh. My eyes widened to see the stars as pleasure burst inside of me. Then he rose above me.

Looking directly into my eyes so I could see his soul, he entered me, thrusting deep inside me as my body shuddered with the pleasure he'd given me. More pleasure washed over me, again and again in rippling waves that moved in tandem to his frenzied thrusts into me.

"Cassie," he cried, plunging then shuddering.

"Sean," I called out as spirit, soul and body soared beyond the stars into a blinding light of pleasure so shattering that my vision went black and my mind went blank.

"Cassie! Cassie!" I blinked, opening my eyes, surprised to find myself wrapped in Sean's arms.

I frowned. "What happened?"

"I think you forgot to breathe and fainted. How do you feel?"

"Exquisite. I saw beyond the stars."

"You did?"

"Yes. Having an astronomer for a husband will prove quite useful."

He bowed his head to mine. "Don't give me your answer until morning, Cassie. There are things you don't understand yet." He pushed me up from the comfort of his lap. "Get dressed."

We did, scrambling in the sand, shaking off our garments before sliding them on. I wished I hadn't ruined the moment. I went to him as he picked up his cape. "The last time you said to get dressed, I didn't like what followed."

He slid his cape over my shoulders. He didn't say anything, but gazed at me, intently serious.

I didn't like the silence. "If you love me and I love you, then why wait till morning before accepting my answer?"

He sighed. "There is only one reason why I would ever let you go now and that is if you don't want to stay."

"I can't imagine why I wouldn't."

"I can. Come, and I will show you."

Sean took me back to the castle, where we entered through

his study. Tonight, as on the other night, there were roses and food and wine set on the table waiting, but the hearth was cold and the candles unlit. He set that to rights immediately, yet instead of lighting all six candles, he only lit two.

"First let's eat and then I have to show you something."

"Show me now."

"No. I want more time with you first."

He poured spiced wine, which, no matter how much he denied it, I still thought had stimulating properties. For as we ate, my body warmed then tingled, bringing a sense of anticipation that had me watching Sean's every expression, his every movement. I settled my gaze on his lips as he slipped tiny bites of cheese and fruit into the heat of his mouth. I remembered just how his mouth made me feel and everything inside of me burned for more.

When he took my hand, I thought he'd lead me to his bedchamber, but he didn't. He led me to the sofa before the fire. Then going to a shelf in the back corner of the room, he returned with a large, ancient looking book, and set it on the small table before the sofa.

"What's this?"

"The Dragon's Curse." Opening the book, he showed me a thousand years of Killdaren history, and whenever twins had been born, one had killed the other. This was why he honestly believed in his impending fate.

"How do you know twins will be born? Are they always born? That seems impossible." So many questions rambled through my mind.

Sean shook his head. "Ask one at a time. No one knows when the twins will be born. Many times they are not, but when they are..." He shrugged. "The evidence is there."

"But why? How?"

"The *Tuatha de Danaan.*"

"The fairies?"

"The queen cursed my family for eternity."

"Why?"

"I am still searching through books to find the reason. It has to do with the spirit of Dragons being born and suffering the depth of betrayal." He shut the book, but left his hand on top as if he couldn't quite let go of it. "There has yet to be a way to break the curse."

"But what if you and your brother had never known of the curse?"

"I don't think it would have changed things. We were born with our hands about each other's throats. My only hope for a life with you is to never see my brother, to continue to look for an answer, and pray we don't have twins."

I set my hand over his. "I believe love can conquer anything. Even this. Is this why you won't accept my answer until morning?"

"If any hope can turn the tide of this curse, it would be yours. But no. There's more. I'll show you in the morning. You've given me life when I've had so little. We've made love in the moonlight. Now I want to make love in the water."

I shook my head, standing and moving away from him. "No. I'm not doing that with you in the sea. I would drown."

He laughed. "I have my own private sea, and I won't have any trouble keeping you afloat."

"What sea?"

"There's a natural hot spring that I've made great use of." Taking a candle, he led me quietly down the corridor past the rooms where Bridget, Prudence and Rebecca slept to his bedchamber. But he didn't stop there. He crossed his room and went into a small corridor, where the air changed, growing warmer and more humid. Then moving through a set of doors, he stopped and so did I. My halt was from surprise. It was a tiled Roman bath with large pools of steamy water. While I stared, Sean stripped. If I'd known of this room in first coming to the castle, I would have braved any obstacle to sink into its steamy waters.

"Come join me, Cassie." He slipped into the water then swam beneath the surface, appearing again in the middle of the pool. Water dripped from his dark hair and slid enticingly over his skin. As before, staring at his mouth brought the heated memory of him feasting on me to mind. My body burned for more. I undressed hurriedly and eased myself into the warm water, holding onto the side until I was sure of my footing. I had yet to learn to swim well; something told me I would in the future. He came up behind me, setting his hands on either side of mine on the tile and pressed his rigid arousal against my bottom.

I went to face him. He stopped me.

"Brace your hands on the tile." He eased my hips up and back until he slid his hot arousal inside of me. Cupping my breasts so that his fingers captured the tips and plucked them like berries, he slid in and out of me so slowly that I thought I was going to die of the pleasure. At one peak he thrust in deeply and held as he nipped the back of my neck at a place that sent fiery shivers to my toes and back to my loins.

"You weren't lying to me," I gasped.

"What?" He whispered in my ear, evoking another shiver.

"You've made quite a study of this subject."

"I'm just beginning to explore what I have learned."

I would have said more, but what he did next with his fingers ripped away any ability I had to think. All I could do was feel until I was so spent my knees wouldn't even hold me upright. Swinging me into his arms, he carried me to his room, dried me off. Then, placing me in his bed, he curled around me.

"I love you, Cassie. With all of my heart."

"I love you too," I sighed and drifted off to sleep.


"Cassie, it's almost dawn. We need to talk."

I turned to him, burrowing against him, needing his warmth. "I dreamed of Mary."

He drew a deep breath. "And?"

"I saw her on a dark cliff looking at the sea. I woke before I could see more."

"Dragon's Point," Sean said. "I'll show it to you some night.

Mary used to go there to paint. There's a family graveyard there. Perhaps your family would like to bury her there."

I could see Mary at peace there, painting the sea. "Yes. I'll speak to my aunt about it later today." I hesitated. "Can you accept my dreams, Sean? I never know when the darkness will come."

"You shouldn't even question that. It is me you need to decide if you can accept. I never know when the headaches are going to intrude, and I may have to live in the shadows of the night forever."

Moving from the bed, he scooped me up into his arms and took me to a wall of curtains across his room. He pulled them open, and there was the sea set softly aglow by the pinkish light of the dawn.

"This is the time that the world is waking, that children are smiling, waiting to play. That men are going off to work and to the sea, and women are gathering to talk about their cares as they pray for those they love. The sun rises up and greets them all, will keep them warm through the day and will ease them to their beds at dusk. This is the time that I go to sleep. I will see none of them, I will hear none of them, I won't hear a baby cry, or run across a sunlit glen to chase my child as he laughingly plays. I live alone in the shadows and have no real hope that it will ever be different. I did have a few brief times in the sun recently, but it always came at a price. The headaches were just at such a point that I could stand the pain. I don't know if I will regain that or not."

He set me on my feet and knelt before me like a dark knight before a queen. "Will you marry me and share my world, Cassie? Can you? Will you dance with me beneath the stars?"

The sun rose against the horizon and he turned from it. I reached out and pulled the curtain shut, welcoming the darkness. I would be here to watch over Rebecca, just to be sure there was no horseman from the sea. I would be here for Bridget, to help with her mother and brother, and to know when she heard from her sister. And I would be here with him forever.

"Yes." I kneeled before him, and cupped his face in mine. What I couldn't understand before, I knew fully now. "Yes. I will share the light of my soul in the darkness with you." I kissed him then, promising all of my heart and all of my life to whatever destiny we would carve out of a bright future in the shadow of the stars.

# About the Author

Jennifer St. Giles, a USA Today Bestselling Author, also writes contemporary romantic suspense as J.L. Saint. She is a nurse and mother of three. She has won a number of awards for writing excellence including, two National Reader's Choice Awards, two time Maggie Award Winner, Daphne du Maurier Award winner, Romance Writers' of America's Golden Heart Award, along with RT Book Club's Reviewer's Choice Award for Best Gothic/Mystery. Website: jenniferstgiles.com jlsaint.com.

I love hearing from my readers and you can find me on Facebook and Twitter. *Midnight Secrets* is the first book in the Killdaren Trilogy and tells the story of how love can make the difference and change the lives of everyone it touches if you let it. So open your hearts and enjoy!

# SAMHAIN
PUBLISHING

www.samhainpublishing.com

*Green for the planet.*
*Great for your wallet.*

PUBLISHING

*It's all about the story...*

Romance

HORROR

www.samhainpublishing.com

CPSIA information can be obtained at www.ICGtesting.com
Printed in the USA
BVOW021624190212

283278BV00003B/2/P